Elisa Adams

Kathleen Scott

R. Ellen Ferare

Saskia Walker

Volume 19

Secrets

Satisfy your desire for more.

SECRETS Volume 19
This is an original publication of Red Sage Publishing and each individual story herein has never before appeared in print. These stories are a collection of fiction and any similarity to actual persons or events is purely coincidental.

Red Sage Publishing, Inc.
P.O. Box 4844
Seminole, FL 33775
727-391-3847
www.redsagepub.com

SECRETS Volume 19
A Red Sage Publishing book
All Rights Reserved/July 2007
Copyright © 2007 by Red Sage Publishing, Inc.

ISBN: 0-9754516-9-3 / ISBN 13: 978-0-9754516-9-4

Printed in the U.S.A.

Book typesetting by:
Quill & Mouse Studios, Inc.
www.quillandmouse.com

Contents

Affliction

by Elisa Adams

To My Reader:

Sometimes a story seems to have a mind of its own, and no matter what the writer does to try to shape it to fit the image they have in mind, something unexpected happens to change everything. This was one of those stories. It took me by surprise, and brought me to a place I hadn't even realized I wanted to go. I hope you enjoy getting lost in Holly and Shane's world.

Chapter One

"What can he give you that I can't?"

The deep voice coming out of the darkness brushed over Holly Aronson like a caress. She closed her eyes for a brief second and muttered a curse. She should have known he'd follow her in here. Maybe on some level she had known. Hoped, even.

When had she gotten so screwed up? "Go away."

The muted sounds of the party downstairs reached her through the open door and a pang of guilt speared her stomach. She should be down there now, helping Andrew see to his guests, not upstairs inviting trouble.

"I wish I could." Shane McAllister stepped through the doorway into the library, his hands in the pockets of his black slacks and his mouth drawn in a grim line. "We both know it's not that simple."

His tie hung loosely around his neck and the top button of his slate-colored shirt was undone. She took in the sight of his mussed dark hair, probably from running his hands through it as she'd seen him do so many times, and her heart skipped. The idea of being unfaithful had never crossed her mind until Shane had stepped into her life.

His blue-eyed gaze played across her skin in a slow, sensual dance. Her nipples pebbled, and the way his gaze darkened told her he noticed. She tugged at the hem of her dress, suddenly wishing she'd worn something a little longer. A little looser. Anything to stop Shane's attention—both wanted and unwanted at the same time. Just because it felt good didn't make it right. Hadn't she learned that lesson a long time ago?

She turned and walked to the window, glancing outside and giving Shane her back. As soon as her gaze dropped to the lawn below, a different kind of anxiety filled her. Shadows moved and twisted in the moonlit yard, most likely caused by the summer breeze sifting through tree limbs, but it made her shiver just the same. In the daylight, Andrew's house was beautiful. Elegant and stately. In the darkness, it made her want to turn around and run.

Irrational. She needed to learn to let go of her fears. The monsters she'd seen in so many nightmares didn't live here.

"Holly."

The hair rose on the back of her neck. Shane's voice came from directly behind her. No matter how quiet the room, he always managed to sneak up on her, and it unnerved her more than she'd ever admit.

"Just go, Shane. I came up here to be alone."

He settled his warm palms against her waist, the action letting her know he had no intention of listening. He leaned in close and his hot breath feathered across her ear. "Don't lie to me. You don't like to be alone. It's the only reason you're leading Andrew on the way you are, isn't it?"

His words stung and she winced. She tried to step away, but his grip tightened. She was stuck between a wall of hard muscle and a window two stories above the ground, and his closeness made a lump form in her throat. How dare he question her motives when it came to Andrew?

How dare he be so right? "Stop it. You know that's not true. I'm not leading him on. I want to be here. I... love him." She stumbled over the words and almost couldn't bring herself to say them. They were true, but not in the way Andrew wanted them to be. Her stomach clenched at the thought of hurting him. He'd always been so good to her, and she'd been happy with her life until his old friend Shane had shown up and thrown her world into chaos.

Just one smoldering glance and he'd made her doubt everything she believed to be true. One touch from his strong hands and she'd known, deep down inside, that Andrew would never make her happy again. Still, she fought her attraction to Shane with every ounce of her being. He was no good for her, and she couldn't let herself fall into his trap. He'd be gone soon, out of her life, but Andrew would never leave her.

Holly stomped her heel down on Shane's foot and he let her go with a low grunt. Her traitorous body cried out at the loss of his heat, but she ignored it. Pursuing what he offered wouldn't be worth the pain in the end. "Leave me alone, Shane. I don't want any part of your sick fantasies."

She rushed for the door, intent on making her apologies to Andrew before heading home for the night, but Shane grabbed her arm before she reached her destination. He hauled her against him, chest pressed to chest, and her knees went weak. He always had this effect on her and it incensed her that he could stir such strong reactions. Her life had been one disaster after another and she usually prided herself on being able to keep her emotions under control, but with Shane, that had proved to be impossible.

"Let me go," she said through clenched teeth, her hands balling into fists.

"Not until you answer my question." Shane's lips were so close to hers his breath brushed her skin when he spoke. He smelled of crisp, clean aftershave and warm, sensual man. The combination was enough to dampen her panties and send a curl of arousal spiraling through her middle.

"What question?"

A hint of a smile played across his lips. When he spoke, his tone wasn't much more than a whisper. "What can he give you that I can't?"

"Stability."

The smile grew. "You mean boredom."

"Caring. Compassion."

Lust sparkled in his eyes. "I can give you that, too, sweetheart. More than you know."

Something inside her twisted and she let out a soft sigh. Her back arched, her body aching for his hands all over her. She leaned closer and her lips parted. At that second, time seemed to stand still. It didn't matter how wrong it was. Didn't matter that she'd made a promise to Andrew. The only thing that mattered now was Shane's kiss.

He leaned toward her, but stopped when his lips were inches from hers. "I won't touch you. Not the way you want me to. Not until you've told Andrew the truth."

Holly wet her lips with the tip of her tongue. "Which truth would that be?"

Shane released her and stepped back. A muscle ticked in his jaw. "Tell him it's me you want. Me, and not him. He deserves to know what's going on between us."

"There's nothing between us."

"That's right, Holly. Just keep lying to yourself."

Her gaze dropped to the floor. Unlike him, she refused to hurt Andrew. It didn't matter how much she wanted Shane. She could never have him, and they both knew that. "Why are you doing this?"

"Because I don't take no for an answer."

She glanced up to see him standing in the doorway. It shook her that he could move so soundlessly. Just another reason why he wasn't a man to be trusted. She didn't know anything about him. "You're going to have to learn. I'm with Andrew. He's right for me. You are so obviously wrong. I don't trust you."

A half smile tilted one corner of his mouth and his gaze turned mocking. "Do you really think you can trust him?"

"I know I can." Andrew had proven himself, time and again, to be the kind of staid, reliable presence she needed. If she let Shane in, he'd tear her carefully rebuilt life apart.

"Don't be so sure. I've known him a lot longer than you have. I know all his secrets. Trust me, honey. With him, you haven't even scratched the surface." He shook his head. "Don't let your guard down, Holly. He isn't worthy of your trust."

With that, he walked away, leaving her alone to digest what he'd said. He'd been trying to shake her. Trying to rattle her faith in Andrew. Trying to plant a seed of doubt in her mind that would leave her questioning every decision she'd made in the past few months.

She leaned against the wall and let her head drop back.

Damn him, it had worked.

Chapter Two

Shane stood in a darkened corner of the room, watching as Holly walked down the stairs, through the throng of party-goers, and right into Andrew's arms. His gut tightened and he narrowed his eyes. It shouldn't have been like this. Every time he closed his eyes, he saw Holly's delicate features and fair skin. Her long, black hair and her green eyes that held a glint of steel behind their softness.

He saw her curves and couldn't help but imagine what it would feel like to have her underneath him, naked and sweaty and screaming his name. Even now, his cock hardened against his zipper.

Andrew was like a brother to him. Had been for too long to remember. But right now, he hated the man with a passion.

The second Shane had seen Holly, he'd known he had to have her. Andrew knew it, and he wouldn't let her go.

What would Holly think if she knew the truth about her so-called prince charming? What would she do if she learned his deepest, darkest secrets?

She'd run, as fast as she could, and would never look back. Because the truth was something an ordinary human would find so hideous, so frightening, that it would be almost incomprehensible.

Shane wouldn't reveal Andrew's secrets to her. To do so would be to reveal his own, and he wouldn't do anything to chase Holly away. Andrew was banking on that fact. He'd all but told Shane so himself earlier that day.

Though music and laughter filled the room, Shane stood close enough to hear Andrew speak.

"Where have you been?" he asked Holly, concern etched on his face.

False concern, of course. Shane's stomach rolled. Since when had Andrew been concerned about anyone but himself? Shane wouldn't buy into the fact that his friend had changed. Holly might be special, but she couldn't work miracles.

"I needed some space. You know how I feel about crowds and parties." Holly ran a shaky hand through her hair as she glanced around the room. Looking for him, no doubt. Shane smiled. She could deny it all she wanted, but he'd seen the lust in her eyes. Lust, and a deep, aching need that echoed somewhere inside him. But she was stubborn and refused to see what was right in front of her, no matter what he said.

"I know," Andrew continued in a soothing tone. "I appreciate the effort you're making for me, though."

Holly's smile flickered before it faded away. "This is an important event. It's the least I can do, after all you've done for me."

"I haven't done nearly enough." Andrew leaned in and placed a kiss on Holly's lips. Shane clenched his teeth. He didn't know how much more of that he could endure before he snapped. If he snapped, the results wouldn't be pretty and they'd surely drive Holly even further away. He needed to do something to prove to her that Andrew wasn't the man she thought he was.

A few seconds later, the perfect opportunity to do just that presented itself.

"I promise to keep this sort of thing to a minimum." Andrew tucked a lock of Holly's hair behind her ear. "But it's an essential part of business. Have to keep the gods of money-making happy."

Shane stepped out of the shadows and walked over to them, settling his hand on Andrew's shoulder. He faced Holly with a smile. "That's the new policy, of course. Ever since they outlawed human sacrifices."

Chapter Three

Holly grasped Andrew's arm, her fingers tightening against the rough fabric of his sport coat. She glanced at the floor, afraid that if she looked at either of the men, they'd know what she was thinking. Afraid that, if Andrew saw her reaction to Shane, he'd know what she'd been doing earlier. It was no use trying to convince herself she'd done nothing wrong. Her thoughts alone had been hot enough to start a wildfire.

Andrew leaned in and worked her fingers off his arm. He slipped her hand into his and gave it a squeeze that should have been reassuring but only managed to drive the spike of guilt deeper into her gut.

"Easy, Holly. He's just kidding. Right, Shane?"

"Right. Andrew never was one to worry about laws and regulations, anyway."

She glanced up at Shane and narrowed her eyes. What would it take to get him to go away? Lately, whenever Andrew was around, Shane wasn't far behind. She couldn't keep living her life teetering between remorse and arousal. "Very funny, Shane."

Humor danced in his gaze, but something darker hovered in the background. Something that made her stomach knot and, despite her mind's warning, sent hot lust racing through her. She stiffened and moved away from Andrew. She couldn't let him see how Shane affected her—though he'd probably noticed weeks ago. Andrew was smart. Observant. He had to know there was something between them.

As if reading her mind, Andrew draped his arm over her shoulder and leaned in to kiss her cheek. She managed a weak smile, but when she glanced up at him, his gaze had focused on Shane. Aggravation was etched upon his face and his eyebrows were raised in silent challenge.

She clenched her hands into fists. Was this all a game to them?

Neither man spoke, but a strange tension crackling in the air alerted her to the exchange between them. Shane took a step forward and Andrew's arm tightened across her shoulders.

It seemed like an eternity before Andrew finally broke the silence. "I've had to bend a few things to get where I am." He pressed a lingering kiss to Holly's temple. "But nothing too serious. Shane likes to embellish the facts to make me look bad. He thinks it'll make him look good by contrast, but he doesn't realize he's only dragging himself down along with me."

Andrew's lips brushed her cheek and Holly waited for some sort of feeling. Nothing came. No spark, no intense attraction like the one she felt for Shane. The same attraction that swelled in her now, in the most inappropriate of situations.

Even standing inches away from Andrew, it was Shane's hands she wanted on her body. Shane's lips that should be on her skin. Lord help her, she wanted the man inside her with every fiber of her being. Her pussy ached for the feel of him stroking into her, bringing her closer and closer to the edge.

Her face heated and her nipples peaked against the rough fabric of her bra. Anyone who gave her a cursory glance would notice. Familiar guilt clogged her throat and she stepped away, feigning a yawn.

Andrew took the bait. "You look exhausted. Maybe I should drive you home. I'll get your car to you in the morning."

"I have to work tomorrow. Besides, I'll be fine. I'm tired, but not too tired to drive. I can make it home."

"Holly..."

She held her hand up to stop his protest. The sooner she got away from both men, the sooner she'd be able to think straight. Shane messed with her common sense, and Andrew's presence wasn't helping matters. "You have guests, Andrew. You can't leave. And I'm perfectly capable of driving the ten minutes to my house. Thank you anyway, but I'll be okay."

Shane cleared his throat. "I don't have guests to take care of. I can give you a ride home, Holly."

"She said she can make it home on her own. No need for the misplaced gallantry."

"Why don't you ask the lady what she wants?" Shane's tone, though frustrated, held a taunting edge.

Holly sighed. The verbal head butting wouldn't get them anywhere. "The lady just wants to go home and go to bed. Alone. Now, if you'll excuse me, I really need to leave. You two can continue your juvenile games without me."

"Let me at least walk you to your car." Andrew took her hand and gave it another squeeze. His gesture tightened the noose of shame around her neck another notch.

"Okay." Being on the grounds alone at night made her stomach churn, though her reaction was probably a remnant from the nightmare she'd spent the past five years trying to forget. "I have to grab my purse. I'll be right back."

The second she stepped into the back hallway, out of their line of sight, she breathed a sigh of relief. If she kept this up much longer, she'd crack under the intense pressure.

She had a decision to make, and, on the surface, it looked like an easy one. Andrew's stability, along with his caring nature and willingness to let her take her time before agreeing to a real commitment, appealed to her broken and bruised heart. After Mike's death, she'd learned that following her heart only brought her pain.

Shane might stir her body, but physical attraction wasn't enough. He was dangerous, and she'd learned that men like him needed to be avoided at all costs.

Andrew was the right choice.

Too bad her body wouldn't listen to reason.

"What the hell do you think you're doing?"

Shane swung his head in Andrew's direction and raised an eyebrow. "Funny, but I was just about to ask you the same question. Why are you suddenly so interested in settling down?"

Andrew's gaze darkened to nearly black and his eyes narrowed. "Why are you suddenly so interested in stealing what's mine?"

Shane blew out a breath heavy with frustration. What was *his*? What a crock. Holly was no more Andrew's than she was Shane's, or any other man's. "She's not your possession. You've only known her for a few months."

"And I plan on keeping her." Aggression soured Andrew's tone.

Shane stepped back and tried to settle his temper. If he got angry, he'd play right into Andrew's hands. Andrew wanted him upset. Wanted him in a rage when Holly walked back into the room. Shane wouldn't give him the satisfaction. "She's not the type of woman who wants to be kept."

"And when did you become such an expert on what my girlfriend wants?"

"Long before you appointed yourself her protector." He ran a hand through his hair and tried to shake off the frustration that had been dogging him since he'd learned of Andrew and Holly's relationship. It had been two months ago, and he'd packed his things and moved to Granville as soon as Andrew had confessed. The knot in his stomach hadn't eased since.

Andrew was supposed to protect her from afar, not move in on her the first chance he got.

"You asked me to look out for her. Did you expect me not to make contact?"

The defiance in Andrew's gaze made Shane curl his hands into fists. He slammed his eyes closed and pulled in a sharp breath. Andrew, like the ever-petulant little brother, was a master at manipulation. Shane saw right through his act, and he wasn't going to play into it any longer.

He opened his eyes and made an attempt at schooling his expression. "This is nuts. Arguing isn't getting us anywhere. She's in more danger now than she's ever been. They're close."

"I know. I've seen them in the shadows, waiting for a chance to get to her."

So had Shane, and it had been part of the reason he'd stuck so close to her. Only a small part. He couldn't force himself to stay away. She'd worked her way under his skin and now he would never be the same.

"Tell me, Andrew, are you planning to do something about it? You're the one she's chosen." For now.

"Of course."

"So what's your great plan? Besides leading her on, that is."

Andrew said nothing, and Shane cursed. "That's the difference between you and me. By the time you've finished thinking about what needs to be done, I've managed to do it."

He started for the door, and Andrew rushed after him. He grabbed Shane's arm just as Shane's fingers curled around the doorknob.

"Where are you going?"

Shane yanked his arm out of Andrew's grasp and faced his lifelong friend with his arms crossed over his chest. "I'm getting in my car and following her when she heads home. Someone needs to make sure she's okay."

Andrew glanced over his shoulder and Shane followed his gaze. Holly was walking toward them. When her eyes met Shane's, her step faltered and she tucked a strand of hair behind her ear.

Andrew stepped between them. "You should leave her alone."

"What are you going to do if I don't?"

When Andrew stayed silent, Shane shook his head. "That's what I thought."

Holly fiddled with the radio buttons, but the channels kept cutting in and out. Strange, but not all that unusual. Her car was old, and she'd need to replace it soon, but she wanted to hold off for as long as she could. A new car would be an expense she couldn't afford on her nurse's salary, and mentioning it to Andrew was out of the question. He'd insist on buying her a new one. Andrew was good to her, but she'd learned long ago that she needed to rely on herself before others.

She finally found a station that came in and left the radio tuned there for the rest of the drive across town to her rented bungalow. The place was small, just three rooms and a bathroom, but it was all she needed. The closeness of the space wrapped around her and gave her comfort more than an expansive house ever could. Normally, she liked living alone, but lately things had been a little out of the ordinary.

The oddities had started when she'd met Andrew.

She grimaced. No, that wasn't true. Meeting him had seemed to intensify things. Her radio and cell phone malfunctioning in Andrew's neighborhood. The sensation of being watched. The sound of phantom footsteps behind her. The feeling that, no matter where she was, she was never truly alone.

A shaky laugh bubbled up in her throat. Nothing like a good dose of paranoia to keep a person from wanting to go home at night.

The paranoia wasn't unfounded. Her mother had always taught her that monsters didn't exist. They were all in her head. That terrible night five years ago had exposed her mother's words for the lies they were.

Monsters did exist. They were very real, and they could hurt. Kill. What she'd seen still haunted her as if it had happened hours ago. It had taught her to be cautious, and to always look over her shoulder.

With Andrew in her life, she felt safe for the first time in years and it wasn't right to let her taxed imagination taint that. After a long night, she needed a hot bath and an hour with a good book, and she'd be herself again.

She parked her old hatchback in the driveway and walked up the path toward the front door. A glance at the house warned her something wasn't right, but it took a few seconds for the problem to register. Hadn't she left the porch light on when she'd left for Andrew's party?

A chill danced across her senses. She wouldn't have forgotten the light. Something had happened to make it go out.

Panic lodged in her throat. She turned around to run and slammed into a solid wall of muscle.

"Going somewhere, Miss Aronson?"

Chapter Four

Strong arms wrapped around Holly and squeezed, threatening to knock the wind out of her. Her pulse pounded in her ears. She writhed and kicked, lashing out in any way she could to try to get away. Once the initial panic subsided, survival kicked in. Whoever he was, he wasn't going to do anything without a fight. "Let go of me!"

"Stop struggling and this will be so much easier."

The voice was masculine, yet raspy and oddly high-pitched. She brought her heel down on the stranger's instep and he grunted, but didn't let go. Instead, he grabbed her hair and yanked her head back, making her scalp burn. She yelped and twisted hard in his arms.

His rancid breath brushed her cheek. "Do that again, and I'll have to hurt you. Trust me. You don't want that."

"Hurt her, and it'll be the last thing you ever do."

The familiarity of the voice nearly made her sob in relief.

Shane stepped around the edge of the house and she caught a glint of something silver in his hand. A knife.

"Let her go. Now." He injected so much menace into the words that even Holly shrank back.

"Make me."

"I thought you'd never ask."

In a flash, Shane rushed at them. The stranger pushed Holly away and she lost her balance. She hit the ground, her hands and knees absorbing most of the impact. Shards of pain shot through her wrists and she collapsed onto the soft grass.

She struggled to sit and saw Shane wrestle the stranger to the ground. His biceps flexed beneath his shirt as he tried to hold the other man down. He glanced up at her, his shoulders heaving and his hair falling across his eyes. There was something feral about him that made her suck in a breath.

He jerked his chin toward her house. "Go inside."

She scooted back on the grass and wrapped her arms around her middle. She couldn't leave him to deal with the threat all alone, but there wasn't much she could do to help him, either.

His eyes glistened silver in the dim light of the three-quarter moon. "Get inside. Lock the doors and don't open them until I tell you it's safe."

A sliver of panic worked its way beneath her bravado. "What's going on?"

"Just go, Holly! If I don't knock on the door within twenty minutes, call Andrew and tell him it's an emergency."

The urgency in his tone prodded her into action. She pushed herself off the ground, grabbed her purse, and raced toward the house. After a quick glance back to make sure Shane was okay, she let herself inside and slammed the door.

The hollow click of the deadbolt sliding into place did nothing to ease her mind.

She pushed back the curtain covering the window next to the door and squinted into the darkness, but she couldn't make out more than shadows twisting and moving around the yard.

An agonizing two minutes later, Shane walked up the steps. Her heart thumped against her ribcage and she let out the breath she hadn't realized she'd been holding.

He pounded on the door. "Holly, open up."

"One second." With shaking fingers, she fumbled with the lock and finally managed to turn the knob. She opened the door wide enough to let Shane in, but the second he'd stepped into the entryway, she slammed the door closed and threw the deadbolt back into place, as if the simple act of locking the door would keep all the darkness at bay. She tugged her lower lip into her mouth and turned to face him.

He took a look at her, shook his head, and pulled her into his arms.

Holly buried her face against his chest, refusing to give in to the tears stinging her eyes. She concentrated instead on the feel of him, warm and alive, holding her in his arms. His breath sawed in and out of his lungs, and he held her so tight it made breathing difficult, but she didn't care. She welcomed the sensation. She was safe now, and she had Shane to thank for that.

Once the anxiety subsided, another emotion started to take root. She inched closer to Shane, wanting to feel every bit of him against her. The heat of his skin warmed her and still she wanted more.

Shane seemed to notice the change between them, too. His hand wrapped in her hair and he caressed her scalp. He kissed the top of her head before resting his lips there, his heated breath feathering through her hair and stirring something low in her belly.

It seemed like an eternity before he pulled away and looked down at her. "Are you okay?"

"I'm fine. I don't even know how to thank you."

"You're not hurt?"

"No." Her wrists stung a little and her knees would probably be bruised in the morning, but that was nothing compared to what might have happened had Shane not been there. "What did you do with him?"

He backed up a step and turned on the entryway light. Several long streaks of blood smeared the front of his shirt. She shuddered.

"It's not mine."

"What—"

He held up his hand and shook his head. "You've been through enough tonight. You don't want the details. Trust me. Knowing what happened wouldn't help."

She frowned. His words raised a red flag in the back of her mind. Why wouldn't he tell her what he'd done?

The possibilities made her head ache. "Okay. Let me call the police. We'll get this sorted out."

Her mind still racing, she walked down the short hallway into the kitchen and lifted the phone off its cradle. A wave of fear washed over her and she slumped against the wall. Her fingers shook too hard for her to dial the number.

Shane lifted the phone from her hand and set it back where it belonged. "Calling them won't do us any good. The police don't deal with this sort of thing."

Her breath whooshed out of her lungs and her palms broke out in a cold sweat. No police. That had to mean...

No. Shane wouldn't have killed anybody. Not even to protect her. "He attacked me! You think I'm going to just let that go? He can't get away with it!"

His gaze snagged hers and held. The pleading look in his eyes nearly undid her. "He won't."

Holly pushed a hand through her hair. The evening had suddenly taken a surreal turn and she couldn't manage to catch her breath. Something very bad had happened tonight, but she couldn't make sense of what it was.

"Is there a body you don't want them to see?"

"There's no body."

"He got away?"

Shane said nothing.

"So there's no body, but he didn't get away? How is that even possible?" She shook her head. "Why won't you just tell me what happened? I'm not fragile, if that's what you're worried about. I won't break."

"He's not dead. Does that make you feel better?"

It should have, but it didn't. At least she knew Shane wasn't a killer.

They stood in silence for a few seconds before Shane reached out and touched her cheek. The touch was brief, but the warmth of his fingers soothed her. "I'm glad I followed you home."

"Why did you?"

"You left Andrew's house in a huff, and it was partly my fault. I wanted to make sure you got here okay."

The answer was so simple and honest that it made her smile. Tears of stress threatened her eyes again, but she refused to let them fall. She might have cried before, in a different lifetime, but tears had no place in her world now. "I'm glad you did, too. Thank you. You saved my life."

"It's no less than anyone else would have done." A half smile curled one side of his mouth, but it didn't reach his eyes. The worry in his expression made her throat clog.

"Is there something you're not telling me?"

"It's nothing important. He's gone, and you're safe, and that's all that matters right now. God, Holly, when I saw him holding you like that, I just snapped. I couldn't let him hurt you."

"I'm fine."

"You shouldn't have come home alone."

"I don't need someone to protect me." Even as the words left her mouth, she recognized them for the lie they were. None of the self-defense classes she'd taken in the past five years had prepared her for the stranger's strength. If Shane hadn't been there, she might have died. Whatever had happened out their on the lawn, she had to remember he'd saved her life.

"When are you going to get it? This isn't about protecting you. Not really. It's not about questioning your strength. I'm not here because you need me."

Her heart skipped a beat and she sucked in a breath scented with Shane's clean, masculine scent. Her knees went weak. "Then why are you here?"

He traced the line of her jaw with his fingertip. She leaned into the touch. "Because I can't get you out of my head. No matter what I do, no matter how many times I try to change my focus, you're right there. I can't even think straight anymore. These past few months have been torture."

"Don't start." She turned her head and his finger dropped from her face. He reached for her again, but she pushed his hand away. "I can't want you."

"But you do."

"Too much."

"Holly, look at me."

She shook her head. If she looked at him, she'd be lost.

"Please."

When she didn't move, he cupped her chin in his hand and her gaze lifted to his. The heat she found there made her mouth run dry. A wisp of arousal curled in her stomach.

His unwavering gaze held hers for an endless time. Discomfort muddied the lust and she tried to glance away, but he held her face still. With just a look he could strip her raw. Leave her vulnerable and needy and craving his touch more than anything she'd ever wanted.

Her nipples pebbled, and she swallowed hard. She clenched her hands into fists.

"Why are you fighting this?" His voice was barely above a whisper.

She ran her tongue across her lower lip. She had to fight it. There was no other way. She hadn't made any promises to Andrew, but he didn't deserve this. "Because it's wrong."

"It doesn't feel wrong." Shane leaned in and brushed his lips over hers. The touch was brief, over in a second, but it was enough.

She groaned. A tingle ran from the top of her head to her toes, stopping to linger everywhere in between. It finally settled between her legs and made her squirm. One kiss and he had her ready to tear off all her clothes and beg him to make love to her.

She'd known it would feel like this. And she'd known that, the second he kissed her, she wouldn't be able to fight against what she wanted anymore. He would have to be the strong one. All the fight drained out of her, leaving her vulnerable and wanton.

She made one last plea. "Don't, Shane. This can't happen."

"It's already happening. Has been for two months. You're only fooling yourself if you don't accept the truth that's right in front of you."

He dipped his head for a second brush of lips and another shiver raced through her. Almost of its own volition, her hand came up, fingers unfurling, and settled on his chest. Part of her warned to push him away, but a larger part wouldn't let that happen. She curled her fingers in the soft fabric of his shirt.

"But Andrew..."

Aggravation flashed in his gaze. "This isn't about Andrew. Don't try to make it into something it's not. It's about you and me, and the pull between us that neither of us can shake. It's just the two of us here right now. No one else is in the room. The only thing coming between us is you."

"You said you wouldn't touch me until I told Andrew the truth."

"Things have changed. I can't be this close to you and keep my hands to myself. I thought it was possible, but it just isn't."

She shook her head and Shane narrowed his eyes. "Don't deny you feel it, Holly. I can see in your eyes that you do."

"I feel it." She tightened her grip on his shirt. "God, I don't want to, but I do."

A ghost of a smile played across his mouth. He slid his thumb across her lower lip before he leaned in again. This time he didn't pull away.

The warmth of his lips against hers made her pulse race. Every nerve in her body screamed out for more. She let go of his shirt and brought her arms around his neck, needing him so much closer than he was.

When her lips parted on a sigh, he dipped his tongue into her mouth to brush against hers. Heat flashed through her and she tightened her arms. With his hand around her waist, Shane dragged her closer until no space remained between their bodies. The feel of his hard cock pressed against her belly dampened her panties and a sigh caught in her chest.

A desperate longing took root inside of her. She needed him. There would be no pushing him away tonight. She'd get down on her knees and beg if she had to, but he couldn't walk out that door.

His lips left hers and, with his nose, he nudged her chin until she let her head drop back. His tongue trailed down her neck, leaving a riot of quivers in its wake, until he reached the spot where her neck met her shoulder. He bit down there, not hard but strong enough to send a shock through her system and wet her panties even more. A ragged moan slipped from her lips.

He lifted his head. "Do you want me to stop?"

"No." If he stopped, she might die. She pressed herself closer to him, wishing she could crawl inside his skin. Her whole body throbbed, and he was the only one who could make the ache go away.

"Good. I don't think I can."

His hands inched up her waist until he cupped her breasts in the warmth of his palms. She arched into him, loving the feel of her peaked nipples against him. Her clothes were only in the way. She wriggled, hoping he'd take the hint, but instead of moving to the zipper at her back, he leaned in and drew his tongue along the cleavage exposed by the neckline of her dress.

His thumbs scraped across her nipples and even through the layers of her clothes it sent a shock of heat through her. Her knees wouldn't hold her up much longer. Even now, she'd started to sink toward the ground.

"Easy." His breath whispered over her skin, making goose bumps rise on her flesh. His thumbs continued to stroke her nipples, driving her to the brink of sanity while he pressed hot, open-mouthed kisses to her skin.

"Shane, please." She arched her hips toward him, needing relief from the exquisite torture.

He leaned his forehead against hers. The harsh rasp of his breathing filled the space around them. "If you keep moving like that, I won't last. I want this to be good for you, but you're not making it easy."

A laugh bubbled up in her chest. As if she needed seduction. He'd already accomplished that. A long time ago. She'd been primed and ready for two months. "It'll be good. I don't want to wait."

"Holly…"

"Please, Shane. I need you." She caught his earlobe between her teeth and nibbled, delighting in his shudder. "Now."

He pulled back and looked down at her, his gaze seeming to search hers for a few seconds before he nodded. "We'll get there. I promise. I've waited too long for this moment. We're not going to rush it."

His thumbs skimmed across her nipples one more time before he stepped away. He leaned back against the counter, and she got a glimpse of the impressive bulge in the front of his pants. She licked her lips.

"Take off your panties."

Shane's command made her snap her gaze back to his. "What?"

"Take them off and give them to me." He stretched his hand out, palm up, and made a beckoning motion with his fingers.

His demand was unexpected, but it made a quiver run through her pussy. Her gaze on his, she dragged the hem of her dress up her hips and hooked her fingers in the waistband of her panties. She shimmied out of them and, with shaking fingers, placed the scrap of fabric in his waiting hand.

He shoved them into his pocket. A sensual grin curled the corners of his lips. "Good girl. Now get up on the table."

Oh, my God. Her legs wobbly with need, she walked the few steps to the table and settled on the cool wooden surface. She brought her hands behind her and leaned back, meeting his eyes. "Like this?"

"No. Spread your legs. I want to see you."

A shiver raced through her. No man had ever turned her on more. Sex in the past had been good. Sometimes great. But nothing nearly as explosive as this night promised to be.

Slowly, she brought her legs apart, inch by inch, until they were as wide as she could get them. Cool air rushed over her pussy and made her moan. Her clit ached and she wanted to touch it, to do something to relieve the amazing pressure, but she held back. Instead, she thrust her chest out and licked her lips.

Shane's eyes widened. "You're beautiful, Holly. So fucking beautiful. I want you so bad."

"Then what are you waiting for?"

He pushed away from the counter and walked closer, his heated gaze never leaving her body. When he stood right in front of her, he pressed his warm palms to her thighs and skimmed them upward, stopping just before he touched where she needed him most. She tried to inch closer, but he only moved his hands away.

"Not yet."

He pushed the spaghetti straps off her shoulders and tugged the material of her neckline down until he'd exposed her lacy strapless bra. Instead of removing the bra, he only pulled it down, too, revealing her breasts to his gaze.

She whimpered. There was something very decadent about sitting in front of him this way, clothed yet bare. Needy and aching for something he wouldn't yet give. Shane narrowed his eyes. His jaw tensed. He took her nipples between his thumbs and forefingers and rolled the peaks, sending shocks through her.

He leaned down and ran his tongue across a nipple before sucking the bud into the moist cavern of his mouth. His warm, wet tongue swirling over the hardened peak proved to be almost more than she could take. It seemed like an eternity that he suckled her, keeping her suspended just before the edge of the cliff, but not giving her enough to push her over. She squirmed and writhed against him, and he moved to the other nipple, affording it the same lavish treatment.

By the time he lifted his head, she was panting, on the verge of begging him to take her. He'd driven her to near madness with his attention, and all she could think about now was finding some relief. Every cell in her body pleaded for fulfillment. She reached for him, and he crushed his lips over hers in a searing kiss.

As his tongue stroked into her mouth, his hands moved down her body. He skimmed his finger across her slick folds and a shot of heat rushed through her. She bucked her hips.

Shane laughed against her mouth. His thumb circled her clit. He broke the kiss and smiled down at her. "Do you like this?"

"What do you think?"

He pressed down on the tiny bud of flesh and her mouth opened on a moan. "I think watching you get so aroused is pure torture."

His fingers moved along her folds, circling her entrance once before he dipped one thick finger inside. The strokes of his finger were like a wave of pure heaven. Her elbows buckled, refusing to support the weight of her upper body any longer. She dropped them to the table.

It had been so long since she'd been with a man, and she'd never wanted anyone as much as she wanted Shane. The combination was a potent one, and she felt the first stirrings of a climax low in her belly. "I don't want to wait any longer. Please, Shane. That's enough."

He chuckled in response and started to stroke a second finger into her in a slow rhythm that had to be designed to drive her mad.

The sensations built in her belly, spreading upward to her breasts and out to her limbs. She pushed up from the table and reached for his waistband, needing his cock inside her instead of his fingers.

Shane pulled his hand away, his shoulders heaving. He let out a short laugh. "What are you doing?"

"No more teasing. Get out of your pants."

His gaze was so hot she felt like it might burn right through her. He reached between them and worked her fingers off his pants, dropping her hands to her sides. It eased her mind that he was shaking as much as she was.

He took a few steps back, and she groaned. At first she thought he'd deny her request, but then his hands replaced hers at the waistband of his pants. Finally. She'd been waiting months for this moment, though it felt like a lifetime.

The rasp of his zipper filled the air and a few seconds later the tip of his hard cock prodded her entrance. She moaned in response. Her pussy softened against the invasion, and he slid inside.

For a few seconds he didn't move, and she relished the feeling of being so full. Five years had been too long to wait.

Shane's fingers tightened on her hips and pulled her close, slamming her against him. That was all it took to push her over the edge. She squeezed her eyes shut and clenched her hands into fists as the orgasm rocketed through her, shattering her into a million pieces of light and sensation. Her body bucked, and he continued to thrust, his rhythm hard and uneven.

The spasms seemed unending. Every stroke of his cock sent another one rushing through her pussy. Her entire body shook with the delicious quivers and a ragged moan escaped from between her lips. Stars danced at the edges of her vision.

Why had she waited so long to admit how much she wanted him?

Shane's thrusts grew shorter, faster, and his fingers bit into the tender flesh of her hips. She arched against him and he groaned, stiffening before he dropped his hands to the table and let his orgasm take him. Only the sound of their breathing filled the silence.

When Holly started to come back down from the incredible high, tears formed in her eyes. The moment had been perfection, and it had changed everything. He'd somehow managed to make himself a part of her, and now she'd never be the same.

It seemed like an eternity before he pulled away, and when he did, a rush of coldness washed over her, and she shivered.

"I don't even know what to say." The uncertain tone in his voice brought a smile to her face. She wasn't the only one who'd been thrown into confusion.

"You don't need to say anything."

He helped her up and smoothed down her dress, but when his gaze caught hers, he frowned. "Why are you crying?"

"It's been a stressful night."

Without another word, he lifted her into his arms.

"Put me down, Shane. I can walk." Though, at the moment, she doubted her legs would be willing to support her. "Where are you taking me?"

"To bed. You look ready to drop. As much as I'd like a repeat performance, I think we both need a few hours of sleep."

She started to protest, but her body wisely told her mind to shut up.

Chapter Five

"How is your meal?"

Holly glanced up at Andrew and blinked. Throughout the dinner, he'd tried to make conversation, but her mind refused to focus on anything for more than a few seconds. Instead, her thoughts centered on Shane, and why he'd snuck out in the middle of the night without saying goodbye. "It's fine."

Everything in her life was just fine. She stabbed a bite of chicken and slipped it into her mouth.

"Is that why you're pushing it around your plate and hardly eating any of it?"

The food tasted like sand. Dry and mealy and lacking any sort of flavor. It had nothing to do with the meal itself, but instead with her thoughts. Her mind had been in turmoil since she'd woken up alone.

She should have expected it, but Shane's disappearing act had blindsided her. It still stung, even more than twelve hours later. She'd been hoping she was wrong about him. That he was different. He wasn't.

When she finished chewing, she managed a wavering smile. "The food here is always good."

Their customary Sunday night dinner was usually a comfortable one she enjoyed, but tonight, sitting in a crowded, dim restaurant held little appeal. She just wanted to be alone and wallow in her self-pity for a little while before she wrote Shane off and got on with her life.

Andrew returned the smile, but it looked as strained as hers felt. Something dark flickered in his eyes before it dimmed. Pain and irritation replaced it.

They ate in silence for a few minutes before he spoke. "Shane tells me someone attacked you in your house last night."

Holly froze. Her fork dropped to her plate with a clatter. Other diners turned her way and conversations around them hushed. "You spoke with him?"

"Of course."

Something in his expression taunted her.

She got the feeling yet again that Andrew and Shane were playing some kind of twisted game. Winner take all. The thought made her gut clench. She wouldn't be anyone's spoils. "What did he tell you?"

"That someone attacked you on your front lawn. Threatened your life."

The hint of steel in his gaze told her more had been said. "What else did he say?"

Andrew's smile fell. He picked up his wine glass and swirled it around a few times before lifting it to his lips for a sip of the dark red liquid. "I'm glad you're okay."

"You know, don't you?"

He shrugged.

"Andrew, talk to me."

"What do you want to talk about?" He swirled the wine and took another sip, his demeanor deceptively casual. Typical, stoic Andrew, so good at hiding his true feelings.

"Something. Anything." She twisted her fingers in the napkin on her lap.

Andrew set the glass down and leaned forward, his eyebrows raised. "Do you want to talk about Shane? It's a subject that interests you, isn't it? I know he's been on your mind a lot lately. Some nights more than others, I assume. Like last night."

She pushed her plate away. "Don't. Please. Just... don't. I didn't mean for things to go so far. It was a product of stress and my neediness. He was there. He'd just saved my life. Believe me, it won't happen again."

He shook his head. Disappointment flashed in his gaze. "You're lying to yourself if you think that."

Holly glanced at her watch. Guilt clogged her throat and she tried to swallow around it. "I'm sorry, Andrew. I really am."

"I wasn't looking for an apology."

"You weren't?"

"No. I've never asked you for exclusivity. I'd been hoping you would come around, but I've never pushed you. At least, I've tried not to. I know your past has been a difficult thing to overcome."

He reached his hand out, palm up, and she slipped hers into it. The sincerity in his tone made her stomach knot. "You haven't pushed me."

"Then why Shane, of all people? Why not someone else? Anyone else, damn it. Why couldn't it have been me?"

She pulled her hand away. His question was one she'd been asking herself over and over since Shane had stepped into the picture. Her heart ached for Andrew's pain, but they weren't meant to be. She couldn't force what she didn't feel. "I don't know. I just…" Her voice trailed off and she looked away. She couldn't explain the connection to someone else when she didn't quite understand it herself.

"Am I not around enough for you?" Andrew folded his hands on the table. "Am I around too much? If I knew what you wanted, I could give it to you, but you don't give me any clues. No matter what I do, you keep me at a distance, never letting me close enough. Is there something I can do to make things better? Give me a hint, at least. I'm going crazy here." Desperation filled his tone.

"It's nothing you've done, or haven't done." She shook her head. He wanted an explanation, not flimsy excuses. "It's something I need to work out on my own."

"I just want to help you, Holly."

The waiter stopped by her side and gestured to her plate, providing a few seconds of relief from the tension. "Are you finished?"

"Yes, thank you."

"You, sir?"

Andrew nodded and the waiter picked up his plate.

"Will you be having dessert tonight?"

Holly opened her mouth to say no, but Andrew glanced her way and raised his hand to stop her. "We'll share a piece of chocolate cake."

The waiter left the table and Holly glared at Andrew. "What do you think you're doing? Do you really want to prolong this?"

"We always share a piece of cake at the end of a meal." He leaned back in his chair and smiled as if the previous conversation hadn't taken place. "Why ruin a good routine? It's always worked for us in the past. No sense changing it now."

"Andrew, this is a really bad idea."

"How do you figure?"

She propped her head in her hand and closed her eyes. Andrew had accepted things too easily. He wasn't prone to temper, but what happened had to have stirred a little bit of emotion inside him. She didn't want to be around when he finally snapped.

"There's no need to punish me for what happened. I told you it won't happen again."

He raised an eyebrow. "No. Don't say that. It's the last thing I want to hear right now. Don't make a promise you aren't able to keep."

"What is it you want from me, then, if it's not a promise?"

His eyes narrowed almost imperceptibly, but he showed no other reaction. That fact worried her more than if he'd exploded in anger. She fought against the urge to scoot her chair away from him.

"Just for you to be happy. Whatever that takes. If Shane is what you want, I won't hold you back. I won't ruin a lifelong friendship and a new one to hold you with me when that's not where you want to be. But I'm not willing to let go just yet.

"What's between you two is bound to fizzle. Whether it's next week, or next month, it doesn't matter. I'll still be here. Waiting for you."

She should have been relieved, but the emotion eluded her. His easy acceptance only made the knot in her stomach tighten even more. If she'd been hoping for a clean break, she wasn't going to get it. He might talk a good game, but his eyes told a different story.

She fought the urge to cover her face with her hands and scream. Why couldn't he just let her go? Did everything in her life have to be an uphill battle with no end in sight? For years, she'd struggled to get her life back together, and one night with Shane had managed to tear down everything she'd worked so hard to build.

The waiter brought their dessert and Andrew picked up his fork. He dug into the cake with the ardor of a starving man having his first meal after weeks of fasting. She shook her head. His comfort with the situation only strengthened her discomfort.

"Are you having some?" He gestured to the plate. "Don't make me eat this whole piece alone. It would be hell on my waistline."

His friendly tone and the wink he gave her eased her mind a little, but didn't drown all the anxiety. Something odd was going on.

She picked up her fork and broke off a small piece of the rich, dark cake. It had little more flavor than the chicken had, but she managed to swallow it. Just a few more tense minutes, and it would be time to go home.

She'd never looked forward to anything more.

By the time they walked out to his car, the tension inside her threatened to explode. The ride to her house was a silent one, and this time Andrew didn't try to fill the uncomfortable quiet.

He pulled into her driveway, but he made no move to get out and open the door for her as he usually did. When she reached for the handle, he grabbed her hand. "Hold on a second."

She settled back into the seat with a sigh. "What's wrong?"

"There's one thing I want to know." He met her gaze and the pain she saw in his eyes struck her like a spike through her middle. "Why him and not me?"

"What do you mean?"

"He's never done anything for you, never taken you anywhere or bought you things, and you slept with him."

On the last two words, his lips curled in a sneer. Holly blew out a breath. She should have known this was coming. Should have expected it from the start. At least he was showing a little emotion.

"He was there. That's all."

The lie hung between them for a few tense seconds before Andrew shook his head.

"Exactly what I mean. He was there, so you just jump into bed with him after one night. I've been waiting patiently, trying not to push you."

"Is that all you've wanted from me this whole time? You just wanted to get into my pants?" She yanked her hand out of his and balled it into a fist. "I should have seen it sooner. All the dinners out, the flowers and chocolates. What an artful attempt at seduction, Andrew. I never even saw it coming."

Regret filled his gaze, and he shook his head. "You know that's not what I was doing."

She glanced out the window. Her house sat back on the hill, the white clapboard tinged blue in the moonlight. "No, actually, I don't." A tug on the handle opened the door and she stepped out of the car. "I don't know anything about you at all. I thought I did, but I was wrong. I think you knew exactly what was going on between Shane and me, and I think, in some sick way, you enjoyed watching it unfold."

"Holly, stop. Listen for a second." He leaned across the passenger seat and reached for her arm, but she backed away.

"Don't touch me right now. I'm going inside. We'll talk later, when we've both had some time to cool off."

"At least let me walk you to the door."

She grabbed her purse off the car floor and tightened her fingers around the strap until her knuckles turned white. "No. I can manage just fine by myself."

He looked away for a brief second, let out a harsh sigh, and turned his pleading gaze back in her direction. "Don't walk away upset. I can't stand the thought of you hurting like this. I love you, Holly."

"It's a little late to play that card now, don't you think?" She slammed the door, but his words still echoed in her head.

She'd always believed him when he'd said it before, but now she was beginning to question his sincerity. If he truly loved her, he wouldn't have tried to manipulate her. He would have done anything he could to avoid making her feel like a pawn in his sick games.

She marched up the walkway, her thoughts racing. After a few seconds, the anger gave way to reason. Though he'd been late to show it, he had a right to his anger. And she deserved it. They hadn't made any promises to each other, but she could have been up front with him from the start rather than keeping her feelings for Shane a secret. And he could have been up front with her about his reasons for wanting Shane to hang around, and why it felt like he was pushing her toward his friend.

As she walked up the front steps, her head heavy and her stomach rolling, a shadow in a dark corner of the porch caught her eye. She froze, ready to run, but then the shadow stepped forward.

Shane.

Her breath whooshed from her lungs and she leaned against the railing. Her body reacted to the sight of him immediately. Her nipples hardened and her pussy quivered, even though she knew in her mind it was wrong. "What are you doing here?"

"I had to see you."

"No, it's too late for that."

He raised his hands in front of him, palms up, in a gesture of surrender. "At least let me explain."

"If I'd known you would have left in the middle of the night, I would have kicked you out a lot sooner. Last night was a mistake that won't be repeated. You can just turn around and go home right now. I don't want to hear any of your excuses."

"Please, Holly. I have a reason."

No reason was good enough for leaving the way he had. Her fingers shaking with anger, she walked to the door and fumbled to insert her key into the lock. After a few tries, she finally managed to unlock the door. "I'm sure you do. Too bad I don't want to hear it. Talk all you want, but I'm not going to stand out here and listen." She turned the knob and let herself into the house. "Go home, Shane. I don't want you here anymore."

Chapter Six

Shane lodged his foot in between the frame and the door just before Holly tried to close it. When she let out a frustrated huff and shot him a glare, he pushed his way into the house and slammed the door behind him.

She might not want to hear his reasons, but the way he saw it, she didn't have much choice in the matter. Until she understood what had happened, he had no intention of leaving.

No. That was a lie. He had no intention of leaving at all, whether she understood or not. One night hadn't been nearly enough. She could pretend all she wanted, but he saw the need in her eyes.

He crossed his arms over his chest. "You were with Andrew."

"Yes. We always go out for a late dinner on Sunday nights. Did you really expect me to rearrange my whole life because we had sex?"

He took in the sight of her wearing his favorite color—red—in the form of a slinky, ankle-length dress that made his mouth water and his cock ache. She'd dressed like that for Andrew, not for him. His jaw tensed. "Did he tell you I spoke with him?"

"He mentioned you called."

Shane narrowed his eyes. Of all the crap Andrew could feed her. An underhanded and deceitful move—but not unexpected. Finally, the real Andrew was showing through the polished exterior. He ran a hand through his hair, trying not to grin at the murderous look on Holly's face. A lock of hair had fallen across her cheek and he wanted to tuck it behind her ear. "I didn't call him, Holly. He called me."

Her glare softened a little, but suspicion laced the edges of her gaze. "He did?"

"Yeah, at around three this morning. Said he had a very urgent matter he needed to discuss right away. Swore up and down that it couldn't wait another second. What do you make of that?"

She said nothing, but the rest of the tension bled out of her expression, leaving her looking hurt and confused. Her throat worked as she swallowed, and she swiped a hand across her eyes. "What are you trying to tell me?"

"That your prince charming knew where I was. And that he knew the perfect time to contact me in order to pull me away from you."

"How could he know that?"

"I told him where I was going when I left the party. The only thing I can figure is that he had me followed to see if I left at a reasonable hour. When I didn't, he decided to prod me along."

"Why would he care?"

"Because he knows how I feel about you. He's always known, and he's been using it against me."

Doubt clouded her gaze and he bit back a curse. He'd said too much. It was time to pull back a little before he lost her trust—if walking away from her early that morning hadn't already done that.

She locked the door before walking down the hallway, leaving him standing alone in the entryway. He followed and found her by the window overlooking the back yard.

"Why would he use something against you?" she asked without turning around. "I thought you were friends."

He leaned against the doorframe and caught her gaze in the reflection in the window. "We are. But we've known each other for a long time. Sometimes I think too long. We've had our fair share of disagreements, and Andrew knows how to play dirty."

"You sound just like him. Both of you are paranoid."

"Maybe we are, but there are things you don't know. His call was the reason I left. He said it was urgent, so I hurried out, thinking I'd get back to you as soon as I could. By the time I got away from him, you'd already gone to work."

Her tongue darted out to wet her lips, and the sight stirred feelings she wouldn't welcome right now. He bit back a curse and tried to push away his arousal, but he couldn't quite manage to quell it. Just being near her was enough to get him semi-hard. In the past two months, he'd spent many a night in silent misery.

All day Holly had been on his mind, no matter how many times he'd tried to banish her from his thoughts. She was even more of a distraction at a time when focus and concentration were vital. If he kept going this way, he'd get himself killed.

She spun around, her hands on her hips, and stalked over to him.

"What was so urgent that you couldn't even leave a note? Or try to call me sometime today?"

Saving your life.

He blew out a breath rife with frustration. He didn't have an answer for her, at least not one he was free to give. If he told her, he'd have to tell her everything. She wasn't ready for the truth.

"I had to make an emergency trip out of town to look into a few things. It took longer than I expected." And had been completely fruitless, but Andrew had set it up to play out that way. He'd wanted Holly all to himself, and he'd gotten her. For a little while. Now it was Shane's turn, and he didn't plan to let her out of his sight again.

Instead of continuing the argument, he lifted the strand of hair off her face. It felt soft between his fingers.

Holly's eyes narrowed. "Don't think you can look at me like that and expect me to let you off the hook."

"Look at you like what?"

"Like you did last night." Her answer was nothing more than a whisper, but the effect was so strong it nearly brought him to his knees.

He cupped her chin in his hand and brought his lips to hers. Kissing her was pure heaven, but the contact didn't last long before Holly stepped away.

"What do you think you're doing?" She glared at him, but he caught a glimpse of burning need behind the anger in her eyes.

"It killed me to be away from you. I don't know what this thing is between us, I just know that I want to be with you all the time."

If he was with her all the time, she'd be protected. And he'd have a chance to quench the ache he'd felt for her for so long.

"This is crazy."

"Yeah. That's what makes it so good."

Confusion reigned in Holly's mind. She wanted to trust Shane, and she'd tried, but had yet to manage it completely. He sounded sincere, and after Andrew's tirade, she wouldn't doubt if he really had tried something to keep her and Shane apart. But she didn't know for sure, and Shane's expression gave away nothing.

What upset her the most was that, even after he'd snuck away without a word, she still wanted him. Her body still reacted to the memories of what they'd done. Even now, her panties were damp and she had to bite back a whimper.

His mouth had been so hot last night. His touch had sent ripples of sensation along her skin. She had to set that all aside now and focus on the matter at hand.

He stepped toward her and she shook her head. "Are you telling me the truth?"

"Of course, I am. Why would I lie to you?"

She was still trying to figure that out. She brushed past him and walked into the living room, kicking off her shoes along the way. Her purse dropped onto the end table next to the couch, and she moved to the window and glanced out into the darkness.

"Talk to me, Holly. Tell me what's on your mind."

Shane's whispered voice came from right behind her and she jumped. "Why do you always sneak up on me like that?"

His hands came to rest on her hips and he pulled her back against him. Despite her aggravation, her body soaked up his warmth.

Instead of answering, he leaned down and pressed his lips to the side of her neck. That was all it took for her to melt in his arms. One night in her bed, and he already knew right where to kiss her to make her whole body quiver.

"I wish I'd been able to wake up with you this morning." He nipped at her earlobe. "There were so many things I wanted to do to you."

She shuddered. "Like what?"

He chuckled, stepped back, and pulled down the zipper of her dress. He pushed the fabric off her shoulders and the satin dropped to the floor with a whoosh. She stepped out of the dress, and Shane kissed her between her shoulder blades before he released the clasp of her bra and drew the straps down her arms. Then he skimmed her panties down her legs, leaving her wearing nothing at all.

"Like this." His hand spanned her hips. His clothes felt rough against her back. She shivered. Her tongue darted out to wet her lips. She'd been afraid of this. Though she'd tried to fight it, there was nothing she could do about it now. Shane was dangerous. Mysterious. The wrong man for her in so many ways.

And she couldn't tell him no.

The sight of herself reflected in the glass sent a shiver through her. Her skin was flushed, her lips parted and her eyes hazy. Shane met her gaze in the window and smiled.

His warm palms skimmed down her body until he reached the juncture of her thighs. He dipped a finger lower and rubbed it across her clit. "And this. I've been waiting hours to do this to you again."

She dropped her head back against his shoulder. The reactions inside her were basic, primal, and she could no more stop them than she could stop breathing. She needed Shane on a level she barely understood.

"Why are you doing this to me?" she whispered.

He circled his finger over the bud of her clit, making her hips arch. "Don't tell me you don't want my touch. That would be a lie."

As if to prove his point, he released her and stepped back. Her legs buckled and she whimpered, putting her hands on the window frame for support. Her gaze focused on the darkness in the yard around her. She shivered. Though the area where she lived was quiet, anyone could look inside the window and see everything.

She started to shrink back, away from the glass, but Shane put his hand on the center of her back and held her there. "Don't move, Holly."

"Let me pull the curtains closed."

"Why? There's no one out there." He inched his hand around her body and cupped her breast. Soon the other hand followed, and he pinched her nipples between his thumbs and forefingers.

She bit back a scream of sheer pleasure. "How can you be sure?"

"I'm not."

The seductive tone in his voice made her pussy quiver. Someone might be out there, watching them from the cover of darkness. The idea shouldn't have turned her on, but it did.

He pressed against her and thrust forward. The feel of his hard cock between her ass cheeks, even through his clothes, only increased her arousal. A sob caught in her throat. He planned to torture her again before he let her come, and there was nothing she could do about it. She refused to beg. That was what he wanted her to do, and she wouldn't give him the satisfaction if he gave her nothing but torment in return.

She bit her lip to stay silent as he trailed a hand back down her body and pushed it between her legs. His fingers stroked along her folds before he dipped them inside her. At the same time, he squeezed her nipple and leaned down to sink his teeth into the flesh above her shoulder blade. The bite was harder than before, and it nearly made her come.

A harsh cry burst from her throat and she writhed against him.

Shane's laugh rumbled against her skin. "I've wanted to do this to you, too. For so long."

He bit down again and a tremor rushed through her pussy. "And as much as I'd love to continue playing with you like this, there are things I'd much rather be doing."

He released his hold on her and she swayed toward the window. She took a moment to catch her breath before daring to turn around. Finally she pivoted, pressing her back against the glass for support. Shane was in the process of stripping out of his clothes.

He pulled his shirt over his head and tossed it to the floor. It landed next to her dress. His chest and stomach were toned, covered in a smattering of fine, dark hairs a shade darker than the hair on his head. Her fingers itched to skim down the ridges of his six-pack, but she held back and waited. Last night they'd barely had a chance to undress before they'd dropped to the mattress and fallen asleep. Tonight, she wanted to look.

His hands moved to the waistband of his jeans. He unsnapped them and dragged the zipper down. He kicked out of his shoes, and the pants and socks were next to go, leaving him standing in front of her in nothing but black boxers. The head of his cock poked out above the waistband and she licked her lips.

She stood rapt while he hooked his thumbs in the waistband and pulled the boxers off. They dropped to the floor and he stepped out of them, walking forward until he stood only inches from her.

Her mouth went dry at the sight of him. Such a beautiful man, and yet so flawed. Puckered, shiny scars marred his chest, abdomen, and thighs. A particularly gruesome one ran across one shoulder. She reached out and traced her finger along the smooth flesh. "What happened?"

A hint of a smile played across his lips. "Which time?"

"Any of them."

He shrugged. "Fights, mostly. Not recently. In another lifetime."

She wanted to question him more, to learn more about the man who was slowly working his way under her skin, but he didn't give her a chance. He pulled her close and kissed her.

She clung to him, relishing in the feel of skin on skin, heat against heat. This was what she'd been wanting for months. What she'd been craving. But now it wasn't enough. She needed so much more.

Shane broke the kiss and took her hand, leading her toward the couch. Once they reached it, he settled her onto the cushions and dropped to his knees in front of her.

A shiver raced down her spine. What did he have planned?

In the next instant, her question was answered. He moved her legs apart and spread her pussy lips with his thumbs. His breath brushed across the wet folds, dragging a moan from her chest. And then he leaned in to kiss her there.

Her back arched off the couch. His tongue played across her clit, licking and swirling as his lips nibbled. She threaded her fingers through his hair and arched toward him. The warm, wet heat of his mouth had her hips bucking and her breath rasping from her lungs.

"*Oh, my God.*" Her words came out on a moan.

Shane drove his tongue inside her and her hips came off the couch. His hands moved to her rear and he held her there, not letting her move more than a few inches while he ate at her with the fervor of a man long denied.

She tightened her grip on his hair, but it wasn't enough. Her hands dropped to his shoulders and she dug her nails into the soft flesh there.

His hiss against her pussy made her throw her head back and scream. The unexpected orgasm rushed over her, dragging her along as wave after wave of pleasure rocked her body. Her vision grayed and her mind threatened to shut down. All the while, Shane held her in place against his mouth, and the feel of his slick tongue only made the tremors stronger.

She bucked against him and pushed at him with her hands, the intensity almost too much to stand. "Shane, I can't take anymore."

He lifted his head long enough to give her a knowing smile. "I think you can."

He brought his mouth back down to her pussy and sucked her clit into his mouth. A second orgasm followed right on the heels of the first. Her entire body shook and shuddered and she could barely draw a full breath. Her hands dropped to the couch and she threw her head back, unable to do anything but ride out the waves. It seemed like hours before Shane finally lifted his head.

"You okay?"

She couldn't manage more than a mumble.

The next thing she knew, she was being lifted off the couch. She ended up on her hands and knees on the soft carpet. Shane's hand caressed her back. His cock prodded her entrance.

"Can you hold yourself up like this?"

"I think so."

"Good."

His hands came to her hips and he pulled her back against him. His cock slid into her, stirring another round of quivers in her sensitized pussy.

Her elbows buckled and she bent them, resting her forehead on her clasped hands. When he came, she felt it with every fiber of her being.

She would never be the same.

Sometime later, Holly lay falling asleep in Shane's arms. She still had no idea how they'd managed to make it to the bed, but she was glad they had. Her muscles ached and she knew she'd be sore in the morning.

He stroked his hand up and down her arm and kissed the top of her head.

"You okay?" The sleepiness in his tone made her smile.

"I'm fine." Wonderful. The monsters from her nightmares licked at the edges of her consciousness, but she pushed them away. Just for one night, she wanted to be normal. No problems, no worries, just a woman who was falling in love with the man of her dreams. The connection that had formed between them when they'd first met had solidified into something strong. Something deeper than she could rationalize.

Too bad she didn't know anything about him.

The thought made her freeze. A sense of foreboding lodged in her throat, and no matter how many times she tried, she couldn't swallow it down. Instinct told her she could trust him.

She just hoped that instinct would hold up when all the secrets around them finally came to light.

Chapter Seven

Holly padded into the kitchen to find Shane at the counter, making coffee. The tension inside her eased a little at the sight of him. When she'd woken up to an empty bed again, she'd feared the worst.

The scene before her was so normal, though, that it set her on edge in a different way. Her heart stuttered and she tried to ignore the warm sensations in her belly. She didn't want a commitment, least of all with someone like him.

He wore only his jeans, loose around his tapered hips. Probably unbuttoned. When he put the coffee can back on a high cabinet shelf, the muscles of his back stretched and bunched under his tanned skin. Slight red streaks from her nails marred his shoulder blades.

A small smile tipped up the corners of her lips. The man was sheer perfection, and for the moment, all hers.

A quick shake of her head brought her back to her senses. She had to get moving. Had to shower and go to work. Life went on. Her obligations didn't care about Shane, or the myriad complications he brought into her life.

Getting on with her life would be so much easier if she could stop thinking about how good he looked standing half-naked in her kitchen.

Or how he'd looked last night, naked in her bed.

She cleared her throat. "Good morning."

"Morning," he said without turning around. "What do you want for breakfast? I'm not much of a cook, but I think I can manage pancakes or something. Maybe eggs, if you don't mind the occasional shell."

"Just coffee for now would be great. I never eat anything this early." She settled into a chair and a little while later, he placed a coffee mug in front of her, along with a small carton of cream and the sugar bowl from the counter.

"Thanks." She couldn't help the smile that spread across her lips. So he was here. That didn't mean he planned to stay forever. "I can see you've made yourself right at home."

"Yeah, I figured since I was awake, I might as well make myself use-ful."

She fixed her coffee and took a sip, but set the mug down when she got a taste of the bitter brew. "Is this the same recipe they use for jet fuel?"

"I've been told it's pretty close." He laughed. "Do you want me to make another pot? I could make it weaker."

"No, thanks. This is fine." She brought the mug back to her lips, at-tempting not to wince at the taste. Each sip served as another reminder of his faults. He did have them, and she'd be better off in the end if she remembered that.

After a few moments of silence, Shane asked, "What did you and Andrew talk about last night?"

The sip of coffee she'd been in the process of taking went down wrong. She sputtered and coughed and smacked her chest until the pain subsided. "Why do you want to know that?"

"Just curious."

She studied his expression, looking for anything that might alert her to his true intentions. She found nothing out of the ordinary, but decided to proceed with caution anyway. Andrew hadn't shown much reaction at first, either. Getting involved with Shane had dropped her into dangerous territory. Finally, she said, "We talked about a lot of things."

"And you're still seeing him."

Yes. No. She had no idea where she stood with Andrew anymore, or what she even wanted from him. "He's my friend. He's never really been much more than that, and I think he knows it."

Shane looked away.

"What's wrong?"

He settled across from her and folded his hands on the table. His expression remained neutral, but the tick in his jaw alerted her to his frustration. "This is a mess."

"I would have to agree."

"So what are we supposed to do about it?"

She shrugged. "I don't see there's much we can do."

"Right. Just go with the flow. Let things play out and see what hap-pens." Tension threaded through the words. He sat back and cocked his head to the side, regarding her through narrowed eyes. "I gotta say, Holly, that's not really my style."

She blinked. Everything about him screamed that he was impulsive.

Reckless. "You don't seem like a planner to me."

"No?" He shook his head and let out a short burst of laughter. "It may surprise you, but I don't do anything without thinking it through first."

The heated look he gave her made her tingle all over. She squirmed in her seat. "Getting involved with me wasn't an impulse?"

"I knew what I wanted the moment I saw you. The first time we spoke, I was a goner." He glanced away, as if his admission hadn't come easily. "I felt a connection between us right from the start. That's not something a guy can walk away from and not regret for the rest of his life."

She bit her lip to keep from smiling, but the smile came anyway. "So you planned this?"

"No." He laughed and shook his head. "I hoped. Did what I could to show you what we could have, if you just gave me a chance. I just never expected so many problems. I thought Andrew understood, but I guess I was wrong."

"So what do you suggest? I don't see any easy way out. Not now. Not after we've... " Her voice trailed off and she waved her hand in the air. Her life had been so simple before Shane. She worked, went home, and a few nights a week got together with Andrew or one of her female friends. The only worries and fears she'd had were the ones she'd long ago stuffed into the back corners of her mind.

Now the worries stood at the forefront, ready to drown her the second she showed weakness. Keeping up her strength got harder with each passing day.

"What are you thinking about?" Shane's voice cut into her thoughts and yanked her back to the present. "You look like you're a million miles away. Does my being here upset you that much?"

"No, I want you here." Her thoughts were in turmoil, but she understood above everything else that she wanted Shane in her life. There would be no more denying it. She didn't have it in her to fight the attraction anymore. He might be the worst of her complications, but he also made her feel safer than she had in years.

She took another sip of coffee and tried to ignore his scorching gaze.

After a minute of charged silence, he spoke. "Can I ask you a question?"

"Sure."

"Why did you start seeing Andrew in the first place? He doesn't seem like your type."

The answer came to her easily, but owning up to it created a problem. To acknowledge her reason would be to admit weakness. She met Shane's gaze and wet her lips with the tip of her tongue. A fortifying breath later, she was ready to lay it all down. "Andrew is safe. That's what attracted me to him."

It had been the only thing that attracted her to him. He was good-looking, in a polished-to-the-hilt sort of way, and he had a charm that she imagined most women would find hard to resist, but it was the way he made her feel protected that had drawn her to him and kept her around even after she'd realized there would never be any spark between them.

Shane raised an eyebrow. "Safe?"

"I've had a dangerous man in my life before. I wanted someone the complete opposite of my husband. Someone who didn't take unnecessary chances. Someone who didn't involve himself in activities that could get him or the people around him hurt."

Shane glanced out the window. The muscles across his shoulders tightened. "What happened to him?"

"He died." Holly shook her head. Just saying he'd died didn't seem like an apt description for what had really happened. It didn't do justice to her nightmares. "No, he didn't just die. He was killed. Murdered." Systematically mutilated. Taken apart right in front of her eyes.

To this day, she couldn't shake the images from her mind, though her memories of the night were a little fuzzy. Stress, the doctors had told her. She'd probably never remember everything that had happened, and she couldn't say that the thought upset her. There were some things better left in the dark.

"You saw it happen?"

She nodded. An errant tear formed in the corner of her eye and she batted it away.

"That must have been horrible."

"You have no idea."

Shane pushed up from the chair and moved to the cabinet. He grabbed a glass and brought it to the sink, filling it with water from the tap. When he spoke again, his back was to her. "What happened to him?"

Holly swallowed past the sudden dryness in her throat. Shane's question was a good one. One she wished she had all the answers to. "Mike was involved in business dealings with some bad people, and I guess he upset them. They found him and... well, they didn't let him get away with whatever he'd done."

Shane's shoulders tensed. He gulped down the water and set the glass on the counter with a dull thump.

"Are you okay?" She stood and walked over to him, reaching up and placing her hand in the center of his back. He jumped, and she frowned at his reaction.

"Yeah. Fine. Just tired. We didn't get a lot of sleep last night." His laugh sounded weak and strained.

What was going on inside his head? He asked the questions, but seemed upset by her answers. Something wasn't right. "Talk to me, Shane."

His shoulders slumped and his head dropped. His back moved as he sucked in a breath and let it out on a sigh. "I'm sorry about your husband. Sorry that you had to see it happen. Were you hurt?"

She chewed on her lower lip for a brief second before releasing it. Her physical wounds had long since healed, but the emotional ones had left scars no amount of time could erase. "They attacked me. I think they wanted to kill me, but someone stopped them."

"How?" Tension laced his tone and she glanced at his hands to see them gripping the sink so tightly his knuckles had turned white.

She swallowed hard. Fear tried to take root in her mind, but she pushed it away. She might not know as much about Shane as she wanted to, but she knew he'd never hurt her. "I don't know. I was in too much pain at the time. All I remember is one minute being tied to a chair, and the next waking up in a hospital with the doctors telling me my house had caught on fire and I was lucky to be alive."

She closed her eyes for a brief second. Bile rose in her throat. A fire.

A cover-up was more like it. Andrew and Shane were the only ones who knew her husband had been murdered.

She'd tried to tell the doctors at the hospital, and then the police they'd brought in at her request, but no one had believed her. They'd called her crazy, and for a long time she'd thought they were right. She'd seen psychiatrists, and had learned early on that it was better to keep her mouth shut.

"I am lucky, I guess." Lucky that she hadn't endured even half the torture Mike had.

Some of the tension seemed to drain from Shane's body and he leaned back against her touch. "Yeah. Sounds like they were right about that."

"Sounds like." She rested her cheek against his back, relishing in his warmth against her, but the unsettled feeling didn't leave.

She stepped away. "I have to get ready for work. If I don't head out soon, I'm going to be late."

She was halfway down the short hallway to her bedroom before Shane's voice brought her to a stop.

"You think I'm dangerous."

She walked back to the kitchen and stopped in the doorway. "Is that what's bothering you?"

"Yes." He turned around and faced her with his hands in the pockets of his jeans. Her gaze dipped to the unbuttoned waistband and she bit her lip. "I'm not dangerous to you. I would never do anything to hurt you. All I want to do is make sure you're safe."

Deep inside, she knew that, but her first impressions of the man refused to leave her mind. Shane was an enigma, and no matter how hard she tried to figure him out, she had a feeling she'd barely scratched the surface.

"I know you wouldn't hurt me." He wouldn't mean to. But when he left, it would hurt. She wouldn't be able to stop the pain.

She wouldn't do anything about it, though. He'd told her when they'd first met that his stay in Granville was extended, but temporary. She wouldn't try to hold him when he left. It would be selfish to do so, and would only lead to resentment in the end. Just as Andrew held no claim over her, she held no claim over Shane, and it would be foolish to think otherwise.

Shane glanced at the clock. "You said you'd be late if you didn't take off soon."

Holly nodded. "Are you going to stick around?"

"No, I have some work to catch up on."

He turned back to the sink and she walked away, the tension inside her worse than it had ever been. She pressed her hand to her stomach. Somehow, she had to find a way to make everything right.

Chapter Eight

Holly yawned and stretched her arms out to her sides. Work had been a killer today. The ER waiting room had been brimming with the sick and injured from the second she'd walked through the doors. Two hours after her shift had been due to end, she'd finally managed to punch out and head home. Now, ten minutes after she'd made it through the door, she could barely keep her eyes open.

She took a quick shower and changed before making her way into the kitchen for something to eat, though it was more out of habit than hunger.

Just as she turned on the kitchen light, a scraping sound caught her attention. She froze, not even daring to breathe, while she waited for the sound to come again. When it didn't, she forced a laugh. Her exhaustion must be spawning hallucinations.

Still, she couldn't be too cautious. She'd moved toward the window to shut the blinds when the sound came again. It was a high, soft sound. Grating, almost like the scraping of metal on glass.

Her heart pounded against her ribs and her stomach ached. It didn't matter whether or not someone was watching her. Didn't matter that her imagination might have conjured up the noises. Paranoia caused everything around her to seem suspect.

Her gaze still on the window over the sink, she walked backward, her hand outstretched behind her. When she bumped into the wall, she reached blindly for the light switch. As soon as she found it, she pushed it down and threw the room into darkness.

Once her eyes adjusted, she squinted out the window, but saw nothing. Not even the shadows moved tonight.

She rushed over to the phone and grabbed it off the cradle, dialing Shane's cell number with shaky fingers.

Ten minutes later, he was pounding on the door. She let out a breath and let him into the house.

His worried gaze met hers. "Tell me exactly what happened."

The hard glint in his eyes and the set of his shoulders made her want to cringe away from him, but she forced herself to stay where she was. He wasn't the one she needed to be afraid of.

Taking a quick breath, she said, "Just what I told you on the phone. Nothing specific happened. I just felt like I was being watched. I heard noises at the window, but... I guess it could have been my imagination working overtime. I had a stressful day at work." She tried to chuckle, but the sound came out as little more than a shaky sigh. "I-I'm sorry if I pulled you away from something important."

"Your safety is my top priority right now. Nothing else even comes close," he told her, his voice barely above a whisper. "Lock the door behind me, and turn off any light in the house that you don't need to see what you're doing. Hit the outside ones, too. All of them. Then go pack a bag with everything you need to get you through a couple days. I'll be right back."

Panic swelled in her chest. No! She didn't want him to leave her alone, even for a second. "Where are you going?"

"To check around the outside of the house. Now please, Holly, just do what I asked."

The tense set of his shoulders belied the calm tone of his voice and she swallowed hard. "Okay. I'll go pack."

Shane gave a short nod before grabbing her keys from the table next to the door and stepping out into the darkness.

It took her ten minutes to shut off the lights and pack a bag, and by that time, Shane had let himself back in. She met him in the kitchen and the expression on his face made her whole body go numb. "What's the matter?"

"There are footprints in the dirt by your back door, and mud tracked up the rear steps. Footprints under the window, too." He gestured to the window over the sink. "I didn't find anyone out there, but that doesn't mean they left."

"They?"

He glanced away. "Yeah."

He was keeping something from her. The idea that he still couldn't be entirely honest with her made her stomach twist. Angry heat washed over her. Someone was trying to hurt her, possibly even kill her, and Shane wouldn't even be up front about what he'd learned.

She narrowed her eyes. "So what happens now? Are you planning to send me to a hotel?"

"You're coming home with me." He glanced back at her, his gaze filled with resolve. "I'm not going to take any more unnecessary chances with your safety."

"I'm not sure if that's such a good idea."

"Don't argue. Remember what happened..." He shook his head. "Whoever this is—they aren't giving up. They're serious. They want to hurt you, and this is nothing to fool around with. You'll be safe at my place."

Her mind reeled. "How can you guarantee that?" How could he possibly know she'd be safe? She didn't know enough about him to take him at his word. Though she'd come to care about him in the two months since they'd met, his secrecy, along with his apparent knowledge about the people trying to hurt her, kept her from trusting him completely.

"I can guarantee it because I'm not going to let you out of my sight until I catch these guys and put an end to the problem."

These guys. It sounded almost like a familiar term. Unsure of what to say, she kept her mouth closed for a few seconds. The night she'd been attacked, he hadn't seemed surprised to see the man holding her. In fact, he'd been prepared, a knife clutched in his hand. He hadn't seemed surprised when she'd told him about Mike's death. Upset, but not surprised. His eerie calm settled like a rock in the pit of her stomach.

When she spoke, she had to clear her throat to get her voice to work. "You know what's going on, don't you?"

He stared at her, but didn't say a word. He didn't need to speak. The answer was right there in his eyes.

"You know who's trying to hurt me."

His nod was so slight she almost missed it.

A sliver of doubt wedged in her mind. Had she placed her trust in the wrong man? "Please don't tell me this has something to do with Andrew." She'd send him packing if this was all about trying to turn her against Andrew. The men might be at odds with each other right now, but she didn't want to get in the middle of what seemed to be a private feud.

"No, it doesn't have anything to do with him. It's about your husband. Let's get out of here. I don't like you being here any longer than necessary."

He reached for her elbow, but she pulled her arm away. "I don't want to go anywhere with you until I know the whole truth. I can't trust you when you won't even be honest with me."

"I've never lied to you. Right now we don't have time to argue." His tone was frustrated, his jaw tight. The worry in his eyes made her swallow hard. "Let's get moving Holly, before it gets too late."

She crossed her arms over her chest. "I'm not going anywhere until you start talking."

Shane blew out a breath and shook his head. When he glanced back at her, frustration etched his gaze. "Wanna bet?"

⁂

Holly dropped her bag on the floor next to the door and crossed her arms over her chest. Her expression gave new meaning to the phrase "If looks could kill". Shane would have laughed at the sight, had the situation not taken such a dangerous turn.

The things that had been outside her window had taken her by surprise. She wore flannel lounge pants and a baggy sweatshirt. Her hair was thrown back into a messy ponytail and her face, pale and free of makeup, looked years younger than her twenty-nine. The dark circles under her eyes worried him most. Those, and the suspicious glare she'd fixed on him.

Her suspicion hit him like a spike through his heart and he had to fight to keep from reeling back. He couldn't fault her for her anger. He deserved every bit of it after he'd all but shoved her into the passenger seat of his car. But he'd only done what he had to. He'd much rather have her angry and alive than dead.

He locked the door and stepped into the room. If he didn't react, maybe some of her ire would cool. "You must be starving. What do you want for dinner? We can order something from any place that delivers."

She raised an eyebrow. "I'm not hungry."

He would have bought into her bravado had he not noticed the way her shoulders shook whenever she drew a breath. Seeing her like this made his head throb. An ache started in his chest. He wanted to pull her to him and never let her go, but he pushed his hands through his hair instead.

"How about some coffee, or some tea? I think I might even have a couple cans of soda in the fridge."

"I'm not thirsty."

"Are you going to be pissed at me all night?"

"Yes. I have a right to be. Does the word 'kidnapping' mean anything to you?"

Her accusatory tone only increased his frustration until it felt like the top of his head would come off. "I did not kidnap you."

"You might as well have. You didn't even give me a choice. It amazes me that you don't see it. Andrew never would have forced me the way you did. He respects that I can take care of myself."

Anger sliced through his gut and he leaned against the wall. She really had no clue what she was up against. If she knew, she'd be grateful to him for getting her away in time. "First of all, don't compare me to Andrew. Just don't. He's not what you think he is. Second of all, he would have done the same thing, given the situation. You don't understand what you're dealing with."

"Since you're suddenly the expert, why don't you tell me all about it?"

A bitter laugh stuck in his throat. Maybe he should have told her the truth long ago. At the beginning. Now, after everything that had happened between them, it was a little late to start. "Go sit down in the living room. Take your shoes off and relax. Then we'll talk."

"Sorry. Not in the mood. I want answers, and I want them right now. I'm not moving until I get them."

Explaining the situation to her would only send her running out of his apartment. Once she knew, she wouldn't run to Andrew, either, and that would leave her with nowhere else to go. He couldn't take the chance of that happening, but he had to give her some information or she would leave anyway. The trick would be to scare her enough to keep her safe at his place without letting her in on something that would make her stop trusting him.

His eyes narrowed. "Do you remember what your husband's body looked like when he was killed?"

Her throat worked as she swallowed. She nodded.

"He was in pain, wasn't he?"

She nodded again. Her eyes widened and she clasped her hands in front of her. "In agony."

"Do you want to take the chance of that happening to you?"

"N-no."

"Then you need to trust me. If the guys who are after you catch you, that's exactly what's going to happen. Cut me a little slack, Holly. I know what I'm doing. You think I have all this information that I'm keeping from you, but I don't. I don't know much more than you do."

"Maybe you should cut me a little slack. I'm not helpless."

He recognized the defense mechanism for what it was, but it still grated on him. Would it be so hard to accept a little help from him when she so desperately needed it?

He let out a breath through pursed lips. "Holly, please stop fighting me on this. I just want to make sure you're protected."

Her shoulders slumped and she let out a watery sigh. "I'm sorry. I'm trying to trust you, but it's hard when you won't tell me what's going on."

"You know all that's important. Someone is trying to hurt you, maybe kill you. I'm working to make sure that doesn't happen. The more you fight me, the harder it's going to be to keep you safe."

She swiped at her eyes. "How do you know all this? How can you be so sure?"

He spread his hands out in front of him, unable to stop the smile that lifted one corner of his mouth. If she'd seen half the things he'd seen in his lifetime...

He shook his head. "I've been around for a while. I've seen things. Up until a few years ago, I made a living protecting people from those things."

Most of the anger evaporated from her expression. She closed her eyes for a brief second and blew out a breath. When she opened her eyes, acceptance filled her gaze. "I'm sorry for snapping, but this is hell on me. It's like pulling teeth trying to get information from you, and that only adds to my stress level."

"You don't have anything to be sorry for."

"You and I both know that's not true."

Her sad smile told him she was talking about more than just the threats to her life. Instead of letting himself think about that, he moved closer and took her in his arms, relishing the feel of her warmth against him.

She shook her head. "I'm still angry with you."

"I know." He couldn't do anything about it, either, and that killed him. She didn't deserve this kind of life.

With a small shake of her head, she wrapped one hand around the back of his neck, bringing his lips down to meet hers.

She swiped her tongue across the seam of his lips and he parted them, surprised at her boldness. She stroked her tongue into his mouth, her fingers tangling in his hair. An urgency he hadn't expected tinged the kiss.

When she pulled away, she started working on the buttons on his shirt.

He grabbed her wrists to still her hands. "What are you doing?"

She laughed. "Can't you tell?"

"Yeah. I can tell." He wasn't stupid. The second she'd touched him his body had reacted. "But why now, in the middle of all this?"

"Shut up and enjoy the adrenaline rush while it lasts, okay?"

He opened his mouth to say something, but then thought better of it. If this was what she wanted, who was he to question her? They would have plenty of time in the morning to hash out what had happened and what needed to be done next. For now, he was just glad she'd stopped glaring at him.

Her movements were frantic as she fought to get his shirt off, and he helped her unbutton it and pull it off his shoulders. Her fingernails scraped across his nipples just before she leaned in and followed the path her fingers had taken with the tip of her tongue. His cock, already semi-hard against the zipper of his jeans, swelled.

Holly's glance told him she noticed his reaction. "Why can't I get you out of my head?"

The same sentiment echoed inside him, and he shook his head. He'd been trying to put her to the back of his mind, but every time he thought he'd accomplished it, he saw her and he was lost all over again.

"I don't want you there," she continued, pushing him toward the door. His back smacked against it and she splayed her hands across his chest. "But I can't seem to get rid of you."

She leaned in and kissed his chest, her hands dropping to the waistband of his pants.

"Holly, stop. This is too fast."

She glanced up at him and stilled her hands. "Too fast? I didn't think men understood the concept. You had your turn the last two times. Now you need to let me have mine."

Suddenly everything made sense. She was feeling out of control about her life, so she needed to take control of something.

He understood the feeling all too well.

His head dropped back against the door. She'd be the death of him yet. Soon she had his pants undone and had freed his cock from the confines of his boxers. Her hand wrapped around him, and she stroked up and down his length. He groaned. It was too slow, too light, and he needed so much more.

A quick glance at her told him she knew it, too.

The feel of her hand on his cock sent shivers down his spine. Shivers that settled low in his gut and drew his balls up against his body. He let her play for as long as he could, but then it got to be too much. If she kept toying with him, he'd come and she wouldn't get any satisfaction.

He pulled her hands away and knelt down to pull her sweatpants off. "Shane?"

"I can't wait. I was so worried about you earlier, and now that I know you're okay..." When she stepped out of the pants and panties, he tossed them across the floor. He didn't even bother to strip her out of the rest of her clothes before he had her pressed against the door, her legs around his waist and his cock hammering into her.

Her climax was almost immediate. She clutched at his shoulders and her pussy muscles clenched around him, driving him even closer to his own release. He wondered if it would always be like this with Holly. So fast, so intense.

Her lips on his neck proved to be his undoing. All thought faded from his mind and he stroked hard into her, pumping her full of his seed.

Once his body stopped shaking, he pulled out of her and let her feet slide down to the floor. He leaned his forehead against hers. "Did I hurt you?"

"Of course not." Her hand stroked down his back.

A desolate feeling settled over him, even as he realized the truth. Somewhere in the past two months, he'd fallen in love with this woman.

When she found out what he really was, she'd never want to see him again.

Chapter Nine

Holly stood at Andrew's front door, her fist poised to knock, but something inside kept her from going through with telling him goodbye. He wouldn't be happy about why she'd come. Wouldn't understand what she needed to tell him. But the words had to be said, and she'd rather do it in person than over the telephone.

She glanced back at Shane's car in the driveway, and she shook her head. Even though she'd told him this was something she needed to do alone, he hadn't been willing to leave her.

And when she came back outside, he'd still be waiting for her.

The idea made her throat run dry. She wanted to trust him, and Lord knew she'd been trying, but there was still so much she didn't know. How was it possible that she found herself falling in love with a man she couldn't completely trust? The two ideas were at odds with each other, and no matter how many times she tried to think of an explanation, one didn't come.

She dropped her hand to her side, only to bring it back up again. One thing in this whole mess was certain. She had to break it off with Andrew. The time had come to tell him she'd never love him the way he wanted her to. She refused to string him along anymore—and she'd tell him that as soon as she gathered her courage.

She could almost hear Shane in her head, laughing at her anxiety, and that imagined laughter was what finally gave her the courage to knock.

She waited, breath held, for what felt like an eternity before the door swung open and Andrew stood in front of her.

"Hey." He smiled, but the smile didn't make it to his eyes. He glanced past her, toward the driveway, and his eyes darkened.

"Can we talk? It's important."

He stared at her for a few seconds, his expression wary, before he stepped back and opened the door a few more inches. "Sure. Come on in."

A few deep breaths later, she walked past the threshold into the familiar, cool darkness. At first, the cavernous house had intimidated her, but she'd since gotten comfortable with the size and dim lighting. Andrew had always preferred the darkness.

The thought made her stomach roll. Shane's talk of her husband's death, combined with the recent attacks, had her questioning her choices in the past five years. She now saw every move she'd made as a potential misstep. Each breath, each spoken word could have been the one to bring danger back to her door.

She began to wonder if meeting Andrew hadn't been a coincidence. But was he trying to protect her, as Shane was, or did he mean to hurt her?

The door creaked on its hinges before it shut with a slam. Holly jumped.

"Are you okay?" Andrew asked. The click of the lock sliding into place echoed through the stillness of the room.

"It's been a long week."

"Why don't we go sit down, then? You look like you could use a rest."

When she nodded, he took her elbow and led her into the small parlor to the left of the entryway. "How are you, Holly? I mean, how are you really?"

She took a seat in a red, antique wingback across from the matching couch. "I'm fine."

"You don't look fine." Andrew settled on the couch and crossed his legs, dropping his folded hands onto his lap. "I've missed you."

She tugged her lower lip into her mouth and bit down for a second before letting it go. "I've missed you, too."

His eyes narrowed almost imperceptibly and guilt swelled in her throat. She hadn't lied to him. She had missed him. He was one of the few people she'd let herself get close to since Mike's death. But she wasn't in love with him. Somewhere in the past few months, she'd fallen in love with his best friend instead.

"Are you sure about that?" He kept his tone neutral, but the sharpness of his gaze let her know he understood why she'd come to see him—and he wasn't letting her off the hook easily.

She steepled her fingers and brought them to her lips. Her eyelids fluttered closed for a second before she opened them again and dropped her hands. "Don't do this, Andrew."

"Do what?"

"You know what I'm talking about."

"I'm not so sure that I do. Why don't you tell me all about it?"

The accusation in his tone stung like a slap across the face.

"Better still," he continued. "Why don't you tell me what you've been doing these past nights? And *who* you've been doing..."

She sucked in a breath of air that tasted stale and dusty. She'd known this would be difficult, but she'd never expected him to make it impossible. His gallant, gentlemanly attitude had morphed into something she didn't recognize. Again, the thought struck her that she didn't know him at all. "You said you didn't care. You told me to do what I wanted to."

"And you obviously did."

"I don't want to argue with you. I just came to tell you I can't see you anymore."

Andrew leaned forward, fire flashing in his gaze. His lips parted and his nostrils flared. "So now he's making you give up your friends?"

"Is that what we are?" At the moment, she felt anything but friendly toward him. Her anger waited just below the surface of her calm façade, fighting to break out and show him how she really felt about his mood swings.

"That's what I'd always thought. I'd hoped for more. It probably wasn't right to. I never should have expected something from you knowing you'd never be willing to give it."

She shifted in the chair, trying to think of something to say that wouldn't set him off again. Making him angry wouldn't solve anyone's problems. "You didn't do anything wrong."

"Didn't I? I should have known to keep Shane away from you." He shook his head and glanced down at his hands. When he looked back at her, regret clouded his expression. "I did know. I knew from the start that I never should have told him about us, but I couldn't help it. He always had everything he wanted, and I was left to struggle to hold on to whatever I could keep. Now things have changed, on the surface, but it's still the same. Shane still gets what he wants, and I get shit."

His words held a hint of menace that shook her. She wet her lips with the tip of her tongue. Andrew had never let on that he'd been unhappy. In fact, he'd seemed to relish the fact that he had enough money to buy whatever he wanted. "You're keeping secrets from me. You and Shane. There's something you're not telling me."

He let out a bitter laugh. "So many things."

"I think it's time you start. I want the truth."

He was silent for so long she feared he'd deny her request. She'd started to push herself up from the chair when he spoke.

"Sit down, Holly. Trust me. You'll want to be sitting for this."

She dropped back into the chair. "Okay. I'm listening."

"I know about your husband's murder." He spoke in barely a whisper, and she had to lean forward to hear him.

"I know. I explained it all to you when I told you I didn't want to make a commitment."

"You didn't need to explain anything. I already knew about it when we met."

An icy sliver of dread wedged itself in the back of her mind. "What are you talking about?"

"There are bad things out there, Holly. Like the creatures that killed Mike. They weren't human. They were monsters. Monsters with fangs and claws and red eyes that shined in the darkness." His expression grew taunting and a small smile lifted the corners of his lips. "Monsters that hurt you, and would have killed you if someone hadn't stepped in and saved your life."

She gripped the chair arms until she felt her nails dig into the fabric. She'd never told him the details. Hadn't told anyone the details, not even the police. Fear made her pulse pound in her ears. "How did you know?" Her voice came out as little more than a whisper.

"I know a lot of things. I know about you, but more importantly, I know about Mike and why he did what he did." His smile turned cold. "I also know about Shane. Everything about him."

Her face heated and she clenched her hands into fists. Part of her wanted to get up and run away from the house as fast as she could, but instinct warned her to stay. Andrew held the key to finding out why someone was trying to hurt her, and she wasn't leaving until she had the answers. "Why didn't you tell me this sooner?"

"I did it to protect you. But now I'm seeing I was wrong. I should have told you the truth from the start rather than try to spare your feelings." He shook his head and glanced toward the door. "Or maybe I should have tried harder to convince Shane to tell you. He's the one you want. You'd probably take the news a little better if you heard it from him."

A soft groan escaped her lips and an invisible fist tightened around her middle. "What news?" Had she been wrong to think Shane would protect her? What was it that they'd kept from her for so long?

"Shane is the one who stopped the monsters from killing you the night they killed Mike."

Chapter Ten

Shane hung back in the shadows outside the parlor door, his hands clenched into fists. He'd used his key to get inside the house, and he was glad he had. It looked like he would have to do some damage control. If Andrew had been within reach, he would have wrapped his fingers around his friend's neck and squeezed until all the life bled out of him. Anger washed over him, but he bit it back. It wouldn't do any good right now. His problems had just increased tenfold.

He would have told Holly the truth. Eventually. But Andrew had just taken the choice out of his hands.

Holly's eyes widened and her face turned a pale white. "You can't be serious, Andrew."

Andrew's head swung toward the door. Shane expected to see a challenging smile on his face, but he only found tension. And sadness. Once Holly learned the whole truth, they'd both lose her.

Andrew motioned for Shane to come into the room before he turned his attention back to Holly.

"If you want to know about Shane, why don't you ask him yourself?"

Her gaze met his, and the fear in her eyes nearly made his knees buckle. All this time he'd been trying to protect her. From the monsters. From himself. In that moment, seeing his choices reflected in her eyes, he realized how miserably he'd failed. He sank against the wall and shoved his hands into the pockets of his jeans.

"How long have you been standing there?" Anger laced the worry in Holly's voice. She glared at him for a few beats before she shook her head.

Too long. He should have walked into the room the second he'd seen her sitting there with Andrew, but he'd decided to hang back and wait to hear what was said.

Andrew had known he was there. He'd known, and he'd told her anyway.

Shane bit back a curse. He should have seen it coming, and he should have done something to stop it.

Then again, maybe this was for the best. He would've had to tell her sooner or later, anyway. He sighed. No time like the present.

"I've been standing here long enough."

"Then you heard what Andrew said?"

He nodded.

"Would you care to explain things a little better?" A sharp coldness filled her eyes, and it was all he could do to keep from turning around and walking away. When she looked at him with such hatred, it nearly killed him.

Shane sighed. "What do you want to know?"

"Why were you there the night Mike died?"

He shook his head. Just like Holly to go right for the jugular. Forget asking the simple questions first. She'd picked the most complicated one. "I was trying to keep you from getting hurt."

"You failed."

"I know. I was late." He closed his eyes and pinched the bridge of his nose. "I'm sorry."

"You should be. But that still doesn't answer my question. I've had it with the way you've been keeping me in the dark, Shane. It's time for the truth. All of it. Now."

He didn't even know where to start. His heart ached. So did his head. His throat had long since run dry. She thought she wanted the truth, but he knew better. The truth would only make matters worse.

There was nothing he could do about that now. If she wanted to know what was going on, he'd tell her. And then he'd try like hell to hold on to her when she wanted to run away.

He moved to the couch and flopped down on the firm cushions. After shooting Andrew a scathing glare, he turned his attention to Holly.

"Your husband made some bad choices when it came to business. He'd pissed off the wrong people, and some of them decided to retaliate. They sent the things you saw to kill him. And you, too."

When he paused to gauge her reactions, she made an impatient gesture. "I've already figured that much out. Tell me something I don't know."

"Mike had come to Andrew and me for help when he found out what they had planned for the two of you. I received some wrong information, and that was how they got to you before I could get there to stop it. If one of us had been there, he wouldn't be dead and you wouldn't have been injured."

"You killed the monsters." The flatness in her tone twisted his gut. She was speaking to him—and looking at him—like he was a stranger. Nothing could have cut him more.

"Yes."

"How?"

He drew in a deep breath and let it out slowly. He'd have to tell her, but he wanted to put the inevitable off for as long as possible. "I'm not what you think I am, Holly."

She stared at him for a moment, her gaze cold and hard, before she continued. "Both of you knew Mike." It wasn't a question, but a statement of fact.

He could only nod in response.

"And neither of you thought mentioning that little fact would be a good idea?"

"No, it wouldn't have been. Until recently, you'd been safe. We'd done all we could to protect you and make sure the people trying to hurt you didn't find you. When they found you, I came here to double the protection."

He hoped she would accept his answer, but he should have expected it wouldn't be that simple.

"You've been protecting me. How long has this been going on behind my back?"

"Five years."

Hurt flashed in her gaze. "I just have one more question. Why are they still after me? Mike is the one who made them angry, and Mike has been dead for years."

"They don't know you weren't involved in his business. People like that always want to tie up loose ends, and they'll do it any way they can."

Holly sat back and nodded, her expression grim. "They won't stop chasing me, will they? I'll always have to check over my shoulder for monsters."

"No."

The answer came from Andrew and both Shane and Holly glanced in his direction.

"How do we get rid of them?" Holly asked him.

"The creatures that are after you don't have the brains to make their own decisions. Someone always has to be in control of them. We find their boss, the man who killed Mike. We get rid of him. Then the demons will stop attacking."

"Demons?" Holly's eyes widened and she shrank back against the chair.

Shane blew out a breath heavy with frustration. Andrew really needed a lesson in tact. When Andrew started to continue his explanation, Shane raised his hand to stop him. "Yes. The creatures after you are demons, but not particularly terrible ones. Lesser demons. They're dangerous only when someone is controlling them, and especially when their controller has powers of his own. Their controller isn't human. He's strong, and he's already shown he's not going to let anything stand in the way of getting what he wants."

"What is he?"

"Humans generally refer to his kind as werewolves."

"Werewolves. How am I supposed to believe all this? If I hadn't seen what happened to Mike five years ago, I'd swear both of you were crazy." Holly's brow wrinkled and she shook her head. "If you know who and what he is, can't you just find him and stop him?"

"It's not that simple."

"With you, nothing is. How do you know what this guy is, and what he's capable of?"

He sucked in a breath, bracing himself for what he had to say next. It wouldn't be easy for him to say, but it would be a lot harder for her to take. "Because Andrew and I were born into the same race. We're not human, Holly."

※⁓⟲⟳⟆⁓※

The bottom dropped out of Holly's world, leaving her dangling over a black hole that threatened to suck her in. She pushed out of the chair, her entire body shaking so hard she could barely stand.

"No. This has to be some kind of a joke." Her stomach threatened to heave, and she placed her hand over her mouth. After a few seconds, the wave of nausea passed. "Stop lying to me right now, Shane. I would have noticed if you weren't human."

She glanced at Andrew for confirmation, but only saw remorse etched on his face.

Shane had told her the truth.

What had she gotten herself into?

A few deep breaths did nothing to calm her down. She had to get out of there. Away from the two people in her life she'd been wrong to trust.

"Excuse me. I need to use the bathroom."

She fled the room, heading deeper into the house toward the bathroom, but took a detour out the back door. A minute later, she found herself out on the street in front of Andrew's house. After a quick glance behind her to make sure they didn't realize she'd left, she turned and ran down the street.

Her heart pounded against her ribcage until she thought it would burst from her chest. Every muscle in her body ached and a throb had started in her temples. How could she have been so stupid? She wasn't any safer with them than she was on her own.

She stopped running and bent over, her hands on her knees. Her lungs burned and she sucked in a few deep breaths, trying to keep herself from passing out. It was at that moment that someone grabbed her from behind.

She struggled to get away, but a hand pressed over her mouth and everything went dark.

Holly opened her eyes to the stench of dampness hanging in the thick air. The floor below her was cold. She reached down to touch it. Dirt. With a groan, she pushed herself into a sitting position.

Her gaze scanned the semi-darkness and panic swelled inside her. A basement room, with bare cement walls and high windows. The only door stood at the top of a stairway in front of her. Her leaden legs might not carry her up the steps, but she'd have to try. It might be her only chance at saving herself from the person who'd grabbed her. Shane? Andrew? Or someone else?

At this point, it didn't matter. She'd have to find a way to save herself. She reached into her pocket for her cell phone only to find the pocket empty.

"Looking for something?"

The familiarity in the voice hit her just before the speaker stepped out of the darkness.

The same dark hair, the same long, lean frame, and pale blue eyes. Her stomach again threatened to heave as she tried to make sense of the image she saw in front of her. She had to be mistaken, because this couldn't really be happening.

"Mike?" she asked in a small voice.

"In the flesh." He winked. "Miss me?"

Chapter Eleven

Holly froze, halfway between sitting and standing. Shock made her head pound. "I thought you were dead."

How was this possible? She'd watched those creatures—demons—tear him apart.

"Only because that's what I wanted you to think." Mike leaned against the wall, his hands in the pockets of his pants. Everything about him screamed casual, as if he hadn't pretended to be dead for the past five years.

She shook her head and sucked in a few deep breaths full of stale, moldy air. How could she not have known? How could she not have guessed what he'd done? She'd been completely blindsided.

The face she'd once thought of as handsome now turned her stomach.

All these years she'd mourned his death... "Why, Mike? Why would you do this to me?"

"Nothing personal. Just business. It's always about business."

How could he be so cold? This wasn't the man she'd married. At least not the man she thought she'd married. The man standing in front of her was a complete stranger.

"You never answered my question," he continued. "Did you miss me, Holly?"

"I did." She swallowed back the bitter taste in her mouth. "Up until about two minutes ago."

The corners of Mike's lips curled into a cross between a sneer and a smile. She'd seen that look on his face dozens of times in the past, but now it took on a new meaning. "Is that any way to talk to the man you pledged your life to?"

He took a step toward her and she scooted back against the wall. "I watched you get killed. I watched them rip you to shreds."

"No, you just think you did. What you saw was an elaborate illusion."

He shrugged as if he'd just told her the weather would be nice that day. "That's one good thing about using demons. They can do things that I couldn't have done on my own. It was believable, wasn't it?"

"What about the fire?"

"Just covering my tracks. I had to make sure you'd never question what you saw—and that the police wouldn't question it, either. The body was a homeless man who'd been living downtown. Had to have a body to char beyond recognition, or you might have convinced the police to start digging into things. You've never been one to leave well enough alone. That's what got us into this mess in the first place."

She narrowed her eyes, but didn't speak. He'd never loved her. If he had, he wouldn't have been able to do this to her. Tears formed in her eyes, but she batted them away. She wouldn't give him the satisfaction of seeing her cry.

All the love she'd felt for him for so long rushed out of her, replaced by a darker emotion. Hatred crystallized inside her.

There had to be a way to get away from him and get help. Now she just had to find it.

"Nothing to say, Holly? I have to tell you, that surprises me." He taunted her with his tone, and with his gaze. "If you'd just kept out of my business, all of this unpleasantness could have been avoided."

Holly bit down on her lower lip. The guy was a complete sociopath. Never once in their three year marriage had she found any hint of his state of mind. Not a single inkling. "I had no interest in your business."

She pushed up from the ground and managed to stand on shaky legs. Her body was numb with fear and anger. She put her hands on the wall behind her for support.

"You can say that all you want, but it's a lie."

"I didn't know anything." At least not really. All she'd learned from overhearing his conversations were sketchy details. Nothing anyone could have proven. "Not anything that would warrant this."

"I wish I could believe you, but I can't. You're sleeping with the enemy."

She tried to school her expression, but Mike's cold smile told her he saw the shock written on her face.

"Do you think I have no clue what you've been doing? I've been watching you for months."

The pieces started to fall into place, and Holly bit back a moan. The sensation of being watched. The sound of footsteps behind her. She hadn't been imagining things. She'd been part of the sick game her not-so-dead husband had been playing. Shane and Andrew hadn't been playing with her. It had been Mike the whole time.

She pushed a hand through her tangled hair. "Why now, after all this time? Why not five years ago, right after I'd gotten out of the hospital?"

"I didn't know where you were. It took me that long to find you. After my... death... I hadn't expected you to move all the way across the country. And Shane and Andrew did a good job of covering your tracks. Their connections saved your life. You had no idea you had such loyal guardian angels, did you?"

She gaped. If he was telling the truth, that meant Shane and Andrew had been watching her back for years. They'd kept Mike from getting to her for all this time—but why hadn't they told her he was still alive?

Suddenly Shane's reaction when she'd told him about Mike's death made sense. Of course, he'd known. He'd been upset because he hadn't wanted to tell her that what she'd seen hadn't been real.

Her head started to ache. "If you wanted me dead so badly, why didn't you do it yourself? Why follow me around for months without doing anything, and then send someone else to do your dirty work?"

"Does it really matter that much to you?" He took a step closer, then another, until he stood so close she could smell the scent of his aftershave. The same scent he'd worn when they'd been together. What used to turn her on now turned her stomach. "Do you really want to know how much I've been enjoying this little game? I couldn't just kill you, Holly. The police would get suspicious. That's how the human world works. I had to make it look realistic. It would have looked like a botched burglary to them, if things had gone smoothly. But your guardian angels stepped in, and I had to change my plans."

Without warning, he cupped her face in his hands and kissed her. His hand felt slimy, his lips cold and clammy against her skin. As soon as he pulled away, she turned her head and spit on the floor.

Anger flashed in Mike's eyes, but after a second, it disappeared. "That wasn't very nice. Is that any way to treat the man you married?"

"Don't touch me again. Ever. You lost that right a long time ago."

"I'll do whatever I damned well please." In one swift motion he grabbed her and spun her around, pinning her between the wall and his body. He leaned in so close his breath brushed her cheek and it made bile rise in her throat.

"There's no way you can stop me." He brought his hands to her hips and slammed her back against him. "I take what I want, Holly. You should know that."

She sucked in a breath and closed her eyes, her mind frantically searching for a solution, but she kept coming up blank. She had no idea where she was, and no idea how to get away. No idea what her husband, a man who wasn't even human, was capable of.

A werewolf. She'd married a werewolf. She should have noticed, should have seen the signs that he wasn't a normal man, but she'd either missed them, or ignored them. Not only was he a werewolf, but he'd been trying to kill her.

Her vision grayed at the thought. What was she dealing with? "You can't have me."

"You're wrong. I will have you, one more time, before I finally give you what you deserve."

Panic made her heart hammer against her ribs. Her blood pounded in her ears so loudly she could barely hear over the rushing. Her position made retaliation impossible. He was going to kill her if she didn't get free.

She twisted, hoping to find some way of breaking out of his hold. There had to be something she could do.

There was. She sucked in a fortifying breath. "Okay."

Mike stilled. "Excuse me?"

"Okay. If you want me that bad, who am I to stop you? But you have to stop hurting me."

"Why do I think you're lying to me?" He loosened his grip a little, but it was enough. He spun her around, and she was ready for him. She lashed out with her hand, raking her nails across his cheek.

He stumbled back, his hand covering the side of his face, and in that second she took full advantage. He'd made a fool of her for years. She'd be damned if she was going to let him get away with that. He stepped toward her again, and she kicked him in the gut. Before he had a chance to recover, she raced for the stairs. She made it halfway up them before he grabbed her ankle and yanked her back down.

She hit the dirt with a thud, every muscle in her body screaming. Mike didn't even give her a chance to scramble away. He lifted her off the ground and slammed her against the wall.

"I knew you'd try something like that. I admire your fight, sweetheart, but it's not going to do you any good in the end."

Through the fog of her panic, she heard the click of a door opening and footsteps running down the stairs. She looked up and saw Shane rushing toward them. Mike barely had time to glance over his shoulder before Shane was upon him. Shane pulled Mike away from her. Mike's arm came around Shane's neck and Holly tensed. The two men struggled, and every time Shane seemed to gain the upper hand, Mike managed to wrench it away.

Then Shane gave Mike a sharp jab to his stomach and Mike froze. He let out a gurgling sound and slumped against the wall. His body slid to the floor, writhing on the dirt for a few seconds before he stilled and an eerie calm settled over the room.

Holly blinked, fighting to catch her breath. In that second, everything inside her fell apart.

She couldn't speak, couldn't think. Couldn't even cry.

Shane's gaze met hers and he shook his head. "Are you okay? He didn't hurt you, did he?"

She'd been dragged down the steps and thrown against the wall. Every cell in her body screamed out in protest. She tried to shake her head, but couldn't even manage a small movement. She slumped against the wall and would have slid to the floor if Shane hadn't pulled her into his arms.

For a long while, she clung to him, her mind blessedly blank. But then everything came rushing back and hit her with the force of a truck. She pulled in a shuddery breath and swiped her hand across her eyes before she pushed Shane away.

He threw her a confused glance, but she ignored it. "What did you do to him?"

He leaned down and pulled something out of Mike's body. When he stood, he held his knife out in front of her. "Silver. Kills werewolves—or aren't you familiar with the folklore?"

She'd heard the tales before. And always dismissed them as fiction. But now, faced with a real, live werewolf, she didn't know what to believe.

"Are any of those tales true?"

"Most are. I don't turn into a mindless killing machine come the full moon, though." He blew out a harsh breath. "You can't believe everything you read in books or see in movies. The change is voluntary, and can happen any time I want it to."

"I see," she answered, but she wasn't sure she did. It all still seemed so unreal. It would take a long time for her mind to be able to reconcile everything she'd learned about him. "So it has nothing to do with the cycles of the moon?"

His answering laugh was a little nervous. "Not exactly. The moon cycles determine breeding times. When female wolves are in heat. The urge to change is a lot stronger then, but still controllable."

She glanced down at Mike's body and shuddered. "But you're not a mindless killing machine, huh?"

"No. I kill when I have to. To protect what's mine."

She swallowed hard. Protecting what was his. He meant her. So many emotions ran through her head that she couldn't keep any of them straight. Shane had saved her life, but he'd also lied to her. What else had he kept from her? How many more secrets did he have yet to reveal? "Why didn't you tell me he was alive?"

"I didn't know." His gaze held hers, and she found nothing but sincerity there. "I didn't put it all together until after you ran out. Then it all started to make sense. I swear, if I'd known I would have told you from the start."

He reached for her, but she ducked out of his grasp. "No. Don't touch me right now. I just want to be left alone."

"Holly. I'm sorry." Hurt flashed in his gaze, but she didn't let herself dwell on it. She had her own problems to deal with. It didn't matter that he was telling her the truth now. He'd never bothered to before.

"I don't want to listen to your apologies right now. I don't want anything from you anymore. Please, just take me home."

He looked down at the ground and pushed a hand through his hair. He was silent so long, she thought he'd deny her request, but when his gaze came back to hers, she saw only acceptance in his eyes.

"Okay. I'll take you home. And then you won't ever have to see me again."

"Thank you."

Chapter Twelve

Holly walked toward her front door, her bag slung over her shoulder. Birds chirped and sunlight filtered through the tree branches, warming her skin. Remnants of the fear she'd lived with for so long still haunted her, and she glanced around the yard to make sure no one else was there.

Her life had been so quiet in the past three weeks. No attacks, no odd sensations or footsteps behind her when she walked.

No *anything*.

She tried to remind herself that quiet was a good thing, but the reminders didn't help. It would be a lot easier if she could get Shane out of her head. She hadn't realized how much she missed having him in her life until he was no longer there. True to his word, he'd left her alone, but having him out of her life didn't make her feel any better.

It was for the best. Too many secrets and lies stood between them. She'd fallen in love with him somewhere along the line, but it wasn't enough. It might never be.

"It's about time you got home. I've been waiting here over an hour."

She froze and glanced up to see Andrew leaning against the porch railing. "What are you doing here?"

"Do I need a reason to visit an old friend?"

"Is that what you call me after months of lies?"

His expression darkened and he crossed his arms over his chest. "I'm sorry. I really do care about you. I always have. I only did what I had to do in order to make sure you stayed safe."

"You failed." She swallowed hard. Vestiges of anger still clung to her, and she couldn't shake them, no matter what she did. Her hands balled into fists. "You and Shane both did. I should hate you for not telling me the truth right from the start."

"You should." He nodded, his expression contemplative. "But you don't."

"No. I don't hate you. But I'm upset, and I have a right to be."

He seemed to take her answer in stride. "I won't deny it, but I want to make sure you understand why. Will you let me explain it to you?"

She wanted to tell him to leave, that she didn't want to hear any excuses or explanations, but something inside told her that she needed to listen to what he had to say. Needed to understand his reasons so she could understand Shane's.

At the thought of Shane, her heart ached. She pushed the pain away. "Okay. I'll listen, but it had better be good."

❦

Shane heard footsteps behind him, but he didn't bother to turn around. It would be Andrew, no doubt, and he wasn't in the mood for another lecture.

Don't give up so easily, Shane. You have to see things from her point of view.

He shook his head. He'd tried. Lord, he'd tried, but in the end, it hadn't made a difference. She wouldn't see him. Would probably never forgive him for keeping so much from her for so long. There was nothing he could do but watch the woman he loved walk away.

A hand rested on his shoulder, and he stiffened. It was too small to be Andrew's. He glanced over his shoulder and, at first, he thought he was seeing things. Holly stood there, her hair in a ponytail and her expression uncertain.

"Hi."

He had to clear his throat twice to get his voice to work. Hope swelled in him, but he refused to give in to it just yet. She might be there to yell at him some more for lying to her. "Hi."

"Can I sit down?" He scooted over on the couch and she settled onto the cushion next to him. "Andrew told me I could find you here."

He let out a harsh burst of laughter. Leave it to Andrew, who had screwed everything up, to try to make it right again.

Shane shook his head. Andrew wasn't the only guilty party.

He glanced out the window. "I gave up my apartment. I'll be leaving tomorrow, so you don't have to worry about me being in your way ever again."

Though he had yet to figure out why he'd taken Andrew up on his offer of a room until he got everything settled. Since he'd moved in two days ago, Andrew had been constantly prodding and poking at wounds that refused to heal.

Holly touched the side of his face. "You can't leave."

"Why not?"

"I don't want you to go."

The answer was simple, but powerful. A rush of warmth raced through him and he bit back a smile. Until he knew exactly what her reasons were, he needed to hold back his emotions. "You told me you didn't want to see me again."

She nodded. Her eyes glistened with unshed tears. "I was angry. Hurt. But I've had a lot of time to think over the past three weeks. I spoke with Andrew, too, and he helped me to understand the situation better. You thought if I knew what was going on, I'd only draw more attention to myself. Maybe you were right. I don't know. I just know that I don't want to be without you. You mean too much to me."

The fact that he was a werewolf still made her a little nervous, but she'd managed to come to grips with it. He was the man she loved. She'd deal with whatever the future held knowing that he'd saved her life not once, but twice. No matter what happened, he would never hurt her.

He clenched his hands into fists to keep from grabbing her and kissing her. "You don't know me very well."

She laughed. "And you don't know me all that well, either. But I'm willing to learn. I don't know how this is possible, but I love you. I don't want you to leave."

He didn't even bother trying to fight it anymore. He pulled her into his arms and kissed her, hard and fast. When he broke the kiss, he couldn't hold back the smile. "I love you, too. I don't know when that happened, only that it did. If you want me to stay, then there's no way I'm going anywhere."

Her eyes sparkled and she leaned in to kiss his nose. "We seem to have skipped a few important steps along the way here. Like a date or two."

"I guess we have a lot of catching up to do." And he looked forward to every second.

About the Author:

Born in Gloucester, Massachusetts, Elisa Adams has lived most of her life on the East Coast. Writing has been a longtime hobby for this former nursing assistant and phlebotomist. Now a full time writer of paranormal and contemporary erotic romance, she lives on the New Hampshire border with her three children.

Elisa welcomes email from her readers. Feel free to contact her at elisa@elisaadams.com, and visit her on the web at www.elisaadams.com and elisaadams.livejournal.com.

Falling Stars

by Kathleen Scott

To My Reader:

I always find the easiest characters to write are the ones who sit behind you at the computer and dictate their lives as you type. Thus, it was with Daria and Raven. I hope you enjoy reading their story as much as I did hearing it straight from the characters.

Chapter One

Daria stood with her arms crossed behind her back in parade rest stance. Her C.O. sat behind his desk, his hands folded in a casual pose. He did not appear to be as tense with the situation as she. His entire future was not riding on a first face-to-face meeting with a warrior-cum-husband.

"I understand your need to get a feel for him before the official state introductions, but I'm not sure I want to anger your father by providing you the opportunity," Captain Aaron said. His bright golden eyes twinkled in mischief. He wouldn't openly laugh at her, not when her bloodlines would see him executed for such an offense.

Daria had known when she joined the corps that she would end up having to marry for the preservation of her royal line, but knowing didn't mean she had to like it, especially when her future husband had been the betrothed of her late sister, Lessia.

"Is my father suddenly dictating corps policy?" she asked, letting a bit of her royal disdain show.

"No, but my commission is dependant on your father's good will."

Daria raised a brow at her C.O. It was only too true. Her father had been known to reassign captains who did not openly support the royal politic. In this case, that would include giving the princess anything she wanted. Daria, on the other hand, never wanted special treatment and had stopped sending transmissions home. What good did it do anyhow? She was sure her father received daily updates on her

"Captain, protocol requires you send four officers with you to the air lock whenever receiving a high ranking foreign emissary."

"I know the protocol, your highness."

Daria winced at the use of her title rather than her rank of Eagle. "I meant no disrespect, sir. I just want the opportunity to observe him in a non-state function. My father need never know."

Captain Aaron leaned forward and nodded. "Very well, Eagle Varta. You've worn me down. But please don't breathe a word of this to the squadron. I'll be accused of favoritism again." He offered her a sly smile. Truth be told, she was Aaron's favorite pilot, had been ever since she pulled his fat out of the fire in that dive bar on Gideon III's orbital spaceport, a shithole of a place on the border of a nasty asteroid field. Then there was that infamous night spent in a hotel room, but she tried not to think of that while in uniform.

"I wouldn't dream of it, sir."

Three sharp bongs indicated an inner-ship transmission. Captain Aaron leaned forward and pushed on the communications center. "Go ahead."

"Sir, the Hohn's ship is docking at the portside air lock."

"Thank you, Tibbons." He clicked off the com unit and stood, pulling his uniform jacket down as he did. "Well, princess, time to meet the hubby."

⁂

General Kristiano Raven, the Hohn as his title commanded, exited the docking corridor followed by his staff and came face to face with the Primon delegation. The C.O. of the *Versailles* came forward and crossed his hand over his chest and bowed in greeting.

"Welcome aboard the *Versailles*, Hohn. I hope your stay with us is pleasant. If I or any member of my crew can be of assistance to you, you need only ask."

Raven regarded the C.O. This was the man who had commanded Princess Daria on many missions, and from all the accounts he'd gathered on her military career, he was also a close personal friend. Raven wouldn't even pretend to like that situation for a moment.

He gave a slight incline of his head to return the greeting, then his gaze slid to the right and stopped. Daria!

Only his battlefield training made it possible to control his reaction to seeing her so close after five years. His palms itched to reach out and grab her to him. To bury his face in her soft hair, then begin the courtship ritual in earnest. She stared straight ahead like a proud soldier and gave no indication one way or the other as to her feelings.

"I have arranged for a small reception in the officers' cantina at 2100. Is that acceptable to you?" Captain Aaron asked.

Raven gave a quick nod. "If I may be shown to my quarters, I would appreciate it."

"Eagle Varta will show you to your accommodations."

If Raven hadn't been looking closely he would have missed the slightly surprised dilation of Daria's pupils. She stepped forward and moved her hand to indicate a narrow dimly lit corridor. "Right this way, Hohn."

Her husky voice did odd things to his insides. It didn't sound at all like her sister's had when they had talked over the voice relays. Lessia's had been slightly higher with a breathy edge to it. Daria's was low and had a slight drawl, like she promised more than just showing him the way to his quarters.

They walked down the corridors side by side; his staff followed. She showed them their quarters as the group passed. The tour she gave him was half-hearted at best, and every few moments her eyes would meet his then quickly look away. Her strides were short, yet efficient, and her hands remained clasped behind her back in the formal Primon military posture. Her correctness drove him crazy.

They came to a stop outside a portal. "If you need anything, please contact the ship's liaison and she will be more than welcome to accommodate you." She hit the entrance button and the door slid open.

A light fragrance of summer sweet flowers and exotic fruits hit his nose. He leaned over to determine if the scent came from her, and drew in a deep breath. "Thank you, princess." He let his lips brush against her ear.

She stepped back and gave him a curt nod before turning on her heel and heading down the corridor. He entered the quarters and slid the panel shut again. So, his little princess did not wish to acknowledge her royal roots. This would prove quite interesting. She was nothing as she had appeared at the ball five years before when he'd caught sight of her leaving through an upper balcony door and out into the night. He'd seen her push through the crowd until she reached her destination and then she'd disappeared.

He'd often wondered if she'd left to meet a lover, but the thought tortured him so, he tried not to poke around at the possibility.

He sank into the sofa and pulled the correspondences from his inner pocket. Damn Ignaki to the very bowels of Hell's Caverns! If he had gotten the right princess in the first place the Hohn would have been married and had an heir by now. But no, the ineffectual advisor had given him the wrong name, the wrong princess, and now he had to try to negotiate another alliance and appear as if he took the youngest Primon royal daughter as a substitute for the dead Lessia. Daria had always been his first choice—his only choice.

He slid the communication disk into the reader and stared at the words that chilled his blood. Hostile takeover of the Riman sector. It appeared his enemies were closing fast. It would take all the firepower of Primon and Jevic to rid the sector of this new threat. The problem was that his advisors had not been able to determine exactly where the threat stemmed from.

He wiped a hand down his face. A reluctant bride might sweeten the anticipation, but it would do nothing to take the edge off his tension. Who was he fooling? Princess Daria might not be looking forward to their union, but she had agreed to the match. Now, if he could only keep her safe until the wedding.

Though Lessia's death had been ruled an accident, Raven couldn't be sure it wasn't an assassin's contract that killed her. He'd looked, exhaustively, but the evidence just wasn't there to be found.

A bong sounded in the room. "Enter," he called, though he should have shown a bit more caution. He sincerely hoped the visitor was Daria returned to get to know him better before the formal state introductions.

His primary aide, Pollack, entered and bowed to him. "Hohn, I have been going over the final arrangements for the state introductions and I'm afraid there is a problem."

"Problem? I employ you so there will be no problems." He raised a brow and remained seated, though his posture changed enough to intimidate Pollack.

The man swallowed. His generous Adam's apple bobbed up and down with the motion. "Sir, the Riman delegation was killed in the takeover of the sector. The middle Primon royal daughter, Bellacore, is married to a Riman diplomat. Primon is readying for battle before the state introductions. Your bride may be engaged in warfare before the proposed date."

"Then we simply step up the date. Try tonight for instance. Captain Aaron has already arranged a formal welcome reception in my honor; we'll use it as an opportunity to have the state introductions. Prince Hefcat will have to preside from planet side. Afterward, I will pledge our fleet to fight alongside the Primon guard." He waved his hand away. "I see no problem."

Pollack coughed. "According to Primon tradition, once the introductions are made, the wedding must take place within seventy-two common hours or the bride returns to the marriage market and may then be offered to another."

Finally, something to smile about. "Worry not. With the princess stationed aboard this vessel I doubt she will have opportunity to slip from my grasp before the seventy-two hour mark. The ship's clergy can perform the Primonese ceremony, then we will have a full formal Jevic ceremony when we reach the home world."

"And her orders?"

"The alliance will override her orders in this instance." As he said the words he wasn't so sure she would agree to being held back from the thick of fighting for the sake of the alliance. Even so, if she felt it her duty to fight, fight she would. The thought troubled him in no small measure.

Chapter Two

Daria continued to shake.

She pumped her fists open and closed to try and work the feeling back into them. They had been clasped so tightly together they had gone numb.

He knew her. He bloody well knew her. Why would the Hohn have wasted his time in finding out not only what she looked like, but what vessel she had been assigned?

She paced around the library, scrubbing her face with her hands. Of course, he knew what she looked like. A man with the Hohn's power and connections would have researched his future wife thoroughly. Oh, he was probably lamenting his hasty decision to push for the alliance now that he'd gotten a lode of her abundant self. He probably hoped she looked like the late and beautiful Lessia.

Who was she kidding? It didn't matter what he thought of her or she thought of him. They would marry and the alliance would save both their worlds. She hadn't served the Primon fleet without learning a few things about intergalactic politics. Not to mention growing up in the palace royale.

A shiver ran down her spine. It had been five years since she'd last saw him. Her sister's funeral. She could remember it so clearly...

Traditional mourning music filled the hall and every so often a sniffle or sob could be heard between the sounds of swelling pipes.

Daria sat with her family, tucked between her sister, Bellacore, and the outside wall. The crimson mourning veil hid her face from the world and blocked the view of curious funeral guests.

Doors at the far end of the cathedral swung open and the Hohn entered with his imperial escort, his long legs eating up the aisle as he hurried to view the remains of his lost love. His stride slowed as he approached the glass-topped coffin. He placed his hand on the top and then bent over double. After a moment he straightened and hurried from the proceedings, not even staying to lend his voice to the choir that would send Lessia's soul to Hialeigha, the Primon afterlife.

Daria shook the memories from her mind. Never had she seen a man brought so low over the death of a beloved. The fact that it was the mighty Hohn himself made the scene even more surreal. No one in the chamber that day ever spoke of the scene, at least not in the royal presence.

A chime sounded, and Daria quickly hit her com unit, grateful for the interruption. "Eagle Varta, you have an incoming transmission from Prince Hefcat."

Her father. She did not want to talk to him now. It was as if the man had some kind of sensor array strapped to his head that alerted him to her thoughts.

"Patch him through." She moved to the visual display and opened the channel so she could see his face.

A low tone hummed before the screen blinked on and her father sat before her with his hands steepled in front of him. She knew that pose. Something troubled him.

"What is it, father?" she asked without preamble. He wouldn't have appreciated sentiment. He was a man of action.

"Disturbing news from the Riman sector. There has been an unprovoked attack on the Riman delegation on route to Primon. I am declaring war on those responsible."

Daria's heart seized. Adrenaline pumped through her veins. The taste of battle filled her mouth. Then her father's last words jarred her back to reality. He didn't mention who was responsible. "You're declaring war on an unknown entity?"

"We don't know who they are, only the model of their craft. It's like nothing we've ever seen. They will be easy enough to identify."

The thought intrigued Daria as much as it terrified her. She put her finger to her lip in thought. Another chime sounded on her father's end of the transmission. "I have another call. I'll let you know more information as it becomes available."

"Do I have your permission to share this with the C.O.?"

"He has already received the information through the chain of command. I wanted to tell you myself." He signed off without salutation or endearment.

The screen blinked out and Daria sat still for a moment to let what her father said soak into her brain. The words were not as significant as the fact he called her personally to let her know. He had never done that before.

The overhead announcement sounded through the library speakers. "Eagle Varta, report to Captain Aaron's office. Eagle Varta, report to Captain Aaron's office."

She shook her head. The day was not getting any better.

For the second time that day she stood before Captain Aaron, though this time control seemed a bit harder to grasp.

"He wants to do what?" she asked and transferred her weight to the heels of her feet and crossed her arms over her chest.

"I don't need to repeat myself, do I? His decision to go forward makes sense given the developments in the Riman sector." Captain Aaron gave a shrug. "I doubt the Hohn would have let this opportunity pass by without taking full advantage."

"Well, it does give me the excuse to skip the spectacle of a formal wedding." An idea that had more merit than not.

Aaron gave her a lopsided grin, gold eyes twinkling. "I knew you'd find some advantage in the idea."

"Yes, well, above all else I am my father's daughter, no matter how I try to avoid the familial ties." Suddenly, her muscles tightened as a terrible thought jumped the synaptic gap and burrowed in her brain like an Akadian sand bore. She had absolutely nothing to wear! It was a totally feminine and humiliating thought coming from the mind of someone who wore androgynous uniforms and used coed bathing facilities. The wardrobe for the state introductions and the traditional Primon wedding gown were back in her room at the palace.

"Is something wrong?" Aaron asked, raising a brow at her.

"No. No." She shook her head. "If there is nothing further, Captain, I would ask to return to my quad to begin preparing for the introductions."

He waved to the door in an informal gesture.

She hurried down the corridors and to the quad she shared with three other Eagles. A quad consisted of four bunks in a small space enclosed only by retractable walls that separated it from the other quads. As were the bathing facilities, all quads were coed with deference made only to rank. Each quad was named for old Earth icons in honor of those long-lost Primonese ancestors.

The quad Daria was assigned had all women in it. Unusual in a ship the size of *Versailles*, but Daria often thought perhaps her father had something to do with the fortunate circumstances of her sleeping arrangements. As if she hadn't known the touch of a man before.

She pressed her palm to the plate to enter the corridor where her quad was located, hoping that her friend Onya still had that sexy red ball gown she'd worn to a dinner with a Riman ambassador during the Gideon III mission. Granted Onya had fewer curves to hide, but the fabric looked slinky enough to expand to fit Daria's generous breasts and hips.

Onya sat on her bunk clicking through a holo album. An excited smile played along her full lips. "You should see these holos Cole sent! He's such a doll."

Cole, short for Coleanthandor Holimatra—the ambassador in question.

"I really wish I had time, but I have a wedding to prepare for." Daria stripped off her uniform shirt and threw it on the bed, then sat down and started to remove her boots.

Forgetting the holos, Onya sat up straighter. "What? Did you say wedding?"

"I'm afraid I did, and if you don't mind, I need to borrow your red dress so I'll at least look like a daughter of the blood." She set the boots under the bunk and stood to remove her pants.

"You want to get married in my dress. Oh, that's so sweet."

Daria closed her eyes for a moment in silent prayer. "I hope it fits."

Onya bounced off her bunk and headed to her locker. "Oh, it'll fit all right. You're going to look so outrageous in this. The Hohn is going to go wild."

Daria held up her hand in protest. "I don't need him to go wild. I just need to look the part of the good little princess."

"Oh." The word sounded disappointed, not excited.

"What's wrong?" Daria moved over to look into the locker with Onya. Her fellow Eagle didn't need to explain further. Something dark and sticky had exploded all over the inside of the locker and the front of the dress.

Not one to be depressed for long, Onya grabbed the dress from the locker and spun away. "You go get your shower and do the preliminaries, I'll get this cleaned and meet you back here."

Rather than dwell over the possible ominous omen, Daria hurriedly took Onya's advice.

The Eagle showers were located at the back of the quads. Ranks from Hawk through Eagle used the same facilities with very few exceptions. She hurried under the showerhead and hit the water, trying not to think of the situation that had gotten so far out of her control.

The Hohn.

How had she ever let her father talk her into joining her life to a man who was the very quintessence of power and authority? She knew and understood the need for the alliance between the two planets, but having lived under the watchful eye of the public during her formative years, it wasn't something she wished to continue into adulthood. That was only one of the reasons she'd chosen the anonymity of the guard. Instead of being the last of the five princesses, she was one of many pilots in the Primon fleet.

Despite the hot water cascading down her body, a chill started low in her belly and continued to travel up to her breasts. She would be expected to consummate the marriage as soon as possible. Dearest Maker, how was she supposed to get romantic with a man that she didn't know, and one that would most likely be comparing her to her late sister? At least she knew Lessia had been too shy and far too romantic a soul to let the Hohn see her before the state introductions. But that didn't mean he hadn't been shone a picture of her older sister. And what a picture Lessia had made. The woman had been unparalleled in beauty and grace, but more importantly, she had been a very dear, sweet woman. She would have made a wonderful wife and partner for the Hohn.

Daria worked soap into a lather and washed her hair. The Hohn was definitely handsome. He looked more like a pirate than the highest-ranking general of the Jevic home world. There was a lethal grace to his walk, and a dangerous glint in his obsidian eyes. His body was big and powerful, and Daria's mouth went dry at the thought of seeing all that male beauty naked.

She stuck her head under the water and rinsed.

"Now there's a sight I'm gonna miss," said a male voice from behind the veil of water.

Daria cleared the water and suds from her eyes and glanced at the man standing against the wall of sinks watching her. He flicked the ashes from his cigarette into the nearest sink and then took a long slow drag.

Falcon Borman was as fair as the Hohn was dark, but he still had a lethal edge to his smile.

Daria turned off the water and began drying off under his watchful gaze. "You coming to the cantina?"

"Wouldn't miss it for anything. I'm looking forward to watching the Hohn swallow his tongue when he sees you." He put his cigarette between his lips and pushed off from the sinks and came toward her. "Need help with that?"

"With what, making the Hohn swallow his tongue?"

Borman laughed. "No, idiot. Drying all that lovely skin of yours."

"Thanks. I think I got it." She raised a brow at him. They had already been down that road and it wasn't a place she cared to revisit, though he was definitely a sexy bastard. "What brings you to my pre-wedding toilet?"

"I'm a little bummed. The boys and I had this big last night of freedom party planned for you. Now it looks like those plans are all shot to hell and back."

"So it would seem." Daria wrapped the towel around her body and fixed it under her arms. "We can have the party when we reach Primon. It can be a welcome to matrimony party instead."

Borman scratched at some very becoming stubble on his chin. The rasp of his calloused palm over the bristle sounded loud in the confines of the showers. "I don't know. I don't think your husband would appreciate the idea of you going out on the town with a bunch of horny pilots that have seen you naked and wet many, many times."

Daria laughed and shook her head. "I think you're making more out of this marriage than it is. The Hohn needed the alliance and the tie of marriage to make it binding."

"You'll still be his wife. And if you were my wife, I wouldn't let you out with us." Bright blue eyes moved down the front of her. "Why did you have to be a princess of all things?"

"I've asked myself that same question a million times. Now if you'll excuse me, I have to get dressed. I'll see you at the cantina."

She moved around him and headed back to the quad. With any luck Borman wouldn't give the Hohn any ideas on how to properly care for a wife.

Chapter Three

Raven studied himself in the full-length mirror. His formal regalia glittered in the ambient light, illustrating a life spent in service to his people. He wondered if Daria would wear her uniform or show off her beautiful body in a revealing gown.

A sly smile pulled up the corner of his mouth. Tonight she would be his. From this day forward, no other man would have the right to touch her, possess her, make love to her.

He would spend his time learning her body. The scent and taste of her. He would discover what pleased her and what made her moan in ecstasy. Hot spirals of desire seared his groin and stirred him to full erection.

A quick glance at the chronometer showed he hadn't enough time to change into a less conspicuous suit. Everyone from here to the officers' cantina would be able to see the bent of his thoughts. And his lovely bride would know how eagerly he anticipated the marriage bed.

After a five-year wait, he would finally be married to his love.

Military personnel and Primon clergy filled the small cantina to witness the marriage of Princess Daria of Primon to the Hohn of Jevic. Raven glanced around the room. It amazed him how the crew of the *Versailles* could turn the celebration from casual welcome to state wedding in only a few hours.

Pollack stood to Raven's right and would act as official Jevic witness to this ceremony. Holos of the ceremony would also be downloaded into the Jevic archives.

The cantina door slid open and Daria entered the room on the arm of Captain Aaron. Her unisex uniform had been replaced by a crimson sheath dress in some clingy fabric that stole Raven's breath and made his mouth water for the taste of her creamy flesh.

Bare shoulders glowed in the low lighting, begging to be kissed. Dark gold hair lay piled atop her head in an elegant do, exposing her long smooth neck and the tiny curls of new hair too short to stay swept up. There was something intensely feminine and vulnerable about that spot on her nape. He would place his lips there later, and kiss it ever so gently before he undressed her.

She turned and her expressive eyes met his across the room. Was that fear he saw, or uncertainty? Her hands were folded together as they looped through her Captain's arm. As Raven moved closer he could see the fingers were clenched. Captain Aaron leaned toward her, speaking into her ear and a sensual smile spread across her beautiful face.

Raven saw red.

Did the captain favor Daria because she was his lover? Did the special treatment received aboard the *Versailles* extend to the captain's bed? He had no doubt she had lovers before him, but the thought of coming face-to-face with one made anger roll low in his gut.

Before he could check his actions, Raven crossed the room, protected in the mantle of the Hohn title, and claimed his bride.

He let his gaze move down her body in a caress, while hers never left his face. He could feel the jade depths of her eyes penetrating his mind and heart. The dress left little to his imagination, and he had a very fruitful imagination where Daria was concerned.

Captain Aaron let go of Daria's arm and nudged her with a shoulder. That seemed to snap her out of whatever hypnotic thoughts held her captive and she moved closer to Raven.

Behind them the large com units came to life with the link to Prince Hefcat and Princess Cordelia.

Captain Aaron moved forward and stood between the view screen and the wedding party. "On behalf of the officers and crew of the *Versailles*, I welcome you Prince Hefcat and Princess Cordelia."

Prince Hefcat bowed in acknowledgment of the greeting and then to the Hohn out of mutual respect, though Raven could see a faint white line around the man's lips. It did not sit well with him to do so. "Though it pains us to forgo the traditional ceremony on Primon, we do believe in the importance of expediency given recent developments. We are grateful the Hohn has chosen to go forward with the marriage rather than postpone." He turned his attention to Raven. "General Kristiano Raven, please allow me to present my youngest daughter, Princess Daria Helaina Varta Kruise."

The hand she extended to him was small, yet capable looking. Her skin looked so creamy and fair next to his deeper rich Jevic coloring. He took her hand in his much larger one and watched a becoming blush rise up into her high cheeks. What a lovely thing she was. "My pleasure, indeed."

"Princess Daria Helaina Varta Kruise, your intended husband and Consort Prince of the Primon realm, General Kristiano Raven, the Hohn of Jevic."

Raven waited to hear that low sensual voice again, but she merely closed her eyes and fell into a deep curtsy over their clasped hands. He knew it was what the Primon royal family held as perfect state introduction protocol, but he wanted more than anything for her to break that protocol. He had read accounts of her exploits off-world and in her squadron and knew for a fact the woman before him held very little regard for her royal image—well, most of the time.

Raven moved his thumb over the back of her hand a few times. It felt so small in his, and slightly clammy. That made him smile. Eagle Varta, the intense and heroic pilot, was nervous. The thought comforted him. If she had been immune to the proceedings, her palm wouldn't be damp.

"At this time we will forgo the customary engagement binding and move straight to the marriage ceremony," Prince Hefcat said. "Cleric Jans, if you please."

A Primon cleric stepped forward and held out a long embroidered scarf. "Princess Daria, Hohn, please step forward and raise your entwined hands."

They stood next to one another, her head only coming as far as his shoulder. A warm thought spread through him at knowing how well she would tuck under his chin when he held her.

The cleric wrapped their hands in the scarf and began speaking in the ancient Primon tongue used only in the holiest of ceremonies. Lyrical and inviting, Raven had memorized the words long ago and now let them swirl around his body and mind, drinking in their essence as he did the fragrance of the woman beside him.

When the service ended, a short reception had Daria's shipmates basking in the revelry of her good fortune. Raven watched Daria sip her drink to all the toasts in their honor, but her glass never seemed to empty. Raven found restraint such as that very pleasing, though he wished she would look at him and smile as she had done to Captain Aaron earlier in the evening.

Daria seemed very popular with her crewmates and a few of the more exuberant females hugged her tightly. Then one impossibly leggy blonde threw herself into Daria's arms. A low oomph exited Daria's mouth and her arms came around the woman to steady them both.

"Onya, you nearly knocked the wind out of me."

The blonde turned a sexy smile to Raven, and leaned in to whisper in Daria's ear. Daria promptly turned red at the comment, her gaze straying to his.

A handsome man with fair coloring and the rank of Falcon came over and captured the woman called Onya by the arms. "Come on, Onya, I heard the ambassador is trying to reach you." The Falcon ran his gaze up and down Daria in a highly possessive glance that made Raven wonder how many men aboard the *Versailles* had sampled her sweetness.

He'd seen enough. He set his glass down on a nearby table and moved closer to his wife. The practiced look he gave the other man had been known to quell an enemy in his tracks. Raven considered any man who looked at his wife with such undisguised lust an enemy. He slid an arm around Daria's waist and moved his mouth to her ear.

"Let us return to our quarters."

Alarm opened her eyes wide. "Now?"

"Yes, now. Though I find this reception highly enlightening, I want only to be alone with my wife."

She swallowed.

"Come, say good night to your friends."

Daria set her drink down, and sent a bewildered look around the room. She nodded good night to her friends, thanked Captain Aaron then allowed Raven to escort her from the room and down the corridors to their quarters.

᠉ᢌᡦᢒᡧᡕᢚ

Heartbeat and respirations were definitely not normal. Total system failure certain. Daria took what was supposed to be a deep breath, but it barely made a dent in her lack of oxygen. Death would soon come to claim her and carry her to *Hialeigha*.

A large warm hand skimmed down her bare back. Desire shot through her and made her knees want to buckle. But she couldn't do this. Couldn't go through with consummating a marriage that should have been Lessia's. At least not yet. Not now, with the memories of how the Hohn looked while bent over her sister's casket swirled in her mind like a meteor shower.

This should have been Lessia's wedding night.

All through her preparations, as Onya fussed over her hair and applied the perfect makeup to her face, a steady stream of words had marched through her mind. The semblance of a speech began to form. Before she could ever lay with the Hohn as his true wife, she would have to let him know she understood and appreciated the love he had for Lessia and would understand...

"You're frowning, princess."

"Huh?" She came out of her musings and turned to look up at him. Dark eyes glittered in anger at her. "Oh. I was just thinking about something."

"I hope you weren't anticipating the marriage bed with such a look on your face. I would hope our first coupling would be pleasant for you."

By the Maker, she wouldn't speak of this in a common hallway. She took a quick glance around and was happy to see no one in the halls but the two of them.

"You have had lovers?" His hand caressed her back again and his breath warmed her ear. They stood in front of his quarters—their quarters—and she waited while he palmed the door opened.

She gave a quick nod to indicate there had been lovers. A glance to gauge his reaction showed none whatsoever. He probably thought her morally lacking for a wife of the Hohn. Though she had never cared what others thought of her, this was the man she was to spend the rest of her life with.

Heat rushed to her face. Why was he doing this to her? Why was she letting him? It wasn't as if she were a tender young virgin on the altar as a sacrifice. Damn it all to Hell's Caverns and back, she was a seasoned combat pilot, time to start acting like one. If he wanted to make love to her pedigree and not her past, he could just go jump out the nearest airlock.

The door slid open and they stepped inside. The appointments were nice and spacious, but Daria barely got a look at the room before she was backed up against the now closed door and the Hohn was bending his head down to her.

Lips, firm but gentle, settled over hers. The Hohn sipped at her mouth, and teased it open. A moan swelled up from her throat and she felt her hands move of their own volition to caress his broad muscular shoulders. He took the sound as encouragement and took the kiss deeper, became more possessive, demanding. Strong hands clutched under her arms and lifted her higher. A thick muscular thigh wedged between her legs and held her in place. The position stunned her in its intimacy, and sent hot throbs of desire through her body to pool in her sex.

His mouth devoured hers. His tongue slipped through her lips and brushed against hers. A low moan filled her mouth and tasted of his un-checked desire. His hips rocked forward, leaving her in no doubt of his desire for her. His long, thick erection rubbed against her stomach.

Large hands moved down her sides, cupping her breasts, molding them to his palms. Instantly, her nipples tightened. He rocked his hips again, and his thigh slid over her already pulsing clit. If she didn't stop the kiss now, she would drown in him. Or come. And it was definitely too soon for that.

Daria pushed away from him, breaking the drugging contact of his mouth on hers. His dark eyes were heavy-lidded with lust. He rested his forehead against hers for a moment, confusing her with their combined scent.

He moved his leg and she slid down the wall. She walked farther into the room, putting much needed space between them.

Something about the man simply got to her on a plane so much deeper than any other man she had ever known. Perhaps it was the implicit power he radiated. Energy floated around him like a force field. Raw masculinity dripped from his every movement, hot as lava and deadly as cyanide.

Daria looked over her shoulder at him standing by the door. His hand-some face was pulled into a slight frown, head cocked to one side. The man unsettled her, even when he did nothing more than stand across the room from her. What was more unsettling was her reaction to him. Sure she'd had lovers before, but even with Borman and Aaron she hadn't felt this overwhelming loss of control.

A vision of Raven draped across Lessia's casket filled her mind and made her breath catch. She turned from him, unable to look in his eyes any longer. This wasn't her husband—not really. This man before her was a hand-me-down from her older sister. She had become a wife by default. In all the years of her rebellion, she had never once envisioned herself taking a husband she knew loved another woman, especially if that woman was her sister.

A hand moved down her neck, startling the images from her mind. She hadn't heard him move from the door. "I didn't mean to scare you. We'll take this night slow if you prefer." Warm breath stirred the hair at her nape before his lips settled there.

Her nipples tightened painfully again under the soft fabric of her bor-rowed dress. She turned around to confront him. "Look, before we jump into anything physical, I think we need..."

Red lights and sirens began to flash and screech overhead.

"All hands to battle stations. Repeat. All hands to battle stations."

Daria moved passed the Hohn, her speech dying in her throat as her training took over and she hurried from the quarters.

"Daria!" He shouted down the corridor at her as she ran toward the quad.

She turned for a moment and stared at his stricken face. "I have to go. I can't fly a fighter in this."

Dark eyes pleaded with her, though no words moved through his tightly clamped jaw.

"It's my job, Hohn. You knew that when you signed the treaty with my father and agreed with the price of my hand." Daria wasted no more time on the one-sided argument, but hurried on to the quad to change into her flight suit.

At the door to the quad she met with a tide of pilots heading in the opposite direction. Falcon Borman stopped and grabbed her arm as he started past her.

"What are you doing?" Blue eyes flashed at her under heavy tawny brows. "Go back to your husband."

She pulled her arm from his grip and moved away. "And let you have all the fun? Not likely."

"You're going to jeopardize the alliance," he shot at her over the tops of the pilots' heads as they moved between them.

That statement stopped Daria and she turned back to Borman. "I sincerely doubt that. My parents' appearance over vid made the ceremony binding. And the Hohn will not go back on his word."

He moved back to her and stood staring down into her face. "I hope for all our sakes you're right. I'd hate to think I gave you up to a man who could never appreciate you like I could."

What he didn't say, but was there in his eyes, was the night on Gideon III she'd spent with Aaron. Even though she and Borman had been apart for months before, he'd still been hurt when he found out about the liaison. Be that as it may, past lovers had no bearing on her marriage, especially with a man of the Hohn's character.

Conviction coalesced between her breasts. She may not know the Hohn as a person, but his reputation spoke volumes. Even if she spent forever in a starcruiser fighting against some unknown galactic threat, the Hohn would never see his integrity questioned by going back on his word, or an alliance no matter what she did in the name of duty.

"You worry about bringing the squadron back to *Versailles* safely. I'll worry about my husband." Saying the word out loud unnerved her as she turned from Borman and started back to the quad. As it was she would be reprimanded for not being on the fighter deck within the five-minute window.

Now on top of the wail of sirens she had the word "husband" ringing in her ears like the tolling of a death knell. Well, they'd just see about that. She hadn't married to help both planets, only to lose her own identity in the process. No, she'd fought too hard to gain her rank of Eagle to throw it all away on a loveless marriage. He might just be the sexiest man to travel the galaxy, but the Hohn had bought her royal blood, not her body and soul.

She moved to her quad and opened her locker to pull out the flight suit. The lightweight material clung to the body like a second skin, as millions of tiny sensors woven directly into the fabric created an interface between the pilot and the fighter's computer.

Once in the suit she ran down the halls and to the flight deck to board her fighter. Another Falcon, by the name of Gray, stood checking off pilots' names on the roster as they boarded their ships to defend the unfriendly skies.

"Glad to see you could make it, Eagle Varta," Falcon Gray said dryly and lifted a steely gaze to her.

Daria didn't make a comment but hurried to the cockpit and strapped herself in, then began to flick controls to bring her ship to life.

The on-board computer whirled to life and a familiar voice buzzed in her ear. "Good day, Eagle Varta."

"How's it hanging, Loki?"

"High and to the right," the computer answered in a crisp tone.

She smiled in spite of the grave circumstances. Loki never failed to come up with great answers for her oftentimes colorful greetings. A sudden hit jarred the ship and the *Versailles* shuddered under the impact.

"Has the motherboard downloaded any info on the attack?"

"Unknown fighters. No distinguishing flags or markings on their sides. Unable to ascertain origin. Attempts to contact ships and negotiate peaceful ends to engagement unsuccessful."

"Must be the same bastards who attacked the Riman delegation."

"That is affirmative. Receiving transcripts from Primon on Riman convoy attack."

"Quad Valhalla, you're up. Prepare to launch," the voice of the deck commander announced over her headset.

"Eagle Varta and Loki copy."

"Eagle Charter and Thor copy."

"Eagle Ramsey and Odin copy."

"Eagle Prussin and Tyr copy."

The rest of her quad mates chimed in. Clearance came and the ships rocketed out of the bay and scrambled into the dogfight happening just beyond the *Versailles'* starboard side.

Screens rolled before Daria's eyes displaying back to her the information Loki took from her flight suit and interrupted as instructions. Primon pilots didn't so much fly the fighters as they gave physiological commands to the ship's computer and the computer self-maneuvered to those commands.

Ships crisscrossed the black expanse of space before her. Laser fire erupted from gunners and explosions rocked the fighter. The unknown attackers were as her father said. They were like nothing she had ever seen. Knife blade sharp, they cut through space with a speed and agility that put the Primon fighters to shame. Even with the biotechnology, the *Versailles'* pilots were being slaughtered.

"Loki, head to the thick of the fighting. It looks like Renaissance quad is having a hard time shaking the bastards."

"Destination redirected." The ship rolled and maneuvered to the seat of heaviest fighting.

"Power laser cannon and ready guns."

"Lasers powered and standing by." The weapons' screen glowed yellow in standby sequence.

Ahead ships exploded and Daria watched in horror as the Da Vinci disintegrated in a shower of a visible wave emanating from an enemy fighter.

"What the fuck is that?"

"Unknown weaponry," Loki answered. "Attempting to analyze data."

"Well, analyze faster." She gripped the gun controls, aiming for the ship that annihilated the Da Vinci and got lock-on. "Fire!"

Impossibly the enemy fighter rolled and fired on her. Sparks flew through the cockpit, showering down on her arm and side. The stench of burnt biosuit and flesh filled her nostrils.

Not good. Definitely. Not good.

Chapter Four

Raven stood on the bridge and watched the dogfight unfold before his eyes. Somewhere out in the chaos, Daria braved the odds. Each time a ship exploded, he glanced over at the display that gave the name of the pilot and ship hit.

His hands were clenched at his sides in anger. How dare she leave their quarters to fight? Did the vows they speak mean nothing to her? But no, they had to. He'd felt the way she reacted to his kiss, felt the tremble of her lips and the pounding of her heart. He had drunk in the throaty sigh she couldn't hide from him. If they'd had more time, he could have coaxed her into bed and put her fears to rest for good.

After she left, he'd called his fleet and alerted the nearest ship to assist. They were barely within range, and he doubted if they'd be able to arrive to the battlefront in a timely manner.

Captain Aaron stood at the command center, barking orders to the frenzied bridge crew. "Make a long range sweep of the area. Those fighters couldn't have flown this far into space without a mother ship."

"I'm not picking up anything out there but our own, and some Jevic signals," a young woman at a console answered. "The enemy may be just out of our sensor range, or they're blocking their signals."

"Try harder."

Jevic fighters flew into the fray, called upon by their Hohn into the battle with their Primon allies. Captain Aaron turned his head slightly to Raven and gave a sly smile. "You could have told me you called in the cavalry."

"I didn't know if they'd be here in time. It seemed pointless to raise hopes if they were late." His watchful gaze never left the screen.

Another Primon fighter took heavy fire and a female voice cursed loudly over the transmission. "Damn it. I'm hit!"

The tech manning the communications console turned a startled face to first Raven and then his C.O. "Loki has sustained major damage."

"I've lost my forward guns and am losing pressure in my thrusters."

Loki. Daria's ship. Raven balled up his fists and held them stiff at his sides. He wanted to hit something. He wanted to rage. But he didn't, he stood there on the bridge of the *Versailles* with Daria's people surrounding him and watched as a lone fighter broke off from the battle and limped back toward the ship.

Static crackled over the speakers. "I'm... losing... on... Loki's..."

Raven held his com unit to this mouth. "Cover that ship. I want it escorted back to *Versailles* without further incident."

"Yes, Hohn," a voice answered as two Jevic fighters pulled away and escorted the broken ship back to the dock.

Aaron held his attention to the fighter that started to drift as the engines failed. "Eagle Varta. Status report."

Dead air greeted his request. "Raise the docking crew."

"Docking crew raised."

"Falcon Borman, release the tow beam and bring Loki in."

"Releasing tow."

Raven watched helplessly as the Loki came back to the *Versailles* not under its own steam. An urgent need to get there planted itself in his sacrum. "Take me to the docking bay."

༚ༀ(༒༺)ༀ

Daria released the halter straps and waited for Borman to manually open the cockpit for her. Pain radiated up and down her left side where the blast had blown Loki's circuits and the resulting fire burned down her arm and hip.

The biosuit had melted in places and in others stung the tender flesh underneath. She plucked the suit away from her hip as pain shot deep into her midsection. This wasn't good. It wasn't good at all.

The cockpit cover slid open and Daria started to stand but Borman stopped her. His face twisted into a grimace at the injuries. "Wait for the medic."

"No. I'm fine enough to walk to sickbay. Help me out of this."

He started to comply then stopped as another figure loomed through the fighter's open top.

The Hohn looked in at her and frowned. "You're hurt."

"Thanks for the update, Captain Obvious, but I think I've figured that one out." She winced when she levered herself to stand. If no one wanted to help her out of the disabled ship, she'd do it herself.

The Hohn reached in and grabbed her around the waist and pulled her to him. The uninjured side of her lay plastered against his chest as he started walking from the hanger bay still holding her in his arms.

His expression was impassive, jaw clenched. Daria had the overwhelming need to reach up and touch that granite-hard face. What would he do? Surely his mind was busy having flashbacks of the shuttle mishap that claimed Lessia's life. Her stomach roiled with the realization.

"You can put me down. I'm well enough to walk." She tried to swing her legs down by bucking against his chest.

He gripped her tighter. "Just direct me to sick bay."

"You really didn't have to carry me."

Dark eyes flashed down to lock with hers. "But I did."

For a moment she allowed her eyes to close and leaned her head against his chest. He felt so solid under her hand and cheek. She could hear the cadence of his heart and the air moving through his lungs. The Hohn was everything of life and vitality.

She popped one eye open to gain her bearings. "Next right and follow the corridor all the way around. Sickbay is at the end."

With the directions given, the Hohn picked up the pace. His left arm rubbed against the burns on her side, making her wince in pain.

"Almost there."

The whoosh of the sickbay doors sounded and Daria heard medics running toward them, but for some reason she found it very hard to open her eyes at that moment. But she had to. The Hohn could not see her weak. He may have loved Lessia for her soft femininity, but he would come to admire Daria for her strength.

"Put her on the exam table," Dr. Crowder, the surgical chief, told the Hohn in a clipped tone.

Daria opened her eyes and gave the doctor a lame smile. "Thought you'd seen the last of me after that scuffle on Remmick, huh?"

"You're a damn fool girl," Crowder scolded, her large gray eyes narrowed under sharp gray brows. "I told you the last time you met with mishap, I wouldn't put you back together again."

"Ah, but this time it was in the line of duty." Daria raised her right hand to the flight suit's zipper and started to pull it down. She glanced at the Hohn standing there beside her sick bed, watching the proceedings as if to ensure she would come to no harm under the good doctor's care.

"You can leave now." She waved a dismissing hand toward the door.

"I think not." It was stated firmly and sounded as much order as protest.

Daria raised a brow in her most imperial manner. "I appreciate you carrying me here, but I no longer need your services. You're free to amuse yourself for the rest of the evening."

A dark smile played at the corners of his sensuous mouth. "I have no intentions of 'amusing myself' on my wedding night, unless the amusement in question features my wife."

Shocked but not speechless, Daria ground her teeth together. How dare he be so impertinent in front of others? "Then at least have the decency to allow the doctor to exam me without you standing there in all your Jevic Hohn intimidation."

The smile traveled up and heated his eyes. "I wouldn't dream of it." He leaned over and placed a lingering kiss on her mouth. "I'll wait outside."

Even a kiss as chaste as that felt possessive coming from him.

When he was gone, Dr. Crowder helped her from the biosuit and began to assess the burns covering her arm and side. "They're superficial only. The one on your shoulder is the worst. I can put some dermaseal on it and you'll be good as new."

Daria ventured a look at the area in question. Angry red welts were eaten into her flesh. "Oh yeah, that's attractive. Wait until the Hohn gets a load of these beauty marks." Lessia had never had a scab or scar in the entirety of her short life, and it seemed Daria had nothing but.

Dr. Crowder looked up from her work of applying the dermalseal. "Somehow I don't think the man will mind."

Daria's heart lurched painfully. Of course he wouldn't, he was probably still in love with her sister. "No, you're right about that I'm sure."

"Why didn't you let him stay? His concern for your welfare is very touching."

"His concern for my welfare is part of his need to control all situations he finds himself in." Daria winced when the doctor hit a particularly tender area. "Besides, I'd rather him see me rude than crying out in pain."

"You're playing a dangerous game."

Daria gave a negligent shrug of her shoulder. "I've played them before."

"But never with the Hohn."

Raven leaned against the corridor wall and listened intently to the conversation going on inside. So, she wanted to put up a brave front for him? His heart swelled with the knowledge. It showed him just how much she cared about how he saw her as a wife, as a partner, but most importantly, as a person.

His com unit beeped. "Hohn."

"Sir, we've been able to intercept one of the enemy craft. We're towing it aboard the *Ramaclesus*."

"Excellent. Keep me informed on your findings. I want the pilot thoroughly interrogated."

"Very good, sir."

He signed off as Daria came out of sickbay wearing a patient gown and holding her body stiffly. "You plan to walk the corridors in that?" She started by him and he got a flash of a very naked, very shapely backside.

"I plan to return to my quad, change into some decent clothes and then get to the hanger bay to find out how Loki is."

He wrapped his hand around the flapping fabric and pulled her to him, closing her gown. "At least wrap the damn indecent thing around you better."

"What? Are you afraid I'll show my shipmates something they've already seen? Get a grip." The words were caustic, but she did hold the gown tighter to cover herself.

They began to walk down the corridor side by side toward the quad. "What do you mean your shipmates have seen you?"

"Coed showers, Hohn. Don't Jevic starcruisers have them?"

The very idea appalled him. And he considered himself an enlightened man. "No. We do not. We have separate facilities for the men and women."

"Seems like a horrible waste of space that could be used for something else." She turned her head to look at him.

"Even so, it is the way of Jevic." A slow smile slid into place. "But you need not use the coed facilities any longer. Our quarters have private showers."

When she looked him again, her mouth held a very bright smile of her own. "That's a real bonus, Hohn."

The quad chambers were empty when they entered. All the pilots were either in the fight, in sickbay, or in *Hialeigha*. She moved to one of the quads and stood near the locker rambling through the contents. Suddenly, she opened the patient gown and let it fall in a puddle at her feet.

With her body in three-quarter view, it was hard to see beyond the curve of hip and breast, but even what he could see had him hard and ready. He traced the length of her spine and curve of her shoulder with his eyes. The top of one shoulder was shiny in the plasticine bandage the doctor had painted on to heal the wound and keep infection out. The injury looked deep and angry to Raven's eyes.

He moved closer to get a better look at it. "Does it still pain you?"

She turned her head and considered the injury then looked back up at him, seemingly unconcerned by her nudity. As well she shouldn't be. Her body was the essence of perfection to him.

From this vantage point he could gaze over her shoulder and down the slope of her high full breasts to the sweet pink nipples at their tips. He ached to caress them, bring them to full hardness and suckle them into his mouth.

"It tingles," she answered after a brief pause.

Unable to keep from touching her, he slid his hands around the front of her, pressing against the softness of her abdomen. "Yes?"

"Hohn." It came out as a sigh beside his ear as she tipped her head back.

"Raven."

"Huh?"

He buried his nose in her neck to nuzzle the spot between her ear and shoulder. "My name is Raven." He roamed his hand up and across her hips and her pleasurable sigh turned to a quick indrawn breath. "Damn." The dermaseal had come off at the touch of his warm hand. It wasn't supposed to come off until dissolved by a specially formulated remover.

Raven turned her so he could look at the area. "That's not right. Let me take you back to sickbay."

"It will be fine. She probably just didn't put it on thick enough there. I was in kind of a hurry to get out." She pulled a lightweight shirt over her head. "I don't think I'll be able to put bottoms on though."

Raven leaned in and riffled through her clothes ignoring her outraged huff. He found a pair of stretchy leggings and handed them to her. "Step into these." When she had and pulled them up, careful not to touch the wound, Raven squatted and took the waistband and rolled it down to the very bottom crest of her hips. It wasn't perfect, but it would do.

The flat plane of her stomach was exposed before him, begging to have his mouth on it. Right on the lower half of her stomach, above the curve of her mound, was the most amazing birthmark. His breath caught in his chest and refused to be expelled.

"Something wrong down there?" Daria asked and shoved at his shoulder to pull away from him. She turned back to her locker and continued to rifle through it.

Raven stood. He watched her in profile for a moment. A most peculiar look passed over her face. "Daria?"

She turned back to him, not meeting his eyes this time. "Did you want to return to your quarters? I'll be all right going to check on Loki by myself. I just need to find another pair of boots."

When she would have moved away from him, he caught her arm. "Have I offended you in some way?"

"No. Don't be foolish. I can't be offended. I'm a fighter pilot. I'm made of sterner stuff than your average princess." She pulled her arm from him and moved away.

"You would tell me if I had? I want no misunderstandings between us." He watched as she sat on the bed to pull on a pair of boots.

She finally looked up at him, a weary smile curled up one side of her mouth. "I think we understand each other perfectly, Hohn."

As she rose and left the quad, Raven stood there and watched her retreating form and wondered why he felt he had just missed something important.

Chapter Five

Mechanics already had Loki torn apart and were looking through his innards to see if repairs were possible.

"I'm really sorry, Eagle," Hawk Conners said as she slid out from under Loki's control panel. She brushed a hand through dark cropped hair and shook her head. "It looks like whatever that was that hit you produced some kind of irreversible damage to Loki's motherboard. I won't know until I get the thing out and back to the repair lab, but for now I wouldn't be too optimistic if I were you."

"So the charge fried it?" Daria asked giving Conners a hand down as she climbed from the cockpit.

The Hawk nodded her thanks. "No, I don't think so. I would think if that were the case you'd have instantly gone black on all screens. You lost power over the course of minutes. It's almost like it took a while for the charge to run through the lines and take them out. And systematically too, I might add."

Daria patted Loki's fuselage as if it would comfort or cure him. "How so?"

"To an enemy, what is the most important element to take out on an opposing forces' fighter?"

"Weapons," Daria answered as the light began to dawn. "My weapons went first, though the place where I took the hit was nowhere near the gun circuits."

"Bingo." Conners touched her finger to her nose. "Next communications, so you can't call for help. Then navigations so you couldn't get back to the mother ship."

"So it's like a computer virus?"

"More like a worm. But yes, essentially I'd say that's what we're dealing with."

Daria let out a long breath, considering the Hawk's words. She ran a hand over her forehead, feeling slightly warm in the hanger bay. They needed to check the ventilation in this part of the ship. It didn't seem to be working. "But you don't think you can repair Loki?"

"I'll try my best, but I'm almost afraid the worm infecting him will crawl into the computers in the repair lab and we'll have a whole other set of problems."

"Damn." The last thing Daria wanted was to press the technicians to repair Loki at the cost of the *Versailles*.

Sweat pooled and dripped down between her breasts and along her spine. "Are the environmental controls broken in here?" She fanned her shirt away from her body.

"Feels comfortable to me." Conners pointed her screwdriver toward Loki. "Let me get back to work and you get back to sickbay. You aren't looking so good."

"Hell of a thing to say to a woman on her wedding night." Daria started to turn away when the entire hanger bay seemed to spin up on its axis and pitch wildly.

"Eagle!" She heard someone yell right before the entire hanger went dark.

⁂

Raven stared down at Daria. Impotent rage rose up in him at seeing her so helpless. Hadn't the doctor looked for more than the surface burns? Apparently not, or she wouldn't now be fighting for her life in a ship's sickbay. All the Gods weeping!

Captain Aaron entered the room and handed Raven a communications disk. "A full log of the attack, the hit on the Loki, and what the techs have been able to ascertain from Loki's motherboard."

"They worked fast." He put the disk in his pocket to read later. Now, all he wanted to do was sit beside Daria and will her into wellness.

Her face was pale and no color appeared in her once pink lips. His heart tightened. She looked dead. Only the gentle rise and fall of her breasts made him aware that she had not taken the spectral road to *Hialeigha*.

He took a seat beside her bed and took her limp hand in his. The skin was too cold to the touch. Tears clogged his throat.

When he felt he had mastered his emotions enough he raised his eyes to look at the Captain. "I'm taking her back to Jevic."

Aaron nodded. "I'll have my people hail your nearest cruiser and have them rendezvous with us as soon as possible."

Jevic physicians were the premiere healers in the known galaxy. If they couldn't help his beloved, no one could.

Aaron turned and left after placing a hand on Daria's shoulder and gazing into her immobile face for a moment longer than necessary. Once again Raven wondered if his wife had been her C.O.'s lover. But it no longer mattered, they had spoken vows and she was under his care now. He would remove her to a Jevic ship and take her back to the home world and out of Aaron's reach. If she lived.

If. Such a small word for such a vast number of possibilities. But she had to live. They had an entire life spread out before them.

Raven moved close to her ear. "Listen well, Daria. You will live. You will fight this with every last fiber of your being. You will come back to me. I've waited five long years to have you, and you will not deny me."

He moved so his lips could caress her cheek. "I love you. Do you hear me? I will not lose you."

It was only a matter of hours before the Jevic ship that had aided them in the attack docked alongside the *Versailles*. With much care, the Jevic physician and the medics transferred Daria to the gurney. The controls were set for stability and it hovered along beside them with no bouncing movement to jar her body. Not that it would have mattered in her case. The injury had caused an infection to spread, the injury wasn't unstable like a neck fracture.

Captain Aaron was at the airlock waiting for them, a concerned look on his face. The couple that had slammed into Daria at the wedding was also there. Both of them wore serious expressions and the man looked as if he were fighting tears. The woman didn't try to fight her tears, but let the river run down her face at will.

Raven bowed formally to Captain Aaron. "I thank you for your hospitality and consideration while aboard your ship. You may be assured if the circumstances are ever reversed, you and your crew will enjoy all Jevic hospitality."

Captain Aaron gave a stiff nod. "I only wish things would have turned out differently. But the Primon fleet will forever be indebted to you for bringing your ships to our rescue." His gaze fell to the gurney as it hovered through the airlock and onto the Jevic ship. "Would you send word as to Eagle Varta's status? She has many friends aboard the *Versailles*, and I'm sure they will be praying for her swift recovery."

Raven thought it was more than a matter of letting her friends know, but he couldn't deny the man his request, even if the truth of his and

Daria's relationship was more intimate than Raven would have liked. "I'll keep you apprised."

In the sickbay aboard the *Ramaclesus*, the doctors stood over Daria, taking blood samples, examining her with all the technology at hand, and desperately trying to determine the nature of her illness. The contagion had attacked with a ferocity Raven had never seen before. She had gone from declaring her fitness to unconsciousness in less than ten minutes.

He stood back away from the doctors, leaned against the counter with his arms crossed over his chest. Several times, Healer Keeta tried to get him to leave, but had finally given up when Raven threatened her with reassignment to a penal colony on the Jevic moon of Epsilon.

As he brushed his hand along his coat, he felt the outline of the disk Captain Aaron had given him earlier. He hadn't time to read it yet. He swiveled a seat around and sat before a console then popped the disk into the reader.

Watching the attack unfold again was disturbing enough, but seeing and hearing Daria's voice as she made her final transmission hurt more than anything he'd ever known. At least it wasn't the last time he'd heard her voice. No at that time, they'd had a misunderstanding, he was sure of it, though he still wondered at the cause.

"Is that the file on the blood the Primon physician took?" Healer Keeta stood over him looking at the display as cells danced across the screen.

Raven came out of his silent reverie to study the screen closely. He glanced down at the file legend and shook his head. "No, it's the file the Primon Hawks made of the computer worm that took out the Loki."

"Tyrees, bring that blood sample here!" She grabbed the sample from her assistant's hand and fed it into the analyzer then pulled it up on screen. Much to the healer's horror and Raven's confusion, an identical picture filled the screen.

"What does it mean, Keeta?"

"It means that whatever infected the systems on the Loki is infecting your wife's systems as well."

"How is that possible? She's not a machine." Fear crept up from deep in his belly and threatened to strangle him.

"The Primon pilots wear biosuits that integrate between themselves and their ships' computers. It must have entered through the burns on her shoulder and hip."

"But why is it still there wreaking havoc on her?" He rose and moved to the bed in order to make sure she had not shut down as the Loki had.

But then no alarms had gone off to indicate a turn for the worse. He had to remain calm. No matter what, he could not lose control before those under his command.

Healer Keeta sat at the console, clicking away at the control pad. "The body runs on its own form of electrical current. The worm had only to follow the electric impulses of the nervous system to find a foothold."

He ran a hand over Daria's brow, smoothing the hair from her face. "Can you do anything for her?"

The clicking stopped. "I can keep her stable, but I need the facilities at the Healers' center to cure her. The *Ramaclesus*, though a well-equipped ship, is not the place where I would wish to test an anti-virus for such an illness. We need to get to Jevic as soon as possible."

At least there was something he could do. He hailed the command bridge to give the order for the jump to light speed.

"Sir?" Keeta came up behind him to put a comforting hand on his arm. "I want you to be prepared for the eventuality of your wife not making it to Jevic. The worm could attack her heart, and once that happens, I will not be able to do anything more for her."

Raven balled his fist in a tight grip. The other hand continued to stroke Daria's forehead. No, she had to survive. He had finally made her his wife. They hadn't time to get to know one another yet, or even enjoy the pleasures of their union.

"Why don't you go and get some rest? The Primon physician told me you've been by her bedside since she was brought to sickbay. You haven't left here since you boarded."

He lifted his shoulders and stood straighter. Did he look fatigued? "I am fine. You take care of my wife; I'll take care of myself."

The healer started to protest, but then Raven's com unit sounded again.

"Sir, we've dismantled the enemy fighter. There's something here we think you should see."

"I'll be there directly."

He took a moment to place a kiss on Daria's still lips and nodded to the healer. "If her condition changes, notify me immediately."

The enemy fighter stood as an awesome spectacle of engineering technology. The weapons worked on pulse waves that emitted a code to attack the primary systems of other ships, but how the targeted ships received those transmissions remained a mystery. However, one the most disturbing revelations had been found when the confiscated fighter revealed no pilot on board. The entire ship ran on remote control from an unknown location.

Clarin, Chief of Flight Operations, wiped a dirty hand across his forehead, smearing grease and some unidentifiable substance on his skin. "So, the doc thinks the biosuit Princess Daria wore infected her with the same virus unleashed in the code?"

"Yes." Raven considered the craft for a moment. He had just finished explaining the physician's theory. He didn't intend to spend much time in the hanger bay. He wanted to get back to Daria as soon as possible. "Send any information on the virus immediately to Healer Keeta."

"I did find something that may be of help." Clarin leaned back into the cockpit and pulled out what looked like an energy transformer. "It's part of the weapons array. When I plugged it into the handheld diagnostic grid, it began to mutate into giving me the same output as the grid. Very strange. At first I thought the transformer powered down and I wasn't getting any output from it, but when I plugged it back into the ship, it worked."

"You're saying it mimics whatever power source it's connected to?" Raven didn't like the possibilities such technology represented.

"Or resemble it enough to find the source of power generation and stop it completely." He handed the handheld grid to Raven. "Its dead. Completely useless now."

How was this supposed to help? Ice ran through Raven's veins. Whatever mutant nanobots were at work within the transformer had invaded Daria's body. He was moments away from falling apart and wanted none of his crew to witness his complete destruction.

"Forward the information to Healer Keeta." He turned on his heel and headed out the door and to his quarters.

Chapter Six

They made the Jevic homeworld just as the twin moons were coming over the eastern horizon. Daria's gurney was transferred from the *Ramaclesus* to the base hospital in the city of Tritan. She still had not regained consciousness and that very fact worried Raven more than he dared admit, though Healer Keeta didn't seem as upset by that as she had the information Chief Clarin forwarded to sickbay.

All information had again been relayed to the base physician and lab where the healers began working on a serum to help fight the foreign technology that invaded Daria's body. Healer Keeta expressed to Raven that the machines looked like living cells and not their much larger mechanized counterparts. She had also marveled that she had not lost Daria's vital signs, but thought that it was merely because humanoid physiology and the continuous course of the circulatory system didn't provide the nanobots with a journey's end. Therefore, the nanobots didn't know where to attack, or more importantly, what system to take offline, or in what sequence.

Raven greeted the high healer and hospital commandant, Raizen, with a stiff nod.

"We've been able to find a serum that will destroy the nanobots, but I warn it does come with some risks since we've only been able to trial it in simulation." The high healer scrubbed a hand over his closely shorn scalp and herded Raven to a console. "I want you to see what we've been able to do in our model."

Raven watched quietly as the serum attacked the nanobots and killed them off one by one. It indeed looked as if the scrum would work, but questions tumbled one over the other in his mind. He wanted no unnecessary risks taken. The medical staff would get one shot and one shot only.

He affected his best Hohn countenance. "Given the fact the nanobots are so clever at disguising themselves within the existing systems, how will the serum know which cells are real and which are the imposters?"

"Part of the risks I mentioned is the very real possibility that the serum will destroy all of your wife's blood cells in order to cure her."

The very thought horrified him. "How will you keep her alive?"

"By doing a simultaneous transfusion with a synthetic blood. When that runs clear of both serum and dead cells, we will transfuse with whole Primon blood products."

"And you think this will work?" It sounded as if it contained more than just "some" risks.

Raizen gave a small shrug of a shoulder. "It's the only chance we've got. Since our healers have never come up against such an invasion before, we're working blind. I wish I could tell you of vast experiences with such a treatment, but there just aren't any."

As the Hohn, Raven gave a nod to indicate his consent to treatment. Even if she died during the process, at least he knew he'd brought her to Jevic and given her the chance at life she deserved.

⁂

Daria could barely make out what was going on around her. Voices would come and go, and every once in a while she could feel someone touch her skin. More often than not, the touches felt like whispery caresses across her cheek and brow. A few times, she thought she felt the sweet pressure of lips pressed against hers. All the sensations were welcome, except for the crawling under the skin.

Violent itching spread from her feet to her head. The very hair on her scalp crawled as if made of deadly Vulsian cape spiders. No matter how hard she tried, no matter how many signals given from her brain to her arms she couldn't move in order to scratch. The screams that welled in her soul went nowhere.

Now, something that felt like ice water filled her veins and caused her heart to spasm and freeze. Excited shouts preceded frantic hands all working to try and save her miserable life. She just wanted to let go, and yet she fought on.

More than once she heard Lessia's soft voice calling to her from behind a bank of thick fog. Behind the veil between worlds, the gates of Hialeigha loomed ominous before her. No, she wasn't ready to step over that golden threshold and leave worldly cares behind. She still had much to do in her life. The fleet needed her. The alliance needed her. Over all the shouts and soft murmured persuasions of her dead sister came another voice, strong and determined. The Hohn's. Only one word dripped from the sensuous lips she could recall so clear in her mind: Live.

The word drummed through her body and chased away the coldness. Peace blanketed her and she finally slept.

Her eyes opened to a strange place. As she looked around she noticed it was a medical bay of some sort, but one unfamiliar to her. A young woman bowed over her and placed medication into a tube inserted into Daria's right arm. As she bent over, Daria noticed the crest of the Jevic healing order on her uniform. So they had come to Jevic, or were aboard a Jevic ship.

Daria tried to talk, but her voice only came out as a low croak of sound.

The startled healer looked up into Daria's face and smiled. "Your highness is awake."

She cleared her throat and corrected. "Eagle."

The healer frowned and entered something into the pad next to the bed.

"Drink?"

"Yes, of course. I'll be right back." The healer walked off, leaving Daria to study her surroundings. Most of what she could see was a bank of displays and a ceiling fashioned out of some dark sound-absorbing tile, but that was the extent of her view.

The strong presence of her husband floated in the air around her. She drank in his scent. He came up on her left, and she turned a smiling face to him before ever seeing his face. The Hohn had taken a seat beside her bed, his expression grim.

Strange sensations filled her body when she looked into his deep obsidian eyes. He had willed her to live, and she had, proving to her once and for all the extent of his power. The thought was amusing, and not something she would use to hyper-inflate his already firmly engrained sense of self-importance.

As his eyes took in her smiling face, the grim expression on his own muted into a smile. "You're awake."

She nodded, still not trusting her voice to work.

The healer came over and brought a cup filled with a thick liquid. When she started to help Daria to sit, the Hohn dismissed her and helped instead.

When she drank her fill, she held up a hand. The Hohn placed the cup on a bedside table and then leaned her back on the bed.

"How do you feel?" He asked and brushed the hair from her forehead. Vague recollections of that same touch during the height of her illness skidded through her mind.

"I feel like I've been hit repeatedly by a very large, very angry pachyderm."

"You had some rough moments, but high healer Raizen assures me you'll make a full recovery." He skimmed a bent knuckle down her cheek.

She looked around her again. "Where are we?"

"Jevic. The command base at Tritan, to be precise."

"I must have been out for longer than I thought."

"About a common month."

She started to bolt up from the bed. "A common month! I have to get back to my fleet. They'll need me. What about Loki? Is he all right?"

A large hand to the middle of her chest flattened her back to the bed. "Stay down. You've been too ill to worry about such things."

"But the fleet…"

"Has managed this long without you."

"Have they been attacked again?" She both wanted to know and recoiled from the answer. If they had undergone another attack while she was incapacitated, she'd never forgive herself.

The Hohn shook his head. "No, thankfully. We have been able to learn a few things from the fighter my forces intercepted during the fight that injured you."

"What things?"

The grim expression returned and he shook his head. "I'll tell you all about it after you get some rest."

"Rest? By your account I've had an entire common month of rest." She started to push up again, but he stayed her by placing that large hand of his on her chest again. "Would you stop doing that?"

A light smile teased the corners of his mouth. "Ah, you are feeling much better." He leaned over and brushed a quick kiss over her lips before standing. "I have some things I must attend to. I will return later in the day."

As he started to leave, she grabbed his hand. "Hohn, please, tell the physician I want to leave. Tell him I'm well enough to go."

The man actually had the audacity to give a throaty chuckle. "Tell a universally renowned Jevic healer that his patient is well? Me? I may have command of all the Jevic forces, but even I am not that brave."

Daria huffed for a moment. She folded her arms over her chest. "Fine, if you are not brave enough, I, sure as Hell's Cavern, am."

He leaned down and kissed her again. This time, however, he lingered over her lips. When he backed away, his gaze bored into hers. "Of that, my love, I have no doubt."

Heat moved through her as he walked away. Had he just called her his love?

She fell back to sleep as the endearment echoed through her mind.

Chapter Seven

It was a few more days before Daria was well enough to be discharged from the hospital. The Hohn was there to escort her to their quarters. However, their quarters turned out to be every bit as impressive as the *palace royale* on Primon.

As he guided her through the massive rooms, servants opened doors for them and bowed in deference and respect. Though Daria had grown up in such opulence she had never coveted it, nor wanted it as an adult. Give her a starcruiser and a C.O. who rode roughshod over his soldiers any day. Living up to the expectation of such grandeur was infinitely more stressful than facing an entire squadron of enemy fighters. That was one of the reasons she chose to leave the *palace royale*. She never felt quite as if she measured up to the standards set by her more beautiful and refined sisters.

"Is this residence provided by the council? Or did you purchase it?" She heard herself ask as her voice echoed off the high ceilings.

"No. It's been the Hohn residence since before the days of the council. The Tritan king lived here once upon a time." He ushered her through a doorway and down a long hall. At the end, double doors opened into a grand ballroom. "When I'm not expected at the command center, we'll reside at my country home."

Daria turned to him. After all the walking through the halls for the grand tour, she was beginning to feel fatigued. "Really? What's it like?"

"Nothing so grand as this." He walked across the ballroom, tucking her arm through his as he did. "When you are feeling better we will have our formal Jevic ceremony in this very room."

"And a formal Jevic ceremony is important to you?" she asked as they came to a stop in the middle of the dance floor. All around them, floor to ceiling mirrors reflected their images back to them.

Eyes warm with desire searched her face. "It is."

The thought of him wanting all the pomp and ceremony made her smile. "Then we will, but I'm really uncomfortable as the center of attention."

His hands came up to hold her face as she bent her head back to look up at him. "How could you be?"

Warm breath fanned her face as he spoke. He was so close she could almost taste him. Deep inside, her heart begged for his lips to claim hers, but her head screamed no, it was wrong to want him so much when he should have been married to Lessia.

Temptation spurred her closer. Fear made her stop just short of kissing him.

"Daria." The word came out as a near moan.

"Hohn."

"Raven," he corrected before lowering his mouth to hers. He parted her lips with the practiced movement of his mouth on hers, and slipped his hot tongue in to slide against hers.

She moaned, pressing as close as she could against the wall of his chest. His hands moved down her face to caress her shoulders. He moved her back from him. His eyes went from warm to blazing. "I've waited so long for you."

"I'm sorry," she whispered. It must have been hard for a man as sexual as the Hohn to forgo his husbandly rights for a month. But who said he had been faithful in that month? She swallowed around the sudden lump in her throat.

"What?" He brought his hand up to her brow and smoothed her frown away.

She shook her head. Bluster had always been easy for her. Confessions were hard.

"Come, I want no secrets between us." He started toward the opposite door at the end of the ballroom.

They walked in silence for a few steps, Daria refused to answer his question. He wrapped his large hand around her neck and guided her while his fingers gently caressed her.

"I remember the first time I ever saw you." He stopped at the door and turned back to the ballroom. "You were at a ball on Riman. I watched you push your way through the crowd. I believe your destination was the balcony garden. I lost sight of you after you exited the garden doors."

She remembered that ball very well. She had attended against her wishes and better judgment, with Lessia. Shortly after the ball, the offer for an alliance and the Hohn's hand had come for her sister. He may have remembered her coarse manners at having shoved her way through the crush of dancing bodies, but he had asked for the hand of her prettier and genteel sister.

Tears stung her eyes and she fought them back. How could something that happened five years before still have the power to bring pain? Jealousy burned her gut. Truly for one who had not wished to marry the Hohn in the first place, her reaction to his confession was definitely strange.

"I looked all over for you, but couldn't find a trace of you."

Her heart pounded behind her breastbone. "I didn't think I'd be missed. I rarely am among the more dignified strains of society."

"Where did you go?" A servant opened the door for them and he followed her into the hallway. "I often wondered what your hurry had been."

Often? Oh, she doubted that very much. These were the words of a practiced seducer. Just how many women had he seduced over the course of his career, from one end of the galaxy to the other? "I thought I saw one of my fellow cadets leaving through that door. I needed to talk to him."

The Hohn grunted. "And did you find him?"

Embarrassment burned her face. Oh, she had found him all right, with his pants down around his ankles and his cock in some woman's mouth. "Yes. But he was a little too busy for conversation at the moment."

He gave her a startled look. "I see."

"Wish I hadn't." Then she shook her head. "No, that's untrue. I'm glad I found out sooner rather than later the type of man he is."

"His character suffered in your eyes?"

"I will not tolerate unfaithfulness in a relationship, regardless of how most royals turn the other way. But then I've never fit in within my own family anyhow."

Suddenly the Hohn stopped and pinned her to the wall. His big body covered hers. His eyes dark and tortured. "Was he your lover?"

Daria didn't like being intimidated, nor manhandled in such a fashion. But there was something in his eyes, in his body language that told her the information was important to him. For once in her life, she decided not to strike out in rebellion and bowed to his need. "No. We were considered a couple, but we hadn't been intimate yet."

"Did you love him?"

"I respected him, but he lost my respect and my friendship that night."

The Hohn rested his forehead against hers. "I pledge here and now,

I'll never be unfaithful to you. I'll never give you reason to lose your respect for me."

She smiled up at him. "Who ever said I respected you?"

He took the joke for what it was and laughed with her. After a moment he sobered and looked directly into her eyes. "I mean it, Daria. It would break my heart if I ever thought you didn't respect me, or had lost faith in me."

She moved to put space between them. "Look, I do respect you, and the uniform you wear. You wouldn't have been elevated to Hohn if you weren't a loyal and honorable man. I do know enough of Jevic government to understand that much. However, I don't really know you as a person. And since the entirety of our marriage has passed while I've been unconscious, we haven't had a real chance to get to know each other."

He took a deep breath and considered her. "Come, we need to get you back to bed. You're looking flushed."

She felt flushed. Right down the airlock and into the void. What did he expect from her, a proclamation of undying love? Well, he'd be a long time waiting for that. She had never worn her heart on her sleeve and didn't intend to do so now. She desired him, but that was far from love. "I am rather tired."

Without further delay, he showed her to the master suite and dismissed the maid who came to help her undress for bed. Daria was too tired to do much more than take off her shoes before climbing up on the high raised dais bed and falling across it in a haphazard fashion.

The Hohn removed his boots and uniform and lay down next to her. "Should you be here?"

"I'm your husband, so I see no harm in napping with you."

Daria gave a sleepy laugh. "No, I mean your duties. Shouldn't you be off intimidating some underling somewhere?"

"No, my love, I'm exactly where I need to be right now." A strong arm hooked around her waist and pulled her so her back rested against his chest.

She turned her head and looked at his naked splendor. Damn, but he was one beautiful specimen of manhood. Jevic skin was naturally darker than Primon. Several shades in fact. Where her body was all pink and pale, his was all bronzed and perfect. Smooth dark hair covered his chest and narrowed at his navel, then became coarse and thick around his genitals. His penis stirred and began to grow under her watchful gaze.

Quickly, she turned back and placed her head on her hands.

Laugher stirred her hair. "You act like you've never seen a naked man before. Do not tell me you didn't get your fill of peeking into the next stall while using those coed showers?"

Of course she'd seen men before, naked men. Lots of naked men. But this was a her husband. Her aroused husband. Her aroused husband who was still in love with her dead sister. But Lessia wasn't here, and the Hohn obviously needed some relief.

Daria put her hand up on her forehead. It was really getting hot in the room, and having him snuggled up behind her wasn't helping matters.

"Do you always sleep naked?"

"Yes. Does it bother you?"

No, it had only made her go supernova. "I'm just feeling a little over-dressed at the moment. And it's way hot in here."

He turned her over onto her back and looked into her face. Something like panic filled his eyes before he tamped the emotion down. He ran a warm hand over her brow. "You feel normal."

"That's not where I'm feeling warm."

A low growl came from his throat. "It may not do to incite my passion after your being ill for so long."

Daria could hardly get a good breath in. The memory of the level of desire he had lifted her to when they were in his quarters on the *Versailles* burned a path down her body. Her breasts felt full and heavy, her nipples tight. Warmth surged between her thighs. "Do you want me?" A glance down proved he did indeed want her very much.

"How could I not?"

"We could take it slow," she suggested as his mouth moved over her face, then down her neck. His hands began to pull her shirt up.

"Slow can be very good, my love." He pulled the shirt up and over her head, exposing her breasts to his hungry gaze. "So beautiful." His tongue came out and swirled around her nipples, first one then the other.

"Mmmm." Daria heard herself moan and could see her body arch into his mouth. She put her hand under her breast and cupped it up to him in offering, bringing it closer to his hungry mouth.

Strong teeth nipped at the sensitive flesh, leaving a trickle of pain before his tongue laved, gently taking the pain away.

Long thick fingers caressed her belly and moved under the waistband of her pants. They moved unerringly through her curls and into the drenched folds of her sex. "My Gods," he murmured.

He slid his other hand over her side and pulled her pants off. He settled between her legs. Her thighs spread against the width of his broad shoulders. Dark eyes centered on her open sex. "I have to taste you, Daria."

A low whimper came from her throat. If he didn't she would die for sure. Captain Aaron had been the last man to go down on her, and that had been a while ago. Right after the Gideon III mission. She'd considered that night a "Thanks for saving my ass fuck." They'd done it several times and many positions that night.

But this was different, this was her husband.

"Please," she heard herself say, becoming detached from the moment as he moved down her body, nipping at her skin.

He rubbed his face against her curls, taking in a lung full of air as he did. Then he was there. His tongue coming out to play with her clit. Circling it with tightly controlled strokes. One, two fingers pushed into her then moved slowly in and out. Daria arched, reaching for the release that hovered so close.

How could he manage to push her to the edge so fast? He'd only begun and yet she had been near climax since he'd first touched her.

A long wet tongue replaced his fingers.

"Hohn."

He kissed her wet center and moved up. "Raven."

Her hands twisted in the bed covers as she fought to hold on to the delicious feelings that slammed through her. The Hohn was an accomplished lover. And he was all hers!

Sensations rippled through her, bringing her back off the bed as her orgasm came in a blinding explosion. He slurped and supped and licked, until he had gotten it all. Then he moved up her body again, keeping her legs wide. Slowly, oh so slowly, he moved into her.

"Daria." His voice came out as a low husky groan.

Oh, by every God, he was hard and long and hot. His sex filled her to overflow and then some. Her body wanted to accommodate his size, but she had stretched to the max as it was.

He moved so slowly she could hardly stand it. But he had promised to take it slow and easy, and she had fallen into a stupor of sensation that she could not wake from. He felt good and right inside her, as if this had been what she'd sought in all her other partners.

He continued to rock into her as gently as his big body would allow. Her eyes slid open a fraction and she gazed at him through the shadow of her lashes.

Dark eyes locked on hers. His jaw set like granite slab. Nostrils flared in excitement, his lips pulled back to show teeth. A single drop of sweat rolled down his temple and splashed on her hard nipple then ran down her body.

Every muscle of his body was drawn taut as he continued to thrust into her over and over.

Damn, but she never wanted it to end. "Make it last," she begged. "Make it last forever."

His hand slid down the back of her thigh in response and straightened out her leg. He turned his head and kissed her ankle. "I will, my love. I will."

Their lovemaking continued at that same slow pace until Daria had moved out of her head and could swear she looked down upon them on the bed. His dark buttocks moved rhythmically, the muscles clenched as he pushed in and out of her. Then she realized she was looking into the shiny reflection of a skylight.

"Are you with me?" She heard him ask as if from a great distance.

No, she had fled her body and now hovered on the ceiling, watching the couple on the bed make love. Her face looked enraptured as she stared at their reflection. Hypnotized by the sight of his movements, she'd never felt so singularly erotic in her life.

"Daria?" He asked again and pulled out of her.

His body leaving hers snapped her back into her mind and she looked into his eyes and frowned. "Why did you stop?"

"I thought you'd left me."

Her body arched up to his. She put a hand to his face. "Finish me. I was so close."

His cock slid into her again, this time moving a little faster and a little more desperately than before.

"That's it, Hohn."

His slick body moved over and in hers again and again. She clamped down on him, holding him inside her. A shout ripped from his throat and bounced off the walls. Hot fluid filled her and she fell. Fell down, down until he caught her at the bottom of a ravine.

She surfaced and smiled at him, even though his face was buried in her neck and he couldn't see it. Hungry lips moved over her neck and cheeks then found her mouth. The sweet taste of her desire remained on his tongue.

"We sleep now," he murmured between kisses. "I won't wake you."

"You'll lie beside me?"

She needn't have asked that question. His eyes drank her in and a slight smile played at the side of his mouth. "Yes."

Daria snuggled down into the crook of his arm and drifted off, body and mind satiated.

Raven looked down on Daria, asleep in the fold of his arm. Tenderness moved through him in a soft, warm rush. He shouldn't have taken her so soon after her illness, but when she'd offered, he could not refuse. And she'd been so ready for him, too.

He placed a kiss on her forehead. Barely a brush of his lips against the smooth skin, but it was enough to make her clutch him closer to her. A pale round breast pressed against his side. The smell of their lovemaking hung heavy in the air.

Everything he'd ever wanted lay in the bed beside him. Now he had only to find the ones responsible for her injury and he could truly enjoy his marriage. There was no way in the heavens he could sit back and allow the culprits to go unpunished. They had killed the Riman delegation, tried to kill his wife, and had begun to harass outposts that were under Jevic protections. It could not continue.

Daria woke.

Warmth radiated up and down her left side. A heavy arm and leg draped over her chest and thigh. Her right arm had fallen asleep in the awkward position. She shifted slightly, careful not to wake the Hohn.

He stirred and held her tighter. If he used much more pressure, she'd be crushed under his weight. As it was, his thigh lay directly over her bladder now and she had a definite need to use the facilities.

She didn't even know where the facilities were.

She moved again. This time he woke.

"What's wrong?" He sat up.

"I have to pee." She scooted to the end of the bed and stood. His eyes raked down her naked body, heating her more than his body snuggled against hers had.

He pointed to an archway, covered by gossamer curtains.

She walked through the curtains and found an entire room, half the size of the grand ballroom. A large tub sat in the center that continuously recycled water. The toilet and sink stood behind a marble wall. A shower stall was off to the right, and could easily fit a party of six.

Decadent and overindulgent, it was every woman's dream. Even the palace royale on Primon didn't have facilities this spacious. After she finished with her most pressing need she walked to the tub and dipped in a toe. Warm water greeted her, and she couldn't resist the urge to submerge herself all the way to her neck.

"Ah," she groaned as muscles she hadn't used in a while unwound.

"Enjoying yourself?" The Hohn stood at the edge of the tub, still in all his naked glory.

She smiled up at him and moved her arms through the water. "I could get very used to this tub."

"If you like, I'll have one installed at the country home." He entered the tub and moved to the side where she leaned back against the wall.

"You'd do that for me?"

"I'll call the contractors first thing in the morning."

As he came to her, Daria leaned forward and looped her arms around his neck. "I should warn you, I might become spoiled if you continue to grant my every wish."

"It's my pleasure."

He made love to her again, right there in the oversize tub. Water sloshed over the sides and ran across the tiled floor. She pushed up from the tub floor to rock against his body and imbed him deeper in her sheath.

"My love," he breathed into her ear, picking up the pace of his thrusts.

The endearment lodged in her chest. It wasn't the first time he'd called her that, and she doubted he'd stop. The truth of the matter was it made her uncomfortable to hear knowing he didn't mean it. He'd mean it if she were Lessia he made love to.

"Kiss me." He held her jaw and moved her face to his, taking her mouth in a possession as complete as if he'd shackled her. He pulled back and stared at her swollen lips before attacking them again.

He bent her over the side of the tub. His hands moved down her side and clamped across her thighs, pulling them wider apart. The position exposed her clit to the brush of his body, sending tremors racing through her.

"Does that feel good, my love?"

"Yes," she managed to pant out before throwing her head back as her orgasm ripped her emotions wide open and left her defenseless. Quickly, she slammed a shield down to protect her heart, and closed her eyes so he couldn't see the vulnerability she knew was there.

He reversed their positions, so she straddled him, impaled on him.

"Move on me. I want to watch you make love to me."

Daria braced her hands on either side of his shoulders and gave a slow movement up and down the length of him. "Like that?" She teased him by making a circle with her hips.

His eyes slid partway closed and yet he still watched her. His mouth opened slightly as his breathing hitched. "Yes, my love. Just like that."

She tried to keep it slow and steady, but having him right where she wanted him, and having him let her do what felt good to her body gave her a rush of power. She began to move faster, bouncing on the length of him.

His hand gripped her hips and slammed her up and down. Together they exploded, their shouts echoing off the marble walls. Daria came back to her body and wrapped her arms and legs around him tightly, giving him a hug along his entire length.

He wrapped his hand in her hair and pulled her close enough to speak against her lips. "I'll never get enough of you."

Daria held him tighter. If she held him tight enough maybe, just maybe, the memories of Lessia wouldn't rise up and strangle any special feelings he may start having toward her. She knew he desired her and that he'd desperately wanted her to survive the illness that had ravaged her for the past month, but that was a far cry from loving her as he had her late sister.

The Hohn's hands moved on her back, creating gentle ripples in the water. "We should probably move before we look like pickled fruit."

A reluctant laugh came from somewhere deep inside of her. Such an unlikely thing for someone like the Hohn to say.

She moved her face and kissed him quickly before pushing up to her feet. The feel of him sliding out of her made them both moan.

As she stood, he held her hands in his. "Are you hungry? I'll ring for dinner if you are."

Daria rubbed their linked hands across her abdomen. "I could probably eat something."

His gaze moved from her face and down to her pubic hair. He studied the birthmark that she'd always hated. Why she hadn't had it taken off long ago, she didn't know. She pulled her hand away from his and covered it.

"Don't hide it," he said and leaned forward to run the tip of his tongue over the mark.

Heat spread from the point of contact out to her limbs and down to the soles of her feet. She rested her hands on his broad shoulders and watched him as he continued to kiss her on that one spot.

Her hands moved of their own volition and ran through his hair. Her palm curved around his head to cradle him to her.

The kisses stopped and he leaned his forehead against her. They remained in that pose for a while, the water drying on their skin.

Finally, he stood and helped her from the tub. They walked back into the bedroom and the Hohn handed her a silk robe from the wardrobe. All along the collar and sleeves were hand embroidered symbols. Daria held the collar out from her and studied them. They were ancient Jevic cartouches, but she wasn't sure of their meaning. Nor was she sure of the meaning of the robe being in his closet. It had a decidedly feminine cut and fit her to perfection.

"What do they mean?" she asked, trying to tamp down the irrational jealousy that flooded her veins at the thought of him having another woman in his bedroom—one that had left a robe behind.

He slid into a similar robe and then touched the metallic threads on hers. His fingers settled on a different character with each movement. "Cherished. Beloved. Protected."

She frowned as her heart hitched. Closing the space between them, she ran her fingers down the front of his robe. "What does yours say?"

Dark eyes glittered in renewed desire. His hand came up to hold hers as she moved it over him. "Protector."

"All that work to say one word?"

"Ah, but in Jevician there are forty words for protector."

A little tidbit she didn't know about the language. She cocked her head to one side. "But not beloved or cherished?"

He studied her face closely. "With some of the words it is implied."

"Show me," she said as her hands continued to trace over the unfamiliar language.

An arm slipped around her waist and pulled her closer. "This word is *po'sa*. It is a family head title." He moved her hand across the soft fabric of the robe, stopping on another character, this one directly over his heart. "This is *ki-hir*, husband."

She let her fingers trace over the symbol, then moved on to one up on his shoulder. "What's this one?"

"*Felone*. Warrior."

"And this one?" Her fingers trailed slowly down past the overlap of fabric and brushed against the bulge where his cock started to harden again.

He didn't look at the symbol this time, but continued to stare in her eyes. "Father. Life giver. *Mayell.*

A smile curved the corners of her mouth. Her hand slid down the length of him, coming to rest on another cartouche. "And this one?"

"Lover." His mouth came down on hers and he backed her up to the bed. When the back of her knees hit, she fell back.

He followed her down and parted her robe. Daria spread her legs for him and as he slid inside her, she smiled up at him. "Is there a word for insatiable?"

The smile she thought she'd get for her question was not forthcoming. Instead he looked down into her face as if he were in the throes of a soul deep pain. They made love, until sweat glistened on their skin, and their silken robes stuck to their bodies.

"It feels incredible being inside you," he said into her ear as his hips continued to rock.

Daria had gone to that place only he could take her. She was beyond speech and could only feel. Her cunt throbbed around his hardness. All sensation centered on the places where their bodies joined. She wanted to tell him how incredible he felt inside her, how just a slight rotation of his hips would make her scream and come. But she didn't. She bit her lip and held onto him tighter, bringing her body up off the bed and curling around him.

The com unit trilled loudly overhead.

The Hohn didn't stop. His strokes deepened. Sped up.

The com unit trilled again.

He quickened the pace even more. Daria lifted her hips to help him and let herself fall. He followed her, whispering Jevician words in her ear. Words she hadn't learned in language classes.

When the com unit trilled the third time, he rolled off her and gazed at the ceiling. "I told the staff not to disturb me today."

"If they are, then it's probably important." She glanced at his profile, admiring his perfectly chiseled features.

"Yes, but not as important as making love to you." He lay there for a few more minutes as the trilling became more insistent.

Daria said nothing as she watched him roll from the bed and walk to the com unit. He inserted the earpiece to ensure she couldn't overhear the conversation. He only spoke three words in the entire conversation: Give the order.

He didn't turn back to her, but moved through the curtains into the bathing facilities. Daria heard the shower start and the door close as he got in.

Shut out. Wow, he wasn't even going to tell her what happened. Granted, as the Hohn, he had the highest clearance of any non-council member on the entire Jevic home world. There were things about the Jevic government she would never be allowed to know.

She sat on the stool next to the shower door. She didn't dare invade his privacy by opening the door. Though they were intimate, she didn't feel that comfortable with him.

The water shut off and he opened the door. "I'll have the staff bring food before I leave. You should rest for the remainder of the evening."

"And where will you be?"

"The command center." He wrapped a drying cloth around his waist and headed back to the bedroom.

"Has something happened?" she called out to him. When he didn't answer, she followed him into the bedroom.

He stood in the wardrobe pulling on his uniform pants. Tension put brackets around his mouth. A frown knit his brow. "I will not be back this evening or possibly tomorrow. Have the staff notify me if you need me."

She gathered the borrowed robe closer to her and tried not to let the distance he was putting between them sting. "Is there anything I can do?"

The uniform shirt flapped open as he sat to pull on his boots. "Not at the moment. Please, go to bed."

Anger roiled low in her gut. "Huh. Good enough to fuck, but not much good beyond that. And they said the honeymoon wouldn't last." She turned to go back into the bedroom. The Hohn grabbed her arm in a move so quick she didn't see it coming.

"Who said?"

Daria looked up and swallowed. The man was a frightful sight when angry. She made her own face as fierce as possible. "No one. It's an expression."

He stared at her for a moment before his features softened. "Forgive me, my love. I'm ordering you around like one of my soldiers. But I do want you to rest. I've been, in your word, 'insatiable' and should have been more restrained after your illness."

"I am tired, so I'll take your advice. But I'm not very good at just sitting about with nothing to do."

A shadow passed over his face and he reached out to touch her cheek. He knew something he wasn't telling her, above and beyond what the communiqué relayed. "When I return, we'll go over your duties as my wife and partner. Until then, you may utilize the library to familiarize yourself with the Jevic wedding ceremony."

"No offense, Hohn, but I have my own job. I'm not saying I'm not honored to act as your partner, but it will have to be scheduled around my duties to the fleet."

He closed the fastenings on his shirt and stepped around her. "We'll discuss this when I return. There is no time to spare."

With that he leaned in and gave her a distracted kiss before hurrying from the room.

"Pompous ass," she muttered.

She hurried through a shower and put on the clothes she came home in. They were the only ones she had at the moment. She hurried from the room and enlisted the aid of the first servant she found. "I need to open a com channel to my father."

The servant bowed at the waist and led her to a small alcove where a com station sat. She thanked the servant and dismissed him before opening the channel. The relay took a long time in coming, but when it did come through, it was not her father who stared back at her from the screen, but Captain Aaron.

"Daria?" he asked in surprise and leaned forward.

"Captain? I was looking for my father."

"He's on board the *Versailles*." A smile broke across his face. "You look well."

"I am." She gave a tentative smile, but there was a surreal sense of urgency that rose up from her sacrum. "What is my father doing on the *Versailles*?"

"Stegos Outpost has been obliterated. Sneak attack."

If Daria hadn't been sitting, she'd have fallen down. Stegos was in the heart of the Primon sector. It functioned primarily as a Jevic substation. How had the aggressors gotten that far inside Primon airspace without being noticed? She needed to get a flight off world and back to the fleet. If the attack was the reason—and Daria was sure it could be no other—for the Hohn's hasty departure then why was he reluctant to tell her about it?

She really needed to return to the fleet. "What's the closest Primon ship to Jevic at the moment?"

Captain Aaron frowned at her. "Why do you need to know that?"

Sometimes it seemed as if the higher the rank, the more out of touch an officer became. "So, I can hop a hide back to the fleet."

"Damn it all to Hell's Caverns and back!"

"What's the matter? I may have just been released from a Jevic med station, but I should be able to help..." Daria started to plead her case, but was cut off mid-sentence.

"No. Not going to happen. You've been relieved of duty. You are no longer a member of the fleet." He leaned forward, crossing his arms one over the other and softened his voice. "I'm sorry. You should have been told before now."

Daria sat in stunned silence for a moment. The Hohn meant to ground her. Clip an eagle's wings and it could no longer sore the skies looking for prey. It could no longer defend its territory. No wonder her husband hadn't wanted to discuss her "job" with her. She no longer had one that didn't serve him and his people. Losing her identity had not been part of any marriage bargain she had made.

"Daria?" Aaron asked tentatively.

She tore her gaze away from a distant point in the hall and returned her attention to him. "Here."

"I'm truly sorry. I wish there was something I could do."

With tears burning behind her eyes, she shrugged. "It's not your fault. But thanks for being honest and forthright enough to tell me."

She signed off then and stood, no longer sure of why she'd wanted to speak with her father. Now to get to the Jevic ships so she could blow off this rock.

Chapter Eight

Daria had never flown a Jevic ship before. The fact that she was attempting to get close enough to steal one was something none of her previous exploits had ever prepared her for. She couldn't exactly ask her husband if she could borrow the keys to the star-cruiser for a day of shopping around the nearest galaxy.

She flattened herself against the hanger door as a squad of pilots hurried by on the way to a transport ship. Their attack ships were probably long stowed in the hanger bay. She'd have no way of getting to them and launching from the transport ship. Too many people were needed to launch out a cruiser to make that risk worth her while, especially if the captain of the vessel was a shoot-first-ask-name-and-rank-later kind of commander.

Her hand lifted up against the door panel as she peered around it. She couldn't very well march across the tarmac and grab a ship either. Her skin would peg her as a Primon before she ever reached her destination. But then, there had been some Primon pilots training on Jevic bases, perhaps no one would think much when they saw her. The only thing to give her away would be the lack of a uniform.

Oh, screw it. She'd make a run for it and hope for the best.

A ship sat not forty meters from her, the cockpit open and awaiting a pilot. Well, she was a pilot and she'd just be taking that ship for a little spin to the nearest Primon base. No one would refuse to give an Eagle, or—she cringed to think of it—a princess royale, a lift into the battle zone.

She checked the way. There were people moving all about preparing other ships and crews to leave the planet. What was one more person moving about? She kept her head up and proceeded across the tarmac and to the ship, acting as if she were doing exactly as she should be.

"Come to, mama," she said as she vaulted up into the cockpit and strapped herself in.

The control panel was foreign to her, but not completely alien. At least the markings were in a Jevician dialect she understood and that would make figuring out the controls much easier. She took a moment to orient herself to the new surroundings. Halfway through, shouts could be heard from across the tarmac.

"Sorry, no time to visit now, boys." She flipped the engines on and turned on the com unit to monitor the control tower. With all the ships lifting off to rendezvous with the other Jevic forces, air traffic in the area was at a premium.

She pushed forward on the thrusters and watched as those running towards her stopped and covered their faces from the heat and force of her liftoff.

꙳꙳(♥)꙳꙳

"Hohn, we have an unauthorized lift off of a fighter from the base," came a voice over Raven's com unit.

"Who's the pilot?" he asked looking up from the star charts of Primon airspace that were spread out in front of him.

"We don't know. No one on the ground crew ever remembers seeing her before."

Raven closed his eyes and let a violent curse fall from his lips. Her. There could be no other woman with enough audacity to steal a fighter from the tarmac of a fully armed and staffed command center than Daria.

"Should we shoot her down?"

"No! Prepare my ship; I'll go after the deserter myself." He rolled up the charts. He could work on the ship after he intercepted his runaway wife.

The meeting room wasn't too far away from the bay where his ship was kept secure. Thank the gods she hadn't taken it out. But then she wouldn't, she'd take a fighter out.

He hit his com unit again. "Patch me through to the stolen ship. Secure line."

"Yes, Hohn." After a few clicks, a channel opened. "Go ahead, Hohn."

He waited until the sound of the dispatcher clicked off and then he balled his fists and let his errant wife feel the force of his anger. "Daria! What in all the suns' blazes are you doing?"

No answer. She was ignoring him. Headstrong female.

"Answer me. You've stolen a fighter from a pilot who needs it. Bring it back and we'll talk."

Still no answer.

A click sounded to alert him that someone wanted to break in on his conversation. "Go ahead." He might as well let the person have his say since Daria refused to talk to him.

"The ship closed frequency. They're going silent running."

Raven entered his ship at almost a run. His flight crew gave him a wide berth, and worked in silence, afraid to speak to him. He took the bridge and stood watching as they blasted into space.

"When you locate the stolen ship, tow it to the bay. Be prepared for hostility from the pilot, but do not use force to contain."

"Yes, Hohn," the helmsman acknowledged, as she punched numbers into the control panel.

A sizable hole ached where his heart should be. Why had Daria run from him? Had he come on too strong with her? Had she decided she didn't want to live on Jevic?

No, most likely she'd discovered the attack on Stegos and thought to rejoin the fleet. But why hadn't she called him to discuss it with him before running off in a ship she'd never flown before? He'd promised to talk to her when he returned.

The fighter ship would be easy to catch. It was smaller and more maneuverable, but the Hohn's ship had more engine power and would overtake the fighter in no time.

"Hohn, we've located the ship."

"Good, let's pull her in. I'll be in my quarters. Bring the pilot there."

❊❀⟨♡⟩❀❊

Daria knew the flight was over when she felt the tow beams engage. She shrugged back in her seat and waited to reach the Jevic ship. At least they hadn't shot her down. Whatever happened, she would plead her case to the captain of the vessel and hope he wouldn't recognize her rank and name.

The ship docked and she was brought to the captain's quarters under armed guard. They'd seemed surprised when they noted she was a Primon. She didn't know what they had been expecting.

The door panel slid open and she was pushed through the portal. It closed with a swish behind her. There was only one other person in the room, and he wasn't happy to see her. Oh, by every deity real and imagined! The Hohn stood across the room from her in all his glory, mad as a wet Telarian jungle cat.

Immediately her hackles rose. How dare he come after and tow her in like a naughty child? Sure, she had stolen a ship from the base, but he had no right to ground her in the first place. She placed balled hands on her hips and faced him. "What do you think you're doing?"

He lifted a brow. "Getting my ship back."

That hurt. Deep down where things she didn't want to admit to herself lived. Way down. He only cared about the ship, not that she'd left him. She swallowed and notched up the bravado. "I was on my way to the Primon fleet. You had no right to stop me."

"No right? I'm the Hohn of Jevic. I had every right to chase down a stolen fighter and see to its safe return."

"If you wanted to protect your precious ship you shouldn't have grounded me."

"Is that what you think I did?"

"I spoke with Captain Aaron after you left..."

The Hohn let out a grunt of disdain. "Couldn't wait to speak with him, could you?"

She frowned at him. "I was looking for my father, who I'm told is aboard the *Versailles*. Captain Aaron answered the transmission, and if he hadn't, I still wouldn't have known you stripped me of my status and had me removed from the Primon fleet."

He walked around the desk that separated them. He nodded his head a few times. "I did this? Is that what you think of me?"

"Who else would do such a thing? You even said we'd discuss my duties to you when you returned."

His eyes closed and he leaned against the desk. "Did you not stop to think that I have no authority over the Primon fleet? I have no say in who it allows into its ranks, even if that person is my wife."

"Then who did?"

"Your father."

"Why would he do such a thing?"

"Because having one daughter die on him, and watching the other fight for her life the way you did was probably too much for him. He was trying to keep you from any more danger."

Daria stood stock still. The Hohn came forward and put a hand on her face.

"I'm sorry. I should have told you sooner, but you didn't mention getting up in the air until today, so I thought you were all right being planet side for now. At least while you finished recuperating."

"You'd let me fly?"

He quirked a brow at her. "Not combat." When she started to protest his hand gently covered her mouth. "I nearly went out of my head watching you under attack. Then this past month watching you, willing you to live was the longest of my life. I know you're capable and strong, but I fear I'm not as strong as you. I want to sleep at night knowing the woman I love is safe beside me."

Daria felt her eyes go wide. He loved her? No, surely he had gotten her confused with Lessia again.

He shifted his hand so his fingers stroked her mouth before he lowered his and took her lips in a long drugging kiss. When he pulled away, he studied her face. "I've been in love with you since that night you escaped the ball and fled to the balcony."

She shook her head. "Then why did you offer for Lessia's hand?"

Red stole up his cheeks. The Hohn embarrassed? Daria hadn't thought such a thing was possible.

"My advisor at the time gave me the wrong name. I never saw Lessia's face until the day of her funeral. If it hadn't been for your royal family's tradition of having glass-topped coffins, I would never have known my love hadn't died in that shuttle accident."

"But you didn't even know me. How could you love me? It was Lessia you spoke to, arranged a life with."

He nodded and let out a long sigh. "It's true, but I did wonder why I never got a sense of that spirit I saw in you that night. To my discredit, I never thought to question my advisor and verify Lessia's identity."

"Poor Lessia." Daria sat down on a sofa and put her hands over her face. "I can't imagine what would have happened if she hadn't died, and you would have not known her identity until the state introductions."

"There would have been nothing for it. I would have honored my word and married her."

Daria looked up at him. "And when you discovered the woman you thought you were to marry was the bridal attendant and not the bride?"

"Probably done exactly what I did to my aide when I discovered the mistake, banished him from Jevic and my service."

The tale was something she could scarcely believe and yet he delivered it so matter-of-factly she had to believe him. And why shouldn't she? He'd admitted to his own failing in the tale.

They were silent for a moment then the Hohn came and sat next to her. He took her hand in his and started rubbing it back and forth. "Do you think you could ever learn to love me?"

"Oh, Raven," she said using his name for the first time and discovered she liked the way it tasted in her mouth. "I don't know. Please just give me time to know you first." When his eyes turned bleak she added, "I'm not averse to trying."

He smiled then pulled her close and held her against his heart. "Thank you for that." He blew out a breath that stirred her hair. "I lament your sister's passing. It was a terrible tragedy, but one of the best moments of my life was looking into her still face and realizing she wasn't my *chekara'*, my beloved." He kissed the top of her head.

A dull throb of pain settled in her gut for him. "How did you discover that the woman you saw at the ball was me? It could have been anyone, and not a woman of royal blood."

"I researched the royal archives and found your picture. That's when I learned you were in pilot training at the academy." A steady movement of his hand up and down her arm lulled her into a feeling of security. For a military leader, he was vastly tender with her.

"And you waited five years to claim me? You ran a terrible risk of having my father give my hand to someone else, or of me finding some space jockey to marry." She glanced up into his face with a teasing smile on her lips.

He shook his head. "It wouldn't have happened that way, at least from your father's standpoint. He wanted the alliance too bad to risk giving your hand to another. Though as headstrong as you are, if you'd have wanted to marry your space jockey you probably would have and damn the consequences."

Daria laughed. "I give that impression, but I do know my duty to my family. A princess's life is not her own, though gods know I've tried for anonymity. The future of the Primon people has always been my first concern. The fact I joined the fleet should be testimony of that."

Raven crooked a finger under her chin and held her face up so he could continue to look into her eyes. "Your sense of duty is only one of the many reasons I knew you and no other could be my wife."

She was content to stay sitting against the wall of his chest, listening to the steady cadence of his heart, and the movement of his breath. The gentle hum of the ship's engines made her eyes feel heavy and she started to fall asleep against him.

"Daria," he said in a whisper. "Let me move you to the bed. I need to return to the bridge."

Of course he did! He was heading into battle. She sat up. "I'm sorry. I've been taking time away from people who need you. That's unforgivable."

He shook his head. "We won't even make Primon space for another day and a half at maximum speed. I do, however, want to gather intelligence and lay a plan."

"Go. I'll be fine here." At a measuring look from him, she added. "Don't worry, I won't steal the fighter again."

"Glad to hear that."

The man was as good as his word and helped her to the bed, then made sure of her comfort before he placed a tender kiss on her lips and left the quarters.

Daria rolled over onto her side, pillowing her head on her arm. Unbelievable! The Hohn had loved her all along, had wanted her for his wife, not Lessia.

Chapter Nine

A light kiss on her ear woke Daria in a sleepy haze. Disoriented, she moved her gaze around. Where was she? On the *Versailles*? But this wasn't her bed, and this was definitely not the quad.

She tried to roll over, but didn't have the power. Oh, her limbs felt like lead. It felt as if she'd dragged herself tens of kilometers up a slippery slope. No handholds to move her along, only the sheer will of her spirit kept her from falling.

"Daria." The low rumble of a voice brushed warmly over the shell of her ear. A hand skimmed over her hip and pressed against her belly.

She knew that voice, that timbre of sound that could ignite every last thread of desire in her. On instinct her body moved into the warm spoon of his. Memory flooded her and her mind cleared. They were aboard the Hohn's personal vessel. And the man himself was pushed up against her, trying to wake her from the veil of sleep.

"Wake love," he urged, his arms tightening around her body and his mouth paying homage to her ear, her neck, her shoulder.

"I'm awake," she murmured, moving her head for better access.

"We've reached Primon airspace."

That information made her sit up and stare down at him. "Why didn't you wake me?"

A crooked smile lifted his mouth and a teasing light filled his eyes. "I did."

"You let me sleep for a day and a half!" No wonder her limbs felt heavy.

"And you needed it." He pushed up from the bed and held his hand out for her to take. "Now, you must bathe and eat. We will rendezvous with the *Versailles* soon. I will not have your father thinking I treat you ill."

Daria shook her head and offered him a smile. "No one who knows you would ever believe you capable of such a thing." She placed her hand on his.

"No, Daria. Only you know I am not capable of such a thing." His hand gripped hers tightly.

No, his image probably wouldn't allow him to show vulnerability. Warriors on their way into battle did not show cracks in their armor.

⁂

Refreshed and in a borrowed Jevic uniform, Daria stood on the command bridge beside Raven as they came within the coordinates where the outpost had once been. Mangled debris floated through space. The outpost that had once been home to nearly fifteen-thousand Jevic and Priman lives had been reduced to nothing more than junk.

Daria could see the subtle change in her husband. Tension radiated from his powerful body. His hands gripped the armrests on the command chair.

Out the portside view screen, the *Versailles* hovered. Experience told her Captain Aaron would have already made sensor sweeps of the area to ascertain the explosive device used.

First the Riman delegation was attacked on their way to the state introductions, and now a Jevic outpost. What was going on?

Jevic and Riman had a strong bond that went back to treaties that had been signed when both planets discovered space travel. They often fought side by side in intergalactic wars, and to attack one without attacking the other was unheard of. When the Riman delegation was slaughtered, it was only a matter of time before those responsible came after Jevic forces.

"We have incoming transmission from the *Versailles*," the communications officer said, as he busily tapped on his console.

"Full middle display screen," Raven commanded.

Prince Hefcat and Captain Aaron, along with the senior officers, sat in the council room around a long oval table. Being only a pilot, and not of a distinguishing rank above most other pilots, Daria had never had a chance to sit in on any meeting conducted behind those closed doors.

Light from the display grids on the wall behind her father and Captain Aaron cast them in an eerie glow and set the stage for what should prove to be bad news.

"Hohn, our initial sweep of the debris is indeed positive for the nanobots you mentioned." Captain Aaron made a motion with his hand. "I would transmit the evidence to you, but Prince Hefcat and I would advise you to come aboard the *Versailles* immediately."

"Very well, prepare your ship for boarding by the *Royal Renegade.*"

Daria startled at the name of his personal ship. *Royal Renegade*, indeed. She turned a brief smile to him which he responded to with a gentle shrug of a large shoulder. He didn't even pretend it hadn't been named for her and her outrageous behavior.

"I'll contact the dock."

Within a few minutes, they were once again aboard the *Versailles*, and Daria breathed a sigh. It felt like coming home, and at the same time it felt a little foreign to her. Raven stood over her seat, looking down on her.

"Will you accompany me? I think your father would very much like to see you, though I haven't told him you're aboard."

"You can be so oddly sentimental at times, Raven."

He took her hand and helped her stand. "Only where you're concerned." He gave her a quick up and down, studying the dark blue Jevic uniform. "You look good in those colors. I think I may just give you your own commission within my fleet when this is over."

"Oh, sure. Dangle a commission during peacetime over my head. You never want me to have any fun."

Daria started to walk toward the door when he pulled her up close and said into her ear, "I assure you when this is all over, you'll know nothing but fun. The only thing better than seeing you in the uniform of my world, is seeing you out of it and lying beneath me."

Heat oozed through her body, but she didn't have time to make a comment. The outer doors swished open and two guards she knew from various missions stood there to escort the Hohn to the council room. They started when they saw Daria.

They both bowed in the proper greeting of commoner to royal, something they had not done while she had been an Eagle aboard the same vessel. It shook her to know they would be so formal with her after all the times they'd gotten drunk and stupid in some run down outworld bar.

She bent to return the greeting. "Please, dispense with the formalities and take us to the council room."

Gyre Vorcan lifted his mouth in a half smile. "As you wish, your highness."

"Ass," she muttered as she and Raven followed behind them down the long winding passageways that led to the council room.

She could have told the guards to leave her to direct her husband to the meeting, but allowed them to continue on. The rules had changed during her illness, whether she approved or not. Stripped of her commission, she was entitled to all the pomp and ceremony afforded her royal blood, and to fight against it would expend more energy than she wanted to at that moment. She needed to save her strength for talking her husband into allowing her to fly combat in the coming war.

The guard entered a code in the security lock then allowed the retinal scan to proceed. The door swished open and before Daria could comment, the guard announced her and Raven with all the long and proper titles they both held.

"Daria!" Prince Hefcat stood and came around the end of the table. For once in his life, he held forth no propriety nor seemed to care for who witnessed his emotions. She was enfolded into his embrace, her head tucked under his chin in a protective gesture that had tears stinging her eyes. She'd been a very little girl the last time she had been held in such a way by her father.

"Oh, by the Gods, my baby girl," he whispered in her ear so only she could hear.

Wrapped in the arms of her father's love proved Raven's words from the day before. Her father had decommissioned her to save her, not to stymie her. "It's all right. I'm feeling much better, Raven saw to that."

Her father pulled away from her and looked into her face. A question burned behind his jade eyes, so much like her own. After a brief hesitation he asked, "You are pleased with your husband?"

"He saved my life, how can I complain?"

"You, never. You simply find a new strategy and get around any problems you encounter." He smiled at her. "You are more like me than any of your sisters ever hoped to be."

Raven moved up behind her and placed a hand on the small of her back. He exchanged greetings with her father then directed her to a seat so they could begin the war conference.

Captain Aaron ran the meeting, beginning with the discovery of the nanobots emitted during the destruction of Stegos Outpost. "We can only speculate why the nanobots were used in this instance, but the theory is the enemy hoped to utilize them as sweepers to clear the area and prevent any possible aid from reaching the station in a timely fashion. Once the wave was discharged, any ships within the area would have been effected and unable to rescue possible survivors."

"Would there have been survivors?" Raven asked. "With the size of the explosion, and the fact it hit the power center, the prospect of survivors would have been remote at best."

Prince Hefcat shook his head. "This enemy leaves nothing to chance. But we have finally made headway in discovering their identity."

"How's that?" Daria asked. If they were close to learning who this stealth enemy was, she most definitely had her interest peaked. They had killed too many of her crewmates and had come close to taking her life in their quest to conquer the sector.

Captain Aaron made a motion with his hand and the communications commander hit a button to send a low gravel-abraded voice over the speakers.

"...sound cannons. Prime the explosives on G-level and prepare to port to deep space." The poor quality and garbled voice made it difficult to understand, but what made it worse was the incompleteness of the transmission.

Daria turned to look at Raven to gauge his reaction. He'd gone decidedly pale, and his hands clenched into tight fists.

"Is that all you have of the transmission?" He addressed the communications commander directly.

"It was hidden inside a signal normally emitted from the Stegos Outpost. Cloaked in everyday sound traffic, it stayed virtually undetected for we don't know how long. Transmission channels on that particular frequency are ignored, and the signal was found quite by accident." Commander Sheehan held her hands folded on the table and gave her full attention to the Hohn. "It was recorded and saved to analyze at a later date. When the attack happened, we went back to the recording to try and discover the origin of the signal. That's when we found the hidden transmission."

"And were you able to determine from what direction the signal came?" Raven's eyes were glittering, hard coals in his tense face. Daria recognized the man beside her as the true warrior spirit that embodied the Hohn persona.

"No. But we," she indicated the command council, "agreed that it had to have originated from a remote location beyond our sensor range."

The Hohn remained quiet for the rest of the meeting, keeping his own counsel and offering no opinions on the remainder of the exchange.

When they finally adjourned, and were once aboard the *Royal Renegade*, Daria stopped him from going directly to the bridge and steered him instead to their cabin.

He resisted at first, but when he would have turned away she moved in front of him to block his way. "Raven, please, don't pretend you didn't recognize something about that voice we heard on the transmission."

He clenched is jaw and looked away from her. Gently, she reached out and touched his cheek, guiding his attention back to her. "Tell me."

"Ignaki."

"Who is that?"

"Ignaki was the advisor I dismissed from my service."

Cold fear prickled her spine. So the attacks weren't as unprovoked as they all believed. It was for revenge.

Daria hit the door locks behind them and the panel slid open. She pulled Raven in the cabin with her and moved to the sofa. "Tell me everything. No matter how insignificant you may think it is." She sat down and raised her eyes to him. He did not take a place beside her as she'd hoped, but began to pace.

"I started to notice his change in behavior after the treaty was signed and the plans for the state introductions made. I believed he had misgivings with the treaty; I had no idea he was trying to cover his own incompetence."

Daria flung her arm in the direction Stegos Outpost had been. "I hardly think he's incompetent. He's attacked the interests of three different planets in the last month, all without detection until today."

"For five years, I've lived with the knowledge that I may have done something that caused your sister's death. I never found a trace to indicate it was anything but an accident, just this horrible gut feeling that refused to leave me in peace."

"And now?" Her throat almost closed around the words, dread stole her breath.

"If there were a way we could reexamine the shuttle, I bet we would find the same nanobots that took down Loki and swept the Stegos wreckage."

Daria didn't know what that would prove and told him as much.

"Maybe nothing. Or it could prove that Ignaki conspired against me long before I ever had him exiled."

When he stopped in front of her, Daria reached out for his hand. Large and long fingered, his hand swallowed hers, the grip firm. "So, how do we find him and those he's conspired with?"

He shook his head and pulled her up into his arms. With his face buried in her neck, he said, "My only thought is to keep you safe. Now I know how personal this war is and I want you nowhere near a battle. We'll rendezvous with the Jevic fleet and I want you aboard a vessel for the homeworld."

Her arms held him tight. "No, I won't leave you."

"Daria." His voice sounded ragged in her ear. "I won't lose you."

A small tremor moved through him, vibrating against Daria. "Look, Ignaki tried his damnedest to kill me and he failed. And if he tries again, he'll fail again, and he'll keep failing until we destroy him."

Raven moved his hands up to her face. His fingers spread so his thumbs grazed across her bottom lip. Passion flared in his eyes, then his mouth claimed hers, hot and hungry. She opened for him, letting him know with action that she accepted his love and protection, even if she didn't totally agree with the protection part. Her lips curled into a smile as he continued to kiss her.

"Does my passion amuse you?" he asked as the humble beginnings of a smile cracked one corner of his mouth.

"Not in the least. I just think you're incredibly sexy when you go all Hohn on me."

Despite the tension of the last few moments, he laughed. "Somehow I don't think that was what brought that lovely smile to your face, but I'll let it go for now if you'll agree to return to Jevic until this is over."

She let her hands fall to his shirt fastenings and began to undo them. "I have a better idea. If you'll allow me to have my way with you right now, I'll stay here with you and continue to administer to your baser needs throughout the course of the campaign."

His eyes nearly crossed. The hands that had been holding her face, moved down to cup her shoulders. "Never use your body to bargain with me."

"Why?"

"Because I'll let you win every time, and to lose so often to one's wife is unsporting."

Daria let out a snort of laughter before guiding him toward the bed. "Contact the bridge and have them move us off the *Versailles* and into deeper space."

Raven frowned and stopped her. "You want to use the *Royal Renegade* as a moving target."

"Yes. But chances are he's well away from here by now. However, I'm sure he knows exactly where you are at all times. He hasn't made a direct attack on you yet, but perhaps the temptation may prove too much if he knows we're both on board." Daria backed up and sat on the bed and craned her neck to look into Raven's eyes. "He tried it on the *Versailles.*"

He shook his head and placed a knee on the bed, forcing her back. "But you won't be on board this vessel for much longer. If I thought leaving you on board the *Versailles* and having your father take you back to

Primon with him would keep you from danger, I'd do so." He pushed her onto her back. "However, after having waited so long for you, the idea of sending you away again has little appeal for me."

The firmness of his erection pressed against her upper thigh. The memory of having it deep inside her made her squirm under his weight. He knew well how to use his body to advantage in bed. A wellspring of want opened in the deeper recesses of her soul. But soon the warm rivulets turned to ice as an uncertain future sprang up before her eyes.

"We need to find Ignaki and stop the bloodshed. The thought of him killing innocents in the name of vengeance, and knowing we could bring our children into the battle if he's not found soon terrifies me."

"He'll not touch our children." Raven promised with a ferocity that made Daria believe as nothing else could. General Kristiano Raven would never allow anyone to harm his progeny. At that moment he looked fiercer than any bird of prey she had ever seen guarding the Primon skies.

"But we get ahead of ourselves," Daria said as she reached up to finish unfastening his shirt. "Maybe we better concentrate on making those children first."

"From fighter pilot to gentle mother so fast. I have the feeling our life together will never be dull." He started at the bottom of her borrowed uniform jacket and began to unhook the clasps.

"I can be a mother and a pilot. You make it sound as if I can only do one thing at a time, but as a woman and a princess, I assure you, I can do many."

She let the conversation drop as his hands skimmed up the inside of the shirt halves and cupped her breasts. Desire tightened her nipples into hard peaks that pressed against the light blue standard issue undershirt she wore.

Raven's glance moved down her body to the rigid outlines pressed against the soft fabric. With his gaze moving up to take her in, he lowered his mouth and began to suck them through the thin shirt. His eyes closed as he worked first one than the other by holding them in his teeth and flicking his tongue over them.

In restless ecstasy, she spread her legs and cradled him against the flat plane of her stomach. How good it would feel to have him take her clit as he had her nipples and flick it in such a manner. The very thought made her moan and push her pelvis against him.

When he lifted his head she could see her nipples clearly through the fabric, made transparent by the wetness of his mouth. He removed her uniform pants and underwear, then rolled her over onto her stomach and lifted her mid-section into the air so her butt rose higher than her body.

"Lovely," he whispered and ran his hand over her. Slowly, his fingers rode the curve of her until they slipped down to trace a path through her wet center. "That's the prettiest thing I've ever seen." He spread her thighs wider, and then his mouth was there, right where she wanted it.

Thick thumbs spread her drenched lips open, and his tongue slipped inside her. Long, slow strokes teased and promised, coming closer and closer to the area where she burned for attention. It felt maddeningly wonderful, almost beyond her capacity to tolerate.

She folded her arms and lay her head down on them, her ass as high in the air as it could go. Little by little, she backed up closer to that questing tongue, until there, just barely, a ghost of the sweet sensation she longed for grazed across her clit.

He moved away from it again then teased his way forward, until she felt the faint caress for the second time.

"Raven," she moaned, as he let his tongue brush against it yet again, this time for a fraction longer.

"You're like the sweetest nectar. I've never tasted anything so good in my life." Then he flicked her fast and hard and she came undone in is mouth. He held her open for him, not easing the torture even when she cried out and shook from the power of her orgasm.

Her breath came in short gulps, and in her dazed state she believed she would get a small respite from the exquisite torture of his lovemaking, but it wasn't to be. Before she could move, he unfastened his uniform pants and mounted her from behind.

The thick hot slide of him inside her made her sigh. Raven's lovemaking was without equal in her experience. The pleasure he gave her reached some deep hidden chamber in her soul, and wound him around her very heart. With every thrust he claimed more of her for himself, and she gladly allowed it.

One long arm slid around her and a practiced finger began to caress her already sensitive flesh. The other hand rubbed her buttocks a few times then teased the entrance of her body where his cock moved in and out in a mesmeric motion. She didn't know what he did next, only felt the wet stroke of his thumb around the circle of her anus.

Her breath caught in her throat. If he did that, if he pushed his thumb inside her while he moved so deep, and his other hand continued to strum her clit, she'd fly apart. Her entire body would unhinge, and she'd never be put back together again.

The room suddenly felt too hot, the air too thick to breathe. She began to gulp to draw breath into her body. Sobs of bliss tore from her throat. Then he was there, pushing his thumb into her, in the same torturous rhythm of his cock. And Daria was lost.

The convulsions came so fast and furious the sound that ripped from her throat was that of a wounded animal. She felt Raven tense against her, and then the rush of his come as it filled her.

He still held her in the same grip, his fingers continued to minister to her even as his breathing steadied and returned to normal. "Again, my love. I want you to come again for me."

She didn't think she could. Nothing could compare to that previous lovemaking. But even as she formed the thought she felt her body begin to climb the summit.

He brought his thumb out of her and gently stroked against the rim of her anus. "When you've gotten used to my size, when you learn to fully trust me…"

She lifted her head and looked at him over her shoulder. It didn't take a great imagination to know what he wanted to do. "I do trust you. Please… yes, please do it, Raven. I want to feel you there."

His cock jerked inside her, and hardened to full erectness. The look on his face was pure triumph. He slid out of her cunt and rubbed his cock against her anus a few times. "I love you so much, Daria," he said, and slid into her unbelievably tight passage.

Tears mixed with passion and pain filled her eyes and spilled down her cheeks.

"By the Gods, don't cry, my love." He started to pull out of her, but Daria moved back to capture him again.

"Don't you dare. You're so unbelievably good…" The words were choked off on another sob of pleasure/pain. If this was his idea of love-making, she'd never survive their first year of marriage. She'd die of overwhelming sexual satisfaction.

The words were like switching on a hyperdrive to his libido. His hand left off the loving ministration of her clit and came back to help the other hand hold her in place for him. Daria rested her forehead on the bed and ran her hand down the front of her body. Her nipples were so erect they ached. She gave them both a loving touch that felt so good she continued to circle them with her fingernail for a few moments, before sliding her hand between her thighs.

Above her, Raven growled low in his throat. "Do you like touching yourself while I'm inside you, Daria?"

She nodded her head and breathed out the word "yes" on a long sigh.

"Mmmm. Stick your fingers inside your cunt for me." The soft stated command made her tremble all over. Never would she have dreamed to countermand him.

The silky movement of her hand through her plump wet folds had her teetering on the edge. Her lips were so swollen it hardly felt like her body—and if Daria knew anything it was her own body. She had touched herself many times in the past, brought herself to climax in the quad showers and her bunk time and again.

"That's it, my love," Raven encouraged. "How does it feel?"

"So good," she murmured, lost to sensation. She stuck her thumb out and brushed it back and forth over herself as she drew her fingers in and out.

Again waves of desperation rolled over her. She needed to come, had to come. But it felt so good she never wanted it to end.

Raven leaned over her and kissed her back, her neck, her shoulder. She could feel the gentle slap of his balls against her lips. She withdrew her hand from her sheath and reached with all her might to brush her fingertips against them.

A long groan filled her ear, and hot breath that smelled of her sex bathed her face. She touched him again and his arm came around her to replace the fingers she'd pulled out of herself. He moved with purpose now, as if fighting to get her off before he came.

Sweat stuck their bodies together and made it more difficult to move against one another, but Daria didn't mind. She liked the feel of his skin plastered to hers. It was as if they had become one being.

She turned her face until their mouths melded. "I love you," she breathed against his lips, and felt the beginning of his release begin to ripple throughout the length of his body. His orgasm was all the answer she needed to know he'd heard her whispered words.

Passion pulled his face into a sublime expression. But she had only a glimpse of it before he hid it in the hollow of her neck, and rested his lips against her nape.

His fingers curled in on her and touched a spot only he could find, and she fell with him.

In the quiet that followed, he held her against his chest, his back pressed to her. The breath against her cheek began to slow, and even out, deepen.

She reached back and caressed his thigh. "Hey, don't fall asleep. We have some plans to make."

His long fingers spread across her lower abdomen. "You should be the one resting," he said and nuzzled her neck. "I think you had it right when you said I'm insatiable."

"Well, according to your account, you're making up for five common years of want." She sat up and started off the bed.

"Where are you going?"

"To take another shower, so we can meet with your staff and plot how to trap Ignaki." With that she turned and made for the shower.

Chapter Ten

A half hour later they sat in the command center surrounded by the Hohn's senior staff and advisors. Off the portside, the *Versailles* continued to comb the area for information that may have been missed on the first few passes through the area.

Raven watched the exchange, but didn't make comment on any of it. Something about the information gathered by the *Versailles* niggled at the back of his brain. He had missed an important fact somewhere along the way. The pieces should have fit together, but so far they hadn't.

Why would Ignaki go to such lengths to destroy him? If the motive was revenge, why blow up the outpost? And the Riman delegation? The direct attack on the *Versailles* he could understand if for no other reason than he and Daria both had been on board at the time.

"Pull up the files collected from the captured ship, and the ones downloaded from Loki," Raven said and flicked a hand at his Data Specialist.

"Yes, sir." She nodded and began typing in the key codes that would access the requested information.

"What are you thinking?" Daria asked, her head cocked to the side in question, a slight frown on her brow.

"Something about the way this all fits together bothers me." He rubbed his hand across his forehead. The beginning of a headache throbbed just behind his eyes.

Information began to scroll across the display screen before him. He'd studied it so much during Daria's illness that he had almost committed it all to memory. Perhaps he was too close to the situation to discover some heretofore unknown pattern. There had to be something more there, something they could use to bring Ignaki down.

Warmth slipped into Raven's bloodstream. Right before they made love, Daria had mentioned the children they would have one day. There was nothing he wouldn't do to make that future happen for them. Their lives wouldn't end as those on Stegos Outpost had...

Raven sat up in his chair. The warmth increased into an inferno as adrenaline fed his system. "Contact the *Versailles*."

Across the table, Daria perked up as well. "You've found something?"

"Remembered." He turned to the communications officer. "Contact the *Ramaclesus* and get Chief Clarin on a vid com."

"Yes, sir."

"Well?" Daria leaned forward in her chair and laid her folded hands on the table. "Are you going to enlighten us, or keep us in suspense?"

"I'm still working it out in my head." Her enthusiasm made him want to smile, but he held the motion back.

"Tell us and you'll have more heads to work it out in."

He studied his officers, who looked back at him with expectant faces. "We'll wait for Clarin."

The Chief of Flight Operations for the battlecruiser *Ramaclesus* came on the vid com a few moments later. He bowed his head in the formal manner in greeting the Hohn. "Sir."

"At ease, Chief. You disabled the weapons aboard the captured enemy fighter, and discovered it could mimic signal outputs from certain devices."

"That's correct."

Raven ran his hand along his chin in thought. "Is there any possibility it could be smuggled aboard a station and activated via hidden signals from remote locations?"

Without hesitation, Chief Clarin nodded. "The fighters ran by remote, so why not give a delayed activation sequence by remote? Sweepers meant to look for explosive devices wouldn't catch such weapons because the only output would be from impulses known as normal on board the station."

Just when he thought he could grow no angrier at the deliberate way in which Ignaki sabotaged Raven's life and career, rage burned up from the very pits of his soul. "And the most efficient way to gain access to a space station in such a manner is through her shipments. Cargo. Supplies. Even clothing… His eyes shifted to Daria as recognition dawned.

"The biosuits," she whispered, even as the horrible thought raced through his mind.

"Are we still linked to the *Versailles*?"

"Yes, sir."

"Hail Prince Hefcat and Captain Aaron."

"Yes, sir."

The Primon leaders came on screen. "You've found something?" the Prince asked.

"Have your tech crew scan the biosuits for the nanobots."

Incredulity skimmed across their Primon features a moment before Captain Aaron gave the order to test the pilots' biosuits.

"Now, tell us where you're going with this," Prince Hefcat commanded in a voice underscored by patriotic umbrage.

"I assure you, I am not accusing your military of sabotaging the alliance, or of blowing up Stegos. The voice on the hidden signal was that of a man named Ignaki who used to be in my service. If my theory is correct, he somehow gained access to biosuits bound for the outpost and other ships in the Primon fleet and planted the nanobots in the sensor relays, to forward information and signals to his operatives, or to detonate the explosives." Raven let a brief glance fall on Daria. "I'll have to look at the replay of the attack on the *Versailles*, but I'm sure what we saw wasn't the actual discharge of a weapon in the strictest terms, but a concentrated signal meant to activate the nanobots in the biosuits."

Captain Aaron's golden eyes turned to where Daria sat. "And why the nanobots could feed directly into the princess's bloodstream."

Raven nodded.

A voice on the Primon end of the connection filtered through the transmission. "Sir, we have positive identification. We selected suits at random and they all came up positive for the nanobots."

The confirmation fell over the group like fresh dirt on a grave. No telling how widespread the contamination had gotten, but it would be easy and quick to detect.

"How many vessels did Stegos supply?" Raven asked.

"At least half the fleet. There should be records, but we'll have to track them down," Prince Hefcat answered. He turned to someone off screen and said, "Contact the rest of the fleet and relay information so they can scan for the 'bots. Have them resupply only from shipments received directly from Primon Central Supply Depot and no other."

The Prince turned back to the Hohn and deferred to his authority. "What do you propose we do to stop this Ignaki?"

"We use the relay signals in the opposite direction. If the signals come to us, they have to originate somewhere. We'll find him at the end of them. And then we go after him."

Hours later Daria lay with her head resting on Raven's chest. Neither of them could sleep. There were too many plans to make, too many simulations to run to ensure success of this latest and most dangerous mission.

Her hand soothed him, running through the silky hair on his chest and feeling the hard muscles underneath. Ever since hearing that the fleet's biosuits had been infected with the nanobots, Daria had seethed with the need to exact her own revenge on Ignaki. How had he managed such a feat without anyone knowing? Her friends had lost their lives at his hands, all in the name of vengeance—maybe even her sister's life had ended as a result.

"Raven?"

"Hmm?" His thumb stroked up and down her arm.

"Lessia's shuttle was piloted by Eagles from the *Desdemona*, a sister ship to the *Versailles*. Their biosuits came from Stegos, I'm almost sure."

Raven rolled over and lay atop her, looking down into her face. Eyes dark as the deepest reaches of space studied her face. "That was five common years ago. I suspect Ignaki of her death, but can we believe your sister died in the same manner as those on Stegos?"

"The weapons had to be tested sometime. Why not test it with revenge on the very person that represented Ignaki's worst failure? If she didn't die when the weapon discharged what would he lose? He had the power to not only give you a chance to have the woman you wanted, but also a means to destroy you."

The proud brow furrowed in misery, and he lowered to touch it against hers. His breath caressed her lips. "Forgive me, my love. I should have pressed harder to solve this mystery before now."

She brushed the hair from his face. "There is nothing to forgive. You didn't know any more than the rest of us what the connection was."

An unsteady laugh tumbled from his mouth and vibrated against hers. "I love you so much, but by all the Gods I don't deserve you."

"Why would you say that?" She didn't find the comment amusing in the least. It was she who didn't deserve such devotion from him.

"Because you would absolve me of having such a man in my employ, and bringing his hatred into our lives, and into the lives of the Primon people." He raised his head and the look he gave her was filled with torture.

Daria lifted her mouth and touched her lips to his. All the tenderness she felt for him, she conveyed with the brush of her tongue against his.

His hold tightened around her. The kiss deepened, consumed. Ignited. She slid her legs apart to cradle him gently between her parted thighs.

The roll of his hips brought his cock to brush against her opening. They'd made love so many times in the past few hours that Daria felt sure she would never be the same again. From the first moment she'd learned her body as a sexual being, she had dreamed of a lover like him.

Hate for Ignaki burned her heart like acid. If he had performed his duty and hadn't interfered she would have been five years married to Raven, and Lessia would have been alive and with a family of her own. And yet, she couldn't resent her experiences in the fleet. They had helped to shape the woman who now lay beneath the Hohn, opening her body and heart to him.

The sweet nudge of him against her clit made her moan. He moved against her again, and then pushed inside. The pace he set was steady and slow, so unhurried, as if he wished to never leave the safety of her body, or give up such indescribable pleasure.

In the afterglow, a germ of a plan started to form in her mind. She sat up on the bed and looked down into Raven's face. His eyes were closed and his breathing suggested he'd finally found some measure of peace to allow some much-needed sleep.

He wouldn't like where her thoughts were headed. Combat missions had pretty much been forbidden for her, but in truth there was no finer candidate than the Hohn's royal wife to draw Ignaki's attention.

Quietly, Daria started to roll from the bed, but Raven's arm tightened around her waist.

"Where are you going?"

"To contact the *Versailles*. I wanted to find out if they ever got Loki up and running." She felt him tense at the confession, but Daria settled back against his chest again, content to stay there for a while longer.

His lips brushed her ear. "And why does that matter to you now? I thought we discussed this and agreed you'd take a freighter commission when it's safer?"

She turned so she could see his face. "We did, but this takes precedence. If it works the way I'm seeing it in my mind, I want to be the one to fly the mission."

He shook his head even before the last of the words fell from her into the space between them. "No. It's too dangerous."

"How can you say that? You don't even know what I want to do."

A chime cut the conversation off before it could escalate into an argument. "Hohn," called the voice over the intercom. "We found the signal origination."

"On my way." He rolled off the bed and put on the uniform he'd discarded earlier when they'd prepared for bed. The look he sent up and down her body made her nipples pucker instantly. "Though I love seeing you naked, especially when I can tell you're ready for loving, I think perhaps you should put on something more modest to attend the bridge with me."

If she had known he planned to have her follow him there, she would have already been half dressed. She huffed and started pulling on her borrowed uniform.

As they entered the bridge a short time later, crew members worked in frantic concert to stabilize the signal and lock down its location.

Raven took the command chair and turned away from Daria as he typed in a code to pull up the information on his console. He studied it in silence for a moment, then. "Cross reference with known star charts. This signal is coming from deep space."

Feeling useless was something Daria had never done well, and in the current climate it was totally unacceptable. Surely her skills could be used for something productive. She watched the charts fly past as the ship's computer traced the signal into the deeper realms of space. Then something flashed across the screen, something she recognized from her time at Gideon III.

"Wait, wait!" She called out to anyone who would listen. "Replay that last sequence."

One of the techs turned to the Hohn for confirmation before complying with the order. His head moved in an imperceptible nod, his eyes glued to the screen.

The charts moved back to replay the previous maps. Daria leaned closer to Raven and fixed her eyes on the monitor lest she miss it the second time. "There. Stop."

A small gap in a known asteroid field could be overlooked by some, but not Daria. She'd flown that field before, knew it intimately. The debris in it was so dense only highly trained pilots with small ships could penetrate, but with a larger opening, almost any sized ship could hide there. And hide well. Especially if the transmissions to and from the ship were hidden inside known signals.

"There's your opening." Daria pointed to the screen. "Any ship hiding in there took that route. Follow your signal and it will take you into the heart of the field."

The Hohn turned and studied her face for a moment, then called to the

Data Specialist. "Can we penetrate that far into the field?"

"Not at this range. We'll need to get closer to it."

"Very well. Pass all information to the Versailles, and let them know we are in pursuit."

Raven turned to her and gave her a cool look. "Now suppose you tell me your plan."

She took a deep breath. "We have to turn the weapons back on Ignaki. I thought if a Primon pilot could get close enough to whatever carried the command signals, we could plant our own bomb onboard. We prepare to negotiate with them to give up Ignaki. If they don't, we do to them what was done to Stegos."

A thunderous expression came over Raven's face, and he turned to look out the front view screen. "Using a Primon pilot with the nanobots in the biosuits would definitely get closer than any other ship could. But why you? Do you mean to kill yourself?"

"No, but it makes sense to send me. For one reason, Ignaki will sweep the ship and find signatures compatible with a Primon vessel and pilot. If he discovers it's me, so much the better. Do you think he'll turn away the possible chance to have the Hohn's wife in custody? Secondly, Loki is infected with those same nanobots as the biosuits. Maybe we can use that to our advantage, if the Hawks got him back in working order." She lowered her voice and moved closer to him, enough that he would be the only one to hear her. "Third, I have to do this for Lessia, and for the life and marriage that should have been hers."

Raven let out a long breath and reached for her. In front of his crew, he put her hand to his mouth and kissed it. "If I give my consent, it's as if I approve of you flying into danger, of possibly killing yourself. I don't want that. I want you here and safe with me."

"And I want to be safe, but neither of us will be until we bring Ignaki down."

"And discover who has aided him and why. And for that I will not sacrifice you." He leaned in and placed a kiss on her temple. "But you've given me an idea on how we can both have our way."

"How's that?"

Chapter Eleven

Once again the *Ramaclesus* and the *Versailles* were docked together like two great mechanized behemoths mating in space. The *Royal Renegade* had docked in the *Versailles'* launch deck and all participants stood in the repair bay looking over the remains of Loki.

"Well, is it feasible?" Daria asked Chief Clarin, as nothing but his feet stuck out Loki's underbelly.

"It's feasible," he confirmed then started to pull out. "He'll fly again, but we'll have to get him very close to the asteroid field and the mother ship for them to pick up his signals."

"Why?" Raven asked, bending down to look up into the ship's innards. "They can track the signals this far to us, why not the other way around?"

"Because this is one lone ship with a very weak signal, and it'll be flown by remote. You won't have the added nanobots from the biosuit to kick up the signal."

"We could always stick one inside the cockpit," Daria offered. "Or rig one to work from the *Versailles'* bridge."

Her father, Captain Aaron, Hawk Conners, the Chief, and the Hohn all looked at her as if she'd lost the rest of her mind.

Daria pointed at Loki. "How do you propose to fly the ship by remote? I say do it the way we have always done it. What are the biosuits if not a means of remote control? We just happen to be in the cockpit while utilizing them." Daria smiled when Hawk Conners and Chief Clarin caught on to her idea.

"Someone explain to me what she means," Prince Hefcat commanded.

"She means to interface with the Loki by running the circuitry of the biosuit to direct link with the *Versailles*. The maneuvers would be the same whether she sits in the cockpit, or in a comfortable chair safely aboard ship." Chief Clarin smiled as he relayed the premise. Admiration gleamed in his eyes for Daria's crafty thinking.

She let her glance fall to her husband who stood in the same stoic stance he had maintained at the airlock the first time she saw him at close range. Now, however, his gaze burned with love and appreciation for her, and her quick mind. It was what she wanted all along, a man to love her not only for the physical side of their relationship, or her ties to the Primon royal house, but one who could be proud of her as a competent member of the crew that had something worthy to give a mission.

Seemingly unaware of the looks passing between his daughter and her husband, Prince Hefcat shook his head. "You are amazing, my dear."

"No, not me." She pointed her head in the direction of the Hawk and the Chief. "They're going to have to be the ones who are amazing here. I'm just the idea person."

Chief Clarin bowed. "Then we better get to work if we're going to make Loki airborne"

※ (♋) ※

As the mechanics worked out the problems with making Loki fly and turning the clever devices against their creators, tech crews worked steadfast on the *Versailles'* bridge to create a place where Daria could once again pilot her ship, if only by remote.

"It won't be the same as being in the cockpit," she lamented.

Raven stroked the small of her back as he stood behind her. "This way isn't without its dangers. If you should take another hit by a ruptured suit…"

Daria turned around and placed her fingers against his mouth. "Then we'll return to Jevic, and high healer Raizen will have to put me to rights again."

He took her hand and held it. "When next we return to Jevic we will stay at the country house and concentrate on nothing but pleasuring each other."

A smile filled her face. "I like your plan better."

His gaze lingered on her mouth, heating her blood to a boil. The man had the sexiest mouth she'd ever seen. Knowing intimately all the pleasure it could bring to her very sensitive female parts had her changing her stance a bit as the rough fabric of her uniform pants brushed against her.

Outside the view screen deep space plunged by as the ship hurtled toward the outskirts of the sector and drew closer to Gideon III. The *Ramaclesus* flew ahead and a little to starboard.

"Princess, we're ready for you to try the relays," a tech called to her.

"Oh, then I better get suited up." She leaned up and brushed her mouth against Raven's and squeezed his hand.

"Would you like to join me while I change?"

He followed her back to their quarters, silent but willing.

The suit hung in the corner of the room waiting for her to don it. The entire idea of putting one of those enemy agents back on her body after nearly losing her life to one made her skin crawl. But there was no choice in the matter. It could be her and no other to fly this mission. For Lessia. For herself. And for Loki if she had to detonate the weapons.

Raven placed his hands on her shoulders as she contemplated the suit. "Second thoughts?"

"No. Just realizing how vulnerable we all were in the fleet. Imagine wearing enemy weapons as close as our own skin, as intimate as our thoughts, and never suspecting it. If I had died in that attack, we would have never known. How many more pilots would have died?"

He slid his arms around her and rested her against the wall of his chest. "Too many."

She turned to face him. He'd asked her when he confessed to her after her capture if she could ever learn to love him, so far the only thing she'd given him was a declaration during the throws of passion. He deserved more. He deserved better. The Hohn, in the brevity of their marriage, had proven time and again he was both noble and loyal. Any woman should be proud to be his wife, and though Daria prided herself on not being like other women, she was so proud he had chosen her and only her one night in a crowded ballroom.

"What?" he asked as his eyes searched her face and the awed expression she knew must be there.

She shook her head to try and order her thoughts. "For months now, since word came of your renewed interest in the alliance, I've been torn up thinking you offered for my hand while still in love with the memory of my sister." When he started to interrupt her, she was sure to deny it, she shook her head. "I know now that wasn't the case. I do believe you've loved me all along. I want you to know that I appreciate you allowing me to be who I am, and loving me despite that."

A small smile curled the corner of his mouth. Dark eyes gazed at her with deep emotion. "I don't love you despite who you are, but because of it."

She swallowed.

Quietly, and with much care, he helped her shed the Jevic uniform and pull on the tight skin of the biosuit.

He knelt at her feet and held the biosuit out. Bracing her hand on his shoulder, she stepped into it. With a soft caress, his hand moved up the inside of her leg, fingers fanned when they reached her thigh. Bare knuckles by accident or design, she knew not which, grazed her mound.

She moaned.

He moved to her other leg and placed tender kisses along the side of her thigh, working his way up. When he reached her, she could feel the wetness pooling. He had only to flick his tongue through her folds to discover her desire for him.

She rested her hands on his head and gently guided him there. "I love it when you kiss me here, and move your tongue inside me," she whispered.

He growled and complied.

Daria pulled back and saw the rapid flick of his tongue as he worked on her. The sound of his mouth working through her wetness along with his excited groans heightened her excitement. The curve of his nose brushed and bumped across her clit, and she pressed closer.

His hands slid around and gripped her cheeks, pulling her tightly to him. Unable to hold back, she came. Long and hard, panting out in ecstasy as the waves crested over her.

Raven placed a final kiss on her. He looked up with hot eyes and licked her from his lips. Then he stood and pulled the suit over the curve of her hips and swell of her breasts as he brushed his tongue over her. She'd never dressed for flight in so loving and gentle a manner before. She would never look at a biosuit in quite the same way again. And now the suit didn't seem quite as deadly as before.

Fully suited, she faced her husband, and he bent down and kissed the tip of her nose. "Go knock 'em dead, Eagle."

⁂

Fifteen minutes later she climbed into the pilot's chair that had been removed from Loki's cockpit and began a start up sequence.

Over the link up from the flight deck came cheers. "We have engine ignition," Hawk Conners' rusty voice filtered through the com unit.

"Good morning, Loki. It's great to be back in the saddle," she greeted the ship in the headset. Silence answered her.

This wasn't right. She needed to communicate with Loki. "He's not responding to verbals."

"They disabled that feature. Try a short flight around the ship and land him again," Captain Aaron said from the command chair behind her.

"Yes, sir," she responded automatically. She wanted to ask why they had disabled voice commands. It was as if she would fly a stranger.

A screen had been installed so she could see what Loki's sensors saw. It wasn't as good as being directly in the cockpit, but it gave her enough of a view to fly with confidence. Instrument panels in front of her lit with all the read outs she would have if seen aboard her fighter. There was no way she would be flying Loki blind, even in this unusual situation.

"How does it feel? Does he handle the way you remember?" Captain Aaron monitored the instruments and visuals from where he sat.

"It seems to be, but it's a little odd without having his engines rumble under me. I'm used to feeling the power." The view took her out of the launch deck and out into space. The images before her started to shudder. "I think I'm losing visuals."

"Working on it," a voice she didn't recognize answered.

The screen popped and crackled before winking out. When it came back on, Daria had to correct her flight path quickly as she headed directly for the *Versailles'* fuselage. "Whoa!"

"Bring him back in. We need to work out some of the bugs," Chief Clarin said.

She turned the ship and came back to the flight deck. When she had Loki safely landed she turned and regarded Aaron over her shoulder. "This plan is only going to work if Loki appears to have a pilot on board. If they get visual and see it's a Primon ship it's over. There can be no mistakes, or they'll blow him out of the sky before we ever get aboard that ship."

"They'll get him working right. Just think, until a short time ago we never thought to see Loki in the air again at all."

"Thanks, Captain Look-On-The-Bright-Side." She stood and stretched the tension out of her shoulders. "I'm going back to my quarters. Have me called when they're ready again."

⁂ ☙(☉)❧ ⁑

The call came as they neared the asteroid field. Daria closed her eyes to fend off the nausea racing through her body. She would have liked another chance to test Loki before the actual mission, but they had run out of time. A transmission from Gideon III relayed that a super freighter from Jevic had been blown to Hell's Caverns and back as it attempted to engage its light drive. A sweep for the nanobots came up positive. It was time for action.

"Wait," Raven touched her shoulder as she started through the door and into the corridor. "I want you to know how proud I am of you. In the short time of our marriage, you've far exceeded all my expectations of you. Your bravery and strength should be the measure of all pilots in the Primon fleet, and indeed my own fleet." With that he leaned over and brushed a tender kiss over her brow, cheeks and finally her mouth.

Tears filled her eyes. How could such a man keep his tender side so well hidden from the rest of humanity? "I do love you, Raven. I think I have since the moment I saw you at Lessia's funeral."

He kissed her again. A long tender kiss that sealed their souls as one. When he lifted his head his mouth pulled down at the corners in worry. "Now, go get Ignaki."

The bridge had been cleared with the exception of essential personnel. Pilots were remanded to the flight deck to await instructions. Daria's father had been taken to his quarters, for security purposes. If all went according to plan, Ignaki would be handed over without the need to detonate the weapons aboard Loki, and the pilots would be used as escort only to bring the evil former aide back to face his victims.

Daria sat in the pilot's chair and once again flipped through the start up sequence. A shock moved through her as a simulated engine vibration began in her seat. A brief smile came and went over her face. Hopefully, the rest of the flight would be as well crafted as that small detail.

When she hit the button for her flight screen to come to life, she was nearly blown away by the image. Instead of the small screen she'd had earlier, the viewer directly before her took up one entire wall. When it blinked to life, she could see as if she were aboard her fighter sitting in the launch bay.

"How's it hanging, Loki?" she asked into her headset, not because she thought he'd answer, but because she needed to stick to her routine.

"High noon, Eagle Varta. High noon

It was so good to hear his voice she almost wept with relief. "I want you to know, Loki, if it comes down to blowing the bombs, I'm sorry."

"At least I'll die a hero."

Daria smiled and felt the tears rise in her eyes. The images on the screen blurred. "You're already a hero."

"Eagle Varta and Loki prepare to launch." The deck commander's voice came over the headset.

"Eagle Varta and Loki copy. Ready to launch."

The signal came and they shot from the launch bay and into the star-filled sky. Asteroids filled the viewer before her, and Daria gave herself over to the instinctual flying bred in all trained Primon pilots. The biosuit relayed her commands and swept through the field, entering not at the same point as the mother ship, but farther away so she could sneak up on them as much as possible.

The output signal from the enemy vessel grew stronger as she moved Loki closer. "Approaching vessel, identify yourself," came a command from the other craft, but the words were hard to understand, as if the speaker did not have a clear command of the language.

Her instrument panel dimmed and then all control of Loki left her capable hands. Daria covered her mouthpiece and turned to Captain Aaron. "They've taken flight control from me."

"Then we play our hand." Captain Aaron stood and pulled his uniform jacket down. "Once Loki is in their landing bay, hail the vessel."

It took another few moments before Loki's visuals showed him being locked into the bay. Grotesque humanoid forms began to move around him, inspecting him.

"Hail now, before they have a chance to discover the bomb and dismantle it." Captain Aaron remained on his feet, and Raven, in all his Hohn glory stood beside him.

"I am Captain Vreelan Aaron of the Primon vessel *Versailles*, and this is General Kristiano Raven, the Hohn of Jevic. We have come in search of the Jevician known as Ignaki. Hand him over to us and we will prepare to negotiate a peace with you. Harbor this criminal and pay the consequences."

The screen filled with a hideous visage. Long pointed teeth stuck up from the creature's bottom jaw and short tusks came out from the cheekbones. His head was bald and covered with a thick skin that looked gray under the lights of their bridge. The relay took a while as their ships databanks searched for the proper translation codes.

Daria wondered if they even had the right ones, but then Ignaki had been able to communicate with someone aboard the ships, so they must know at least some of the common tongue.

Finally, the leader spoke, his voice low and garbled. "We are Scullins, and we will not surrender. The Ignaki foretold of your attack, and he has proved right."

"The Ignaki has misled you," Raven barked. "Our races did not even know of your existence until he brought you to our attention. We have only attacked you in defense."

A large clawed hand pounded on the arm of his chair as the Scullin captain became enraged. "No! 'Tis not a lie. He has foretold your attack, and now you are here. Scullins know of Hohn. The Ignaki left to die on your order."

"The Ignaki should have died as he has saw men of his own people killed on his order. The Ignaki is traitor to his own kind."

"Eagle, we have limited control back for you," Chief Clarin said into her earpiece.

"Enough to shoot off a warning shot from the cannons?"

"You betcha'."

"Loki, lock on random target and fire."

"Locking on."

The laser cannon fired and ripped a hole in the side of the ship. Gravity controls in the bay were lost and Scullins free floated, some sucked out into the heart of the asteroid field.

"Prepare to launch Jevic squadron," the Hohn spoke into his the comm unit on his lapel.

From her periphery, Daria could swear she saw Captain Aaron stiffen at the command. This was nothing they had discussed in meetings, but it would make their work a whole lot easier.

Not to be outdone, Aaron hailed the flight deck. "Prepare to launch quads."

"If you don't hand over Ignaki and agree to a truce, we will blow your ship all the way to Hell's Caverns and back," the Hohn said.

"Scullins better fighters, faster ships."

"Not since we discovered your hidden signals inside the Primon bio-suits. You have no way to tip the battle in your favor now."

"Still better fighters."

"Not unless you want to blow your ship up yourself. You launch your fighters and begin to fire, and the ship sitting in your docking bay will rip your ship to pieces. It's loaded with the nanobots you used to ignite your explosions."

"Scullin ship has women and children on board. You would not kill innocents."

The Hohn raised a brow. "Did you take that into consideration when you disintegrated Stegos? You killed fifteen-thousand aboard that station, and not even a quarter of them were military personnel. They were merchants and scholars and mothers and children. All innocents."

"Prime laser cannon again," Daria said to Loki. If the men were going to dick around and flex their muscles, she was going to act. At least another blast might scare them into some action.

"Laser cannon primed. Ready to fire at will."

"Fire!"

The blast ripped a hole in the inner seam of the ship and decompression started almost immediately. The view screen showed Scullins scurrying about to try and breach the hole.

"The next blast will take your entire ship out as you did to Stegos Outpost. Hand over Ignaki and agree to a truce and live." Raven had his hands to his sides, his fists clenched in rage. "You have exactly five seconds to make your decision or we blow you up."

The Scullin commander appeared unmoved, until Raven began to count backward from five. At two he raised his hand to give the command.

"*Tosh!* Wait!" The commander yelled. "We will agree to terms. Will hand over the Ignaki as show of good faith."

The Hohn raised his hand to his chest and bowed in the formal manner. "We will launch a Jevic ship to bring him back to the *Versailles*. If I sense any treachery on your part or the part of your men I will give the order to blow the ship. Is that clear?"

"Clear." The Scullin leader bowed.

Epilogue

In the aftermath of what became known to the alliance as the Great Asteroid Crusade, Ignaki was brought back to Jevic to face a tribunal for treason. He was found guilty and executed before the public in the city of Triton.

Before going to his death, he admitted responsibility for the death of Lessia. He said he'd wished only to cover his mistake and allow the Hohn to marry Daria. Remorse for his mistake was not long to linger when the Hohn dismissed him from service. At that point, Ignaki had already been in secret negotiations with the Scullins for over two years. It was unclear exactly what his intentions were in doing so, and those were secrets he took to his grave.

The Scullins were earnest in their want to cleanse the sins committed against the planets of Primon, Jevic, and Riman. Their technologically advanced civilization surpassed even those small devices that proved to be so destructive to the Primon fleet. And yet they marveled at handmade goods and clothing from all the other planets they began trading with. Silks were a special favorite, especially for the Scullin females.

Daria stretched out in the shade of a large *Ingoth* tree whose plate-sized leaves were thick with a sweet nectar that if drunk gave a burst of euphoria. But she didn't need any such drug to feel euphoric, for at the moment Raven lay beside her and traced the line of her breast in a lazy fashion.

It had been six months since her last mission and every day, she became more and more at ease with her new position in the Jevic fleet. At first the thought of an admiralty to a force not hers by birth, but by marriage, had felt wrong, but when she discovered that in the Jevic tradition the Hohn's wife always held such a title, she relaxed and enjoyed the commission. She wondered why he had teased her about being a freighter captain, but then she had learned over the months that, though tender, Raven had a rather off-beat sense of humor.

He turned to her and looked down into her face as a breeze lifted his hair and blew it back. Overhead a bird called, and insects buzzed in the grass.

His erection brushed against her thigh.

She looked over at him and shook her head. "Again?"

"Yes. Again." He smiled a lecherous grin. "I'm what you call, *feronin,* insatiable."

Daria let out a laugh that moved up into the tree and higher still. So the Jevic did have a word for insatiable after all, and here she'd been thinking it was "Raven".

About the Author:

Kathleen Scott lives in New Jersey with her husband, cat, and a plethora of characters in her head. You can visit the website she shares with MK Mancos at **www.mystickat.com**.

Kathleen Scott

Toy in the Attic

by R. Ellen Ferare

To My Reader:

Santa Cruz is a California beach town that cherishes individuality. A walk down Pacific Avenue can be counted on to illustrate the point. You might spot a young woman wearing nothing but two squares of duct tape and a pair of jeans, or a man wrapped in strategically molded aluminum foil. Fortunately for most people, no one is required to follow a creative dress code. Visitors can safely leave the foil and duct tape at home.

If you ever do decide to visit, be sure to check out more than just the boardwalk. There are funky shops, wonderful bookstores, and good eats just a few blocks in from the beach. You can find some some nice Victorian B&Bs, too, but I'm sorry to say that none of them offer the extra amenities featured in this story...

Dedication:

To Shannon, who can always be counted on to help find plot holes and positional improbabilities. To Ed, who was still willing to answer the phone even when the third CPU chip didn't work. To Mag, Nat, and Arianne, who had better not be reading this. And, of course, to Jacques, my most valuable research assistant. Long live research!

Victorian's Secret

The man and woman at the neighboring table were young and amorous, and completely oblivious to the cries of "Get a room!" from the other bar patrons. Gabrielle Roarke watched the pair in jealous fascination, finding it extremely unfair that they had chosen to sit next to her. Their spelunking, as she'd decided to call their mutual exploration of mouths and shirts, only served to remind her how long it had been since she'd had a date.

This whole trip to Santa Cruz was a mistake. She'd known it the minute she'd driven into town, and seen the gloomy bed and breakfast where her friend Rachel had asked her to stay. Gabrielle's visions of a pleasant all-expenses-paid vacation in a swank hotel had vanished with her first glimpse of her destination, sending her scurrying off to grab a bracing drink and postpone the inevitable check-in.

What she really wanted to do was drive back home. Damn her promise to Rachel. If the woman hadn't looked so pitiful when she'd asked for this favor, Gabrielle would never have agreed to come. Now she was stuck here. Days of rain and solitude stretched ahead, just because her friend wanted her to try out a creepy old Victorian hotel that could have starred in a Hitchcock movie. *Joy.*

Depression settled around her like a gray fog. The steady drizzle outside was typical winter weather for coastal California, and it matched her mood perfectly. She morosely signaled to the waitress for another margarita. If she was really going to spend the night in that dismal house, she needed a little more fortification.

The lovers next to her leaned into a slow, languid embrace that flirted with illegality and was intimate enough to stir an amoeba to lust. Gabrielle was much higher on the evolutionary scale, and hastily looked away as her body flared in sympathetic response to their passion. Her second drink arrived and she tossed it down in four quick gulps, welcoming the sudden cold pinch at her temples. The mild pain provided only a brief distraction from the floor show; unable to stand the view any longer, she rose from her table, paid for her drinks, and fled.

It was a short walk to the hotel, with one stop at her car to retrieve her bag. The rain had slowed to a gentle mist that bathed and cooled her face, but did nothing to cool any other part of her body. She kicked at a wet pebble on the sidewalk and tried to ignore how badly she wanted to be doing what that couple in the bar had been doing. Sometimes she wished her brain was wired differently, that it didn't demand some deeper connection before she could get naked and sweaty with a man.

She came to a halt in front of her assigned lodgings for the night. The place had grown even less appealing since the afternoon. It loomed over her in the fog, silent and completely dark, aside from a porch light casting a feeble glow on the wooden steps and veranda. There was barely enough illumination from the dim bulb and the gathering dusk to make out the numbers of the address and the NO VACANCY sign hanging on the front door.

Vacancy or not, Gabrielle had been assured there would be a room available. "I've heard there's a special suite in the attic," Rachel Ducroix had explained. "You have to know to ask for it. You're due some vacation time, right? If I pay all your expenses, would you drive down there and check the place out for me? See if it's suitable for my employees? You can stay there as long as you want—I'll cover it."

Then she'd launched into a hurried explanation of how she needed to find a better hotel for her programmers to use on their trips to Santa Cruz. An acquaintance had recommended a little place within walking distance of the best shops and restaurants. It sounded promising, but Rachel wanted someone she trusted to look it over for her. Since all her employees were busy at the moment...

She'd paced the room while she talked, with little trace of her usual poise. Gabrielle's heart had ached for her when she glimpsed the mingled hope and grief in her friend's eyes, recognizing that look only too well. They hadn't been friends for very long when Rachel's brother had vanished, but she had worn that same expression for months after his disappearance, even while fiercely insisting he wasn't dead. It was clear that something had stirred up her old memories of him. Her emotions were in a turmoil, and she was not her usual self.

Only someone with a heart of stone could have refused her request after seeing that unhappy, troubled face. So Gabrielle had agreed to go inspect the hotel, and on a whim, had taken every vacation day she had due. Weeks of free time stretched before her, and she'd been looking forward to it. Until the rain and the lovers and the unwelcoming house she was supposed to stay in had made her realize how miserably lonely she was going to be.

She stared up at the hotel and resolved that most of her holiday would be spent somewhere else, even if it meant Rachel wouldn't be footing the bill. The old Victorian made her skin crawl. Though it didn't look particularly run down, it had an aura. A very unpleasant aura. The place radiated unfriendliness, and all the windows seemed to stare at her like unlidded eyes in the darkness. With a sigh she trudged up the walk, wondering if a third margarita would have improved the house's curb appeal.

The door opened almost immediately to her knock, and a meticulously dressed woman stood silhouetted in the entryway. She was thin and angular, and though the fine lines on her face revealed her age, the rest of her was as trim and toned as the body of a woman decades younger. Her dark eyes glittered like a snake's as she stared out at her visitor. "What is it?" she asked, her voice colored with a slight European accent.

Gabrielle glanced at the sign, then back at her. "A friend of mine told me that this is a good place to stay?" Even she could hear the question in that statement.

The other woman considered her and her small overnight bag, with a gaze as unwelcoming as the house. "Didn't you see the sign? My rooms are full."

Gabrielle found that difficult to believe. From the look of things, there wasn't another soul anywhere inside the building. She hid her skepticism and said merely, "I'd heard that you have an attic room you usually don't rent out, for those who know about it."

"Ah." A small smile twisted the woman's mouth. It was not a pleasant smile. "Yes, that room is available. How many nights were you wanting?"

"Two, I think. No more than three. Depends on how things go." *Depends on how long I can stand it.* She wasn't looking forward to her stay at all—both the house and its owner needed a major karma adjustment.

The door opened wider and the woman gestured her inside, then shepherded her to a stairway at the far end of the foyer. "Maximum stay is seventeen nights. After that, you're out."

"Seventeen? Why not two weeks or a month?" she asked, curious.

"It's the rule," was the curt response.

Conversation died after that. They climbed to the top of the stairs, where her guide opened what looked like a tall cupboard and led her into a room occupying the entire third floor. It was bare and minimal, but not as cheerless as the rest of the building. Small gaslights along the back wall had been rewired to provide a soft glow from bulbs shaped to resemble candle flames. The floor was of yellow pine, burnished by decades of sunlight to a glowing gold, and the walls were papered with a textured weave of earth tones. Windows liberally scattered along two walls gave the occupant an aerial view of the streets below. A barebones bathroom had been jury-rigged in the left corner: a toilet, sink, and tiled corner with shower head, separated from the rest of a room by a carved wooden screen providing minimal privacy.

The middle of the attic was occupied by a huge brass bed, and a tall dresser of faded oak sat against the back wall. Besides those two pieces of furniture and the plumbing, the room held nothing except an object draped with a dust cloth, about four feet tall and irregularly shaped, placed by the bed. It was hard to tell what it might be. A sculpture?

The landlady noted where her gaze had fallen and smiled a slow, inscrutable smile. "Enjoy your stay. Feel free to make use of the amenities." Still smirking, she withdrew from the room.

Gabrielle waited until the door was safely closed before tossing her bag onto the mattress with a sigh of relief. "That woman is creepy," she muttered. This was definitely not a place she'd recommend to Rachel for her employees. Prosaic though her programmers were, even they wouldn't be immune to the bad vibrations from house and hostess.

After stashing her belongings in the dresser and shoving her bag against the wall, she walked over to the only secret the room held: the odd, cloth-covered thing positioned near the bed. Curious, she reached out to see what lay underneath. Before her fingers could touch it, all the hairs on her body rose, as if static electricity, or the caress of an unseen hand, had brushed her skin. The veil of fabric slithered to the floor in a pool of white silk, and the hidden object was laid bare.

It was a sculpture, as she had guessed. A sculpture like nothing she'd ever seen. She faced a life-sized statue of a man kneeling with legs spread, his head thrown back and face contorted in an expression of pleasure/ pain any consenting adult would recognize. The artist had captured him at the height of his ecstasy, just as the shudders of orgasm were cording the muscles in his neck and chest. He wore nothing but his skin, and his erection was thrust forward as if clutched inside a woman. One hand was raised to cup the breast of his unseen partner, the fingers of the other curved around her invisible waist. Gabrielle could picture exactly where the woman would be—straddling him, chest to chest, thrusting with him as he climaxed. It was the most stunningly erotic thing she had ever seen, and it reawakened the ache in the lonely, sex-starved area below her belly.

She reached out a hand to touch the muscles of his chest, and the contours felt real, though cold and metallic, as if her fingers glided over chilled skin. Even the individual strands in his shoulder-length mane had been sculpted, the down on his arms, the thatch where his penis jutted. She closed her hand around his forearm and was amazed at the lifelike feel of it. It took no great imagination to fantasize she was touching a living body instead of a statue that was anatomically correct in every possible way.

Whoever had posed for this work had been in excellent physical shape, with a body most women only dreamed of holding—muscles sculpted and defined without being overdeveloped, buttocks so perfectly formed her fingers itched to splay across them, an impressive erection that would fill a woman completely. Her mind presented her with searing images of her own body entwined in an embrace with the original model, and she sighed. Just what her hormone-activated imagination needed—another reminder of how empty her bed was going to be tonight.

The metal under her fingers grew warmer. A flare of light— Was it light? Or heat? Or something her mind couldn't recognize, so categorized as both? —swelled around the statue, and she blinked. Heat crept up her arm and spread through her, waking an insidious tide of desire. All of her body throbbed as if in response to a lover's caresses, and she blinked again, uncertain and a bit wary.

Glittering motes of gold threaded through her thoughts, soothing away her uncertainty. *You've been wanting a man,* they whispered. *There's one here, for you to take with no commitments, no risks. Look at him.* Her gaze fixed on the statue kneeling at her feet, while her mind floated in golden fog. Before her light-muddled brain realized what the rest of her had decided, she had walked the few steps to the door and shot the deadbolt home. Her hands slowly unbuttoned her shirt as she returned to the statue, her fingers working almost of their own accord. The shirt slid to the floor. The rest of her clothes quickly followed. She approached her frozen lover completely nude, as bared to his gaze as he was to hers.

His toned shoulder was firm and warm under the hand she placed there to balance herself when she knelt, straddling his legs. Her free hand encircled his erection to guide him in, and that, too, was as heated as a man should be. He filled her completely, rubbing with gentle friction as she sheathed him to the hilt. With a sighing breath she leaned forward to fit her breast into his raised, cupped hand, as if she were the missing half of the sculpture. The splayed fingers of his lowered wrist pressed against her hip. She closed her eyes, drifting in a haze of honeyed light and mindless arousal while her body ached for more than a frozen embrace. "Damn. I wish you were real," she whispered.

The hand on her breast tightened, and the erection inside her throbbed and jerked. Her eyes flew open as the statue clutching her gasped, a choked, shuddering sound. He thrust into her once, forcefully, and she saw the metal sheen fade from his face and hair even as his muscles spasmed and his body contracted in the little death of orgasm.

She was straddling a flesh and blood man. A naked, wide awake, flesh and blood man. The knowledge penetrated the numbing fog in her head, and she tore herself off him to stumble back against the bed, panting. The awakened heat inside her and the trickle down her inner thigh told her more clearly than vision that the man before her was real, all right. Real and already used up for the night.

He groaned and fell to all fours, flushed and breathing hard, his face hidden by a curtain of black hair. "H-hello," he panted. "Hell of a way to meet someone, I know."

The world had shifted into a bizarre and unbelievable place, as if she'd fallen into a Lewis Carroll rabbit hole. She stared at him. The mist and margaritas wreathing her brain stopped her from sensibly fleeing into the hallway. "Um," she said intelligently. "Who the hell are you? What are you doing in my room?"

The head of the ex-statue lifted, and a small smile curled the corner of his mouth as his breathing slowed to a normal rate. "Wasn't it obvious?"

"Well, yes." Only her foggy disbelief saved her from the blush that threatened. "But—but you're alive! How can you be alive?"

He rose easily to his feet. "You woke me. For my services, I would imagine."

"Services?" Her eyes dropped to his fading erection. "Some of your services," she pointed out, "seem to be unavailable."

An eyebrow lifted. "Give me a little time, woman. And there are other things we can do in the meantime." He padded over to her as if he were an invited guest, and took hold of her shoulders, pressing her back onto the bed, legs trailing to the floor. Another wash of golden light spread from his fingers. She lay quietly on the covers and watched him kneel beside her, waiting to see what he had in mind.

It occurred to her to wonder why she wasn't trying to escape or take charge of this whole situation. Her acceptance had nothing to do with the sheer attraction of the man leaning over her, though he had a masculine beauty that would turn heads anywhere, the planes and contours of his body as perfect as if sculpted by a master hand. His face was no hardship to look at, either—square, firm jaw, aquiline nose, eyes the green of a cold arctic sea. It was a face that could haunt a woman's dreams.

Dreams. She seized on that as the reason for her strange languor—she had to be dreaming. If so, she fervently hoped she wouldn't wake any time soon. She murmured lazily, "How about if you take it slower next time? Quickies have their place, but honestly…"

He flashed her a stunningly attractive grin. "Believe me, it wasn't quick for me," he assured her. "I'd been building up to that one for two hours, fifteen minutes, and… What's the date?"

"Huh?" She expected her dreams to make no sense—they usually didn't—but that question was weirder than the usual illogic of dreams. "Today? It's January 15th."

"…and six days," he finished. "Including the time spent as a statue, of course."

"Of course." The oddity of that statement penetrated her sluggish brain. "I do realize that statues don't come to life," she assured him. "I know this is a dream, and you'll be going away when I wake up. Which is too bad."

Fingers reached out to stroke her breasts in one light, teasing touch, and she quivered. Everywhere. "We'll call this a dream, if you like. But there's no reason to end it for awhile," he said softly. "It's been a long time since I made love to a woman like you. Plain ones, desperate ones, . old ones, yes, but not a woman with such high, beautiful breasts," as his hands cupped their contours, "and such lovely legs."

She studied his face. There was something in the angle of his cheekbones and the set of his green eyes that seemed strangely familiar to her, especially when he smiled. She wondered who he reminded her of, what known person had crept into her sexual fantasy. It was a good sexual fantasy, whoever he might be, the most erotic dish her imagination had ever cooked up. "I could use a good orgasm right about now," she whispered.

He grinned and bent to kiss her cheek, then his lips traveled down her neck to fall on her right breast. The warm tugging of his mouth on her nipple immediately sent waves of desire pounding through her, and she made a small sound. He lingered there for a long time, his tongue tasting and tracing the curves of each breast. When his mouth abandoned them to nibble and lick his way further down her body in a slow, erotic path, he left a trail of heated flesh in his wake. She moaned when she felt him back away from her to crouch between her splayed legs. His breath warmed the skin of her inner thigh as he kissed her, tantalizingly close to where she wanted him to be. Her fingers slid into his hair, and he glanced up at her with a tiny smile before lowering his mouth to the wet, hot places aching for his tongue.

He ignored the most sensitive areas first, merely licked and teased the swollen skin still damp with his sperm. His tongue stroked and penetrated every fold and opening, lapping at her like a cat. Each touch sent a blaze of fire through her nerves, and she moaned as his mouth caressed her in a teasing rhythm. She hovered, aching and trembling, in an exquisite agony that seared her nerves with waves of heat. Using only his mouth, he held her suspended in a shivering web of fire that made her cry out for the feel of him inside her. His lips inched higher and his fingers slid inside her as if he knew what that wordless cry had meant. She began to shudder as his tongue reached the very center of her arousal and slowly, gently traced its contours.

She had never been a screamer with her previous lovers, but all restraints were lifted with this man. Her moans swelled into loud, vibrant cries as she arched her back and pressed into him, wordlessly begging for more even as her hips jerked and she fell into a wild series of shudders. He gave her more, his mouth never leaving her as his fingers thrust and rode her spasms. Then, when she thought they were finished, he began all over again.

When he finally lifted his head to climb back onto the bed and sit cross-legged beside her, she was as limp and glowing and incapable of standing as a jellyfish. She'd never fantasized oral sex like that before, and certainly not such a trio of firework-studded climaxes. "Wow," she managed. "That was incredible." Then she opened an eye to stare up at him. The last traces of the golden haze that had wrapped her thoughts were gone, and she finally, truly understood that there was a strange man sitting on her bed. She said drowsily, "You're no dream. My imagination isn't this good."

He chuckled. "No, I'm no dream. I'm real enough. But you knew that, sweetheart."

"Did I? You gave a really convincing imitation of a statue caught in true coitus interruptus."

"Stop," he said, his voice suddenly weary. "No need to pretend you don't know about the curse."

"Curse? What do you mean?" She raised herself on one elbow. "Is that why you were frozen like that? Someone cursed you?" Viscerally, she already knew the answer to her question. Some primitive part of her, inherited from a distant, preliterate ancestor who used rocks for tools and believed eclipses were caused by demons, had recognized the magic in those flashes of golden light. "You really were turned into a statue," she said wonderingly.

He turned his head to look down on her with skepticism. "I'm finding it hard to believe in your surprise."

She shrugged. "I only came here because a friend asked me to. She didn't say anything about you. Believe me, she would have mentioned you if she'd known."

"A friend." He reached out in one swift motion to seize her shoulders, and jerked her upright. His careful calm was gone. "What's your friend's name?"

"None of your business." She shoved his hands away and crossed her arms across her breasts, the last of her post-orgasmic sloth chased away by his sudden tension. The reality of where she was and what she had just done crashed down on her. *What am I doing here? I just had sex with a man I don't know at all. And he's cursed, too. He could be anyone. A serial killer. A man who kicks puppies.*

He sensed her discomfort and shifted back from her, though his gaze didn't leave her face. A flare of something—she would have sworn it was hope, though that seemed odd—flickered in his eyes before he suppressed it.

"All right," he agreed easily. "It's none of my business. And to answer your question, yes, someone cursed me. That witch downstairs. She was angry that I'd upset her daughter." He grimaced. "I only gave the girl a one night stand, and she wanted more."

She wasn't really listening to him. Her thoughts were more focused on the fact that she was sitting next to a naked man she knew nothing about. *Except that his hands and mouth are amazingly talented.* That stray thought was firmly shoved into a cage and locked away where it couldn't do further harm. "I can't believe I just had sex with a complete stranger," she grumbled, and scrambled from the bed to yank on her discarded clothes.

"I don't think you can call us complete strangers anymore," he pointed out. "Though it's not really your fault. The curse has a... let's call it an encouraging effect on women when they first wake me. It's probably worn off by now." He eyed her almost angry movements as she dressed. "It's definitely worn off by now," he amended. "But if you want formal introductions, I'm Gavin. And you are...?"

"Gabrielle." Armored with clothing, she felt ready to turn around and face him again, which was a mistake. He sat cross-legged and completely at ease on her bed, beautiful and nude, his erection quite obviously reawakening. She averted her eyes, but not before he could spot the appreciation in them and give her a knowing grin. All that gorgeous flesh was making her weak, she decided, so she marched over to the dresser and dug out the extra large t-shirt she'd brought to sleep in, with a pair of jogging shorts. The shorts would be tight and a bit revealing, but she was fairly sure he could cram those sleek hips into them. She tossed the items onto his lap. "Here."

"What are these for?"

"They're clothes. C-l-o-t-h-e-s. You know? Things to wear outside when you don't want to be arrested? Cover up a bit, please. I don't want you to freeze when you leave."

"This is a change," he remarked, rising to his feet. "Most women prefer me with clothes off." Voice muffled inside the shirt as he pulled it over his head, he said, "If you're going out, bring back some food, will you? I haven't eaten for a week."

The t-shirt fit him perfectly, but the gray shorts did little to hide the incredible sculpting of his lower half. Deliberately turning her eyes away from the attractive southern exposure, she pointed at the door. "I'm not going out, you are. It's been nice, but I don't sleep with guys I don't know, and I don't know you. Out."

"I'd love to do as you ask, but I can't leave this room," he said patiently, as if to a dim child. "Remember? The curse?"

"Sure you can," she told him, and manhandled him towards the door. He allowed her to drag him forward—a man six feet tall with musculature like a Greek statue could easily have resisted. She wrestled the door open and pressed against him to push him through.

"You smell wonderful," he told her as she braced an arm to each side of the door frame and shoved. "Like sea and salt. Like a woman who's been thoroughly loved."

"Out." She shoved harder, and he yielded to her, stepping backwards onto the top step, where he froze and stared down at his feet with an odd expression.

"I don't believe it," he whispered.

"What? That I would say adios after you gave me the best orgasm of my life?"

"No." He raised his head to grin at her. "Though that's good to know. No, I can't believe you got me out of there. I've been trying to get past that door for years."

"You've been stuck in here that long? With no television or internet or books or anything?" To Gabrielle that was a horrible punishment, much worse than being a frozen statue. "Because of the curse?"

He nodded. "It's been almost three years, if you count the time spent as the Man of Bronze." Turning, he advanced carefully to the second stair leading down, as if expecting to be yanked backwards by some invisible leash. His next step was slightly less cautious, and then he was exuberantly running down the stairs. "Come on," he called over his shoulder.

"But—" She'd finally got rid of him, and he expected her to come along? With a sigh she thought of the thin clothing he was wearing and the icy rain that was now pounding a loud, fast rhythm on the roof above her head. The least she could do was see to it that the man was suitably dressed before she sent him away. She grabbed her raincoat and scurried after him to the front hallway, its shadowy foyer as dimly lit as the porch.

Clouds and Rain

The landlady had heard them clattering downstairs, and was waiting by the door when they entered the hall. Her eyes snapped to Gavin, and her expression was not happy. "You shouldn't be out," was all she said, but the words were sibilant and hissed.

The man halted to stare at her with a focused, intense hatred, his face cold and forbidding. "You can't stop me."

"True. But you'll turn into something worse than a pumpkin, and permanently, unless you're back in the attic by midnight," she warned, then switched her venomous gaze to Gabrielle. "Glad you're enjoying the facilities here," the woman said, "but the furniture doesn't leave with the guests."

"Of course," Gabrielle agreed, and took her companion by the arm to drag him out the door. He was like a growling dog, legs stiff and feet planted. If he'd had hackles, they would have been raised.

She pulled him outside and onto the sidewalk, where his t-shirt was immediately soaked by the driving rain. "Come on," she said. "I noticed a thrift shop not too far away. Let's find you some better clothes and a coat before you go home."

"You heard the witch. I can't go home," he snapped, glowering at the front of the dark Victorian house they had just left as if he itched to set it on fire. The words he muttered under his breath sounded like curses, and not of the magical sort. At her urging, he shook himself and turned his back on the place to stride down the street, still tense with anger. She trotted beside him, her shorter legs matching his pace with difficulty until he calmed a little and slowed to accommodate her.

Once he had walked off some of his rage, she could see his attention shift to the world around them. His eyes flicked everywhere, examining the cars as they hurried past in a spray of water, the houses huddled in the steadily falling rain, even the irregular patterns of the cracks in the sidewalk they followed.

"You really haven't been outside for a while, have you?" she asked.

"No. Not from lack of trying." With a visible effort, he dragged his gaze from their surroundings and refocused on her. "I think the difference was that you wanted me to go out. All the other times I tried, my partner either wasn't there or had other ideas."

"That doesn't make any sense. Why would it matter what they wanted, or what I wanted?"

"You're the boss," he said simply. "Pretend I'm a genie, and you're the one who let me out of the bottle. Kind of like that."

They walked down the street, side by side, while she considered his words. "So instead of three wishes, I get three orgasms?"

He laughed then and flashed her a wicked smile. "Oh, no, many more than three," he assured her. "We'd already be done, otherwise."

She was instantly aching and ready for him. A few strokes of those fingers of his and she'd be at number four, here on the sidewalk in the pounding rain. As if sensing what she was thinking, he reached out to pull her to him. She almost let him, and then the sight of him soaked to the skin, rain dripping from his hair and plastering the thin fabric of his shirt to his chest, roused her better impulses. How could he possibly be interested in sex when he was almost shivering with cold? *Besides, you don't even know him, remember?*

"This way," she said instead, and led him several more blocks to the thrift store, where they found a cheap leather jacket and some pants and shoes that fit him perfectly. To replace his wet t-shirt, she picked up a long-sleeved gray sweater with the original tags still attached. The last item she grabbed was an ugly purse woven of two slabs of suede and a black leather thong, which her companion eyed with a lifted eyebrow and a quizzical glance at her. She paid for everything with Rachel's money, which seemed only fair, since it was her friend's fault she was having to buy clothes for a stranger. She knew Gavin couldn't foot the bill. If he'd been hiding a wallet anywhere on that magnificently nude body when she'd discovered him, she would have noticed.

The woman at the register rang up the items absently, her gaze glued to the wet man standing on the other side of the counter, his soaked t-shirt and shorts clearly highlighting his assets. He smiled when he caught her staring, and winked at her. She positively glowed under the impact of his smile.

While he was off changing, Gabrielle worked on unthreading the leather binding from the hideous purse. "Here," she said when he pushed back the dressing room curtain, and offered the thong to him along with a comb. "Want to pull back your hair?"

He gave her a smile similar to the one that had poleaxed the cashier, and used the gifts to slick back his damp mane and tie it into a ponytail. She'd been sure he would be used to wearing it that way, and she'd been sure he would look amazing. It was nice to be right on both counts, but she hadn't expected the tight ache that flared in her belly at the sight of him dressed and groomed and eyeing her with a quizzical stare. *I'm just hungry*, she tried to tell herself, but she knew better. What she hungered for wasn't food.

"How about dinner?" she said hastily. "You did mention you were starving."

Green eyes glinted with an expression she couldn't fathom as he gazed down at her. His nostrils flared, like a predator testing the air for the scent of prey. "Eating sounds good," was all he said, but her heart stuttered and then shifted into overdrive at the look that flashed briefly in his eyes. She was fairly certain he hadn't been thinking of food just then, either.

They found a Thai restaurant only a block away. It was almost full in spite of the rain, and it took some searching to find a table. Gabrielle ordered a spring roll and soup, and then watched the man across the table from her eat enough to feed a family of three. Her dinner companion's attention was focused solely on his food until two teenage girls with breasts the size of honeydew melons brushed by the table, talking loudly into flip phones lit with neon blue lights. His eyes immediately left his plate and he gazed after them in obvious fascination.

She nudged him discreetly with her foot. "Hey, lover boy," she said. "It's not polite to stare."

"Did you see how small they were?" he said, gaze still fixed on them.

Her jaw dropped. "If those are small, what do you call mine?"

"Haven't seen yours," he said absently, then, with more interest, turned back to her. "Does yours glow blue, too? Show me."

She stared at him, and then blushed as she pulled her phone from her purse and handed it over. "I thought you were checking out their breasts," she admitted.

"Those were nice, too. But not small," he remarked, turning the device over in his hand. "Impressive. Phones have certainly shrunk in size. How new is this?"

"Pretty new, but it's a basic model. I didn't want all the extra bells and whistles." She watched him press keys and poke around in the interface. "I gather that you like electronic gadgets?"

He grinned. "As much as I like women. You should see some of the things I have at home. Had at home." His grin faded and he stared down at the phone. Hand fisting around it, he asked slowly, "Do you mind if I call someone? I'd like to let my sister know I'm all right."

"Sure, go ahead. As long as it's in the U.S." He nodded and went to stand in a private corner near the restrooms while he called, a piece of cell phone etiquette she appreciated. She watched him smile as he greeted whoever answered, and the smile lit up his face. It was obvious he loved his sister. He spoke quickly, and then, after a pause to listen, his face grew grim. An argument broke out, not heated, but a definite disagreement. The conversation dragged on for a few minutes longer before he ended the call.

He was quiet and reserved when he returned to the table. An awkward silence settled between them, similar to the tentativeness of a first date. It was as if he didn't know her but suddenly wanted to, and it made him cautious. At one point, he took a deep breath and opened his mouth to say something, then closed it, and voiced nothing further until the bill came.

When the waitress placed it in front of him, he smiled at her with the warmth he seemed to give all women whose paths he crossed. He reached for his pocket automatically, then laid his hands slowly on the table. "Even if I still had my wallet, the credit cards would all be expired by now. Do you mind footing the bill?" he asked Gabrielle, his reluctance obvious.

"Why not? I had to dress you. Might as well feed you, too."

His eyes narrowed at the remark and he rose from the table. "You'll be reimbursed," he said stiffly. "I'll see to it." He stalked over to the door and waited, arms folded, while she settled the tab. *Oops. Good going, Gaby. Rub his nose in it, why don't you.*

The clouds had temporarily stopped pelting the streets with water, which made for a drier walk back to the hotel. An unconformable, chilly silence stretched between them, the temperature drastically lowered by Gavin's icy quiet. Gabrielle finally cracked under the strain. "Okay, I'm sorry. I knew it was stupid thing to say the minute I heard it come out of my mouth. Do me a favor and forget I was so rude."

"You weren't rude. Merely truthful." A gust of wind shook the trees above them, releasing a sudden shower of droplets onto his bare head. He lifted a hand to wipe the water from his face. "And I meant it. You'll be paid back."

"But—" She groped for words to explain. "In spite of what I said, I don't want to be paid back. To me, this evening was like a date. You're making me feel like it was a business transaction." It didn't seem necessary to tell him that someone else was footing the bill, anyway.

His chilly reserve faded. "A date? You want this to be a first date?" His voice dropped, and his next words burrowed under her clothes to caress her skin like questing fingers. "I'll bet you don't usually have three orgasms on a first date."

His tone and the sight of his chiseled face illuminated in the headlights of a passing car brought memories of that same face leaning down to kiss her neck, her breasts, her thighs, and she found herself floundering in a wet, hot sea of desire. She shivered and turned away. It had been quite clear to her all evening that most of the women he met couldn't help reacting to him. Her pride wouldn't let him see that she'd joined the ranks of his conquests, ready to stare dreamily into his eyes, or better yet, feel his body moving against her in a steady, rhythmic dance. With an effort, she squashed every trace of those last traitorous thoughts from her face. "Uh—no, I usually don't. So three's enough. How about if I drive you home now, wherever that is?"

He shook his head. "Didn't you hear the witch? I have to be back in that attic by the stroke of midnight or I'll be a statue forever. She doesn't make idle threats." He reached out to seize her arms, and she shivered again at the heated promise in his gaze. "You've paid for the pleasure of my company, so you might as well enjoy it. And I promise you—what I gave you this afternoon was only a taste of what I intend when we're alone again."

Though desire grew in her to a throbbing ache and she knew yielding to him was inevitable, she wanted to resist him for a little while, wanted to show him she would not immediately come running if he crooked a finger. Not like all the other woman he'd smiled at tonight. Though why it mattered, she couldn't have said. "N-no reason to go back to the hotel yet," she stammered. "You have about five hours left until midnight. How about if we head somewhere else until then?"

A small, satisfied smile curled his mouth, and he released her. He knew he'd won. "Wherever you like," he conceded, and strode beside her as she led the way to her car.

Neither of them had much to say as she drove out of the city and over the mountains to the urban sprawl beyond, a trip of over an hour on the rain-slicked curves. She focused on her driving in a desperate attempt to ignore the prickles of sexual awareness tingling through her, while her passenger sat and stared out the window, buried in thought. When they pulled into the parking lot of her destination, the biggest electronics warehouse she knew, it took a minute for him to rouse from his reverie. She waited for his reaction when he finally realized where they were, and was rewarded by a brilliant smile.

"Fry's," he said reverently. "You brought me to Fry's. I love this store."

She trailed after him as he sprang out of the car and trotted towards the front entrance. "I thought you might. I have a good friend who's as addicted to tech toys as you seem to be. This is the first place that idiot would want to go if rescued from a time warp."

He stopped in the doorway so abruptly she ran into him, and he turned to face her, his gaze dark and predatory. "Just how good of a friend is he? Are you lovers?"

Gavin's wolf-like stare swallowed her voice, and she stared back at him for a long minute before rediscovering it. "*She* is not my type," she managed finally. "I prefer men. As I'm sure you noticed."

His teeth flashed in a smile that wasn't at all reassuring. "Who is your current lover, then?"

"No one. Unless you count the man who seduced me in my hotel room today." She poked him in the chest. "Not that it's any of your business."

His smile faded and he studied her face, then bent slowly to kiss her. Even before their lips touched, she could feel her body warming in anticipation. She hadn't yet felt his mouth on hers, though it had visited almost every other part of her anatomy. A surprisingly fierce desire for his kiss shot through her like a jolt of electricity.

The embrace was wet and deep and thoroughly arousing. It was the kind of embrace that usually signals the end of foreplay and the beginning of fast and furious penetration. She expected such kisses when stark naked and already slick with sweat and desire. Not when in a public doorway where she couldn't follow up on its promises. She moaned.

He broke away from her and grinned, then turned without a word to lead the way inside. She followed him, cursing the effect he had on her. It wouldn't have surprised her if every male in the place could sense the pheromones pouring off her, could see how swollen and aching she was to finish what he'd started. All that reined in her anger at his cavalier ending of their kiss was the swelling at his groin and the pounding of his heart she'd felt before he pulled away. At least she had company in her frustration.

Soon after, she left him poring over a box of computer parts, discussing something called overclocking with a fellow customer. Gabrielle drifted to the book section and browsed the shelves, then found her way to the music and movies. She'd graduated to the television sets when he came looking for her, signaling he was ready to leave until his gaze fell on the bigger flat panel screens. His eyes widened, and he bent to study the specifications on the sales tickets. After ten minutes of waiting, she wandered off, shaking her head.

An hour later, he found her lounging near the cash registers as the store closed, reading a magazine she'd bought and eating a candy bar. His eyes were glazed and orgasmic.

"You take as long in here as my friend Rachel does," she commented. "You should meet her—you two would make a great couple."

His vision cleared and he turned his devastating gaze to her, favoring her with that smile that had melted waitresses and cashiers all evening. "I have met her," he admitted. "She's my sister. That was her I called on your cell phone at dinner."

It all clicked into place then. The strangely familiar features. The change in attitude after he'd made that phone call. The brother she'd never met, who had vanished without a trace a few months after she and Rachel had become friends. "You're her missing brother," she said in a strangled voice. "Oh, God. She sent me down here to screw her fucking *brother.*"

Coitus Interruptus

She ran outside into a driving rain, feeling angry and betrayed. How could Rachel do such a thing to her, and not tell her? Send her completely blind into this?

Footsteps splashed in the puddles behind her as he followed her like a shadow. "Gabrielle, wait!" he yelled. "She didn't know about the curse. Damn it, would you listen to me?"

She raced up to her car and groped for the keys, unable to find them inside the chaos of her purse. His hands reached from behind her to cover hers, steadying her shaking fingers. "She didn't know," he repeated firmly. "I asked her to send someone to scout the place. That's all I told her." He dropped his chin onto her head and pulled her against him. Cursing herself for a weak fool, she let him wrap his warmth around her. "The witch's spell doesn't let me give details. I only told her I needed someone she trusted to check out the attic room."

Ice cold rain pattered down on her, blocked only slightly by her raincoat and the warmth of his body pressing against her back. She desperately wanted to believe him. "You've never been out of that room. How did you talk to her?"

"My last visitor left me alone with her purse for a few hours. She had a cell phone."

She pushed him away and he reluctantly released her. Her groping fingers finally found the keys and she unlocked the door, then, after a slight hesitation, unlocked his as well. He walked with pantherlike grace to the other side of the car and slid inside, saying nothing as she shook the raindrops from her coat and tossed it into the back seat before joining him.

Her voice broke the silence abruptly, like the fall of a hammer, as she drove from the parking lot. "So what now?"

"Well," he said after a pause, "Rache said you took several weeks of vacation. I want you to spend them with me. In Santa Cruz."

Her car swerved abruptly into the next lane, and the hulking vehicle she cut off flashed its lights in an automotive middle finger. She cursed and brought them back to where they should be. "Why?" she asked bluntly. "I've found out what she needs to know."

"Because I want you to. You can stay for up to seventeen nights—that's the most the witch will allow. We can have some good times in seventeen nights."

She eyed him suspiciously. "Is this a curse-related thing? You have to screw me blind for seventeen nights or you'll turn into a toad?"

He shrugged. "It's an attraction-related thing. I like you, and if you leave, God knows who that witch will find for my next visitor. Someone ugly and armed with a whip, most likely." When her mouth curved, he added, "With bad body odor."

"I only booked the room for three nights," she protested.

"She'll extend it. She's used to guests who suddenly want to keep the room longer than they expected," he said confidently.

Her eyes met his, and her nipples leaped to attention when she saw the fire in his gaze. "We'll see," she said weakly, but he sensed her agreement. His smile wasn't triumphant, it was warm and full of promise, and he leaned forward to kiss her ear.

"You won't regret it. Keep your eyes on the road," he whispered, and unbuckled his seat belt.

His breath warmed her throat, and he nibbled at the base of her neck as his hands coaxed her sweater out of her jeans. Fingers grazed her side, then traveled slowly upwards to the plain, utilitarian bra she wore. She vowed to change to a lacier version the second she was reunited with her luggage. His fingers found the front hook and undid it with a simple flick, and her breasts eagerly nestled into his palms. One hand continued to caress them while the other focused on her fly, stroking her bared belly as he parted the zipper. Her foot accidentally pressed down on the accelerator as his finger slid under the edge of her thong. "Stop it!" she sputtered. "I'm going to wreck the car!"

"Pull over, then," he suggested, and tugged her jeans downward. Even as she swerved to the next lane she was raising her hips to accommodate him, and her thong and pants were down around her thighs as she pulled into the shadowy parking lot of an office complex, silent and emptied of its daytime crowds.

She turned off the engine and said, "I can't believe you did that. We could have died."

"There are worse things than death," he said, and found the knob to recline his seat, then hers, laying her out before him like a feast. Her body quivered, remembering the exquisite feeling of his hands and mouth on her that afternoon. Rachel had once said that her brother never bragged of his conquests, but no woman who'd ever had him had been the same afterwards. Gabrielle believed her friend now. She wanted him so badly she couldn't think, couldn't talk. No other man had ever affected her like this.

Her legs shifted and split apart in blatant invitation, prevented from spreading as wide as they wanted by wet, clutching denim. "You can't move," he noted, and bent to work her legs free.

The rain-dampened jeans were reluctant to slide off her skin, and took some coaxing. Her tiny thong went more easily. He stroked it appreciatively as he untangled it from her ankles. "Better?"

"Yes." Her voice was husky and unrecognizable. "Much better." Eyes closed, she felt him lean over her, and wondered where his touch would fall. A warm puff of breath caressed the inside of her knee, followed by tiny strokes of his tongue as he traveled slowly up her leg. The ache between her thighs grew to a hot, heavy throbbing in anticipation of his kisses, and she moaned when he passed it by with only a few tantalizing licks before moving on to her upper body.

Her breasts were taut and heavy with arousal as he pushed her sweater higher and exposed their curves to his gaze and the touch of his mouth. She cupped them in both hands and arched her back, offering them to him in a mute plea. His lips closed around a nipple and he suckled it to fullness, while his fingers drifted lower, lower, and lightly massaged the sweet, growing ache. The windows fogged as she panted and shifted restlessly in her seat.

"I want you in me," she whispered. His hand obeyed at once, curling two fingers to enter her with teasing slowness while his thumb continued to stroke its soft, erotic dance. A glow spread through her, and she could feel her legs start to tremble. "No, your cock in me."

He hesitated, then opened his fly with a quick flick of his fingers. His erection sprang free, more than ready to take over for his hands, and she saw it thrusting eagerly through the slit in his clothes as he settled back in his seat to lie next to her. "Come here, then. I don't fit under the steering wheel."

She surged from her seat and climbed onto him, straddling him awkwardly on the narrow seat. His hands slid up her thighs and he seized her hips, lifting her into position above the rigid flesh jutting above his pants.

"I haven't done this in a car since high school," she panted. Her folded legs settled to each side of him, and her hands locked around his raised arms. "Give it to me. Now."

He sheathed himself inside her with one smooth push, and his hard, hot erection completely filled her. A sense of fulfillment spread through her as he slowly slid in and out, the cloth of his pants rubbing against her as the two of them moved together, his arms flexing rhythmically as he helped her rise and fall in time to his strokes. Though she rode him, he was the one who set the pace, his hands gripping her waist and urging her faster, faster, as the friction of each stroke built her hunger into an intolerable heat. The aching glow inside her quickly flared and expanded into a cascade of rippling contractions. She moaned and clenched around him, and his hands slid inside her sweater to cup her breasts while he rocked with her.

The last of her spasms had barely faded when he carefully lifted her off him. His cock rose painfully stiff from the shadows between her legs. He tucked it back inside his fly and zipped it out of view.

There he was, completely dressed and ready to appear in public, while she crouched above him, disheveled and wearing nothing but skin from the waist down. *Good thing the windows are fogged up*, she thought blearily, and reached out to touch where he was still hard. "What about you? Doesn't seem fair that I should have all the fun."

He summoned a faint smile, but it was obvious he was in difficulties. "I'm fine."

"No, you're not. How about a little mouth-to-dick resuscitation?"

"No resuscitation needed, sweetheart. It's still alive and kicking." With a none-too-gentle shove, he urged her over to her side of the car. She barely avoided the steering wheel as she fell back in the driver's seat. "Let's go," he ordered, sitting up and readjusting the back of his seat. "We're done here."

In her experience, men never refused an offer like hers. Ever. "I think I should be insulted. Afraid I'll bite you?"

He turned his emerald eyes on her and his gaze was intense enough to set her afire all over again. "No," he said. "I'm afraid I wouldn't last more than a second with your lovely mouth on me."

She started the car and waited for the overloaded defroster to clear the windows while she struggled back into her wet jeans and returned her seat to a vertical angle. "That's one of the nicest things anyone has ever said to me," she finally said.

"Then all your previous male friends have been boneheads," was his frank answer, as he closed his eyes to signal that the conversation was over.

They drove in silence to the hotel and parked on the street in front. The rain had lessened to a light drizzle, almost a mist, that coated their faces with tiny droplets as they headed slowly up the sidewalk. He held the door for her, and she saw his jaw was clenched and his face grim as they entered the house.

The landlady was waiting for them in the foyer, nattily dressed in leather pants, angora sweater, and spike heels. "Have a nice time?" she asked, her mouth twisted in a slight smile.

"Wonderful," Gabrielle told her brightly. Her roommate merely favored the woman with a cold stare before silently shoving past her to climb the stairs. Did the witch stagger back before his shoulder actually brushed against her, as if an invisible barrier prevented him from touching her? Gabrielle was almost certain that was what her eyes saw. *That would explain why he doesn't try to choke the life out of her. I bet he's already tried. Several times.*

The woman's knowing gaze moved from his retreating form to her guest, and she smirked. "How many nights will you be staying, then?"

"What's the maximum stay again?"

The witch's lips curved into a cold smile. "He's very good, isn't he? Seventeen nights, payable in advance. No refunds if he freezes up earlier."

Fingers shaking from her sudden rage at those callous words, Gabrielle had to fumble in her purse for a long few moments before she pulled out a credit card. "Here. Seventeen nights then."

"You won't regret it." Their gazes locked, and Gabrielle felt a sudden thrumming in the eerie aura that filled the house. "Make sure I don't regret it, either, little girl." The witch's right hand lifted to trace a pattern on her guest's cheek, and the smile on her lips grew into something feral. "I'll bring the card up to you after I've run it through. Enjoy your stay."

Gabrielle was sure her shivers were visible. "For what I'm paying, I'd better," she mumbled, and fled upstairs.

Her roommate was waiting halfway up the first flight. "How much are you paying?" he asked curiously.

"No idea. But rooms with a view never come cheap. Particularly the kind of view your room has." She rubbed her arms and shivered again. "Why am I suddenly so cold?"

"What you need is to be warmed up," he said as they reached the top of the stairs and he opened the door to the attic. "I can take care of that for you." He stepped into their room, then turned to favor her with an exaggerated leer.

She remained standing where she was. "You know, I think I need a little alone time. You can have my nice, comfy bed tonight, and I'll go sleep somewhere with a less creepy landlady. See you in the morning."

"What?" He stared at her, then charged at the doorway. It stopped him cold, as if he'd hit a wall, and he grunted at the impact. A frustrated fist rose to pound on what appeared to be open air. "Gabrielle, don't even think of leaving yet! Get in here."

"You really can't come through that door without my help, can you?" She took a step toward him, and his fingers immediately closed around her wrist to pull her all the way inside with a savage jerk. "I wasn't going to leave," she assured him. "I just thought you deserved some punishment for not telling me you were Rachel's brother. It was supposed to be a joke."

"It wasn't funny." Seizing her by the shoulders, he stared down at her, face taut with anger and another emotion she couldn't identify. His grip on her tightened as if he wanted to shake her, and then his eyes dropped to her mouth. She saw the kiss coming, and eagerly rose to meet it.

His mouth was hard and angry at first, but then as she softened under him, he slowed his assault, cupping her face in his hands to taste her at a more leisurely pace. He kissed the corner of her mouth, then nibbled at her lower lip, his tongue flicking out in an invitation she willingly accepted. The kiss slowly reintensified into a hungry and demanding embrace, and he backed her to the wall, pressing tightly against her.

They had left the door wide open. There was a knock on the doorframe just as she reached the same stage of throbbing arousal he had tormented her with at Fry's. She moaned softly in frustration. Gavin raised his lips a bare half inch from hers and said, "Go away."

"I don't think so," the witch answered, and walked into the room on her stiletto heels. She held out a little clipboard with a credit card and printout attached. "I need a signature on this."

He didn't move, forcing Gabrielle to wiggle out from between him and the wall to take the offered clipboard. Once she'd worked her way free he turned to stare out the window, his gaze remote and inscrutable. She examined the bill and winced at the total before scribbling her name on the appropriate line.

"By the way, is there a convenience store nearby?" she asked. " I need to buy a few things. I wasn't expecting to stay so long."

The witch nodded and gave directions, but her gaze was speculative as her eyes flicked from Gabrielle to the man standing stiffly by the wall. A tiny furrow appeared in her forehead. Her heels clicked in a brisk staccato when she left, her head still turned to study the silent pair. Gavin didn't look away from the window even after she'd gone, and the room's atmosphere cooled as his gaze narrowed and his thoughts went to some distant and isolated place. It was clear he'd lost all interest in exploring Gabrielle's mouth. She sighed.

"There's still an hour until midnight," she pointed out. "We could go to an internet café, if you want. Or we could buy some wine and pick you up a newspaper."

"I think I'll stay here and take a shower," he said in a remote voice.

"Oh." Her disappointment was obvious even to her own ears, and she cringed. *Way to go, Gaby. Just because you can't stand the thought of leaving him behind with that horrid woman, you don't need to sound so... so clingy.*

He turned, refocusing on her with an effort. "There are other ways to pass the evening, if you like," he offered.

Puzzled he would suggest such a thing when his mind was obviously miles away, she eyed him suspiciously, and then the light dawned. "Oh, I see. If you think I might be interested in sex, you have to switch into stud mode, don't you? Because of the curse."

"Are you interested?" he countered, neither confirming nor denying what she'd said. That was confirmation enough for her.

If he could ignore the fires lit by his kisses before the landlady had burst in on them, then so could she. "No," she lied. "I'm going back out to get a few things we might need." She hesitated, then swallowed her pride. There was no way she was leaving him alone with that weirdo on the ground floor. "Please come? We'll be back before midnight. You don't want to stay here alone with the Halloween freak, do you?"

He studied her face. "Why? Are you worried about what she might want from me while you're gone? No one can touch me except my current mistress, and she knows that. Besides, she's already had her turn. How do you think I got cursed in the first place?"

"You mean you—and she—ew!"

His mouth twitched. "Don't look so horrified. Yes, we did. She came up to me in a bar in Silicon Valley, and after a lot of innuendos, offered to take me to a nice love nest she had in Santa Cruz. Next thing I knew, I was screwing her, she was chanting some bad poetry, and—here I am."

"But she has about as much sex appeal as a snake! In spite of the heels. You actually let her seduce you?"

He shrugged. "She's a good looking woman." A slight frown creased his forehead as memories resurfaced. "Even so, I wasn't attracted to her. At all. I knew something wasn't right from the start—her eyes were so empty—but I still went home with her. Do you suppose there's such a thing as a love charm?"

"Wouldn't surprise me, after everything else." She wrapped her hands around his arm. "Now I'm even more determined not to leave you behind. Come with me. Please?"

"It's that important to you?" At her nod, he said slowly, "Then I'll come." He walked with her through the doorway, then dropped back to follow several steps behind, a silent, almost chilly presence as they descended the stairs.

The witch was inevitably lurking by the front door, and she let them out without a word, her dark eyes fixed intently on them both. Gabrielle tried not to think of the image his story had conjured—a woman's body writhing with pleasure in his expert hands, taking what he had to offer even while coldly weaving the spell that would imprison him. The witch's eyebrow lifted at the sight of Gabrielle's hostile expression, and her questioning gaze followed them outside. Gavin didn't even acknowledge her existence as he brushed past.

Once in the car he reverted to his normal behavior, and Gabrielle had forgotten about his cold but brief reticence until they returned to the hotel, bags in hand, a few minutes short of midnight. There again he adopted a chilly reserve between the front sidewalk and their room. She was beginning to suspect he didn't want their landlady to know how well the two of them were getting along. The deception seemed a good idea to her. *The witch would probably toss me out on the sidewalk if she knew he had an ally. Without a refund, either.* She followed his lead and walked in silence until they reached the room.

Any thoughts of immediate and wild sex vanished when she saw the fatigue on his face as he collapsed on the bed, and she wondered how long it had been since he had last slept. Time spent as a statue didn't seem to count, from what he'd said. She dumped her purchases against the wall and went to brush her teeth, and when she finished she found he'd already stripped and fallen asleep under the blankets.

With his face completely relaxed, the resemblance to his sister was undeniable. He had the same sweeping cheekbones and thick black hair, though his nose was stronger, more aquiline, and his mouth was firmer. A dusting of beard sprinkled his cheeks. After staring down at him for a long, long time, she quietly showered and dressed for bed in her spare nightshirt, then, after a moment's consideration, put on her sexiest thong, a black scrap of lace.

When she slid into bed beside him, he rolled over immediately and gathered her into his arms, still breathing regularly and deeply. Nice reflex, she thought drowsily, and spooned herself against him for the night, back pressed to his chest. He was erect and hard, and fit nicely between her buttocks when she snuggled into him. She pulled the blankets over them both and fell asleep, feeling strangely safe and content.

❦

Gavin liked women; he always had. Big breasts, small breasts, tiny waists, wide hips with flesh to hold—each woman had her own special assets, and he loved exploring them all. There was nothing better than the taste of a woman hot and ready for his touch, or the feel of her shudders around his cock when she came.

Admittedly there had been many females in his bed, even before the witch had cursed him. None of them had ever affected him the way this one did. His sister had sent him help, as he'd asked, but he grimly wished he'd thought to tell her to send an ugly, unlikable friend. He knew he would never last all seventeen days with this one.

Gabrielle made a soft, sighing sound and pressed her bottom against him. His erection was already throbbing, demanding to be buried inside her, and he stirred restlessly. He hoped she wouldn't ask him to screw her. If she did, he would have to do as she asked, and it would all be over.

Usually he brought things to an end within a day or two. Rare was the visitor who tempted him to hold himself back. After a brief fling with his latest guest, he would let the orgasm come, and oblivion would hit. Then the world would shift and a new woman would be impaled on him. It was tantalizing at first. Who knew what the next armful of flesh would be like? Would she be fat, thin, sensuous, restrained? Few of them were restrained, actually. Restrained women didn't usually screw statues.

The longest he'd gone so far in this dance of endless partners was three days, and that had been near the beginning. Soon after, he'd decided *What's the use?* and then fallen into a routine of ending each interlude once he had some sleep and some food. It had seemed hopeless until this small woman came at his sister's request. How had Rachel known the right thing to do, with the little he'd told her? He hadn't been able to tell her much. His words had been restricted by the curse and by his pride.

Sometimes he could laugh about the curse. It was ridiculous when stated in bald terms. He had to keep each visitor happy, while keeping himself from being too happy. Simple as that. One ejaculation, and he would be stiff from head to toe until the next sex-starved lady happened along.

It had been a close thing, in the car. Gabrielle had demanded full pen-etration, and he'd had to give it to her, but in another minute she would have been embracing a frozen statue.

A friend of his sister wouldn't be stupid. She would figure out the terms of the curse, he was sure. He only hoped she would do it soon, before she asked him to go too far and he could no longer hold himself back. He wanted every one of those seventeen nights with her, even if she couldn't find the clues to freeing him. She was like a breath of fresh air in this stale, miserable place.

His bed partner shifted slightly away from him, her breath purring softly. He peeled the blankets back from them both to look her over, and the view was as lovely as he remembered. Her shirt had ridden up slightly, and the two rounded curves of her buttocks were bared to him. He cupped a palm over one, and stroked it. Her slight moan encouraged him, and his fingers wandered to the tiny band of elastic tracing the natural cleft there, hooked it, and slid it slowly down. The lace between the vee of her legs was damp. She was hot and ready, as she always was. He wondered if all her lovers had found her so easy to arouse.

He pulled her against him and reached around to touch her between her thighs with one hand, tease a nipple with the other. His knee coaxed her legs apart, and she moaned again, pressing her bottom into him. His cock immediately demanded to give her what she asked for, but he disregarded it. He had to, though there was nothing he'd like better.

"We bought some champagne," she reminded him sleepily. "Let's open it. I want to taste it on you."

He ignored her and licked the delicate area at the back of her neck, then bit down softly while gently massaging below her clit. The folds under his hand swelled into welcoming valleys.

"Okay, forget the champagne," she hissed, and twisted in his arms. Her mouth fell onto his chest, then kissed its way lower, until her breath tickled the base of his cock. He searched for the strength to push her away, and couldn't find it. His fingers, wet with her juices, seized her hair as her lips traveled like a brush of silk up his erection. Her tongue teasingly flicked the tip as she rolled him onto his back. He groaned and coaxed her head down, felt her open to take him into the hot, wet tunnel of her mouth. Licking and sucking, she swallowed him, then retreated until her lips barely kissed the encircling ridge near the tip. A blinding rush of blood and need and desire swept through him, and he pumped his hips to meet her as she descended again, and again. An orgasm hovered, ready to crash through him. All his control vanished with this woman. He felt like a clumsy teenager about to stain his pants.

He pushed her mouth away almost roughly, and sprang to his feet. *Alcohol. Alcohol will help.* "You're killing me, woman," he growled, and stalked over to the wall to search through their recent purchases.

She rose to her knees and stared after him. "Did I hurt you?" she asked finally.

He took a deep breath. "Hell, no." He found the bottle of champagne and pulled it out, beaded with condensation. It was still chilled. "We forgot to buy glasses."

"I thought we'd use the one in the bathroom."

He fetched the lone glass and speedily popped the cork, then tossed back three full measures of the champagne, regretting the waste. It was an unexpectedly nice little wine for a convenience store find, but then, this was Santa Cruz. Padding back to the bed with the last of the champagne in his glass, he gently pressed Gabrielle back onto the blankets. She went willingly, but the look in her eyes was puzzled and a tiny bit hurt. He wanted to reassure her that her technique had been very, very nice, but that would lead to explanations he couldn't give. She would have to figure it out on her own.

Tilting the glass slightly, he straddled her belly and poured a few fizzing drops onto her breasts. Her uncertainty vanished and she closed her eyes, gasping softly as he bent to suck and lick the wine away. The cold champagne beaded her nipples into taut buds, and he swirled his tongue around them, while stroking and kneading the sides of her breast with his free hand. Between licks and nibbles, he continued to sip the last of the drink, waiting for it to take effect. It had been over a decade since he'd had to rely on alcohol for staying power, but he knew his limits. Tonight, he needed it. Badly.

He was well fortified with wine when she reached up to take the glass from his hand. "My turn," she whispered. His breath caught and he dropped to his hands and knees above her, then turned a half circle to face her feet. With one languid hand she lifted the glass and bathed the sensitive tip of his cock in bubbles, then reached down to set the glass on the floor. His erection hung poised above her mouth, and drops of champagne fell onto her lips in a slow, gentle drip. She licked them away with a sensual swirl of her tongue, then pressed her palms against his buttocks and urged him down. He lowered himself carefully into her, letting her decide how deep and how fast to take him, and buried his face in the warmth between her legs.

Her lips closed around him, sucking and swirling in an imitation of her hot, wet cunt that made his blood pound. He moaned and barely held back from thrusting wildly into her face. Her fingers curled around him and stroked, cupped his sac. His reaction was immediate and hard—he felt a surging in him, restrained only by willpower and the slight slowing of the champagne. He focused on the taste and smell of the moist folds his tongue explored, the walls clutching and heaving around the three fingers he gave to her, the curly hairs where his cheek nestled. He took the pleasure she roused in him and poured it back into her, thrusting with fingers instead of cock, licking with tongue instead of giving her the friction of testicles against her sensitive skin. Her mouth fell from him as her opening swelled and widened in the final stages leading to orgasm, and he backed off slightly, wanting to hold her at the edge as long as he could.

She moaned, "Please! Please. Finish it." Her hands clutched his thighs, as if squeezing them would bring his head back down to the swollen pink of her aroused flesh. He stroked the folds slowly with his fingers and watched her ease away from an explosion, then caressed her with mouth and tongue and brought her back to a slow, deep, rippling orgasm that took her in a beautiful series of shudders and spasms. He twisted during the last of it so he could watch her face—he found nothing more erotic than a woman totally lost in the pleasure of her own body. Nothing.

He'd spent many nights in this bed, but none of them had been like this one. Gabrielle was insatiable and hungry and hot, and had a body a man would die to explore. He did explore it, everywhere, always pulling back before allowing himself to go too far. She tried several times to bring him satisfaction, but finally accepted that he wouldn't let her and took the pleasure he offered instead. It was many hours past midnight when the two of them fell into an exhausted sleep, his cock still aching and hard as a rock.

Butterfly Effect

When her eyes opened she knew it was late morning, or possibly lunchtime. The man beside her was sprawled on his back, the body that had pleasured her so thoroughly during the night now completely relaxed in sleep. She could see that his erection had finally faded, but she knew she'd left him in the lurch last night. He hadn't let her do anything about it, and no matter how she stroked him with lips or inner muscles, he'd held himself back. It was an amazing performance, but she didn't see the point. Why would he deny himself? Why would anyone, man or woman?

It had been the most mind-blowing night of sex she'd ever had. Hands down. If he'd wanted to impress her, he'd done a good job. Rachel had been right about one thing: After a night with Gavin, she was ruined for anyone else. What a lover. Even the most basic of positions was amazing with him. On all fours from behind, he knew exactly where and when to place and move his fingers while he thrust into her. Side to side, he had a trick of positioning her upper leg at an angle that made the slightest rub ecstasy. The man was good.

Maybe he hadn't come last night because he'd seen it all, done it all? Maybe he'd been slightly bored? She wasn't so experienced as to think she'd given him a memorable night, but she thought she'd performed well enough to satisfy any man. Why hadn't he been satisfied?

She slid from his grasp and staggered to the shower, where she spent long minutes letting the water pound on her while she considered strategies. This one-sided pleasure wasn't at all fair to him. He might be cursed to be her sex toy, but he deserved a little fun of his own.

And that was when it hit her. The clues had all been there, if she'd been smart enough to put them together before.

Stupid, stupid me. He'd said he was cursed to pleasure his mistress, and only his mistress. She'd taken that to mean other women were off-limits, but he'd meant more than that. He'd meant that, he, too, wasn't allowed release.

"That's twisted," she whispered, and shut off the shower. "That woman is really evil. Who'd do that to someone?"

A voice spoke from the other side of the filigreed screen. "I see you've figured it out."

"Ejaculation turns you back to stone. Am I right?"

"Yes." He stepped onto the tiles with her and curled his arms around her, pulling her back against his chest. "The witch was really unhappy when I resisted her daughter's advances. So she made me into a sex slave who can never have any fun of his own. One little orgasm, and I'm frozen. At least until the next lucky girl comes along."

"Her daughter was your first client, I'll bet," she said angrily. She really wanted to throttle that woman downstairs.

"Yes, she was the first to take me for a test drive, so to speak." He was surprisingly calm about it, and even sounded almost amused. "She would have done better to wait until I understood exactly what had been done to me. Her turn was one of the shortest."

"But—didn't she come back? I'd think the bitch would want lots of repeat visits." Her fingers curled, as if wrapping themselves around the neck of either the witch or her daughter.

"Magic doesn't work that way. Like the genie, remember? You get your one shot, or your three wishes, and then it has to be someone else who steps in to rub the—er—lamp."

Anger smoldered in her at what the woman and her daughter had done out of sheer selfishness. The daughter had known that a one night stand was all he offered, but her craving for more had warped his life into what it was now. He seemed to have put behind him his own anger and frustration at what she'd wrought, adopting an almost mocking view of things. Disrupting the balance he'd found would do him no good, so she buried her fury and attempted a lighthearted tone. "Well, on the positive side, the curse must have taught you some incredible staying power."

"True." After a pause, he spun her around and cupped her face in both hands. "Though not with you. I'm not sure I'll manage to last another day with you, much less until the end of your stay," he said roughly, and his mouth fell on hers, his erection brushing against her belly. Even as she melted into the soft, welcoming flush of desire his touch roused in her, she realized what she had to do.

Her hands rose to grasp his wrists and peel away the fingers cradling her jaw. His hold reluctantly loosened, and he watched through half-closed lids as she pulled away from the warm caress of his lips.

"I'll make it easier for you," she stated, retreating a step. "If you can't have fun, then neither can I. No more one-sided orgasms."

"None?" He reached out to trace a circle around her nipple with his index finger. "At all?"

"None," she repeated firmly, removing his hand. "Until the seventeenth night, when it no longer matters. Then we can both have some good times."

His mouth curled into a lazy, sensual smile. "Two weeks of foreplay? Sounds fun. Not easier, certainly, but fun."

"Uh, that wasn't what I meant. I was thinking more of long hikes in the mountains, going to good restaurants, watching movies—that kind of thing."

"Those, too," he agreed easily. "Unfortunately, you'll have to pay for it all."

"You can pay me back. Rache once told me you're still nice and flush, in spite of your disappearance. My conscience will have no problems presenting you with all the receipts, once you're out of here."

His face sobered and he lifted her chin with a finger so her eyes met his. "I will get out of here, Gabrielle. And when I do, you and my sister will be the first ones to know. That's a promise." He bent his head and very lightly brushed his lips to her mouth, and then her forehead, as if sealing a vow, then pushed her away. "Now, get out, unless you've changed your mind about the one-sided orgasms. I want a shower."

It took great will power to walk away from him, her imagination filled with images of wet, warm rivulets of water running in trails down his face and chest and dripping from their intertwined bodies while he thrust into her, over and over and over. She went and sat on the bed, her thoughts in turmoil.

As her best friend's brother, he deserved better than this. There had to be some way to help him. In all the fairy tales she remembered, it was always possible to break the spell if one knew how. Was there some way she could get the witch to tell her? Trick her into giving away the secret? Or... maybe...

On an impulse she knew the man showering not ten feet away would greatly dislike, she dug out her cell phone and pressed the redial button. There was only one ring before it was answered.

"Gavin! Don't hang up on me again, or I'll rip out your entrails. Where are you? Where can I meet you?" Rachel's familiar voice sounded desperate.

"It's me. Gabrielle."

"Gaby." A long, heavy sigh seeped from the speaker. "Are you okay? I'm not sure what I sent you into, but Gavin was angry with me for doing it. Though he asked me to, the cretin." Rachel was the only one she knew who used words like that in her everyday vocabulary. "Just what is happening down there?"

"You'll never believe me. But you have to anyway, because we need your help."

"Anything. Tell me what to do. There's no one in the world I love more than you two."

"I need you to go to a little shop in Aptos for me, and talk to the owner there." And she proceeded to explain why.

The shower had fallen silent, and so had the voice at the other end of the phone. "You're shitting me," her best friend said finally. "Please tell me this is a joke."

"Nope, it's not, and I have to go. Do it for me, please? Quickly?"

She didn't wait for a response, but ended the call as her roommate appeared from behind the screen, toweling his hair. There were no towels covering any other part of him, and she took a moment to appreciate the view in all its thrusting glory.

"Does your blood ever flow anywhere else?" she asked curiously.

"Not recently. Who was on the phone?"

"Work. Just letting them know I'd be gone longer than I thought," she explained with an innocent air.

"You're a lousy liar." He took the device from her and cycled through the menus to find the list of recent calls. "My sister? Did you have a nice girl-to-girl chat?"

"She's still mad at you for hanging up on her. Why did you leave her in the dark? She didn't know anything."

He walked over to the window and stared out at the dismally gray day. "I suppose she knows it all now."

"A lot of it. Enough to help us."

"Us? There's no us in this." He leaned his forehead against the glass, eyes closed. "It's just me and the curse, sweetheart. Your role is to enjoy a few weeks of purchased time and then get out. I wish you hadn't told her."

His words hurt her. A lot. He was the one who'd asked her to stay, and now he talked of purchased time? "Rachel deserves to know what happened to you. She loves you." *And she has a way of solving problems*, she thought to herself, but she said nothing of that. It was unlikely her idea would bear any fruit and she didn't want to get his hopes up.

"You think I want her to know how low I've fallen?" he asked fiercely. "Because there's nothing she can do about this. Nothing. That bitch downstairs has made this curse impossible to break."

"Oh, I don't know about that. Anything's possible." She studied him, then added innocently, "How do you break the curse, anyway?"

He looked at her then, his gaze shuttered. "You have to find the answer for yourself. I can't tell you. And I don't know for certain—I just have my suspicions."

"How about a hint?"

"You've been given hints. They're there, if you know to look for them," was all he would say.

An insistent knock shattered the silence, and she grimaced. Gavin returned behind the screen to dress as she went to unbolt the door. It was the witch, of course, hovering outside the doorway with a tray of croissants and coffee in her hands. "I see you're finally up," she noted with one of her twisted smiles. "What time will you be checking out today?"

Gabrielle seized the food. The sight and smell of it made her realize her stomach was as empty as the woman's eyes. "Why would I be checking out, when I've paid for sixteen more nights?" It was an effort to keep her voice level, when she longed to toss the coffee in the woman's face for all the twisted things she'd done to the man behind them. *Stay calm, Gaby. She can't suspect you're different from the others. You're supposed to know all about the curse already. You aren't supposed to be angry and shocked.*

The witch's smile faded and she stared at her guest with a cold, glittering gaze. "Most don't like staying in the same room with him, once he's refrozen."

"He's not refrozen yet. That would be a waste of his talents, wouldn't it?"

The odious woman's eyes flicked to the corner where Gavin was dressing and her eyebrows arched in surprise. She left without another word, closing the door behind her with the suspicion of a slam.

She hadn't expected him to last even one night with me? Interesting. She wondered how long he usually stayed around for his visitors.

When he emerged from the bathroom corner, he was wearing his pants of the night before and nothing else. His long hair hung loose to his shoulders, still damp from the shower. She'd left him most of the pastries, and he fell on them like a starving wolf. They disappeared with incredible speed while she watched in fascination, sipping her coffee. It was excellent coffee.

He smiled at her with his charm turned on full force once the last crumbs had vanished, apparently ready to ignore their previous conversation. She wasn't. "Since I've 'purchased' your time," she said coldly, "you're coming with me. I've been wanting to see the butterflies at Natural Bridges. You are going to take me there."

"It would be my pleasure," he agreed. "Give me a minute to finish getting dressed, and I'll drive you."

They ran the gauntlet of the witch's gaze as they crossed the foyer, and her cold eyes followed them, intent as those of a hunting falcon. Gabrielle found it difficult to summon even the pretense of a polite smile when she met the woman's stare. It was a relief to escape outside, away from both the house and its disquieting owner.

The little Toyota was parked only half a block away. Gavin took the keys and drove them easily through town, heading north as he followed Gabrielle's directions. The blocks slipped past and the unease she'd been feeling in the witch's presence faded. She relaxed, idly watching the man beside her. His hands on the wheel and his powerful body in control of her tiny car reminded her of when he was on her, in her, steering and controlling her with the same expert skill. Arousal stirred in her body as she watched him drive, and he somehow sensed her rising sexual tension. One hand came off the wheel to stroke her cheek, then traced the outline of her jaw. "What do you want?" he asked quietly. "You only have to ask."

She pushed him away. "I know. I paid for the privilege, as you so recently reminded me. Park here—that's the visitors' center."

He pulled up and turned off the engine. "I shouldn't have said it. You're the only one who didn't come up to the attic with that in mind."

"True. I came because your sister asked me to. Because you'd called her for help. So don't treat me like all those others."

Hand on the door, he said, "I haven't, almost since the beginning. You aren't at all like the others."

"What do you mean?" she asked suspiciously.

They exited the car and eyed each other across its roof. "Well," he said with a sudden grin, "you're beautiful. They weren't, or usually not. And you were startled when I came to life. They weren't. They were all friends of the witch's daughter, so they knew all the details of the curse."

"All the details? Like how to wake you up?"

"All the details."

"So I was the only one who climbed on top of you believing you were just a statue?" She winced.

His voice deepened, roughened. "I've regretted that I was asleep when you did. Tell me what I missed."

The words were like an electrical current pouring into her already wired body. "Not much. I'd barely started when you woke up," she said in a husky voice that sounded very little like her own. She wanted nothing more than to climb onto the hood in front of him and wrap her legs around him and feel his mouth and cock and fingers work her to ecstasy. The way he shifted uncomfortably told her he was thinking along similar lines.

Instead, they walked from the car without touching, in a silence broken only by the irregular murmur of the nearby sea. She kept her distance from him out of fear she would be arrested for indecent exposure if she let her hands stray. His reasons, she suspected, were similar.

There was a path leading from the visitors' center down into the butterfly grove, and they headed towards it. She'd been here before, but when they reached the bottom she knew at once that he hadn't. He stopped at the edge of the viewing platform, an arrested expression on his face as he absorbed the sight of hundreds of thousands of monarch butterflies floating above them and hanging from the eucalyptus trees in tightly packed clusters. Clouds of flitting wings wove a pattern of orange and black above their heads. The ranger on duty at the observation site warned them not to touch the creatures, and they stood obediently frozen when two or three at a time would drift down to land quietly on them, cling for a few moments, and then float upwards again.

"I knew monarchs wintered here," Gavin said finally, "but I pictured a few hundred perched in the trees. Nothing like this." He held out a finger patiently, and waited to see if one of the butterflies would choose to land on it. One did, almost immediately, and clung to his fingertip, wings sweeping up and down in a slow, steady pulse, like a heartbeat. Something squeezed in her chest as she watched him, dark lashes half closed as he held the creature up to encourage it to fly free, a small smile quirking the corners of his mouth. His green eyes and black hair were all wild Celt, as were his fair skin and the muscled outline of his shoulders under the jacket they'd found. She'd been with handsome men before, but none of them had attracted her so strongly. It wasn't only his looks and his smoldering sexuality. It was the way he had of appreciating the unique beauty of whatever held his attention, whether it was a woman in his bed or a fragile butterfly cupped in his hand.

The insect flicked its wings and launched upward, mingling with thousands of others to lose itself in the shift of colors. She strongly suspected she was like that butterfly, admired while in his hands, but just another fluttering satellite once she rejoined the faceless crowd.

They were both silent as they headed back to the car. Instead of unlocking it, he led her past it and down to the rocks by the ocean's shore, where they climbed onto a promontory of white, eroded stone jutting into the sea. The rock was wet from days of rain, and spray from the wind-chased waves dusted their faces.

Her cell phone rang, loud and clear. She pretended not to hear it over the sound of the surf, but Gavin recognized the ring tone it played, a snatch of the theme song from his sister's favorite movie. "That has to be Rachel," he stated, not even a question. "Answer it."

"Yes, boss." She dug the phone out of her purse. "Hey, Rache. Where are you?"

"In Aptos, at the store you suggested. They want to meet you, and him. Can you come now?"

"I don't think that's wise," she started to say, but the phone was snagged from her hand and Gavin cut into the conversation.

"Hello, sis," he said. "Tell me what you just said to your friend here."

The two of them fell into a discussion, and as it progressed, it became obvious his sister was asking for all kinds of details on his curse: how many women he'd had, how long he usually stayed unfrozen, whether he could touch women not involved in the spell. He answered her questions levelly, but Gabrielle could see how white his knuckles were. She grabbed the phone back.

"Hey, it's me," she said. "Enough is enough, okay? You win. We'll drive over there. See you in about twenty minutes." And she ended the conversation, before he could wrestle the phone away from her.

Wind swept in from the sea and pushed against them with invisible fists, smelling of brine and rain. Gavin stared out across the waves, his expression hooded. "There were people there with her. She says they might be able to help us break the spell."

"I know," she admitted. "I told her to talk to them. They're witches too, but nice ones." *Or one of them is, anyway. I've never even met the others.* She crossed her fingers, hoping she wasn't making a huge mistake.

The next gust brought a spattering of droplets that warned the weather was about to change. "Let's go see them, then," he said at last.

Toil and Trouble

They drove to Aptos in a heavy downpour. There were few tourists this time of year, and they easily found parking directly in front of the whimsical little shop that was their destination. It was just as Gabrielle remembered, its windows filled with displays of crystals, esoteric self-help books, and ceramic casts of mythical creatures. She'd stopped there after a day at the beach the previous summer, and after talking with the redheaded proprietress for awhile, the woman had mentioned she was a witch with her very own coven. At the time Gabrielle been amused and skeptical, but the past few days had made her a firm believer in such things. With luck, this witch and her coven would be the real thing and not some new age wannabes.

Rachel was waiting for them in the doorway, and there were three middle-aged women clustered around her, dressed in clothing that wouldn't have looked out of place in the sixties. There was a lot of flowing gauze and tinkling jewelry and long, curly hair. All three pairs of their interested eyes immediately locked on the man getting out of the car.

"Hello," he greeted the witches, smiling at each of them as if he'd never been more glad to meet anyone in his life, and they preened under his gaze like doves in heat. Then he turned to his sister and opened his arms. Rachel flew into them and hugged him tightly, ignoring the fact that she wasn't actually touching him. Her cheek rested several inches above his chest and her hands pressed the air at his back in an aborted embrace, as if he were coated with an invisible layer of ice that prevented any real contact. Though he'd explained that aspect of the curse on the phone and his sister had been forewarned, it still twisted Gabrielle's heart to see he truly couldn't hold any other woman, not even family.

"I knew you weren't dead. I knew it." Rachel's voice was husky with emotion.

He said nothing, merely held her as closely as the spell's barrier would allow. The others waited quietly for several moments before one of the older women cleared her throat and suggested, "How about if we go in out of the rain?"

The two siblings pulled apart, and Rachel summoned a smile. "Yes, let's. I don't want you to get soaking wet while I scold you."

"Scold me?" His eyes rested on her face as if she were a thing more precious to him than life, and a small smile hovered on his lips. "For what?"

The six of them entered the little shop, which was warm and welcoming after the chilly rain outside. "For telling me nothing," she answered. "For insisting that I send someone else to see what was wrong. For making me promise not to come myself."

Gabrielle spoke up then. "I don't think it was a problem you could have dealt with."

"There are few problems I can't deal with, Gaby." She thought about it for a moment, and blushed. "But in this case, you're probably right."

The trio of witches had sidled closer to encircle the lone man in their store. "So this is your brother?" one of them asked, the redhead from the earlier visit.

"Yes." Rachel sighed, and took her friend's arm to pull her aside. "It never ceases to surprise me how women trip all over themselves to fall at his feet," she confided in a low whisper. "It gets extremely tiring, believe me. Aren't these ladies old enough to know better?"

"It doesn't surprise me at all. It's hard to believe he's still single," Gabrielle commented, with an eye to the three women. They were talking animatedly with Gavin and he was laughing at whatever they'd said. The conversation hadn't turned difficult, yet.

Rachel shrugged. "I'm not. Our father wasn't a strong believer in the sanctity of marriage. He frequently screwed around, and everyone knew it. It almost broke Mom's heart." Her mouth curved in a wry smile. "Gavin inherited our father's wanderlust, but he saw what Mom went through. He'll never settle down, because if he did, it would be for keeps. Which means the chances of his someday saying the marriage vows are about zero."

Watching the four others engaging in a lighthearted flirtation, Gabrielle said slowly, "I understand now why you never introduced me to him."

Her friend's hand closed on her shoulder and turned her to meet a worried gaze. "Gaby. You're falling in love with him, aren't you?"

"Maybe." She lowered her eyes and tried to appear philosophical. "But I know what he is. I don't have any illusions, don't worry. I just want to get him out of that witch's hands."

"I wish I could give you some hope, but there's none," Rachel said sympathetically, and hugged her. "But if anyone ever won his heart, I would want it to be you."

The senior of the witches, a brunette with smile lines fanning from her eyes and mouth, signaled to all of them to follow, and led the way to the back of the store. The shop's owner locked the front door and reversed the Open sign. "It's not as if we'll be flooded with customers in this weather, anyway," she observed.

The room in the back was simply furnished, with a small altar against one wall decorated with shells and stones and a burning candle in the middle. Everyone sat in a circle on the floor and the witches dropped their flirtation to adopt a businesslike tone.

"From what we understand," the redhead said, "your curse is related to sexual activity."

"Yes," Gavin agreed stiffly.

He then recounted in cut and dried terms how he had first become a statue, and how he was awakened each time. They knew to ask leading questions when he reached areas he wasn't allowed to discuss. Gabrielle carefully kept her gaze fixed on the floor as he explained, so she wouldn't see her friend's expression when it was made clear exactly how each visitor brought him back to life.

When he mentioned the maximum stay of any of his guests, the witches stirred with interest. "Seventeen," the oldest of the women murmured. "A day short of eighteen."

"A powerful number, eighteen," the redhead agreed. "Divisible by six and nine and three. A day for significant events."

"Then it takes eighteen days to break the spell," stated the third witch, a tiny woman with thick black hair. "That's obvious. The question is, what are the parameters?"

"Eighteen days, with the same woman," said the shop's owner with assurance. "You need the time factor, the sacrificial factor, and the atonement factor. Every curse has all three. The eighteen days is the time factor. We've got the atonement, too—his obligation to serve every woman who comes to him. So what's the sacrificial?"

"No orgasms for him," Gabrielle said. They nodded, as if discussing tea cozies.

"Then I think I know how to break the spell," said the smallest witch slowly. "Just remain together for eighteen days, and be sure he has no orgasm until midnight of the last day. That should do the trick."

Rachel favored the women with an incredulous stare. "Seventeen days of Gavin and Gaby together with no sex? You need a reality check, ladies."

"We didn't say no sex, merely no ejaculation for him. If it's too difficult for a young thing such as Gabrielle to help with, maybe someone with more experience should step in?" the redhead suggested hopefully.

"Doesn't transfer," the oldest of the three pointed out gloomily. "Have to start over, wake him ourselves."

Their gazes fixed on Gavin, who smiled encouragingly back at them. "We'll give you the address, just in case," he said. "It would be nice to have some witches on my side for a change."

Rachel sighed. "I'll write it down for you. But let's hope it won't be necessary. I'd like my friend to free him, if she can."

"How? The landlady won't let anyone stay beyond seventeen nights," Gabrielle protested. "That means I have to leave the morning of the eighteenth day. Even if we last so long, how do we steal the rest of that final day?"

"We can build a barrier here to protect him," the redhead explained. "Bring him here and we'll raise wards around you both to keep you safe until midnight. Then the two of you can break the cycle."

"Break the cycle?" Five pairs of eyes looked at Gabrielle, and she blushed. "Right. Got it. Break the cycle."

"We'll come," Gavin assured them with a sideways glance at her, and reached out to caress her check lightly with his hand. His sister noted the gesture and her eyebrows shot up in surprise.

After exchanging phone numbers and addresses with the witches, they left the shop in a thoughtful mood. The rain had paused in its assault, and Gabrielle wandered down the sidewalk to gaze in the windows of the neighboring shops, allowing the siblings a little time to say goodbye. Gavin had decided it was best to part company with his sister here, to prevent the landlady from suspecting he had outside allies.

Rachel's words repeated like a liturgy in her head as she stared sightlessly at the store displays. *He'll never settle down, because if he did, it would be for keeps. Which means the chances of his someday saying the marriage vows are about zero.* And, *I wish I could give you some hope, but there's none.*

She didn't want marriage, at least not yet. But she did want some kind of longer term relationship with him. He was smart and amusing and incredibly gorgeous and the very devil in bed. Yes, she was falling in love with him. And yes, she knew how stupid that was.

She had fifteen—no, sixteen more days. That was more than he'd given any of his other visitors. She would have to be content with that.

He stopped beside his sister's car, a sporty silver two-door she must have purchased since his disappearance, and watched her search absently for her keys. It was obvious she had something to say to him, out of earshot of her waiting friend. Her hand fished a keychain from her purse and she pressed the car's remote. The vehicle beeped softly in welcome and unlocked its doors, but she made no move to get in.

"So," Rachel said finally. "What do you think of my best friend in all the world? A woman I would hate to see hurt in any way?"

He turned to look at Gabrielle, poised outside a souvenir shop, examining a rack of postcards in the window as if they were as rare and worthy of attention as she was. "I've never met anyone like her before. Why didn't you ever introduce us? You've known her for what—close to three years? I was still around for part of that."

"I wanted you to leave her alone. I've seen you break too many hearts." Her head rose, and she stared at him challengingly. "I still want you to leave her alone. She's special."

"That's a bit difficult right now," he reminded her. "And I know she's special. I'm not stupid. She's the most fascinating woman I've ever met." He left it at that. He couldn't tell his sister about the incredible sex, the incessant desire to drive himself into Gabrielle and feel her muscles rippling around him in a tight and intimate caress. Then there were the simpler pleasures—watching her face while she talked, feeling her body curled against him while she slept. His sister didn't need to know those things. Saying nothing further, he impassively returned Rachel's stare while she studied him.

"Don't hurt her," she said softly.

He had no intention of hurting her. He intended to take her to places she'd never been, and pain would play no part in it at all. With luck, in a few weeks they'd have their midnight rendezvous with the witches in Aptos, and the curse would be broken. Then all restraints would be lifted. He smiled at the thought as he watched his sister climb in her car and drive away.

Stairway to Heaven

It was after dusk when they returned to the hotel. The witch had opened the door and was standing on the front porch as the two of them came up the front walk. *She must live in that hallway—how else could she always be waiting for us every time we go in or out?* The look she gave them was burning and angry, and Gabrielle's eyebrow lifted as she nodded politely and followed her roommate up the stairs. The woman seemed openly hostile to her now, not just cold and unfriendly.

Safely in their attic nest with the door closed behind them, she asked Gavin, "What's with her? She glowers at me as if I were a child molester or something. I'm the one who should be glaring at her, not the other way around."

"She knows that you're different from the others, and it worries her," he said, and sat on the bed to remove his shoes with a contented sigh.

"How does she know? Because I'm taking you outside?"

He fell back on the covers and closed his eyes. "That, and because I'm still here."

His threadbare coat had fallen open to reveal the contours of his body, only slightly hidden by the clothing he wore. A suspiciously large lump under his fly told her that certain ideas weren't far from his mind. She took off her jacket and walked over to the window while she kicked off her shoes, reminding herself, *That erection doesn't mean he has the hots for you, girl. You're just the nearest piece of tail.*

"Yes, you're still here," she agreed. "That can't be so rare. It's only the second day. I would imagine most of your visitors want to enjoy your services for longer than that, once they've met you." She reached out a finger to touch the glass, cold and damp with condensation.

"You're forgetting something. Ultimately, I'm the one who decides how long each woman stays." His voice was warm and low. She turned to see that he had risen and was walking over to her with a fire in his eyes, one that promised heated encounters if she let him get too close. She tried to back away, but he trapped her against the window and seized her arms. "You're the only one I've wanted to stay awake for," he said, and, eyes fixed on her, he slid his fingers down to grasp her wrists, then raised them to pin them above her head with one hand.

He watched her while his free hand unzipped her skirt and allowed gravity to pull it to the floor. She stood wearing nothing but a scrap of lavender lace and a mohair sweater. The cold of the window pressed against her back and buttocks, and she hung suspended from his grip. Her eyes closed as his fingers teased the waistband of her thong, stroked the edges of the lace, then slid upward, high under the soft mohair, to encircle and pinch her right nipple. She moaned at the heat that seared through her. He continued to watch while he stroked her and held her prisoner, his hand wandering from nipple to groin and leaving hot, aching flesh wherever he touched.

She fought to free her hands and touch him back, but the corded muscles in his arms pinned her easily in place. Because of his strength she didn't have a chance of breaking free, but she instinctively struggled while his fingers dipped briefly inside her, then drew slow, leisurely circles over and under the lace of the thong. The cold behind her, the wet warmth he spread on her skin, the combination of her growing excitement and her primitive need to escape his imprisoning hands, grew into a deep, spreading ache that widened and flared into something frighteningly intense. He pressed his whole body against her, fingers coaxing her to welcome that growing orgasmic wave, while his mouth descended to her ear.

"You know you want this," he whispered, and his tongue followed his words inside the sensitive shell, tracing its spiral with tiny flicks of damp heat.

She climaxed in a mind-shattering explosion, her moans building to a cry that brought an answering groan from him. When she went limp, he released her wrists and pulled her to him, holding her tightly as if the contact would calm the pressure at his groin. She could feel him there, huge and insistent and throbbing painfully, his erection demanding its own release.

She didn't dare move—he was a man on the edge of losing his control, and she knew the slightest friction would erase all restraints and resolutions and he would take her, right there, against the wall. It sounded wonderful.

He inhaled shakily and pushed her back, eyes still afire and muscles tense. His stare raked her, from the one breast still exposed below her pushed-up sweater, to the hairs peeking around the lace of the displaced thong. Without a word, he turned away from her to head for the bathroom.

"What happened to the 'no orgasms for either of us' bit?" she managed to ask in a choked voice.

There was no response except the noise of the shower turning on. After several minutes no steam had risen from behind the screen, and she realized he was taking a cold shower. A wave of feminine pride surged over her, as satisfying in its way as the pleasure he'd given her. He knew exactly how to make her feel desirable and beautiful, and not only through the way he worshipped her body. Did he treat all women so well, or was she...? No. She remembered Rachel's warnings, and buried any hopes. *Consider this a one-night stand*, she told herself firmly. *Well, a seventeen-night stand.* Hearts could easily be lost in seventeen nights. She hoped hers wouldn't be too shredded when this was through.

That interlude by the window was the last time he dared touch her in a sexual way, though he smoldered with tension. So did she. The two of them were firecrackers whose fuses had been lit, and it was only a matter of time until the explosion. She sensed that the next time her clothes were off, nothing would hold him back.

Neither of them wanted to ruin this chance for his freedom. They adopted a careful wariness around each other, avoiding casual contact unless absolutely necessary. Dressing in front of each other was no longer an option, and sharing the bed was a thing of the past—Gavin now slept on the floor, in a sleeping bag they bought on the third day.

They did a lot of shopping at first. Rachel had given her brother a wallet that held his credit cards and driver's license, all of which she'd kept renewed and up to date. Gabrielle's opinion of her friend had increased exponentially at the sight of that wallet and what it implied. It showed that Rachel had never doubted her brother was still alive, and had done everything she could to keep his life intact.

After purchasing him a wardrobe, bedding, and some electronic toys he believed to be indispensable, their outings switched to movies and dinner, jogging on the beach, hikes in the hills. He drove her everywhere, and everywhere they went, women trailed after him in droves. He'd looked splendid in the buff and in second-hand clothes. Dressed in designer labels and a tailored coat, with hair carefully slicked back and caught in an aristocratic ponytail, he was irresistible.

Not one of those women who tripped over themselves to wait on him or ring up his tab or follow him through a door was ever ignored by him. They each received a smile that lit his face, as if they were each special and unique. He left a trail of warmed hearts and aching wombs in his wake, and Gabrielle was not immune, either. Even knowing what he was, she fell in love with him.

She couldn't help it. He, too, loved secondhand bookstores, the same oddball movies, and some of the same music. He even sat through a few chick flicks for her, and she returned the favor by watching some cinematic car chases with endless explosions of gunfire for him. They both enjoyed hiking, and talked easily about their pasts and futures while following trails between the coastal redwoods. On the seventeenth day, they fell into a discussion of their jobs. He told her of how his start-up had been on the verge of a buyout by a bigger firm, but then the witch had come and he'd never known how it turned out. It was Gabrielle's pleasure to bring him up to date.

"The buyout went through. Rache and your lawyer saw to that. They negotiated a sweet deal for you, too—you were given enough stock to wallpaper the Louvre."

He eyed her quizzically. "My sister told you this?"

She nodded. "My company was contracted to design the new logo after the buyout. You weren't around to okay my design, so Rachel handled it and explained why. We'd only recently become friends. I hadn't even known she had a brother." She paused at the top of the hill they'd climbed and stared down at the Pacific, its froth of whitecaps a reminder of past storms. "She said something else, too, that made no sense at the time. It does now."

"What did she say?" he asked, curious.

"That it was safe for me to visit the office now that you were gone." She turned to face him squarely. "We both know what she meant. She'd been trying to keep me from meeting you."

The simmering sexual tension between them boiled up and threatened to overflow as he gazed down at her. There was no hint on his face of the warm, inviting smile he gave other women. His eyes were burning and intense, and the hunger in them made all of her throb. "Wonder why," he growled, and turned to head farther up the path at a near run. He came nowhere within touching distance for the rest of the day.

That evening when they entered the old Victorian house, their hostess barred the steps and looked them over grimly. "This is your last night," she said coldly. "Make good use of it, since you've obviously wasted your other ones. Checkout is at ten."

"Thank you," Gabrielle answered politely and shoved past her, fingers curled and stiff from an overpowering desire to throttle the creature. She heard the witch muttering softly, and her body reacted to the inaudible words as it would to nails scraping on a blackboard.

When they reached their room, Gavin said grimly, "I think she was casting a spell on you. I don't know what it was, but it can't be good. Do you feel anything?"

"No." She tried focusing inside herself the way all those meditating monks did in the movies, with a complete lack of success. It would help if she knew what she was looking for. "I feel fine," she said with a shrug.

"Still. We need to be careful."

He didn't sleep at all that night. The hours crawled by, and he stayed completely dressed and far away from the bed, though from his silhouette as he paced back and forth she could see it wasn't due to lack of interest. He was within twenty-four hours of freedom, and no hormonal urges were going to rule him when his goal was so close. She dozed intermittently, her dreams filled with dark images and vague warnings.

An hour before dawn, he stopped his pacing to bend over her purse and pull out her cell phone. She heard him flip it open and said drowsily, "You're supposed to ask before you dig in a girl's purse. You might be attacked by a loose tampon or a tube of lipstick or something."

He straightened and walked a few steps closer to the bed. She felt his gaze on her, absorbing her mussed hair and her skin wrinkled with sleep marks, unflatteringly illuminated by the harsh light of the phone's display. "Do you know how beautiful you are?" he said with disarming irrelevance as he pulled out a crumpled business card and turned his attention to dialing. She blinked, speechless.

A sleepy female answered on the other end, and after he identified himself, she came awake, her voice immediately friendly and welcoming. It was the redheaded witch, whose name Gabrielle had never registered. Her roommate, of course, knew it. He briefly discussed what the harridan downstairs could and couldn't do, and then signed off with warm thanks.

She stretched and yawned. "Evelyn, huh? I didn't think she'd ever introduced herself."

"Of course she did," he said, surprised. "They all did."

"Of course they did," she sighed, "once they laid eyes on you."

He grinned and returned the phone to her purse. "She says we should be all right, but to wait until the last moment to check out. The less time there is for the old witch to hunt us down, the better."

The first hint of dawn was lightening the sky to silver when he came to settle on the bed and trail a finger down her cheek. "Gabrielle, I want to see you when this is over."

"You do?" she asked warily.

He ran a hand through her hair, rearranging the tousled strands. "I have some things I want to say to you, but they should wait until I know I'm free. I probably shouldn't make plans for a future when I don't know whether there will be one, yet."

She reached up to touch one corded arm, and slid her hand down its hard curves to his wrist. "There will be," she said confidently. "We'll beat that woman." *Plans for a future?* What did he mean? Her heart thrummed in her chest as he caught her wandering hand in his palm.

"We will," he agreed, and bent to brush her lips lightly with his before retreating from the bed.

At precisely ten o'clock, she opened their door, arms loaded with her suitcase and two weeks of assorted purchases. Gavin followed, a totebag of his acquired clothes in one hand. He'd told her he wanted his other hand free, just in case.

The witch was waiting for them on the narrow stairs, hand outstretched to block the way. "He's not leaving," she hissed. "He can't, and he knows it."

"Why can't he?" Gabrielle asked with matching hostility. "Give me one good reason."

"Because he's mine," the woman spat, almost desperately.

Gavin's eyes narrowed into angry green slits. "I belong to no one," he told her in a cold voice, and raised one powerful hand to grip her neck. Several inches from her throat it stopped abruptly, as if he'd run into a wall. The two of them glared at each other. "No one," he repeated, and with a visible effort, dropped his hand and strode purposefully down the stairs, not looking back. Gabrielle followed him, the skin between her shoulder blades prickling. She felt the witch's stare on her, and it was not a friendly one.

The older woman trailed behind them, muttering under her breath again, and the prickling sensation increased. Gabrielle was never more glad to see anyone than when they opened the front door to find three middle aged witches on the steps, dressed in jeans and sweaters, their necks hung with crystals and a trio of five-pointed stars.

"Gavin!" they chorused, but it was his companion's arms they seized. They chivvied the pair of them to the curb and loaded them into their car, ignoring Gabrielle's protests that she could drive separately. Evelyn pulled into the street with a squeal of tires and sped to Aptos without killing anyone, though the traffic laws she broke numbered in the dozens. They came to a screeching stop in front of the witches' shop, where they accidentally sprayed two waiting customers with water from the puddles left by an earlier rain. Evelyn gave the pair a hurried excuse and sent them on their way, while her friends escorted the fugitives into the back room.

The witches' hideaway had undergone a major redecoration. Chalked on the ground was a huge star in shades of brown and gold, and within its center pentagon, a futon had been laid out, covered with olive green sheets patterned with Celtic knots. Three pairs of hands urged Gabrielle and her companion inside, tossed them some food and bottled water, and then set to lighting the candles placed at the points of the star.

At first the women's movements were rushed, but once they sat and began to chant, the sense of hurry dropped away, as if time had no place in what they did. The words they recited wove a pattern of simple rhymes that set the air to humming, and throbbed against the skin. Then, as the voices fell silent, a golden pentagon of light flared up from the floor to enclose Gabrielle and Gavin in a sparkling, three-dimensional barrier.

"Whew," Evelyn said. "That should hold for now."

"For now," the older brunette echoed warningly. "We need to call in the big guns on this one. That woman is strong."

Evelyn turned to the pair inside the pentagon. "Sorry about the rush. We weren't planning to put you in there until close to midnight," she explained apologetically. "It isn't really equipped for a twelve-hour siege."

"What changed?" asked Gavin as he dropped to his knees on the futon, pulling Gabrielle down with him. She went willingly, happy to feel his touch again after days of abstinence. When she pressed against his side, his arm encircled her automatically as if she belonged there.

"We grossly underestimated her. We'd never heard of her, so we thought she would be small stuff. She wasn't. She isn't. Danielle, go call Eric, would you?"

The tiniest of the three witches, her black hair escaping into disorder from a loose ponytail, nodded and left the room.

"Have we put you in any danger?" Gavin asked immediately. "If so, tell us what we can do to help."

"Actually, the person most in danger is the woman beside you," the brunette said, her gaze worried. "She's lucky to be alive."

Agony and Ecstasy

Gabrielle's skin prickled as all the tiny hairs on her arms rose to attention at the witch's words. "What?"

"She was putting a death curse on you when you came out of the house," the woman explained. "We kept it off you until we could raise the wards, but it's still trying to get at you. Don't even think of setting a foot outside that star until the witch is taken care of."

She felt the arm around her tighten possessively, and Gavin said, his voice hard, "She won't."

"That's for sure," she agreed fervently.

"We couldn't do anything about the spells already on her, though," the brunette added. "I've never seen such a layered assortment of love charms and seduction glamours. Weeks' worth, I'd say. She really wanted you two to see some action."

"Love charms? On me?" she said slowly. Her gaze snapped to the man beside her, and he grinned.

"You don't need them," he assured her. "I'd have had just as tough a time keeping my hands off you without them, believe me."

She bit her lip. Two weeks was an incredibly long time to sustain such an aroused level of interest. Now that she knew how his interest had been maintained, her lingering delusions crumbled. "Of course," she agreed, and pulled away.

The two witches seated outside the barrier smiled and rose to their feet. "We'll leave you alone now. Call if you need anything—we'll be out in the shop all day," Evelyn said. "No one will enter without asking your permission," she added delicately, and the pair of them swept through the curtained doorway.

An uncomfortable silence crept into the room, heavy with unspoken thoughts and speculation. "Thirteen hours without a toilet is a really long time," Gabrielle finally said. She wouldn't look at him. A burning gaze induced by magic didn't have the attraction for her it had held a few minutes earlier.

"Not in your company," he answered.

"Get a grip, Gavin. You're only straining in your trousers because of the witch's love charms. Don't let her dictate your moves."

His arms snagged her again, and weak woman that she was, she let him hold her. "She's not dictating my moves," he said slowly and clearly, as if she were particularly stupid. "The only effect her charms are having is to destroy my self-control. Long, drawn-out lovemaking is not in the cards. So we'll sit, and we'll talk. Until I can have you." A hand cupped her chin and tilted her head back to meet his gaze. "And I will have you. The instant midnight strikes."

She stared into his eyes, and was lost. She groped for something to say that wouldn't reveal how her heart, or what was left of it, lay in his hand. "No toilet and no sex? I won't survive," she said at last.

"Me, either," he agreed, and raised his voice. "Evelyn? We have a problem here."

Evelyn's face peeked through the drape over the doorway. "Yes? What problem would that be?"

He waved a hand at the packages of food and the water bottles. "We're missing one small amenity."

"Handcuffs?" she asked brightly. Then, considering the matter, she said, "Oh. A chamberpot. Hmm. Let me think about this."

Her face vanished from between curtain and door and they heard voices conferring in the outer room. The conference went on for a very long time, which the waiting pair considered a bad sign.

When she popped back in again, it was to give a regretful shrug. "We'll have to lower the wards to bring anything inside. It's best to wait until our friends arrive, so they can help keep the curse off while we toss stuff to you and rebuild the wards. Any other requests while we're at it?"

"Right now, that's all I can think of," Gabrielle said, legs tightly crossed. "How long until your friends get here?"

"Only a few hours. By dinnertime at the latest. Maybe you shouldn't drink the water," she suggested, and returned to the shop.

Gavin laughed at Gabrielle's muttered curses. "She has a point."

"Yeah." She lay on her stomach on the futon and considered the pile of food. "There's not even a book to read."

Stretching out beside her, he wrapped one warm, comforting arm around her. "We can always sleep."

She snuggled against his chest and listened to the beating of his heart.

Its rhythm was steady and fast, faster than she'd expected. "Your heart doesn't sound like sleep is what you have in mind."

"I'm used to it by now," he said simply. "Who needs Viagra when they have you?"

Or a witch's spells, she thought.

The two of them lay quietly, and he began to talk. He told her stories of his childhood with Rachel, recounting some of the scrapes the two of them had fallen into. In spite of the seven-year gap between the siblings, they seemed to have been quite a pair. She smiled sleepily as he provided her with all kinds of blackmail material on his sister. Listening to the sound of his slowing voice and heartbeat, she relaxed in his arms and drifted into slumber.

A loud discussion outside their doorway awakened them several hours later, followed by a polite request to enter. The warm body wrapped around her gently untangled himself and sat up, calling, "Come in."

She was still rubbing her eyes and trying to remember where she was when seven people swept into the room. All were women but one—a thin, old man wearing poorly fitting slacks and a Hawaiian shirt. Three of the women they already knew, and the other three were young and stunningly beautiful. Gavin's connoisseur eye lit up in appreciation.

"Hello," he greeted them. "Have you come to help us, too?"

Evelyn gestured at the elderly man and the youngest of the newcomers. "Alisha and Eric will be entering the star with you. Don't do anything to make them step on the chalk, okay?"

Alisha held a round hand-thrown pot in her hands, fitted with a lid. "Okay, let's do this," she said in a business-like voice, but the sultry glance she sent Gavin's way was obvious to everyone. The other witches smothered smiles.

Five of the women moved to the points of the protective star, and quietly began to chant. A prickling chill washed over Gabrielle's skin, and then the elderly man stepped carefully over the lines to come hold onto her arm while his partner walked in, just as carefully, to set the pot at their feet. "This is just for emergencies," the witch explained. "You can each use the bathroom now, if you're quick."

As Eric's fingers closed around her wrist the shivering feeling eased a bit, but not completely, and he frowned. "I'm having trouble holding it off you," he said in a strained voice. "Let's hurry. And careful—stay off the chalk."

He escorted her to a small bathroom tucked in the back corner, and waited outside while she used the facilities, the door left cracked open at his request. "For my protection on you to be effective, there can't be any barriers between us," he explained. "Sorry, but it's how our magic works. Your modesty will have to suffer a bit."

She shrugged this aside—a door slightly ajar was nothing compared to the relief of finally seeing a toilet.

Once she and her roommate had finished in the bathroom and returned to their refuge, fresh candles were placed at the five points of the star. The witches lit the tapers and resumed chanting as Eric stepped back outside the chalked pattern. A faint golden shimmer rose up from the floor. It had grown to waist height when Gavin sucked in a deep breath, and fell to his knees. "Damn," he whispered, and then the wards snapped into place.

"Clever bitch," one of the witches said in disgust. "She snuck that one in while we focused on the death curse. What was it?"

"Lust spell." Eric's forehead wrinkled in a maze of creases. "Primitive but incredibly strong. Got both of them."

The man beside Gabrielle turned his head and pinned her in a gaze that roiled like an arctic sea, dark green and turbulent. She felt a hot, answering surge of heat as she met his stare. His face held no charming smile aimed at lowering her defenses. This was nothing but a raw male inflamed with desire, and her body knew it, responding by swelling and aching and generating a welcoming wetness ready to accommodate him. She, too, felt the pounding waves of desire, but she could see he was in worse shape. Lust gripped him completely, had driven away all traces of the civilized man she knew.

She took a step backwards as he rose to his feet. "Gavin," she said softly. "Can you fight it? You only have a few hours left."

He was past words and, in answer, reached forward to seize a fistful of her sweater and jerk her to him. She was aware of a soft susurration of voices and the rustling of seven departing bodies, but only dimly. At that moment, the world meant nothing to her. She could only think of the man whose hands were on her, roughly struggling with her clothes.

They were no longer wearable when he finished tearing them off her. Neither were his. The sizzling heat that had been inflaming both of them for weeks had swollen to a conflagration, and there was only one way to extinguish it. His erection throbbed, already glistening with a small droplet of semen. In the candlelight, his skin gleamed as if oiled, highlighting the sculpted muscles of his body and the planes of his face as he reached for her.

She knew from experience how expert and careful his lovemaking could be. That was a learned behavior, a far cry from the primitive instincts that drove him now. There would be no attempt at foreplay, which was fine with her. She didn't need it or want it. All she wanted was for him to sheath himself inside her.

Rough fingers gripped her and spun her around, then pushed her down to all fours. She cried out in pleasure as he slammed himself into her, deep and hard, and began thrusting with powerful strokes. Each stroke rocked her forward with its force and drove her arousal higher. She was aware of nothing but her nerve endings swollen and stimulated by the rough but steady friction and the intermittent rubbing of his sac against her. His hands gripped her waist, trapping her exactly where he wanted her, and his shouts crescendoed with hers into almost animal cries.

The sex was raw and fast. The pulsing fire of it flared and consumed them, and as she screamed in ecstasy he shoved into her in a final series of hard, possessive thrusts she recognized, thrusts that would end with a shudder and a sigh as if a bit of the soul had left his body.

And then he stiffened inside her, and around her. She felt his fingers change from warm flesh to curved metal arcs as the belly pressed against her froze and grew motionless, and the erection inside her altered from blood-swollen flesh to lifeless bronze. She screamed, not in pleasure this time, and pulled away from him. Reason returned as the witch's spell lost its hold, and she twisted to look at him, desperately hoping it wasn't true.

But it was. He was gone, frozen in the throes of his orgasm. He'd missed freedom by a matter of hours. And she'd let him do it.

They left her alone with his finely sculpted body for hours before they returned. When they came through the curtain they found Gabrielle wrapped in one of the futon's sheets, sarong style. Gavin was covered over like a piece of abandoned furniture. She'd first tried draping the other sheet around him like a cape, his face exposed, but she hadn't been able to leave him that way. The clenched jaw, the backflung head, the impassioned expression on his face were part of a private and intimate moment. She didn't want to share that moment with anyone.

She was huddled on the futon, leaning against him, when the seven of them came in and stood outside the chalked lines, their eyes filled with sympathy and compassion.

Redheaded Evelyn was the one who finally spoke. "Gabrielle, it will be all right."

She raised her head from her knees and blinked. "How? How could it possibly be all right? I can't wake him ever again—he told me that."

Eric nodded. "Of course. That would be typical. But—"

"I want to make that witch suffer," she interrupted fiercely, and rose to her feet, keeping one hand touching, always touching, the veiled statue beside her. "I want to beat her to a pulp."

"It's been taken care of," Evelyn reassured her, pushing straying strands of her auburn hair out of her face. "She won't be doing such things ever again, to anyone."

Gabrielle's hand froze where it rested on the sheet. "What do you mean?"

Five of the witches settled at the corners of the star, while the elderly man explained, "She broke many taboos when she put a death curse on you. Usually our hands are tied when dealing with a rogue witch—our magic is only to be used for good, you know. But when there's a death curse on the loose, all our restrictions are unbound."

"You killed her?" She eyed the seven of them. "I hated her, but—killing her in cold blood?"

The old man smiled gently. "We can't kill," he reassured her. "But we can take away a rogue's power, and her memories of doing harm. That we can do."

"I see." And she thought she did. The witch had been stripped of the power she'd worn like a shield, and left to molder in her old house, aware that she had once been capable of great things but not sure what they had been or how she had done them. Aware that she was nothing, now, compared to what she once was. She nodded. "That's a good punishment. But I still want to punch her in the face."

The five witches began chanting softly, as Eric said, "You can come out now. We've banished the death curse."

The glittering barrier shimmered, then receded to floor level and disappeared. She turned to the frozen man beside her and laid a hand on his shrouded shoulder. "Can you banish this curse, too?" She hated how pleading her voice sounded.

Evelyn stepped inside the star and wrapped her in a motherly hug. Tears immediately flooded her eyes, and she bit her lip to dam the flood.

"Courage, child. It's almost over. You know how this curse has to be broken," the redhead said softly. "Your friend has to complete the eighteen days."

"Then would one of you…" Gabrielle couldn't finish the phrase. She knew it was necessary, and she would trust these women with her life—she had, actually. But the thought of someone else completing the final moments of her lover's frozen ecstasy made her hands clench into fists.

"One of us?" The witch's brow furrowed. "That's right, you don't know. We asked the rogue about the exact terms of her curse, and we didn't have it quite right. All you had to do was remain with him for eighteen days. Statue or not. Those love charms and lust spells she put on you were acts of desperation—she hoped you'd walk away from him if he was frozen."

Hope stirred, as gently as a breath of air. "Then—if I'm here with him at midnight—"

"He'll awaken. Permanently. As long as you've never left his side."

Her mind raced back to all those times she'd gone out of the hotel to buy coffee, or a newspaper, or a bottle of wine. Each time she'd insisted that he come along. Each time.

"I was pretty far away from him in the electronics store, once," she remembered. "How far away is too far?"

"As long as there were no closed doors between you, you're okay. The distance doesn't matter." Laying a hand against the younger woman's cheek, the witch whispered, "Gabrielle, even if you've failed, one of us will help him. If not tonight, then eighteen days from tonight, he'll be free, I promise you. We know the parameters now."

With a reassuring smile, she turned to help her friends erase the chalked markings on the floor. Gabrielle stood as still as the statue beside her, one hand still on his arm, searching through all her memories of the weeks spent with him. Was it possible? Had they really never had a closed door between them? She couldn't think of a single time they'd been apart since she'd awakened him. Luck, a hatred for public restrooms, and a powerful attraction which she'd been silently cursing, had saved him. Because she couldn't stand not to be near him, he would be free at midnight.

"How much longer?" she asked. The wild flare of hope swelling in her vibrated in her voice.

Danielle consulted her watch. "Four hours."

In four hours, it would be over. At midnight, he would be free to return to his sister and his home, free to take up the reins of his life again. Though it would mean goodbye, she would finish this, see the last of the eighteen days to its end without asking for anything in return. Because she loved him.

"Then I have a favor to ask of you all," she said. And she explained what she wanted.

※⸙(ʊʊ)⸙※

At five minutes before midnight, the room had emptied of all living bodies but Gabrielle. Candles burned everywhere, on stands of wrought iron, hammered silver, and pewter, twisted and curled into fanciful shapes. New sheets of soft ivory satin covered the futon. Small tables arced in a semicircle around her, loaded with the foods Gavin had told her he liked: sushi, toasts slathered with tapenade, pastries from the awesome French bakery up the hill. Champagne sat in a bucket of ice at the head of the bed.

She'd washed up as best she could in the tiny shop bathroom (without closing the door), and she now wore a thin gauzy wrap the same color as the sheets, held by three ribbons tied across the chest. Evelyn had lent it to her, forcing her to revise her opinion that sex after age forty was a staid and boring thing. Underneath she wore nothing but a black lace garterbelt and silk stockings, also courtesy of Evelyn.

Her hands reached for the sheet draped over her lover, and she pulled it off slowly, as if unveiling a work of art. He was a work of art, the sculpted essence of passion and desire. Droplets of sweat patterned the bronze sheen of his forehead. His hair was mussed and tousled, and his eyes were clenched shut as he held his partner down and made her his with one final, timeless thrust. Gabrielle ran a hand down his arm, stroking the metallic contours of muscles taut with effort and unleashed need.

He was beautiful.

The numbers on the clock loaned by the witches advanced to 11:59. She knelt in front of him and backed up against him, lifting her robe to bare the skin of her thighs. She could feel his stiff, dead fingers close around her waist as she slid into position and buried him as deeply inside her as a man could reach, and waited.

※⸙(ʊʊ)⸙※

He floated in a blackness that wasn't truly sleep. There was no conscious thought, only roiling memories of lust and bodies rubbing together in the dark. His mind remembered nothing, was nothing but a tangled mass of emotions trapped in limbo while time drifted by like a leisurely river, winding its way past his feet as he crouched, frozen, in the darkness.

There was no awareness of what he was, or of what happened to him. There was only a dim knowledge that he had been in this place before, and would be here again, though one memory struggled to materialize out of the obliterating shadows. Hope, brought by a woman. A woman he wanted. Desired. Loved. He reached for the memory, but it faded back into the darkness.

Then warmth encircled him in a familiar grip, tightened and flexed around him in a pleasurable rhythm that called him to life with an irresistible sexual pull. He had arms again, a body again, and he found himself clutching the hips of some lusting female impaled on his cock. Memory returned in a flood that threatened to drown him even as an orgasm shook him, an orgasm meant for another woman he knew with sickening certainty he would never see again. He swore and pulled away from the stranger, closing his eyes, but not before he'd seen where he was—somewhere new, lit with a glut of candles illuminating a mockery of a lover's feast. The female who'd awakened him had been mostly covered in a silken wrap of some sort, and he had no idea if this new mistress was ugly or beautiful, but it didn't matter. He'd failed. The curse was not broken, and Gabrielle was gone.

"Oh, God, oh, God," he whispered, and he couldn't force his eyes open or spit out the words acknowledging the next woman he was doomed to please. He couldn't do this again. Even the magic that had always forced him to his feet to serve his latest mistress wasn't able to make him stir. It had no effect on him at all. As if…as if it wasn't even there.

His eyes snapped open. This time he recognized the room, in spite of the added candles and tables crowded with food. And he recognized the woman who'd turned to kneel in front of him.

Gabrielle.

She smiled uncertainly. His reaction hadn't been what she'd expected at all—that curse of revulsion as he pushed away from her had cut her to the core. "Gavin," she said, her voice tentative. "We did it. You're free now."

He took a deep, shuddering breath, and reached forward to seize her and pull her into his arms, not to kiss her as she expected, but merely to hold her so tightly her ribs creaked. "I thought you were gone."

And then she understood. He'd believed he was with some new woman, still under the witch's magic. Her arms wrapped around him as her heart swelled with a love she knew he neither wanted nor needed. Voice muffled by his chest, she said, "It turned out I only had to stay at your side for eighteen days. It didn't matter if you went metallic for part of it."

He was silent for a minute, and she knew his mind was searching through memories of all their outings over the past weeks. "So we broke the curse without even knowing the terms," he said at last. "Amazing."

His chokehold on her loosened, and his hands rose to cup her face. "Thank you. For everything. I can never, ever thank you enough." There was none of his usual charm as he gazed at her, only an intent, serious expression. She supposed he saw no need to waste his heart-tugging smiles on someone who was already snared.

She extricated herself from his arms and rose to her feet. "Rachel is my best friend. I couldn't leave her brother in the lurch."

A hand shot out to jerk her back down beside him, and the gaze he focused on her was burning and intense. "Look at me and tell me you only did this for my sister. Tell me I mean nothing to you."

A flare of anger saved her from the tears that threatened to shame her. "You want to hear it? You like to see your conquests grovel at your feet? Well, then. Gavin, I love you. I've never met a man like you before, and I never will again. Is that what you want to hear?"

"Yes," he said, and with a quick twist had her sprawled on the futon beneath him. "That's exactly what I want to hear." The kiss he gave her was as searing and possessive as the sex they'd shared that afternoon, though no love charms or spells still clouded his mind. She reacted to him as she always did, breasts taut with desire for the touch of his hand, thighs dewed with juices. His quick fingers had already untied the three virginal bows that fastened her robe, and he cupped her breasts in his palms as he deepened the kiss.

When his lips left hers to descend to a sensitive nipple, she breathed out, "Why?" as her hands dove into his hair.

At first he didn't answer, instead deliberately teasing her skin with light touches of tongue and teeth until her breasts were flushed and moist from his caresses. Then he lifted his head to regard her with solemn eyes the color of smoky jade. "Because I feel the same. I want you in my life for always, Gabrielle." He reached to brush a stray tendril of hair away from her face. "Have you ever thought about marriage?"

"Marriage?" She stared at him. "As in no more screwing anyone else?"

"Yes," he agreed. "That's the only kind I'd ever want. And I want that with you."

The warm glow kindled by his words was more satisfying than the arousal his touch had ignited, but she didn't allow either one free rein quite yet. Suspicion lingered that he was confusing relief at escaping the witch with stronger, more tender feelings. "I think you're getting carried away by your gratitude," she protested weakly.

He rose over her, straddling her, and placed his hands on her cheeks to shake her head gently. "You're an idiot," he said, amused. "I've never wanted a woman as badly as I want you. I want it all: your body, your company, your warmth beside me every morning when I wake up. I love you, Gaby, and I'm asking you to marry me. If you'll have me."

At last she allowed the joy and desire inside her to flare into full brilliance and she smiled up at him. "If I'll have you?" she echoed, her body screaming for his touch, her pulse racing at the sight of his possessive stare. "Oh, I'll have you all right. But only on one condition."

An answering smile lit his eyes as he lightly stroked a thumb across her lower lip. "And what might that be?"

"Screw me. Now. I've been waiting for you to wake up for *hours*."

He bowed, low, as if she were Aladdin and he newly released from the bottle. "Your wish is my command, mistress." And he set to his appointed task with an enthusiasm that made the wait well worthwhile.

About the Author:

R. Ellen Ferare has held a wide variety of jobs, but only two have lasted over the decades. One comes with an irrevocable clause of permanent employment. If you have kids, you know what job that is. The other is writing, which is her way of restoring balance and poverty to life when she wearies of a regular paycheck.

This is her first foray into the land of Secrets. If you enjoyed it, please visit her web site at www.r-ellenferare.com, or drop a line to r.ellen. ferare@gmail.com.

What You Wish For

❧☙

by Saskia Walker

To My Reader:

This magical tale was inspired by a magical place—Cornwall—the rugged, southwest peninsula of England. When I was a young girl, we used to visit the county often, and it set my imagination going with its myths, legends and its beautiful landscape. It was the sort of place you could imagine wishes coming true....

Wouldn't it be lovely if we could get what we wished for? My heroine, Lucy Chambers, does just that and I hope you'll enjoy her wishes coming true as much as she does.

Sweet dreams!

Chapter One

Cornwall, England

Lucy stirred in her sleep. She was in the dream again. Through the ether, he called her name. Recognition flooded her and she reached out for him.

Coiling under the open window, the midnight mist entered the room, wavering over her body. It wore the man's image, taking his form as it moved against her exposed skin, catching the warm, moist area between her thighs. It teased her gently, caressing her skin with the most intimate of lover's touches. Her body pulsated with desire. She fought through her slumber, moaning in response to his call, tangled in the sheets and clutching at the air.

He was there, she could sense him, but still she couldn't touch him or hear the words he whispered. She cried out when the physical experience embraced her body deeper still, her legs opening, her fingers clutching at the pillows.

Only the night witnessed the muted sounds of pleasure from her mouth when waves of pleasure climbed inside her, threatening to drown her in a tide of ecstasy. Finally, they rose to a peak, and then crashed over her whole body. She floated, weightless. As a final surge of spasms flowed through her inner sex, her body shuddered with release, and Lucy awoke.

She lay, stunned and confused, until she began to realize what it was, what had happened to her. She'd had an orgasm in her dream. Her thighs were damp and her body was still in the throes of orgasm, something that had never happened to her in her sleep. She closed her eyes tight against the familiar surroundings and tried to recapture the image of the mystic man that had brought her such pleasure. Only a vague shadow of him was discernible, but in that moment he had seemed so real, as real as the energy and heat that still flowed through her body.

Hitting the "off" switch on the wallpaper steamer, Lucy Chambers stepped back and tried to assess her progress. Energized by her latest nocturnal adventure, she'd been working on the office all day, but she only seemed to discover more layers of history as she went. Stripping the multiple layers of wallpaper felt a bit like going back in time, she mused.

The cottage was at least two hundred years old, she had known that when she bought it, although no one was sure of its exact build date—a fact that annoyed her immensely. She was tenacious in her quest for knowledge about the building and was hoping to discover some clue as she gradually renovated the place, over the next couple of years. The wallpaper in this room alone charted the past eighty or so years and as she worked, her mind traveled into the time when it had been new, wondering about who had lived there and why.

She turned to the window and stretched her aching limbs, yawning and watching as the sun lowered on the horizon. It was late evening but the midsummer light meant that she'd been able to make full use of the day. She rested her forearms on the windowsill, stuck her head out of the window and breathed deeply the heady scent of roses and honeysuckle that rose from below. The room overlooked the front garden, the old stone wall marking its perimeter, the wrought iron gate and the meandering slate path. It was a magical, lush garden with well-established shrubs, ferns and flowers, and a lawn that looked deep and luxurious enough to sleep on.

It was that fairytale quality that had made her fall in love with the place from the moment she saw it. It was also why she had decided to set up her office in that upstairs room, so she could spot her visitors arriving and enjoy the view while she worked. At the back of the house there was a large, unkempt vegetable garden and orchards that went on for acres, but it would be a long time before she got to grips with all of that. She had to get her office up and running as soon as possible. Her web clients wouldn't wait around for her to makeover her new house before they got their updates, and it was far too competitive a marketplace to take any risks.

Above her head a bird chirruped somewhere in the thatch. She craned her neck but couldn't spot its hiding place. That was another job for the list. The thatched roof needed an overhaul, and soon. The cottage was less than half a mile from the rugged Cornish coastline, and she'd have to be ready for the onslaught of the winter weather. However, right now it was time to wrap up for the day, eat, and run a bath. She'd earned it.

She sipped a large glass of chilled chardonnay while she zapped a meal in the microwave. She couldn't be happier, well, she almost couldn't. She smiled to herself. The cottage was a dream come true and her web design company was doing really well. She had almost everything she desired, but she had to admit that it would be nice to have someone to share it all with. A soul mate, a lover.

If only he were real, she mused.

Ever since she'd moved to Cornwall she'd felt the magic of the place, especially at night. The Cornish peninsula was a beautiful, wild and pagan land—a land of legends and myths, where even the mists rolling in from the sea seemed to whisper about the infinite possibility of dreams and magic. It had certainly brought magic into her life, and in the most unexpected ways, because since moving there Lucy felt she had become a true sensualist. She was experiencing recurrent erotic dreams about a mysterious stranger, dreams that left her with a heightened awareness of her own sexuality and desires—dreams that left her hankering for more.

They were just dreams, she reminded herself. But she'd heard her name being called the last time. That made it so much more real and every time she thought about it she felt restless with desire.

The sound of the phone ringing snapped her out of her reverie. Putting down her glass of Chardonnay, she reached for the receiver.

"Hello Lucy, it's Enid, just a quick call because I am about to go back on duty; how's it all going up there on the far moor?"

Enid's voice, mellow as honey, made her feel warm, at home. Enid was the local nurse and Lucy had met her during her first week of house-hunting in the area, the summer before. They'd struck up an immediate friendship in the queue at the post office. Enid was a rather eccentric type—Lucy had to admit—with a quaint, old-fashioned way about her. She had a rolling Cornish accent, the friendliest smile on the planet, and time for anyone.

Lucy had made friends easily with her new neighbors when she moved down from London, but it was Enid who'd taken time to get to know her and made Lucy feel part of the community. She kept her up to date with gossip, laughing with her when the going got tough with the house renovation.

"Enid, good to hear from you." Lucy sat down, the chair cushions springing up against her back, settling her in. She smiled. "It's going well. I've got to make serious strides though; my parents are visiting in a couple of months, and they've been really negative about me taking this on, on top of starting my own company, you know."

Enid gave a sympathetic sigh. "You've made some ambitious choices in life, but it's in you to do so."

"Yes, you could say that. I'm always ready for a challenge."

Enid hummed to herself happily on the other end of the line, like a doting aunt. "We like your spirit, Lucy, we welcome it."

"You'll have to come over and see the changes at the weekend. I think I've uncovered ten different wallpapers in the office alone."

"I'll look forward to it. I'm glad it's going so well; it will be good to see some life in the old place again." She paused. "Then all you'll need to do is meet the man of your dreams."

"Man of my dreams?" Lucy repeated, somewhat guiltily. She felt as if she'd been caught musing over her nocturnal escapades.

"You're a strong, independent young woman, but you still need some male attention, a passionate mate, a soul to share things with."

Lucy chuckled. "Tell me about it." She couldn't deny it. "Alas, I haven't met any dashing heroes on my trips to the local DIY merchants, and my social life is on hold."

"Oh it will happen, Lucy, it will happen."

Lucy chuckled again. Enid had a way of making her feel warm and sure about the world. "I'm still trying to find out when this place was built," she commented, glancing around as she spoke. "No one seems to know for sure."

"As you've probably noticed," Enid replied, "we Cornish encourage mysticism and vagueness, it makes us feel even more special than we already are... but I'm sure you'll find out soon enough."

"True. The local builder's merchants swore they know everything about the buildings in the area, but they haven't a clue about this one, although as you say they may just be keeping me in the dark. The librarian reckons the house is mid eighteenth-century though."

"You'll discover everything you need to know," Enid's tone grew mischievous, "even if you have to go back in time yourself to unearth the facts."

"Ha, you may be right." The joke really tickled Lucy. "I'd really love to know."

Enid hummed happily again. "And are you wearing your lucky locket?"

"Yes, I am." Lucy's fingers went to her collarbone, where the silver heart-shaped locket Enid had given her nestled. The thoughtful gift had surprised her, for inside it was a cropped photo she had taken of Lucy standing by the door of the house, early on in the renovation. It was a touching gift, and Enid had told her it would bring her luck throughout her task here.

"Good, good. Well, my dear, I've got to be on my way. Mrs. Davith needs one of my special teas or she won't rest tonight, but I'll call you soon for a proper chat and, meanwhile... sweet dreams."

Sweet dreams indeed, Lucy thought as she put down the phone. If only she knew. What would Enid make of her dreams about the man?

Knowing her, she'd get all mystic, her strange green eyes bright with humor, and then she'd relate some Cornish proverb about longing and need conjuring men from out of the ether. She chuckled aloud at the thought of it. There was a deep-rooted sense of time and history about parts of Cornwall though, a spiritual quality about the folk there. Even the local nurse seemed to trade more on herbal brews and old wives tales than modern medicine.

Lucy sighed. She was a single woman, that was the hard truth, and she had to have sex soon or otherwise she might lose her marbles. Even so, she couldn't help wondering if it was her desire to have the dream about the man that made it happen over and again. It was shortly after she'd moved into the cottage that he had first walked through her dreams, a tall, dark stranger who watched her with intense blue eyes and spoke to her with words that infuriatingly slipped away on the misty landscape that existed between them. Each night as she drifted off she wondered if the dream would occur again, and it was almost as if her prayers had been answered, because the dream was getting more frequent and more real.

She topped up her wine glass. She certainly wouldn't mind sharing her life with someone as sexy and enigmatic as he seemed to be. She took her glass and her stroganoff ready-meal into the sitting room, where some order had been established amongst the renovation chaos. Sitting down in the most comfortable armchair, she reflected on what the local librarian had told her about the place.

Whilst she hadn't been able to offer a full history, she'd said local legend told of a white witch who'd lived in the area years before the house was built, but that kind of story was rife in Cornwall. She'd also spoken about the mysterious disappearance of a traveler, a man rumored to be staying there. In particular, the disappearance captured her attention. It led Lucy to wonder about ghosts and haunting. Were her dreams actually visions of spirits? Was the man she saw the mysterious traveler who had disappeared?

She rather liked the idea of her new home being the stuff of possible legend, but she had to admit that her experiences were definitely more

dreamlike than waking visions of a spirit world. Figments of her imagination, most likely, she decided. She finished her supper and went to run
a bath.

Inevitably, thoughts of the man still wavered at the edge of her consciousness and that night, when she donned her favorite silk shortie PJ's
and slipped between the sheets, his image moved back into her conscious
mind. God, he was gorgeous, she thought and smiled into the darkness.
What an absolute hunk. And what a powerful orgasm. Could she bring it
on again? She'd certainly give it her best shot.

As she drifted into the arms of sleep, Lucy wished that she were drifting into the arms of her lover instead. The last thing she remembered was
thinking that she really ought to get up and close the window because the
sea mist seemed, eerily, to be everywhere that night.

⚜

When Enid got home from her visits that evening, Wellington, her cat,
was waiting expectantly.

"Mrs. Davith rests well," she informed him. "And Lucy dreams of her
man every night." She put down her bag of tricks, poured a large sherry,
and sat down in her rocking chair.

Wellington followed her over and jumped onto her lap with a litheness
defying his attitude and size.

"So, what do we think, Wellington, do we think Lucy's ready?"

Wellington blinked at her, his gaze steadfast.

"Yes, I thought so too."

The cat settled into her lap, curling his limbs under him.

She reached for her trinket box and pulled out a handful of beads.
"Each bead is a soul in time," she whispered.

The cat looked on judiciously.

She selected two beads—a pearl with a rosy sheen, and a rugged piece of
dark jet—and strung them on a thread, knotting them together securely.

Lifting her glass, she curled the tethered beads into the palm of her
hand and smiled at Wellington. "Here's to the future," she whispered.

Wellington blinked and purred.

⚜

Lucy's dream was vivid. Even though it was weighted with sleep, her
skin hummed with anticipation. She moved beyond it and floated through

the ether. She felt as if she were traveling, seeking him again.

Rolling restlessly, she wandered in the mists of her dream world, her body alive with sensation, tossed from need to want and cast up on the shores of desire. Breathless, she sensed his presence moving closer through the swirling mists. She clutched at the pillows, desperate for release.

He was tantalizingly near, his handsome face looming over her, his eyes wild as he watched her. His breath moved across her skin, drawing a moan from her lips. A voice murmured her name. She reached for him, but he drew back, as if leading her. She struggled to follow, her will to find him fighting leaden limbs to reach out. She saw him walking ahead of her, reached out and touched his back. He stopped walking, began to turn. Then, through the mists, she heard voices in conversation.

There were voices on the stairs.

She wakened with a start, pushing back the sheet and sitting bolt upright. There was someone in the house. *Burglars!* Her heart rate shot up instantly, the blood rushing in her ears. She strained to hear, leaning forward on the bed. Sure enough, she heard a floorboard creak. Then, incredibly, a voice boomed out.

"Be on your way, Nathaniel, and thank you for your hospitality. I'll send you word of my whereabouts when I'm settled."

What in hell's name was going on? The back of her neck prickled with tension, the palms of her hands fast growing damp. She pushed back her hair and tried to make sense of what she was hearing. It had to be burglars, and there seemed to be at least two men, but they were chuckling and talking to each other in a very strange way.

What the hell were they doing in her house?

She climbed out of bed and crept across the floor so that she could hear more clearly. Moonlight carved a passage across the room and she went to step past it but froze when a board beneath her foot creaked. *Dammit.* She stopped dead.

"Five years will turn over soon enough, and I'll do all I can to clear your name in preparation for your return. Until then, safe travel aboard the *Gloriana*. Rest well and take this purse." The sound of disagreement followed. "Take it, please. Take these few small gifts to speed your passage. You'll be comfortable here, oh and I left you a flask of rum and some food to be sure of it." There was laughter and a mumbled thank you. "Just be clear of the house before mid-morn. The servant girl comes up from the town and I didn't have time to tell her anyone would be taking rest here."

"Aye," came the reply. "I'll need to be on the lookout for the Gloriana by then."

The sound of mutual backslapping reached her, and then one set of footsteps faded away down the stairs. One of them was staying, that much was clear. Silently, with her breath trapped in her lungs, she waited. Downstairs, she heard the front door closing. Then another floorboard on the landing creaked and the door to her bedroom was rattled and pushed wide open.

A figure stepped into the room and into the wedge of moonlight that spilled from the window, revealing the intruder to her startled gaze. *It was him.*

The man from her dreams, tall and fierce looking, but this time he looked solid, real, and he appeared to have a weapon hanging from his belt. A sword? *Could it be that he had a sword?*

Burglars didn't run around chatting at the top of their voices and wearing swords, surely not–not even in eccentric old Cornwall. She had to be dreaming. Yes, she realized with a sudden sense of dizzy relief.

I'm dreaming about him again, right?

Nevertheless, caution had automatically taken hold of her and she stepped back into the darkness against the wall, but not quick enough and not before the intruder caught sight of her. He stared at her and then after a silent moment, he laughed, heartily. He dropped a bundle from his shoulder to the floor by his feet, and then strode past her toward the window, presumably looking for his partner in crime.

"Well, Nathaniel," he said, as if voicing his thoughts to the darkness below. "Old friend, you are a true gentleman. I didn't realize that you'd be seeing to my wish for a wench for the night."

"A wench?" Lucy repeated, astonished, then jumped at the sound of her own voice.

He turned back to her and walked over. Snaking his arm around her waist, he pulled her up against him. Lucy swore in disbelief when her feet left the floor. He was well over six feet tall and very strong.

He spun her into the light to look her over, the moonlight flashing on his teeth as he smiled. "Oh yes, and you are a pretty wench aren't you? You'll be a fine way to pass my last night on English soil."

Yup. I'm dreaming. Like last time only... better.

"Well, I guess I should thank you," she stumbled, feeling rather oddly as if she was in some kind of role-playing game. Was that what dreams were like, when you were actually in them? And since when did she have the power of analysis in the depths of slumber? She pushed the thoughts away and tried to get into her role. Because she didn't want the dream to escape, now did she? If she thought about it too much she might just wake up. And lose the glorious feeling of those powerful arms around her—heaven forbid. "I've been called pretty before, but never a wench."

He gave a deep belly laugh. She felt it rumble right through her body, crushed as she was against him. God, he was strong.

"What should I call you then, lass?"

"Lucy," she managed to mumble, before he buried his face in her hair, breathing deeply of her scent.

"Mm, you smell good, Lucy, like damsons."

"It's probably my shampoo or bubble bath."

"Double what?" he asked as he leaned over, taking her with him, and snatched up a small, leather-covered object from somewhere behind her.

"Bath."

It struck her as odd because, glancing down, she didn't recognize the small table standing there by the bed. In fact, the bed looked different, too. The dream had changed everything in her room. And the conversation seemed odd, surreal. But it would, wouldn't it? That's what dreams are like, she kept reminding herself.

The object he had lifted was some kind of bottle, and he uncorked it with his teeth and took a long drink. He stared at her thoughtfully as he swallowed. The heady aroma of potent rum flared through her nostrils. It was so real.

He offered the bottle and she took it tentatively.

The pungent alcohol swirled into her mouth. She swallowed.

Hang on a minute. If he thought the other guy had arranged for her to be there, did that mean she was supposed to be like... like a woman of the night, a prostitute even? Lucy laughed aloud at the idea, nearly choking on her rum.

"Too strong for you?"

"No, I, um, it's fine." Could she really play the part for him?

He turned away from her and pulled the curtains wide open, flooding the room with moonlight. When he turned back, he looked her up and down and nodded approvingly. He stroked his hands over her bare shoulders and then weighed her silk covered breasts quite deliberately in strong, warm hands, drawing her breath from her lungs when his thumbs ran over her nipples.

He chuckled and began to unbutton his coat, a thigh-length number made of heavy felt and leather. The shirt he was wearing clung to the heat of his body. Well cut pants and knee-high boots showed off his long, strong legs. She couldn't help staring at the strange clothing he was wearing. Especially the pants. Tightly fitting, they revealed every bit of him, including the rather impressive bulge at his groin. The fabric looked like soft suede, and it was tucked down into his rough leather boots. In contrast to his heavy jacket, the shirt he wore beneath it was soft cotton, and it flowed over his powerful chest, at once hiding yet revealing his physical power.

"You're like a warrior or something," she commented, barely realizing that she was speaking her thoughts aloud.

"No warrior, although I've had a few tussles in my time."

He said it quite suggestively, and she smiled. She wouldn't mind tussling with him, perhaps she could play the woman of the night, the wench. He didn't seem to mind her eyeing him while he stripped, and with the Dutch courage from the rum, Lucy began to relax and enjoy the dream. Why the hell not? Maybe it would go all the way, like it had the last time. But she hadn't remembered any details like this, no, and she prayed she would remember it all when she awoke this time.

As soon as he had taken off his jacket, he pulled the shirt off and dumped them both on the floor. Oh yes, she thought, her eyes growing wide as she watched him strip—please let me remember every detail. He was well built, his shoulders large and powerful, his belly hard with muscle. He strode toward the bed and grabbed her wrist as he passed, pulling her down beside him. He was strong, and he obviously wasn't used to taking "no" for an answer. He pulled her into his lap.

Lucy was spellbound.

The man grinned again and stroked his hand over her cheek.

This was turning out to be one magic dream.

"Now, what manner of under garments are these?" he asked, staring, quite perturbed, at her shortie PJ's. "And how does a man get rid of them?" With one finger under the spaghetti strap at her shoulder, he shifted the silk chemise around, watching as it moved over her breasts, still peaked from his earlier touch.

"Up," she murmured, gesturing toward the hem of the top, breathless with anticipation to see what might happen next.

He didn't waste a moment. He stripped the chemise over her head and then tugged at the waistband on her shorts while eyeing her bared breasts appreciatively. His eyebrows were up and he had a half smile on his face as if now amused by what she was wearing.

"Gone, and now for the drawers."

Drawers? That tickled her to no end, and she felt laughter rising inside her.

He tugged her shorts off, jostling her weight easily on his lap, and she wriggled to assist in their removal. The bulge of his cock brushed against her leg. Not only was he as hard as steel and his hands sure and knowing, but his gaze was so hot that she felt restless with tension. He began exploring her more demandingly when she panted against his ear. His hands molded and stroked her breasts. His cock was hard against her thigh. The atmosphere between them crackled with anticipation. Her entire body was pounding with desire.

"What should I call you?" she asked, breathlessly.

"Cullen, and if you hear bad things said against me when I've gone on the morrow, don't listen, Lucy, for I am a wrongly dishonored man."

"Oh, have you been a naughty boy?" she remarked, going with the flow.

His eyebrow quirked and he looked at her, as if he was amused by her remark. "Not as 'naughty' as they might have you believe," he said, looking at her, as he stroked his hand over the soft down of her pubis.

He lifted and rolled her onto her back on the bed with ease, his large hands roving over her with the expertise of a sexual connoisseur, seeking out the most tender and responsive places to touch her. She was helpless under the assault. She'd never met a man as sexually confident and demanding as Cullen. Within moments, his hands were inside her thighs and he stroked the length of them, as if admiring the softness of the skin there, before he probed into the hot niche at their juncture. Fire swept through her and down, to meet his fingers where they stroked her intimate places to the melting point. He was so blatant and demanding. She hummed her approval. He kept looking at her to observe her reactions, while he stroked her with strong, firm fingers.

"Ah, sweet heaven, you are inviting, and ready for me, I see."

"It's hardly surprising," she managed to mumble, before she was brought short from further comment when his thumb met the hot kernel of her clit and roved back and forth over it, relentlessly tormenting her. With his free hand he pushed two fingers inside her, where her sex clenched and tightened, aching with need.

Oh, but he was torturing her.

He withdrew his hand, strands of liquid warmth from inside her clinging to his fingers. He growled and took them to his mouth to taste her. "Ah, you taste good, wench." His eyes glittered as he looked down at her spread legs.

In ordinary circumstances, she might have had a twinge of embarrassment at such a forthright sexual approach from a stranger delving between her legs. But the combination of extreme sexual arousal and the surreal dream-quality of the whole encounter negated any such misgivings. She was hot for it, she was writhing on the bed, her entire body on fire with sensation. She beckoned him closer still.

"Heh, that's good," he said, taking her invitation.

She swore aloud when he bent his head and she felt the warm lap of his tongue stroking firmly over her clit. The inflamed morsel of flesh reared up in demand for contact and then throbbed unbearably. His tongue thrashed against the sensitive ring of flesh that opened into her sex. She moaned and arched and rested her hands around his head, drawing him closer. She could hear his hungry gulps as he devoured her. She grew frantic as the sensation built towards its peak. His teeth latched over the stiff little organ, his tongue lapping at it from beneath. The riot of nerves condensed, then peaked and burst. Her hips bucked, a deep, long shudder coursing through her body.

"Oh my, you are a lusty sort, Lucy love," he commented a moment later, while she was still battling to regain her breathing pattern.

She barely registered his remark, because he had knelt on the bed between her legs and she was clearly aware of the very impressive erection he had pulled out of the pants he was wearing. This was crazy. She'd never had a dream this real, well, not that she remembered. My God, if only all her dreams were like this! She felt the smooth, rock-hard head of his cock probing her entrance. He'd already sent her into one red-hot orgasm, and she'd barely recovered. She trembled, melting into the pillows, staring at his fabulous body and the cock that was going to feel so, so good.

Her hips arched to take him and she reached up to his shoulders, and yes, when he thrust inside her, it felt like the answer for everything her body craved, his shaft pushing high up inside her and touching her deepest places. A cry of ecstasy and intoxicated, joyful laughter escaped her open mouth. He kissed her, his tongue pushing into her mouth, bringing her the taste of her own desire, and she grabbed at him, her hands alive to the feel of hard muscle under them, her whole being wanting to clutch and cling to his magnificent body.

"Come on, my pretty, let me at you." He grasped her buttocks into his hands, lifting her easily from the bed and angling her hips as he lifted her higher still, thrusting hard and fast in a rolling rhythm.

"'Let me at you?' Christ, aren't you deep enough?" Again, she laughed, the sound escaping her in an exalted victory cry. She had never been probed so deeply and so thoroughly before, and Cullen's stamina truly was the stuff of dreams.

He joined her obvious pleasure. "Oh, yes, I love a wench who can take it, you're a supple little thing, aren't you? Can't remember the last time I enjoyed riding a woman like this." Even as he said the words he pulled her roving hands together and latched them over her head in one mighty fist, taking full control of her body.

She bit her lip, cursing under her breath, her head rolling as she was thoroughly possessed and submitted to his thorough probing. Her throat was burning, her entire body locked into the experience. He began to buck at the hips, his cock swelling even more as it rode up against her cervix, jamming into her most sensitive places.

Surely, if he came there, it would be too much to bear, too much exquisite agony? But she didn't have time to contemplate it any further, because he ran his thumb over her swollen clit just as her rammed home again and his cock leapt. Her flesh closed, melting and throbbing in a series of dynamite-fuelled spasms as he unloaded himself deep inside her.

He stayed with her for a few moments, and they both savored the intense climax, rocking together in the moonlit room. With regret, she felt him pull out. He rolled onto his back.

"Can we do that again before I wake up?" she whispered, her entire body trembling in the aftermath.

"Yes, lass, we'll do it again, and over again, until the sun rises and I have to leave to board my ship. Suits me fine, that does." And with that he began fisting his cock in one strong hand.

She couldn't believe it. She'd said it jokingly but he was ready to go again. His cock was lifting before her very eyes, although it had hardly subsided since the last round, and then he sat up onto the edge of the bed and lifted her onto his lap, so that her legs splayed open and her glistening sex was thoroughly exposed to him. He murmured admiringly while he touched her there, and then he rubbed his cock against her sensitized flesh, sending a hot wave of renewed lust through her.

Dreams were never normally like this, she reflected, before he maneuvered her onto his cock and glided inside her, filling her to the hilt.

Chapter Two

Cullen awoke with a lazy yawn then cursed under his breath when he glanced at the window and saw that the sun was high in the sky. It was near mid-morn. He hadn't meant to fall asleep at all. His time with the wench had been particularly satisfying, though, and it was no wonder he had drifted off.

He looked down at where she slumbered in the bed, her hair a splendid mess upon the pillows. She was a curious sort, and she had said the strangest things. It was almost as if she were from a foreign land, but she claimed to be English. She had a healthy appetite for pleasures of the flesh though, and his time with her had gone far too quickly for his liking.

He leaned over and pushed back some strands of hair from her cheek with one cautious finger, admiring the pretty upward-tilt of her nose. He hadn't meant to wake her, but when her eyelids fluttered up, he couldn't help smiling.

"I must go. I have to get within sight of the harbor soon."

She sat up with a start and looked around as if surprised. Surely she remembered what had passed between them the night before? After taking in the details of the room, she shrugged, and turned her attention back to him.

"Is the ship coming for you now?"

She looked disappointed. That pleased him somehow.

"On the turn of the tide. But I have to get beyond the village to watch out for its approach. I'll take shelter at the cliffs past the harbor. I'm known in the town and I wish to avoid questioning."

She stared at him, her expression heavy with thought.

She was such a pretty wench, with those dark brown eyes and wild hair the color of polished mahogany. When he reached the Indies, he would have to write and thank Nathaniel McBride for supplying him with such a timely distraction. She was not only pretty to the eye, but she was also adept at her trade. In fact, she seemed to know more about how to respond to a man and give him pleasure than any other woman he had ever known. He was quite fascinated by her. He hadn't thought he could go at it four times in a row, but that thing she'd done with her mouth...

She suddenly moved with deliberation, pulling her heavy hair back and knotting it at the back of her neck. "I see no reason why I shouldn't come down with you."

Cullen was surprised at her words, but when he pondered them, he supposed there would be no harm in it. It might be a long day for him, waiting for the Gloriana and contemplating his sorry state. In his heart of hearts, he had no desire to leave on the accursed ship, which would make it an even more difficult wait. She would be the perfect distraction, he decided, and his body agreed, the blood quickly thundering in his loins as he glanced over her feminine form. So beautiful. So ripe for plunder.

He stood up, grabbing his clothing and quickly pulling it on. "We'll have to hurry, the servant girl is due and we will have to find you something practical to wear." He frowned as he looked down at the floor where the strange, silky undergarments that she'd been wearing the night before lay in an abandoned heap. He'd never seen anything like it, and she didn't seem to have any other clothes in the room. They didn't have time to hunt for her gown and petticoats, which he assumed she had left elsewhere in the house. She could collect them later. Besides, the gown would no doubt be totally impractical, some gaudy affair that would hamper her movements. He reached for his knapsack. Pulling it open, he brought out his spare shirt and a pair of breeches. "These will have to do."

She was looking about the room. "It's not my bed," she commented. "The things are different in the dream."

He didn't understand what she meant, but his thoughts were already elsewhere. They'd have to make haste for the sun was moving across the sky with each moment that passed. He had no idea what time the tide was due to turn and when the Gloriana would approach. He pushed his possessions into his knapsack then snatched up the flask of rum and the bundle of food that Nathaniel had left for him. There was bread and cheese wrapped in a cloth, accompanied by four shiny, red apples. He shoved them all into his knapsack and knotted it closed.

They were almost ready to leave. She had wriggled into his breeches and was pulling the excess material into her hand and tying it in a knot at her waist. She looked adorable and, wearing his clothes, would pass for a ragamuffin lad if it weren't for her beautiful hair and her striking beauty. He glanced down at her pretty feet, still bare. "Where are your shoes?"

She looked around the room. "I don't know."

He shook his head and walked over to a cupboard in one corner of the room. After some efforts rooting around amongst the contents, he pulled out a pair of pink dancing slippers complete with ribbons. They were no doubt expensive, but they would have to commandeer them if she had misplaced her own.

"What year is this supposed to be?" she asked, peering at the slippers as if she'd never seen anything like them before.

Supposed to be? Perhaps she wasn't at her best first thing in the morning. "1806," he answered cautiously.

She stared at him as if in shock. "And who do these belong to?" she blurted, when he handed them to her.

He shrugged, feeling rather perturbed by her strange attitude. Where had the attentive woman of the evening before disappeared to? "I imagine that they belong to Nathaniel's aunt; this is her house. She's away on a tour of the North. She is a devout scholar of botany and went there to sketch."

"Is this her home?"

"Yes, her father's, too, until he passed away." He supposed that she hadn't seen a house as grand as this before, which might explain her curiosity. "He had it built."

It was as if he had told her she was the sole heir to a grand fortune, because her eyes suddenly lit up.

"When, when was it built?" She grabbed his arm, her expression fascinated. When he shrugged, she tugged at his arm most insistently. "The year... it's important."

"Well, let's see." He cast his mind back, with some effort. "I was a lad. Nathaniel and I used to stay here shortly afterwards, in the early 1780's, so I suppose it was 1779, maybe 1780..."

When she threw herself against him and squeezed him in a mighty grip, he was almost winded because he was so startled.

"Good, good," he said, wondering if she was perhaps short of some essential thinking matter. Had Nathaniel sent him the village simpleton to take care of his needs? Whatever it was, her odd attitude only seemed to endear her to him even more, for he found he wanted to take her under his wing and protect her. Something to do with her voracious appetite for pleasures of the flesh, no doubt, he told himself with a wry smile.

"Now, come on," he urged, snatching up his knapsack and his sword. "Let us be on our way, or the Gloriana may leave without me."

As they stepped out of the door, the remaining mist whispered away from the surface of the dew-covered grass, slinking off into the green undergrowth. The air was fresh and high with earthy scents. The sky was livid, the horizon a hazy blur of red-streaked clouds. In the distance, two gulls circled. Lucy took in the sight, her senses filling with the experience. She felt terrific, exhilarated, and more alive than she ever had felt before. All that hot sex, she thought to herself. Then Cullen grabbed her hand, and she was pulled along with him, quickly covering the length of the path and out, into the road beyond.

Except, it wasn't the road.

She realized that the road wasn't actually there, where it should have been. Instead, there was only a narrow dirt track. Wild grass of the type found on the moors was heavy and thick beneath the thin material of her borrowed slippers. There was no sign of the road whatsoever, and Lucy blinked away the strange feeling of disorientation.

It's a dream, she reminded herself, but something had begun to niggle at her consciousness. Perhaps it was the fresh air in her lungs. Perhaps it was the vital, undeniable presence of the daylight. Or perhaps it was Cullen's very real, very fierce grip on her hand, and the look of his powerful shoulders as he guided her across the open land toward the coast. No, it was all of those things and the most basic: the grass, the feeling of the damp grass under her feet, springy, resistant. Real.

And if the grass was real...

She looked at the man who had made passionate love to her all through the night. She eyed his hair, flowing free to his shoulders. She took in the concentrated, determined look in his eye when he glanced back to make sure she was with him.

If the grass was real, did that mean he was real, too?

"Wait." She pulled her hand free of his and stopped dead in her tracks. They'd covered over half the ground to the coastline. In moments, the cliffs would be in sight.

"Sorry, too fast for ye girl?" He flashed a quick grin, but his brow was still furrowed.

Everything he had said to her in the dark of the night came tumbling in on her consciousness.

"My God, this is real." Her words seemed to string out into the atmosphere and weave away from her. Disorientation swamped her. The sense of fun from the night before had gone, whisked away with the advent of morning. All that was left was confusion and doubt about her sanity.

Cullen moved closer. That helped, marginally.

"Real?" His expression was confused, but he smoothed back her hair where it was blowing across her vision, and he looked at her in the most tender way.

Get a grip, she told herself. There had to be an explanation. "You said you were leaving England, yes? Tell me, what is this about? Why are you a dishonored man?"

"Did Nathaniel not to tell you?"

Uselessly, she shook her head, unable to do more than that to urge him on.

"Yes, well, I s'pose you've a right to know, before you spend anymore time with me."

She noticed then how devastatingly handsome he was. In the clear light of day, she had her first real chance to admire the handsome line of his mouth and the strong, angular thrust of his cheekbones.

"T'was a duel. Ach." He raised his hands in disbelief. "I overheard some upstart besmirching my youngest sister's name."

A duel? She stared down at the sheathed sword that hung at his hip. It all seemed so alien to her. How could she possibly take it in?

"Like any man worth his salt," he continued, as if he'd had to deliver this explanation many times before, "I took him aside and told him to mind his mouth. The dim-witted, headstrong young wretch challenged me. Ach, it's all the rage amongst the young bucks. They don't understand the consequences. But still, it had to be done." He shook his head forlornly. "I gave him every chance to call it off, and then the young fool started in on my second before I'd even taken off my cloak. He'd come straight from a tavern where he'd had a belly full of ale the night before. He didn't know what he was doing. Practically collapsed onto his own saber before we even readied ourselves to see him off with a bit of a scare and no more." He looked at her with a sheepish expression.

"Did he die?"

"Near enough, but he's recovering now." He sighed again. "It was an accident, but it falls to me to carry it, and so I must do the honorable thing and leave England for a term of five years. I'm taking this damnable thing with me," he slapped the sword at his hip, "to remind me of my sins." He glanced at the landscape around them. "I love this land, Cornwall, I shall be hellish sad to leave."

His expression was deeply wistful, the like of which Lucy had never seen on a man's face before. Oh, maybe Laurence Olivier in some old movie, but not for real. This guy was battling with true, deep emotions, trying to stand by his duty, despite his convictions. Presumably the lad who had challenged him had been too scared to fight with him and who could wonder at it? Even she could see he would be a formidable opponent to a novice.

Tearing her gaze away from his face-which was hard while he was look-ing at her for her understanding of his predicament–she looked toward the coast where the landscape was clearly visible in the light. His words and the images they spun tumbled through her mind, and she hugged herself as she tried to get a grip on reality. They were on the downside of a bluff she didn't recognize, but beyond them she could just about make out the town of Newquay, with its jetty reaching out into the sea.

It was there, all right, the town that she knew so well, the town that was her home now, but it looked strangely different. The jetty was smaller, the harbor undeveloped. The older, core streets of the town were clearly visible, instead of being nestled in a larger cluster of roads and houses as they usually were. It was the last bit of proof she needed. Somehow, she had been transferred to a different reality, a different version of what was her own place, her home.

"What year did you say this was?" Her voice quavered.

He squinted at her as if surprised at her remark. And why wouldn't he be? He probably thought she was one sandwich short of a picnic.

"The year of our lord, 1806. Why do you ask?"

It was two hundred years earlier.

"Oh, hell, no reason." She gave a hysterical laugh and shrugged use-lessly, hitching the makeshift belt on her pants up and throwing caution to the wind. "I'm stuck inside some weird dream, and it's all getting far too real for my liking."

He frowned. "You do say some odd things, woman."

She loved the way he called her "woman." In fact, she quite liked it when he called her "wench." He stroked her arm soothingly. His touch sent shivers right through her, shivers of delight.

"The sky bodes heavy with a storm," he commented, eyeing the horizon warily, and then looked back at her. "Do you not want to come down to the coast with me after all?"

"Yes, I do." *What the hell else would I do with myself, stranded here in 1806?*

"You look quite pale, are you unwell?"

"No, well, it's probably shock. Listen, Cullen, there is something I must try to explain, although I'm sure you won't believe me. I'm not from here. I mean, I am, but I'm not."

"I thought you were different, lass."

"You could say that…"

"You're not a whore at all, are you?"

She gave another hysterical laugh. *A whore?* "No, I'm a web designer."

"A what?"

"Oh, it's a job, it's what I do, and it's like…" How the hell did she explain the Internet to some guy in 1806? "It's like… drawing." *Sheesh. What a cop out.*

He shook his head thoughtfully, and looked at her as if she were slightly mad, then took her arm, protectively. "Come on, we'll talk more when we get down to the shore."

❦

Cullen frowned. The town was active. It had to be market day. Folks traveled from far and wide to buy and sell their wares in the town, and he didn't want to have to stop and explain himself to anyone he knew. He hurried past the outlying houses, skirting the busier streets. When they reached the far side of the town, he cut in toward the shore and the caves at the cliffs. Nathaniel had told him there was a boat lodged in an old cave that they used to frequent as children.

On the horizon, he could make out the shapes of the fishing boats heading back in to the harbor with their catch. The cliffs reared up at their side, and he craned his neck, trying to spot the outcrop of rock that would indicate the old hiding place. The winds were lifting and the sea was getting rough. At the shore edge, seaweed rolled on the crest of the edgy waves.

Just as he began to think he'd missed the entrance to the cave, they came upon it and he pointed it out to Lucy, ushering her inside. It was just as he remembered it, smaller perhaps, but sheltered and haven-like. There was a drifting tide of sand against one wall, from the high tides of the spring. Against the other sat the rowboat.

"Nathaniel thought of everything. I'll be able to row out to the Gloriana when she sails into the harbor without drawing too much attention to myself. They are collecting a cargo of tin and Nathaniel has paid them a good price for taking me on. I just don't want to make a fuss in the town."

One glance at her told him she wasn't taking his words in. He sighed and dropped his knapsack. He had a look around and reassured himself the cave was safe enough to give them cover until the ship dropped anchor. Once he'd seen it pass into the bay, he could make his way on board with the least attention.

Now he had time to tend to the woman.

She was shocked at his tale, no doubt. He glanced over to where she sat huddled against the rough wall of the cave, her eyes focused vaguely on the mid-distance, her thoughts far, far away.

He squatted down beside her and pulled her into his arms. "Now, tell me, what has startled you so? It's as if you've seen a ghost."

"Oh, trust me, ghosts don't scare me." She gave a weak smile. "It takes more than that to spook me. Although I have to admit that I'm pretty spooked right now."

She had a faraway look in her eyes. They gleamed with some knowledge that he didn't understand. She was a strange, fey woman. "There's magic at play here."

"You aren't kidding." She gave a disbelieving laugh.

"No, I meant you, lass, it's witchcraft, isn't it? I'm in league with a witch." Even as the thought had occurred to him, he realized that the idea didn't shock him as much as it might have done. Cornwall was full of tales of white witches and those not so white, women who could weave magic with their words and spells.

"I wish I were, because then I might understand this or have some control over it."

"Tell me what you mean, tell me about where you are from, your place."

Even as he asked her–and yes, he did mean to find out what was behind her sudden change of mood and her earlier comments–he brushed his fingers over the shirt that bunched and nestled between her soft, full breasts, and stroked the malleable flesh, weighing it gently and sighing as it took its effect on him. Something about the wench made him grow drunk on her presence.

Was it witchcraft?

He would never tire of looking at her—he knew that much with certainty. She was so pleasing to the eye and had a peculiar way about her that he hadn't found in any other woman, some spark, some lack of shame or the like. No simpering maiden, and he liked that, he hungered for more of it. It would be difficult to leave Cornwall, doubly so since she had come along.

"The place I live in, well it's here, but it's not here." She looked sad. "I think I've gone back in time, I mean, I've come back in time... to you."

Whatever he was expecting her to say, it wasn't that. Come back in time? Her brain was surely addled.

She looked at him with sudden, dark intensity glistening in her eyes and then she looked away and stared at the cave walls. "You think I'm mad, don't you?

"What you are saying makes little sense. Maybe you gave your pretty head a bash last night." He was eager to draw her attention back to him.

"Maybe I did." She gave a sad laugh.

He sensed confusion in her, rather than madness, and wondered if she were weaving some strange tale to amuse him. Her eyes were still focused on the far wall of the cave. "You're not from these parts, I can see that, but you've no need to try to impress me with tall tales." He sighed.

"No, Cullen, please listen." Her eyes shone with tears, and she gripped his arm with sudden desperation. "I thought it was a dream, but it isn't." She shook her head. "I'm meant to be in the future, two hundred years from now."

Two hundred years hence? He laughed heartily, then he caught sight of the reprehension in her eyes and guilt stole into his heart. He stared at her. "What makes you think you are from a different time?"

"I live here, here in Newquay, but in the twenty-first century."

Annoyance hit him. "This is ridiculous."

She shut her eyes, one hand clutching at her hair, the other on the locket at her throat. "How can I explain it, when I can't even understand it myself?" She growled with frustration. "If only I could show you," she murmured, seemingly to herself.

He stood up and paced across the cave, turning back to look at her. She was yearning for his understanding, he felt her reaching across the space to him. He shook his head. No, it was nonsense. It had to be madness.

"Wait," she said, clambering to her feet. She darted toward him, holding the locket she wore at her throat. "Look here." She held the locket up to him, her hands shaking as she prized it open. "Look inside."

He was wary, but did as she requested. Inside the locket was a small miniature likeness of Lucy, standing by a doorway. It was incredible work, for it looked almost real, as if she were standing right there inside her own locket. It was the strangest thing he'd ever seen.

"Can you see it, the cottage, see how different it looks?"

He glanced at the doorway, the walls. Astonished, his gaze ran over the miniature again. The beams above the doorway were well worn, as if they had been there many years, the plasterwork in dire need of attention. It was indeed the cottage, though. Nathaniel's aunt's home. "It is as if... as if it is old already." He said it without thinking.

She nodded vigorously. "Yes, you see, this is a photograph of me in my own time, at the house. See how different it looks?"

He felt uneasy. "The artist has painted it this way."

"No, it is not a painting. It is what we call a photograph. In the future, we can capture an image like this, with a device called a camera."

He shook his head, understanding far from being within his grasp. And yet... He looked at her. Her eyes were filled with hope.

Everything about her was different, that much was true. And she didn't even own her own shoes, for heavens sake. Could it be true? It made sense of her strange ways though, and the foreign things she had said. He couldn't deny that. Confusion battled within him, his mind and his heart at odds.

"If it is true," he couldn't believe he was even considering it, "how have you come back to 1806?"

She shook her head. "If I knew that..." She slumped and sat down again.

Every instinct in his body told him she was telling the truth, or at least believed in her convictions, but reason defied it. He squatted down beside her. "I want to believe you, I see your likeness in the miniature and the age of the cottage there, but I cannot wrap my thoughts around it."

"You aren't the only one. I moved to Cornwall and found myself living in a place where pagan traditions are kept alive and mysticism is everywhere, but this is far beyond my understanding."

Her expression made his chest tight.

"You moved here?"

"From London. I bought the cottage where we met. It was derelict."

"The place was abandoned?"

"Well, it hadn't been lived in for a few years when I bought it."

She was speaking the truth, as hard as it was for him to accept. But what did it mean? His mind moved beyond the obstacle of reason and ran with the possibility. "If your words are true, it makes our curious meeting even stranger, don't you think?

She nodded. "Oh, yes. I was asleep in my own bed, and then I woke up in your time."

Yes, he saw it now, how shocked she'd been, standing there in her strange undergarments. They were different in every way, and yet they had been drawn together for some reason. There was an odd similarity of their situations though. "You are lost. I'm trying to find a home. We seem to share the fact that we are wandering souls, Lucy, in search of our destiny."

"Yes, it's true," she murmured, looking into his eyes. "I wonder if that's why I'm here. I dreamt of you often, before. You spoke to me in the dreams, but I couldn't understand the words, not until last night."

Something inside him knotted. He felt drawn to her, and he also felt a strange sense of recognition, some sort of identification with what she had said. It was as if they stood together on the edge of something very significant, but what? What did this mean? He didn't understand it, but he felt compelled to believe.

He moved closer and drew her into his body with one hand, offering comfort. "I heard a tale about a man who had traveled from the future, in London last year. My sisters were all talking of him."

"And what happened to him?"

"I have to admit that I took little notice."

Her face fell. "Me neither, I mean, I've seen time travel described in books and movies too, but never thought about it being truly possible..."

"Movies?"

She stared at him in silence for a moment. "Oh, never mind, it's something from my time that you don't have yet. Kind of like books... believe me, it would take hours to explain. I really wish we had the time, though."

She rested her hand around his neck and looked at him so beseechingly, his heart leapt in his chest and he drew her closer again, wrapping her into his arms.

"I will have to leave here soon, my voyage will begin today." He spoke the words that he felt inevitable, but he didn't want to leave her. The idea of it had begun to feel very, very wrong.

She clung tighter to him, crushing her breasts against his chest. He rested his hands against her back, holding her close while he looked down into her eyes. She was so warm and inviting, and the liquid fire of her spirit was reflected in her gaze. It made his blood surge, and he longed to couple with her again. "Can I find a way to distract us both from our troubles, Lucy, love?"

"Oh, yes. I'm quite sure you could." She trailed her fingertips down his neck and over his arms, squeezing the muscle there. "Just the touch of your hand on my breast, yes..." She gave a low growl in her throat in response to his hand enclosing her warm flesh. "Your touch makes the worried thoughts slip away. I truly believe you could make me forget anything and everything." She tangled her fingers in his hair.

The nature of her response captured him in an instant. Her eyes were growing darker, the atmosphere between them heavy with reciprocated carnal longing. The heating of their blood was so well matched, he was full to overflowing with the need to lock his body with hers. They clung hungrily to each other, their curious sense of identification arresting them in a magic embrace.

"Come then, let us pass the time more pleasantly." He bent his head to kiss her rosebud mouth, before turning his attention back to her bountiful breasts, so beautifully outlined through the thin material of his shirt. Pushing his hand beneath the fabric, he lifted the shirt away and circled one breast with his hand, caressing it and taking the nipple into his mouth, tonguing it, then grazing the peak with his teeth.

"Oh, that makes me go weak at the knees," she murmured. "You really can push all thoughts out of my head."

"Good." He liked that she expressed herself to him, that was unusual in his experience. He turned his attention to her other breast, tonguing it fervently.

"Oh, Cullen, you've mastered me so thoroughly." She gave a husky laugh but it was edged with a note of desperation.

Something twitched inside him, an urge to possess her, completely, and it was fiercer than anything that he'd ever known.

He stood up and abandoned his coat while Lucy kicked off the borrowed slippers and stripped her shirt off. He took a moment to rest a kiss between her breasts then jerked the baggy breeches down her legs. She moaned softly when he tested her. She was already wet and slick between her legs. His glance flickered to her face and she smiled. Her blazing eyes ate him up. She was so lusty, her instincts and desires thoroughly blatant.

"Let me look at you, too. I want to savor you," she whispered, showing that she also regretted the thought of their imminent separation. "You're the most incredible man I've ever met."

Pride soared through him.

She circled him, touching him longingly.

He took pleasure in her need for him, and when she dropped to the floor in front of him and whispered, "Cullen, I'm desperate for your cock," he almost came undone there and then.

"Hellfire, woman, what are you trying to do to me?" He couldn't help himself. She was incredible. His heart thudded loudly within his chest, his body on fire for her. He pulled off his boots and began to take off his shirt. She looked eagerly at him as he undid his breeches. His cock sprang out, hard and ready for her. She took it in her hands, trembling. His fingers slid into the rumpled mess of her hair and he held her head as her tongue darted out and licked at him. When she plunged the gleaming shaft into her mouth and ran its head against the roof of her mouth, he cursed again. She drew back and her tongue ran over each hot ridge of skin, moving over the swollen head with deliberation. She plunged again and again.

He all but cried out for mercy, brimming with pleasure. Her fingers slid down and held his sac. She moved fast and well, and she was bringing him to seed very quickly. He gripped her shoulder with one hand, the other closed on the stem of his cock. His head fell forward, his legs flexing, his cock spurting into her pretty mouth, his seed dribbling down her chin and onto her breasts.

He looked down at her, his mouth open, his hair falling forward, shadowing his face. She looked up at him, her eyes flashing with pleasure. Then she leaned forward to lick him, rubbing her breasts against his hard legs.

Her movements against him quickly made him hard again. He pumped his slick member in his fist and then dropped down beside her on the floor of the cave. He moved his hand up from her belly to her neck, sliding the moistness of his juices on her skin and between his fingers, massaging her nipples with the rich offering, firm and slow. She moaned as she lay back, her eyes filled with longing, with challenge. She looked so very beautiful, her cheeks glowing with her fire, her eyes so dark and full of passion. He moved forward and she gave a low guttural moan when she felt his cock at her hot little hole, signaling her approval. That was good, because he was desperate with the need to be inside her. He grabbed her legs, pulling her body nearer with a jolt.

"Pardon my rush, but I am eager for more of you." He whispered low against her ear, the tension of holding on almost threatening to undo him for a second spill right there and then.

"Believe me, I want it, too, hard and fast," she murmured.

The things the woman said, she was wanton. It took a lot to weaken a man like him, but those words nearly did it.

"Feel my heat." She took his hand and slid it down to her groin so that he could feel the needful damp, cloying heat emanating from inside her.

"God in heaven, you are on fire..." He moaned quietly against her mouth and kissed her deep. His cock reared up again, demanding contact. He heard her breath quicken when she tested him with her hand. She was unbelievable, a canny witch all right, one who could entrance a man with her passionate ways. The light caught her expression, wild and filled with desire for him, and he had to be inside her.

She leaned back against the rock, bracing herself as she edged his hardness inside her sensitive niche. "Cullen," she cried.

"Oh yes," he replied as he eased his way inside, groaning as he experienced the grip of her flesh on his. "This is too good. God help me, I may miss my ship, but I can't miss out on this."

She gripped his shoulders when he filled her to the hilt, bruising up against her most sensitive parts, then he began to move against her. She grasped at him, her legs locking tighter on him. She was so eager, it made something in his chest roar with pride and possessiveness.

He held her hips down with his hands and jammed into her hard, throbbing against the moist walls of her enclosing flesh. As her body rose up toward him, one arm sliding round his neck, he leaned down and sank his mouth onto her shoulder, his teeth grabbing at her flesh. She made a sound, a cry, and fell away from him again. He rode her, but kept them close, moving in deep thrusts, their bodies clinging together in the gloom. The dank smell of the cave, combined with the heady smell of their mating, filled the atmosphere.

"Cullen... I've never had it like this, it's so hot," she whispered.

He could only mutter incoherent words in response. She leaned further back and his body pivoted against her. He was crushed inside her, the angle affording him access to her deepest spot. His manhood was massaging the very core of her womanly flesh and he was already near to shedding his load. He was rigid and pounding inside her hot, wet grip. And she was close to her end, too. Her hands tightened on his shoulders, her head rolling. He cursed under his breath and ground into her deep and hard, riding her against the cave floor insistently. She began to tremble and a low sound escaped her mouth. He felt her spasm, and he thrust deep and fast, driving them both over the edge of the precipice within seconds.

Chapter Three

When Enid awoke, she glanced at her bedside tale. The tethered beads lay comfortably on the small velvet cushion where she had placed them for comfort and safekeeping.

On the bedspread beside her, Wellington stretched.

"It seems things are going well between our two lovers," she murmured, rubbing Wellington behind his ears. "I think we can safely say that making them part at this time would be very cruel, don't you think?"

Wellington seemed to smile.

Enid reached for her spectacles and plumped up her pillows. She pulled back her hair and wrapped it into a loose bun, sitting up and focusing on the window.

The sunshine filtering through the curtains told her the day was good. But the Cornish weather had an uncanny ability to change at the most inconvenient of moments, throwing the best-made plans into confusion. She smiled. Clever, creative minds would always find a way to make the best of any situation, and she was sure that Lucy and Cullen would find the right path, no matter what.

While the passion between them had rolled and thrashed, wild and uncontrollable, the weather outside had become dark and unruly. The sky was stormy, the waves crashing up against the distant rocks. Cullen rose to his feet and walked toward the entrance of the cave. Lucy watched him with a pang of regret.

When she moved, the surface of the rock felt rough against her back, sending an after-tremor of pleasure through her entire body. Would she ever recover from being so thoroughly well shagged?

"Accursed weather."

"What is it?" she asked, pulling the baggy shirt on and joining him close to the mouth of the cave.

"If it stays like this, the Gloriana won't be able to come into dock."

The waves were wild. "Because of the rocks?"

The local history was filled with tales about ships getting into difficulty at the jaws of the rocks outside the harbor, large and dangerous stony outcrops known as the Bedruthen Steps. Would this keep his ship at bay and would she have more time with him as a result? Lucy felt a wave of longing spring up at the very idea, her heart aching for every precious moment she might spend with him.

"The rough seas will hold them off. The Gloriana might not be able to come into the bay until the morrow." He pulled on his clothes as he spoke. "I'll go up to the headland to take a look."

While he was gone, Lucy darted out to the shore's edge and splashed her face with icy water, then she sat inside the mouth of the cave and tried to work out what the hell had happened to her. As logically and rationally as she could manage, she worked through events to see if she could figure out how she had traveled back in time. There were the dreams—she couldn't discount them. Some element of destiny was being played out, that was for sure. But there was more. She had wished for him to be real, as she fell asleep the night before. He had said he wished for a wench. Was that the key, that the two wishes fulfilled one another?

How would she travel back? It would have to be by the same means. Therefore she had to wish it. At the cottage? Did it have to be there? They'd both been there when it had happened, she supposed. When Cullen left on his ship, she would go back to the cottage and wish...

A shiver passed right through her bones, when she considered what might happen if it didn't work, if she was left here alone, without him, but in his time. The idea of him leaving was, in itself, making her despondent, let alone the rest.

"There's no sight of it and no hope for several hours with the weather like this."

She jumped at the sound of Cullen's voice and looked up to see him coming back into the cave, his hair damp and windswept.

He stared at her silently for a moment, as if deep in thought, before rejoining her. "Might as well rest up and eat and forget about it for a while."

"Well, my lovely, tell me more about the place where you are from," he encouraged and opened up his knapsack to share the food with her.

The wind wailed outside and they huddled together, sharing the meager meal and talking. Gradually, as the day passed, she began to tell him about life in the future, her time, her version of Newquay and the cottage.

"So you own the 'derelict' cottage in the future?"

She smiled, touched that he had remembered. "Yes, I'm renovating it. It had fallen into disrepair, time has taken its toll. There have been many different owners, some with dreadful ideas of what might look good in a house." She grimaced. That made him laugh. "I'm trying to make the house live again and it needs to be sound before winter. Most of the jobs I can do myself, others I need to hire someone to do."

"You do this alone and you don't have servants?" He looked amazed.

She laughed. "Not many people have servants in the future. It seems lazy and wrong to our world. Only the idle rich and royalty still do that."

He listened attentively. "Is that why you wanted to know when the cottage was built, because it's yours?"

"Yes, that's it exactly. No one in the neighborhood seems to know and I was so keen to find out. Now you've given me that answer."

"Only that?" He lifted one eyebrow quizzically.

"No, much more than that... Cullen, I've had the best time..."

"I, too."

She watched him thoughtfully, the pair of them quiet as they took each other in. Something inside her felt full, yet ached for more. "And your life, what is it like? Tell me about yourself."

"I am Cullen Thaine, the second son of a nobleman, so I rest easily within my family. I oversee Hollingswell, the family's Cornish country estate, alongside my father, but the true responsibility falls to my older brother."

"Hollingswell Hall?"

He nodded.

"Hollingswell still stands in 2006."

His eyes gleamed with interest.

"It's what's called a Heritage House now. A private consortium bought it and it's open to the public. For a fee, people can visit and experience the heritage of the house and its grounds."

He shook his head, his forehead wrinkled as he tried to picture it. "Imagine that... time served us well."

"It's a beautiful estate."

"It is," he replied, looking deep into her eyes as they shared the moment and the image of Hollingswell.

"What do you oversee?" she asked, wanting to know more about him.

"Land, the tenants. I'm not one for life in the town, if truth be told. I don't fare well in genteel society." He grinned. His smile had a maverick quality about it that tickled her. "I'd rather be out overseeing the land. I often work with the tenants; I enjoy their company. I learn from them as they do from me, and it makes for a good bond, even though my father thinks I'm a heathen. He swears I'm not one of his offspring."

She chuckled. "And you oversee your little sisters, too?"

He looked pleased that she had remembered. "Yes, I also oversee my troublesome little sisters."

She couldn't imagine it, having to duel over such a trifling affair, but she knew from her school days that matters of honor were treated very differently in the past. "What will your life be like, in the colonies?"

"I don't know, an adventure, to be sure. I must fill the time well, make something of the challenge." He gave a wry smile.

"I sense you don't particularly want to go."

"I have to go somewhere. I'd rather stay here, I love this place, have done since I was a child. We grew up at the Cornish estate and I often stayed here in Newquay with my friend, Nathaniel. Cornwall is my home."

She would rather he stayed there, too. Her mind had begun working overtime. She wondered if he would take on an adventure of a different kind... "Cullen, when I tried to find out the history of the cottage, there was a story about a disappearance, a traveler who had gone missing. The librarian said it was just a rumor, but perhaps, perhaps it was you that the rumor was about?"

He nodded, pursing his lips as he contemplated it. "I'd fit that description, but maybe one day I will return." He gave a tight smile. It wasn't wasted on her.

He didn't want to leave his beloved Cornwall, but he had to go away from here for at least a few years. If she could work out how to get back to 2006, perhaps he could come with her and spend his exile there instead. The strangeness of the whole situation, together with the red-hot sex and the growing attachment she felt for him, had made her thoughts wild and ambitious. "I know it sounds far-fetched, but if I made it here, I must be able to make it back to my time. And, if I can, maybe you can come with me."

"To your time?" He was frowning as he tried to make sense of her words.

"Yes, here, but in my time. You'd get your wish to stay in Cornwall for the years you have to be away."

He nodded, his gaze still searching her face for answers, as if she truly were a witch or a magician, not just some lost soul hoping to make this real.

Her confidence faltered. Would it even work? "Do you want to try it? I mean, I have no idea if it will work, but we can try. If it doesn't work, you can be back here at the harbor when the ship docks tomorrow."

Fear and hope riddled her, fear of being stranded here, or worse, stranded here alone without him. He kissed her again, redirecting the flow of her emotions. The desire to be with him churned through her.

"So, instead of spending five years in the colonies, you think I could spend five years away with you in this future world you spoke about, in your… place?" He looked her up and down, and a slow smile spread over his face.

He was flirting with her, and she liked that, but she worried that he had to take the situation seriously.

"Cullen, you have to want it, I mean, five years. It's here, but it's… well." How did she explain it? "It's just, different."

"I'm not sure I understand what you're telling me, Lucy, and I'm stuck on the idea you may be using witchcraft on me." He paused to smile again and indicate he didn't mean to have her burned at the stake. "It all seems so incredible, but hell and damnation, I'm willing to give it a try as much or more than any other adventure, if it involves being with you."

"Oh, Cullen." The fact he'd go along with her made her feel braver about the whole thing and happier, too. "And there's no one special you'll be leaving behind, a girl, another wench?"

His eyebrows shot up when he sensed her curiosity. "Oh, there'll be a few broken hearts, I'll warrant." Then he pulled her into his arms, and reassured her with a kiss. "Take me with you, cast a spell if you can, witch, I'm willing to go where you wander."

He really didn't know what he was letting himself in for, she thought, but something told her it was the right thing to do and his faith in her only seemed to confirm that notion. She held onto that feeling, she'd maybe need to feel that sure later on, when she had to figure out how the hell to get them back to the future.

"What do we have to do?"

"Go back to the cottage, I think. I feel we need to be there, because that's where we both were, when we wished." And then it hit her. "Wait…" Her mind was whirring. "The librarian, the woman who told me about your disappearance, she also mentioned that a white witch had lived up there, years before the house was built. She said the witch used to grant wishes to those she favored." *Could it be true?*

They stared at each other as the implication sank in.

"A wench wasn't all I wished for." He looked thoughtful. "I also wished to stay here in Cornwall."

She took in the significance of what he said and nodded. "And I wished for you to be real, to be with me in my life." Her heart was full of hope.

Cullen stood up, pulling her by the hand with him. "Right then, it's meant to be, let's do it." He glanced at the opening of the cave. "The sea mist is rising by the moment. Let's make our way back now before it gets any heavier."

The mist was rising, fast and wispy, and it trailed their footsteps as if it were so many eyes following them.

Once more they hurried past the town, and Lucy ignored the tug she felt when she saw the lights within the cottages, wishing that security were theirs, too. Like a mantra, she kept repeating her wish, to get them back to her time. She couldn't face thinking about what would happen to her if it didn't work. Cullen would be safe and that thought made her stronger, because his life had now become as important as her own. She started to battle a rising sense of panic. When they reached the cottage, they had to stay in the hidden shelter of the trees beyond the foot of the path until the coast was clear.

"It's my home, yet it looks different, it feels very strange."

Cullen gave her a reassuring squeeze. "I hope I get to see it in your time too."

"So do I," she whispered.

She watched, enthralled, when the serving girl came out of the house after her duties for the day were done, locking the door behind her. She stared at the basket the girl had hanging over one arm, the embroidered shawl she wore over her shoulders and her strange, old-fashioned dress, austere and black. Seeing her come out of the cottage that was her home felt so odd and yet strangely emotional. Lucy had been given a magical glimpse into the history of the cottage, a glimpse she would always cherish.

"She's locked the door. How will we get in?"

"Nathaniel keeps a key hidden under a rock."

"Ah." Lucky, she thought. Was luck truly on their side? She could only hope that would be the case.

A few minutes later, when they were sure the house was silent and empty, they made their way inside and back to the room where they had met. Once there, she turned to him and allowed her gaze to absorb his handsome face.

"I don't even know if this will work, but I have to say this, in case it does… this might be your last chance to back out. I feel you have to be really willing and believe in the possibility that we can travel through time, and not just think you're humoring some half-wit and you'll be back at the shore for the boat in the morning."

He laughed.

"Cullen. This is serious."

"Yes, yes. I'll be serious. I cannot help being happy at the prospect of being by your side a bit longer. I've nothing to lose, and everything to gain." He took her in his arms and held her.

She couldn't help smiling at that, now could she?

"Just be sure you're ready to try for it… anything could happen. I suppose it might not work, but if it does, it will be a strange adventure for you, like this has been for me."

He ran his hand down the length of her hair and then rested his fingers against her cheek, cupping her face.

"I'm sure," he replied. His mouth touched hers, opening her lips with tender inquisitiveness, tasting her as he went, lifting her head with gentle nudges until she looked up at him. She trembled when he ran his hands over her and desire coursed through her body.

They were both sure, they both wanted to try.

The sun was low in the sky and they lay on the bed in the growing darkness, holding each other and considering their fate. She prayed to the God she'd never previously thought worth praying to. Hypocrite, she told herself. But nothing was the same now, not beliefs or dreams, because something incredible had happened to her. She had Cullen wrapped in her arms, and his hands were strong and possessive against her back.

"You said you wished for a wench, yes?"

He nodded.

"And I wished for the man I had dreamt about every night to be real, to be there in my bed with me."

He groaned and his hands squeezed her bottom so that she rested up close against his growing erection.

"Cullen." She laughed softly, looking up at him, dizzy with desire and something else: hope. Could they make this work, could it possibly work? "We both need to wish, to be together, in my bed… in my time."

Fear gripped her heart. Could she still be dreaming, had this all been one long, vivid dream? But she didn't want to lose him, not yet. Her fingers closed on his shoulders, tightly, clinging to him as if he might be taken away.

"I wish you were my wench, now and whenever."

She sighed. "I know one thing for sure. When you hold me like this, every-thing else fades way, and you're the only thing that is truly real for me."

"Good, I would be glad to be the only thing that mattered to a woman like you, Lucy love. I want it, too. I believe…"

He did. She could see it. He had faith and hope in her wild words. Her heart ached. "Please," she whispered to the heavens, to the cottage around them, and the spirit it held, "please let this work."

And then he stopped her whispers when he kissed her again, gently at first, until the kiss became more demanding, until everything else slipped away and there was only the two of them, adrift in time. She cupped his fiercely handsome face in her hands, holding him. A misty ether engulfed them. She opened her mouth and her soul to him. She believed. She tasted him with her tongue and with her whole life force, willing them to be joined and carried forward two hundred years.

She felt her hair lifting, she felt him moving against her, his hands rov-ing possessively over her body. Her shirt fell open, his hands moved inside, then lower. In her mind's eye, they were naked and entwined, amidst an ethereal dreamscape quivering with stars. She sighed against his mouth. This was pure magic, he was pure magic. His arms were strong and felt invincible around her, and she coiled within his embrace, their hearts and spirits afloat in an ever-changing sky of light and color.

Her legs were locked around his hips, holding him there. His cock entered her. Like a lightning rod it pulsated with energy, fusing them together. Their spirits soared, wrapped together and tangled in destiny's embrace. A rush of air, powerful and unchecked, roared up around them like a whirlwind, fierce and swirling with stardust.

In her mind, she spoke to him. *Cullen, you're real, and you are my dream, my dream come true.*

And he knew, he knew what she meant and he returned the love she gave, tenfold. Stars glistened around them and the sky of colors pulsated, rising and falling in time with the driving power of their physical em-braces. In the moment of their mutual orgasm, time stood still and faded into complete darkness.

Chapter Four

Wellington was sitting by the fire, content.

Enid yawned. She took one more look at her handiwork, admiring the pendant she had fashioned that evening. The two beads were meant to be together, each complimented the other so well. She had put them on a silver chain, a heart-shaped loop fixing them in place. She dropped it into her trinket box, closing the lid, happy with her creation.

"Tomorrow should be fun," she said to the cat as she took off her spectacles. "Poor old Cullen, I wonder how he'll fare in this modern time."

The cat gave her an admonishing glance.

"Yes, I know, I'm naughty, but I'll keep watch. The spell can always be undone… if need be."

A bird sang its morning song close by. Lucy fought against the slumber that held her captive and found she was still wrapped in Cullen's arms. She could barely bring herself to open her eyes, frightened that the wish might not have worked. So, with curious fingers she tugged at her neckline, hoping to discover she was back in her shortie pajamas, but no, she was still wearing his shirt, although it was askew and her breasts were bare. She opened her eyes with a deep and audible sigh, and then rolled over and sucked in her breath when her gaze met the vision around them.

My room. She was still wearing his clothes, yes, but they were in her room, back in her time.

The sun was pouring through the window, as if it was the start of a bright new day. Everything was just as she had left it, her very own wrought-iron framed bed and the gilded mirror over the dresser. The stripped pine floorboards awaiting their varnish, the old oak wardrobe and the framed prints on the walls. She jumped up and rushed to the window. Yes, there was the road, and the garden was just as she knew it.

Cullen moved and sat up on the edge of the bed, his hair awry and his clothes undone. She broke into relieved laughter at the sight of him. He was scratching his head and looking around with a bemused expression on his face. She knew the feeling.

She pointed through the window. "Look Cullen, the road!"

He came to her side and peered out just as the hourly bus trundled by.

"Hellfire!" He leapt back, pulling her with him. "What was that?"

"That's the bus, it goes into Newquay." She smiled at him. "Like a horse and cart, but quicker."

He nodded, warily, his hand taking hers as if to reassure himself, and then he grinned as he looked across the view from the window. "It really is Cornwall, but it's somewhere else, too…"

"Yes, that's it exactly. I hope you don't regret this."

"Why would I?" His genuine expression reassured her, quelling the rising doubts about what they had done.

"It's very different. I don't know how I would have coped in your time, without you."

"But you didn't have to, and I am here because of you. Don't you think things would have been very different for me in the colonies?"

"Yes, but not quite as different as this."

The phone on the bedside table rang and Cullen turned to look at it in surprise.

"It's a telephone. It lets you talk to your friends even if they are far away." She smiled at his expression of disbelief as she picked up the receiver. "Hello."

He stared at her, incredulous.

"Enid, yes, I'm fine."

"I'm so glad to hear it." Enid gave her happy hum. "I was trying to get hold of you all day yesterday."

That meant that time had progressed in the future, too, and that would work well for Cullen when he wanted to travel back again. She eyed him up and down, her heart beating. Perhaps she could convince him to stay, rather than going back to his time. "I-I've been away, but I'm back safe now."

"What manner of witchcraft is that?" He stared at the handset, his head on one side as he tried to make out the voice emitting from the earpiece.

She smiled and put her finger to her lips, hushing him, and then she beckoned him nearer so that he could hear, too.

"Is that a man's voice I hear?" Enid asked, and gave a delighted chuckle.

"Lucy, have you got a man over there?"

Cullen cautiously bent his head alongside hers.

"There is someone else here. I guess you could say he's a traveler of sorts."

"Well I hope he's everything you dreamed he would be. Is he a true charmer?"

Lucy wasn't surprised by the amused tone in Enid's voice, but right then she was more concerned with reassuring Cullen, who looked deeply puzzled. "Er, yes, he is, but I better go play hostess. I'll call you back later."

"Do I get to meet him?"

"Yes, yes, I guess so. I'll call you back."

He stared at the receiver even after she had hung up. "You are a witch, to be sure."

"Not really, although there are lots of magic things here, as you'll soon see." What would he make of the modern version of Cornwall, the surfers and the holidaymakers? It was going to take him a while to get used to living in the new millennium, but Cullen Thaine was about to be socialized, super quick.

"But, you know," she added, "if you think I'm a witch now, wait until you see some of the other magic things I can do." She winked at him, thinking of all the fun they were going to have together.

He captured her in his arms, looked into her eyes, and lifted a speck of stardust from her hair. "Oh, I know all about the magic things you can do, Lucy love."

"And I you," she replied, slipping her hands around his neck. Was it witchcraft? Well, there was certainly magic at play because her wish to have him made real had come true. But where would that magic lead them now? If the ache in her heart was anything to go by, there was more at stake between them than just a passionate affair.

⁂❀(ʊʊ)❀⁂

Enid gazed out the kitchen window, taking in the vision of Cullen stalking through the orchards, stripped to the waist, with a basket of early windfalls clutched easily under one arm. With the sinking summer sun blazing low on the horizon behind him, he looked so handsome, every bit the ideal match for Lucy. "Oh, yes he really is a charmer."

Lucy sipped her wine distractedly, her fingers on her silver locket.

"What's he doing out there?" Enid asked.

"He claims he's earning his keep."

"Ah, a gentleman through and through." She glanced back at the window. He was giving several of the trees a close inspection and looked deep in thought as he checked out their condition. She smiled gently as she turned back. "He's every bit as handsome as I remembered."

Lucy's head snapped up. "Remembered?"

"Yes, I met him once before, when he was but a lad. Late 1700s, it was." Enid nodded at Lucy, letting the message sink in.

Lucy swallowed, her face growing pale. Her hand shook and the glass of wine dropped from her fingers, crashing to the floor. She clutched her head in her hands, her pretty eyes huge as she stared down at the mess, aghast.

Enid set down her glass. "Allow me, it's my fault, I should have broken the news more gently, and when you were sitting down." She went to the corner of the kitchen where she spied a dustpan and brush.

Lucy grabbed a sponge and mopped up the spilt wine. As Enid swept up the glass, Lucy turned to her with a frown. "It was you, you that made it possible?"

"You two were made for each other, I hope you will forgive a little meddlesome matchmaking."

"But how…?"

"Cornish magic, my dear, Cornish magic."

"Are you the… the white witch?"

"Oh, you could say that. I prefer to think of myself as a healer, a granter of wishes. Some people balk at the term 'witch'. Alas, it's got rather a bad reputation." Her eyes narrowed, her concern growing. "Now sit down before you pass out. You've turned quite pale."

Lucy obliged, leaving her to finish tidying.

Enid chuckled. She did like giving people surprises, although she had been a little naughty there. She poured a fresh glass of wine and put it in Lucy's hand. Lucy's gaze followed her every action. Enid could sense her thoughts dashing this way and that, fitting the puzzle together.

"You gave me the locket, so I could show him… so he would believe it enough to try?" Understanding filled her gaze.

Enid nodded and chinked their glasses, looking her over with an inquisitive glance. "Well, my dear, you're positively glowing, so I don't think it's done you any harm."

"No, I… he's made me very happy. I don't know what to say. Thank you?"

"Be happy, that is all I ask."

"I am. I think we both are. Should I tell him—about you, I mean?"

Enid thought on it for a moment. "Let him settle in first, it's a big jump. I lived through the time in between, but he has a lot to take on. Leave it a few weeks, I'll tell you when. And remember, I'll be here for you whenever you might need me. For anything."

"Okay." She gave a weak smile.

"I can see you're rushing forward in your thoughts and meeting the problems head on."

"You can tell?"

"You're worried in case someone finds out."

Lucy nodded.

"Relax, it's unlikely." She paused. "You're also concerned because you're falling for him and you're worried about how you'll feel if he leaves."

Lucy gave her a sad look. "Yes, you're right, I can't deny it. I love him desperately, but one day he'll be gone, when his time comes."

They both looked back at Cullen, who was now striding in their direction, his glorious physique adorned only by the baggy shorts Lucy had picked up for him in one of the surfer shops in Newquay.

Enid put her hand in her pocket and pulled out a muslin bag filled with her special brew. "Here, have one of my teas as soon as I've gone, it will help you relax and you won't worry Cullen."

Lucy raised her eyebrows but took the tea, tucking it behind the kettle when she heard the sound of the latch.

"Enjoy it while it lasts, that is what you must do," Enid added in a whisper.

"I will." She paused when Cullen entered the room and set the basket on the floor. "Cullen, come and meet Enid."

He strode over and lifted her hand in his, every bit the gentleman she had remembered watching from afar. She chatted and watched them together for a while, marveling at how Cullen was adapting to his situation. Most of all, her heart warmed at the sight of them together. They were very much in love.

Her work was done. The magic here was now all their own.

She hummed happily as she got into her mini and drove back down to the Newquay, where she had moved many years before, to be nearer to the folk of the town she had been part of for so long.

Chapter Five

Enid's tea did indeed relax her nerves. Lucy cradled the cup in her hands, dreamy eyed. "How do you think people would react if they found out the truth about us, about you?"

"What do you think?" he asked, one eyebrow lifted.

"I don't know."

"I think you do."

He was right.

"I can tell you how folk would react if it were 1806," he said. "They'd treat us as fools. Or worse, they'd say the madness had taken us." He let her ponder his words.

"Yes, you're right, and I suspect it might be even worse here in our time. Some things have improved, some have regressed. There's always the fear that science or the media would take too close an interest." She couldn't even contemplate that, bringing that on him. And Enid.

"This is our secret, our knowledge. Let's keep it that way."

She nodded her agreement.

"Now," he said, moving closer and running his hands over her back as he drew her against him. "Let us speak about something else of great importance." He kissed her forehead, then her eyelids, and then he moved his mouth along her jaw line, his warm breath swamping her senses.

Her head sank back. "Great importance?" she repeated, vaguely, her nerve endings fluttering at his every touch.

He kissed her neck, running the tip of his tongue under her jaw, releasing a tremble in her limbs. "Yes, the orchard."

"The orchard," she repeated again, mindlessly this time, as his fingers wound their way through the buttons on her loose cotton shirt. She was getting wetter by the moment.

"I've been taking a closer look, familiarizing myself with it." He pushed her shirt back over her shoulders. It fell away from her body, pooling on the floor. Her bra soon joined it. His head dipped, and he ran his tongue first over one nipple and then the other, even while he attempted to carry on the conversation. "We want it to flourish again and I think we need to go about this in the ancient way." His hand tugged at the waistband of her cut-off jeans, and then he fumbled with her zipper.

"Cullen." She rested her hands on his upper arms, drawing him up and steadying herself with her fingers clasping around his warm, tanned muscles. "If you are going to have a conversation with me and expect me to understand a word you're saying, you're going to have to stop undressing me at the same time."

He grinned. "Ah, but I must. I'm readying you, Lucy love, because I want to couple with you."

Hearing him say that always made her heart race. "Now that part I understand," she purred, "but what is it you are saying about the orchard and why?"

He drew her up against him and nodded toward the window, where the sun had disappeared and the moon now spilled over the tangled, overgrown trees. "Back when I used to help the tenants with their land, I learned about such things. The Cornish believe in keeping the ancient traditions alive, especially when it comes to nature."

No wonder Enid liked him and wanted to help. He was truly a Cornish man, keeping the traditions alive. "That's true enough, even today," she managed, while pivoting her hips against his, enjoying the feel of his hard body against hers and the promise of lovemaking to come.

"Sometimes the ancient ways are the best." He cupped the back of her head in one strong palm.

"Oh, I'm not about to argue with that, especially with you in my arms." That tickled her, even more so when she thought about Enid's involvement.

He smiled and stroked her hair. "Let us follow nature's way and bring the orchard back to life." He bent and kissed her again, his tongue encouraging hers, then he continued hauling her cut-offs and her knickers down her legs. She laughed as he knelt and finished stripping her, leaving her barefoot.

He stood up and looked for her agreement with a lifted eyebrow.

"Okay, whatever you say about the orchard, I'll take your advice." She sidled back against him. "Now, where were we?" She didn't have a clue what he was going on about, being close to him was much more interesting.

He darted one hand between her thighs. "You're very hot."

She was, but she shivered at his touch, nevertheless. "It's been a hot day, and now you're making me even hotter, Mr. Thaine."

"Let's go outside into the night and cool off. There's a full moon, the light is good." He undid his shorts, stripping off alongside her. "Come on." His gaze was demanding as he looked possessively at her, his cock already half risen and tickling against her thigh.

Outside, naked? She picked up her glass and took another swig of wine. She offered it to his lips and he drank from her hand.

He watched her set it down and then grabbed her hand, leading her out of the house.

After the heat of the day, the late evening air was cool against her naked skin. The hum of insects and sounds of the night resonated somewhere deep in her mind, but most of all she was focused on him, on how his magnificent his body looked in the moonlight, strong and sure as he stalked through the grounds with her in tow.

They passed quickly through the gardens and into the orchards beyond, where the moonlight falling between the leaves cast eerie patches of light to mark their path. He led her deep into the heart of the orchard, where the oldest trees stood and the first of the planting had taken place, many years ago. There, the lines of trees radiated out from an old stone marking the center spot.

"Do you think this was her place, the witch?" She touched the stone reverently, wondering about Enid, the mysterious woman who had lived so long, who had granted their wishes through time.

"I've been thinking that myself." He glanced around at the trees, starkly outlined in the moonlight. "She's brought us here, Lucy, for the eternal circle of life, so it could live on."

He was so right.

He drew her up against a tree, and into his arms. His eyes were wild in the moonlight and she breathed deep, her heart racing, the atmosphere heavy with the scent of the undergrowth and of their desire.

His hands moved over her, down over the curve of her belly and around her hips to her buttocks. He molded them in his hands, lifting her easily so she was crushed against his erection, huge and solid now against her belly. She whispered his name and her sex clenched with need.

"We must offer it up to the earth for the sake of a good harvest." His voice was husky. "Feel nature all around you and let it be inside you. Trust me," he added, when he saw the misgiving in her expression, "it's nature's way, you'll see."

With that dark, suggestive smile he was giving her, she wasn't about to argue. She moved against him, kissing his chest, tasting the salt from his skin, absorbing the rhythm of his body into her own. Somewhere nearby, she heard creatures rustling through the undergrowth, but it only added to the strange mysticism of the experience. She let it enfold her, breathing deeply the scents of the earth and echoing the distant sound of an owl in her soul. "I trust you. I can feel it," she murmured, her body pulsating with desire.

He took her roughly, turning her to face the tree, spread-eagling her, pushing her up against the tree trunk with his hands and moving her against it with his first deep thrust.

He drove again, and again, filling her completely, moving her entire body. She moaned into the night and the night answered, the stars brightening and the branches at the edge of her vision lifting on the ebb and flow of the night air. Nature was all around them and alive, within her. Cullen was strong at her back, and inside, mating with her, fierce and elemental.

She pivoted against the tree, offering herself to him, eager to be marked with his rising sap, riding his thrusts with abandon. His hands roved, spreading her buttocks, stroking his hand into her forbidden places, touching her there, probing inside her with a shocking but gloriously hard finger, claiming every part of her body for the earth. Sensation spiraled through her, every part of her claimed by him. He grunted aloud, his finger working against them both from inside her, his cock fit to burst.

Their mutual victory cries filled the air. She felt herself sexually bared as she'd never been before, a creature at one with nature. When she came, her entire body shuddered.

He pulled out midway, his semen spurting down her legs and onto the soil. "Open your legs wide," he panted, "you must give it up to the earth."

It felt strange, but so right and true. "Yes," she whispered, clutching at the tree, her breasts studded with rough bark, her thighs slick as their fluids trickled down toward the earth.

He whispered words of love to her and stroked her arms where they were pressed up against the tree, until their bodies grew cool and the evening mists wisped up around their bare feet. Then he turned her in his arms, looking at her in the moonlight.

"Pleasured, my love?"

She was trembling. It had been aggressive sex and more, it had been somehow sacred. "Yes, pleasured, lots of pleasure."

"Good, because it could take all summer," he commented, quite seriously.

"What?"

He nodded toward the rest of the orchard. "We'll need to do the same for the rest of the trees."

She threw back her head and laughed joyfully, wild, free and satiated as she'd never been before.

Chapter Six

A month later, Lucy cursed as she darted around the house, pulling things into shape for the impending visitors. Her family was due to arrive at any moment. She wasn't anywhere near ready. How on earth would they get through this?

A mere two months ago, her biggest worry had been her parents' critical words about her recent life choices. Now there was the sudden presence of a rather compelling, but mysterious man in her life to explain.

The dining room was just about in shape to sit everyone for a decent meal, but several unpacked boxes were still stacked by the Welsh dresser, and she wanted them out of the way. Pulling the top box open, she cursed at her disorganized packing. Reaching inside, she pulled out a hairbrush. "I've been looking for you since I moved here." She'd had to buy another.

She rolled her eyes, rested it on the dresser and rooted about inside. It looked as if she'd just emptied a drawer into the box when she'd packed to move down here. She hauled an armful of stuff out, smiling wryly at familiar old magazines, a bottle of moisturizer, two half-read novels, a couple of sex toys and a cuddly toy. It was mostly bedroom junk. With any luck, she could get it upstairs before they arrived.

"There's a car pulling up at the gate," Cullen shouted from the hallway.

"Oh, bloody hell." Wrenching a drawer open, she shoved the stuff inside and pushed the boxes toward the window, where she covered them with the curtains.

Darting through the house, she watched with her nerves shot to hell as her parent's car pulled up at the doorway and the family prepared to invade the house. Taking a deep breath, she put her arm around Cullen and fixed a smile on her face.

"Are you ready for this?" she whispered to him, knowing deep down he was more ready than she would ever be. He looked downright gorgeous in his twenty-first century clothes. His shaggy hair was just brushing the top of his collar, making him look like a rugged rock star relaxing at home—relaxed, self-assured and sexy as hell.

"Ready and willing." He smiled down at her, squeezing her affectionately against his side as he joined her in waving a greeting toward the three figures unfolding themselves out of the car after their long journey. "And I want you to know that I'm already beginning to wonder if I'll ever be able to make that wish to leave your side."

She put her head back, accepted his kiss and savored his words. Yeah, he knew her so well already that he knew she needed the boost, but hell, a girl could get used to hearing that kind of comment from her time-traveling lover. "You're too good to me."

"I'm sure you will make my attentions worth my while." The smoldering look in his eyes would melt ice.

"Be good, for now," she warned. "And where the hell is Enid?" She had invited Enid over to help field any potentially awkward moments. With any luck, she would wave her magic wand-or whatever the hell it was she did-and make everybody happy and accepting.

"She'll be here," he comforted.

"Ah, this must be the mysterious new man in your life," her mother said as she approached. The mention of a romantic interest had resulted in the trip being brought forward a whole two weeks, and Lucy had cringed at her mother's instant curiosity.

"Mrs. Chambers." Cullen grasped her outstretched hand. He bent over it, making an instant impression.

"Margaret, please," she murmured, and gave her daughter an approving smile.

Amazing what a bit of old world charm could do, Lucy mused wryly, as she hugged her Dad and gave her brother Jeremy a high-five. Jeremy was the biggest worry, a rebellious fourteen-year-old, he wouldn't be polite or hesitant about commenting if Cullen made an error. She could only put her trust in fate that this would go as smoothly as possible, and she had been nagging fate a whole lot more recently, she noticed.

They are just here for one afternoon, she reminded herself. That evening the folks would be continuing on their way for a week's holiday touring the coast, and the danger of discovery would be over for the time being.

Mercifully, Enid turned up just as they'd all been given the grand tour of the house, ushered into the sitting room, and presented with a welcome drink. Her family had only been in the house for twenty minutes and already she could see Cullen was greatly amused by them.

Lucy introduced Enid, who looked tickled to bits with the situation. She had her fading blonde hair in its usual bun, but she was wearing a smart fitted dress Lucy hadn't seen before. She had an amused look in her eyes. Lucy couldn't blame her and, besides, she knew Enid would be a big help. Enid at least understood that urbanites from London would find Cullen alien in his ways. Lucy could only hope it would all hang together.

"How's it going?" Enid whispered, as she hugged Lucy and gave her a comforting squeeze.

"Great," she replied through a fixed smile.

"Don't worry, he'll be fine. Believe me, I bet he'll charm them."

Somehow that remark didn't help.

"Now that is kewl," Jeremy declared just at that moment, grabbing Cullen's sword off the mantelpiece.

Lucy winced.

Cullen strode over to where the teenage lad was experimentally waving the sword about like a light saber, and glanced over Jeremy's graffiti-print hoodie and baggy pants with a humor-filled expression. "Cool? Well, I suppose 'tis cool to the touch, but it will warm in your hands soon enough."

Jeremy squawked. "He's funny."

"Funny, and very macho," her mother whispered, approvingly. lifting her sherry glass in Cullen's direction and winking at the other two women.

Macho? Lucy blushed furiously. What was worse, the fact her mother had never approved of her boyfriends, or the fact that she described the one from 1806 as if he were some 1970s beefcake? The travesty. Well it could be worse, she supposed, at least her mother seemed to approve, that was a first. And he did look gorgeous in snug blue jeans and a classic white shirt.

"I say," her father declared when he saw the sword. He abandoned his scrutiny of the plasterwork on the ceiling and joined the scrutiny of the sword. "Are you into reenactment?"

Cullen glanced in her direction, eyebrows lifted.

And she'd thought she had prepared him for every possible conversation topic. "It's an heirloom," she blurted.

"Oh, how lovely, a man with heirlooms," her mother murmured into her sherry.

"Oh, he's got heirlooms like you wouldn't believe," Lucy responded, wondering why she had even bothered trying to prepare him. He seemed to be coping fine—unlike her—and was demonstrating sword moves to Jeremy and her father, both of whom were enthralled, as was her mother, who was watching with starry eyes.

Enid patted Lucy on the arm. "I think he's dealing with things very well. You can tell him tonight if you like," she whispered, and then winked.

"You haven't told us how you met Cullen," her mother said, joining them.

Enid looked at Lucy.

Lucy looked at Enid.

Lucy drew in a deep breath. "Well, he was traveling through... the area and we um, met when he called at the cottage... because he needed directions." She was so bad at fibbing. Had she got away with it by mangling the truth?

"Some girls have all the luck," Enid chipped in, smiling cheerfully at Lucy's mother.

"They certainly do," her mother replied. "I'm pleased for you my dear. At least something good has come of you burying yourself down here in the sticks."

Glancing at the clock, Lucy realized she could get on with serving up lunch. The distraction would help.

"Cullen, could you carve the roast for me?" They had prepared for this one. "The carving knife is just over there in the welsh dresser." He loved technical gadgets and had taken to the electric carving knife as one might expect a swordsman might.

He nodded over at her and stepped sideways to the dresser, reaching for the drawer and grappling about, the sword still in his other hand while he talked his eager audience through a complicated fencing move.

"Oh, dear," Enid said, her hand covering her face, as Cullen looked at the object in his hand and then took in the changing expressions on the faces of his audience.

Lucy stared in disbelief, her jaw dropping.

Cullen glanced again at the silver dream-machine vibrator he was holding in his hand. "Hellfire," he said, "that's not the thing you taught me to use the other day, is it?"

There was a moment's silence, then Jeremy sniggered and Enid chuckled. Lucy swallowed hard. How could this have happened? Then she remembered, the stuff she shoved in the drawer. Bedroom stuff. Cullen's confused expression remained. Her heart went out to him, even though he had no clue what he was holding. Her mum and dad both turned their astonished faces toward her to see what she would say.

"He's got such a sense of humor," she announced, fixing a smile on her face and marching over to extract the object from his hand. "Wrong gadget, lover," she whispered.

"Oh, so what does that one do?" he asked, looking at the shiny surface and the on-off switch with interest as it was snatched from his hand and shoved back into the drawer.

"If I live through this embarrassment, I might get to explain," she whispered in response, wishing the ground would open and swallow the both of them. One thing was sure-life wasn't going to be dull with Cullen Thaine around.

❧⟮ⵌ⟯❧

"I knew something was wrong the moment I saw your face," Cullen said as he kicked off his boots that night.

Lucy lay back against the pillows, watching him, chuckling.

"Well, now you understand why."

"I'm not sure I do." He feigned a confused expression. "Explain it to me again and, this time, I'll concentrate even harder." He gave her a devilish smile as he sat down on the edge of the bed. He picked up the vibrator and toyed with it in one hand.

He'd already had the practical and technical explanation. She decided to give him the more intimate explanation this time. "When I used to get hot for you, after I had dreamt about you but couldn't touch you," she licked her lips, remembering, "I'd wake in the night and I'd need to feel something hard moving inside me, while I imagined you were there, taking me over the edge."

"You pleasured yourself then?" His eyes were gleaming with interest.

She nodded. "I used to play with myself, sliding my fingers inside me, where I was wet from my dreams about you. It was the closest I could get to having you inside, while you weren't here. A vibrator feels even more like a man's cock, and it moves... women enjoy that. I used it when I lived in London and I wanted to feel that pressure, like a man's cock." She put her hand on his thigh, squeezing it.

He smiled darkly. He knew she was teasing him, urging him to get into the bed and make love to her. But he had that measured look about him. He wasn't about to cut to the chase just yet. "Hmm, I might have to take one of these back to my time," he mused, directing his attention to the vibrator, "if they make such an impression on women."

She gave a low growl and sat up as her mouth reached for his. "You're so bad." She began to undo his shirt buttons. "Please don't say that," she whispered against his mouth as she kissed him in small demanding bites, drawing him closer.

"About other women?" He kissed the tip of her nose.

"Yes, that too, but don't talk about going back to your time, not yet." Her hands instinctively clutched at his shoulders. "I'll get my five years, won't I? Promise me that much; you know I love you."

He smiled and kissed her deeply before he answered. "And I love you, too. You've given me sanctuary, and I promise you five years, at the very least." He looked thoughtful. "Let's not discuss it anymore now. I have my new gadget to play with." His eyebrows lifted and his smile was wicked.

With the tip of the vibrator, he pushed the hem of her short nightdress up, exposing the tops of her thighs. He ran the tip into the warm groove at their juncture, teasing the sensitive skin of her mons. "I want to find out exactly how this works."

Her heart began to thud, naughty thoughts racing through her mind. He liked to watch her touching herself; he wanted to see this in action.

"You want me to demonstrate?" She opened her legs, her fingers slipping into the heat between her thighs. She ran one finger over her clit, watching his eyes narrow and his smile tighten a fraction.

He watched her movements for a moment and then reached over to her wrist. "No." He pulled her hand away. His tone was demanding, his eyes glittering with erotic suggestion. "Allow me."

Oh yes. She inhaled slowly. He had a thoroughly determined and devilish look about him. A dark tremor of apprehension passed through her body.

He stood up and finished undoing his shirt buttons, dropped the shirt to the floor, then held her around her upper arms and eased her back onto the bed. He climbed over her, his suede-covered thighs straddling her hips, capturing her. His hands moved down her arms to her wrists. He yanked them away from her body. She let out a small growl of surrender, her head rolling on the pillow.

A shadowy smile passed over his face, partly hidden in the hair that fell forward as he bent over her body. She watched his bare chest, exquisitely masculine, as he lifted her nightdress and pulled it up and over her head, watching as her breasts bounced free. He kissed her deeply, thrusting his tongue into her open mouth, before he moved back down the bed, yanking her legs apart as he climbed off the mattress.

"You're wanton," he whispered with admonishment, looking down at her, "You're such a wild woman."

Fluid seeped from her exposed pussy, the chastisement in his voice and the accusation of her uncontrollable lust were answered by her inner self, regardless of what she might have said. "It's your fault."

He reached for the vibrator and bent over her again. Burying his head between her spread legs, he tasted her with the very tip of his tongue. Bolts of pleasure roared up from that tiny movement, suffusing her groin with heat and a delicious sense of anxious need.

"So wet, so delicious, so ready... I want to take you to your peak, I want to see it happen."

She moaned, feeling sure that her peak wasn't far away at all, and desperate for him to take her to it and force her right over it. Cullen, however, had other ideas. She heard the flick of the switch and the low hum of the vibrator. He traced it down between the damp folds of skin framing her opening, teasing her, then up and over her clit, causing her to moan and wriggle on the bed.

The cold, smooth hardness of the vibrator nudged inside her, the heat of his eyes following its movement and her every response. Instinctively her body responded, her hips rocking forward onto the hard shaft. The vibrator began to hum louder and she let out a loud moan of relief as the reverberations spread through her entire nether region. He rested his other hand over her mons, his palm nudging her clit closer to fruition.

"Seeing you like this is making me hard as rock."

"Cullen..." she pleaded. "I want you inside me. I want to feel your body," she rasped, "your chest, pressed against mine"

He smiled at her plea. "Not till I see you pleasured."

Shock waves darted through her body. She was being teased and stretched unbearably. He was rocking the whole contraption back and forth, jolting out a steady rhythm, filling her with sensation upon sensation. She doubted she could take much more, and then she felt his thumb stroking the hard nub of her clitoris, and she cried out, her body racing between ecstasy and frustration.

Using a vibrator wasn't usually like this. This was different. This was hellishly different, with him in control and watching her with those eyes, eyes that had haunted her dreams for so many nights. Now, when there was so much more between them, to feel him watching her so keenly, reveling in her pleasure, controlling it—it was too divine. She ached for him, ached in every way. "Cullen…"

He muttered something unintelligible as he bent over her, his tongue lapping at her clit. The vibrations traveled all through her and into his mouth as he sucked the swollen bud gently, a beautiful stark contrast to the rigidity inside her. Lucy lost sight of the room, her body jerking spasmodically, as waves of pleasure roared through her. In the distance, she heard her own voice crying out.

Cullen switched the vibrator off, easing it free from her body. He cast it aside, his eyes dark with passion. She could see that he was desperately aroused; the sight of him that way sent an after-tremor through her sex, drenched but suddenly bereft. "I want you, inside me."

He stood up, eyeing her possessively as he undid his belt. Her eyes dropped from his as he climbed out of his pants and she saw his cock rear up, long and thick, its head beautifully defined and dark with blood. He came back and lay over her, his cock pressing against the engorged folds of her sex. He rested his hands on her breasts and stroked her, his palms held over the hard nipples, his broad hands clasping her breasts rhythmically.

She breathed deep the musk scent of his body, it swept through her like a cloud of smoke, immersing her senses in its cover. His closeness overwhelmed her with a new rush of sensations. She loved him, she was intoxicated by him, she was thoroughly absorbed by his presence. She sucked hard at his mouth, grazing him with her teeth. His hips were moving against hers, pressing his erection between her thighs, and it was driving her wild. "Please, Cullen, please," she pleaded.

His eyes flashed at her, his mouth in a passionate curl. Then he reached down and pressed his fingers inside her. "You're mighty swollen. I might use that thing on you again after all."

"I'd rather it was you." Her hips reached for him.

He gave a victorious smile and entered her. As he drove the full length of his shaft slowly inside, she cried out with pleasure. She felt so exquisitely full and yet bordering on pain. He had driven her to distraction with that bloody vibrator and now he was moving so in tune with her body that she felt as if she was about to come again, every time the swollen head of his cock crushed against her, so very deep inside.

"You want this, do you?" He rammed home.

"Yes, please," she begged, clutching him deeper. She felt a sob at the back of her throat and fought it back.

"You are so beautiful, and when you reached your pleasure, you looked like a goddess," he whispered.

She felt like her heart would burst, pleasure and love filled her to overflowing. She was in ecstasy, the ache in her chest caused by the thought of losing him melted slowly through the liquid fire he poured through her body. As their movements became more fevered, she bucked her body up against him, her body arching. Her legs climbed up around his hips, locking him in against her. The mutual pleasure of it shot between their locked eyes. Their bodies were harmonized. They moved in quick, even strides, barely parting but to press close together again.

He turned his face into her neck, drawing his tongue along her skin, his breath like a warm sirocco sifting the sands. Their movements were building speed together, perfectly attuned, and rhythmic. They were pacing, ever faster, towards crescendo. As the orgasm came close, his hand slid over her pubic bone, pressing her mons down as he moved against her. His brows were drawn down, his eyes intense, a bead of sweat sliding slowly down one side of his face. His mouth opened and each quick stride drew a harsh breath from him. Heat welled from her womb as if a heavy, hot liquid was held in her pelvis. A shock wave hit, it buoyed up against the full head of his cock where it had lodged itself deep and hard inside her.

"Oh yes… yes," he murmured, his eyes afire with passion. She felt his whole body arch and bow against hers. Her sex throbbed and gripped his cock as it heaved and lurched, their bodies falling still in the moment of mutual climax.

He gave her a tender kiss, then rolled onto his back, taking her with him, staying inside her while he could.

She chuckled, tethered to him like that, yet feeling strangely afloat in the afterglow. Afloat, drifting. Lost in time? The thought brought her down to earth, and she sighed.

"I know how it happened," she said rolling free of him and settling on her pillow beside him.

"What?"

"How we traveled through time to be with each other."

He lifted his brows.

"It's Enid. She's a witch, she matched us."

He thought about it, and then bent to kiss her. "It makes sense. She's a Cornish enigma to be sure."

"Does it make any difference? I mean, knowing how…?"

"No, it's good to understand it more fully, but the important thing is this." He laid his hand on her arm. "We are here together, instead of me being heaven-knows-where for my exile, while you tried to manage this place alone and keep your business going as well."

Her heart filled, emotions welling inside her. Surely she couldn't live without him? "Please don't talk about your exile, don't talk about leaving," she begged, the words blurting unbidden from her mouth.

"No," he replied "we won't talk about it. Let's just enjoy what time we have together."

She nodded, curling against him.

Would that be enough, though? Would that ever be enough?

Chapter Seven

It was a beautiful morning, just a few days before Midsummer's Day and fast closing on the end of their first year together. Cullen stood in the orchard, contemplating that fact while watching the sunlight push through the heavy canopy of leaves above. He surveyed the crop of apples. The boughs were heavy with fruit, some even trailing down to touch the ground at their tips. He was proud of the progress they had made and he doubted nature and her muse, the white witch of legend, could have been more pleased than he was.

Things were looking good and he gave a heartfelt sigh. It was a heavenly spot. The sun dappled across the grass below, turning it into a moving carpet of light.

When he heard his name being called, he glanced across the orchard toward the gardens. Lucy was walking down the path toward him, holding two glasses of freshly crushed apple juice. He smiled at the sight of her, admiring the way she moved as she walked. She was a vision. She'd filled his life. He had never met a woman like her, and he doubted he ever would again. "You're like Eve, tempting me with your apple nectar."

"Heh, you better believe it." She set down the glasses and sidled up to him to give him a long, slow kiss. "If I'm Eve, this must be the garden of Eden."

"Paradise…" He breathed her scent in. "How's it going?"

"Really well. In fact, it's almost done."

She'd been designing him a website, a guide to living in England in the early 1800s. It was a bit of history, and he hoped it would be useful to people who might be interested. They'd had a lot of fun putting the material together. The fact that she'd done it for him was very special. Not that he fully understood the technicalities of the Internet, even after nearly a year of struggling to do so. He left it to her, turning his hand instead to the house and land. He had taken on two local retired gentlemen to maintain the gardens and fruit bushes, and he had ensured Lucy would have a good crop of fruit and vegetables all year round. He'd also been able to negotiate a contract to supply a small local hotel with apples and summer fruits. Whatever happened, he was proud to have given her a bit of security.

"Thank you." He took her into his arms and kissed her forehead. Lord, the feel of her was so good. Would he ever truly be able to give that up? "Thank you for that and everything." He looked down into her eyes. They had long ago declared the depth of their love for one another.

She looked at him wistfully.

He knew what that wistfulness was about. They had vowed never to speak of their parting until the time came to deal with it and she was steadfast about that vow. At Christmas, Lucy's mother had sent her a framed embroidery for the cottage that read, "Home is where the heart is." It was Lucy's mother's way of telling her she approved of her life in Cornwall, after all, but he knew that Lucy had hidden it away from his eyes. She was trying so hard not to remind of his home, nor to pressure him into staying, and he loved her for that generosity of spirit.

"Take that worried frown away, my love," he added and smoothed his thumb across her brow. He knew what caused her worry. She thought today's planned trip to Hollingswell Hall, his family estate and the place where he'd grown up, would make him want to go back in time earlier. They'd visited the place almost as soon as he had arrived into 2006, but for him that was a startling discovery, part of his manifold leap forward in time and understanding. This time was different, yes, and he knew she feared the worst, that he was homesick. The fear was written all over her beautiful face.

He did need to see Hollingswell Hall right now, to strengthen his resolve about what was the right thing to do. And, more than that, there was something in particular he needed to do there.

"Yes, we must get on our way." She adopted a breezy smile and glanced at her watch. "I've got our picnic basket ready, and I called and checked, the first afternoon tour is at two-thirty. So let's get on our way and we can have our picnic on the grounds, before we take the tour."

"Do we have to view the place with the tour guide?"

"Yes, because it's only a small Heritage House, that's the way they run it, for security's sake."

He nodded, disgruntled, for he felt sure it would make his task more difficult to achieve.

Something was wrong. He'd barely said a word to her during their picnic. In fact, he'd hardly eaten anything at all. He seemed to be a million miles away. With an ache in her heart, Lucy had to face the fact that he was homesick. He'd wanted to come here today because he was missing his family, that's all there was to it, and she had to toughen up and accept that fact.

The first time they had visited, he hadn't even wanted to go inside the house. It had been enough for them to walk the grounds and marvel at what had changed and what was the same.

Now, he wanted to go inside, he wanted to do the full tour. He obviously needed to connect with his old life.

And there she was hoping he might stay.

Up until a few days ago, she'd been almost certain that he would stay. He seemed content, they were so deeply in love. Life was perfect. She tried not to count the days until his five years were up, but it was hard not to be reminded, not to savor every moment and wish for more time.

The tour guide rapped her clipboard against her thigh and ushered the party of tourists together for the commencement of the tour.

Cullen cursed under his breath. He had taken an instant dislike to the guide for some reason, which was something totally out of character for him. In their year together, she hadn't witnessed him clash with anyone. Presumably he couldn't bear to see what he felt were strangers lording about in his family home. He had a scowl on his face that could turn milk.

With each passing second, her chest grew tighter, her hopes for the future fading as she felt him being lured away from her by the past. "Cullen?" She took his hand and he looked at her as if he'd forgotten she were there. "Are you okay?"

"Yes, yes." His tone was terse, but he gave her hand a quick squeeze.

The tour group set off, moving along a red carpet walkway through the grand downstairs rooms at an agreeable pace, while the guide delivered a non-stop catalogue of facts with a superior expression on her face.

Cullen's gaze darted about the artifacts on display while he muttered to himself, catching the guide's disapproving glance on more than one occasion.

Lucy kept a close watch on him. His expression remained tense and disapproving until they entered the large parlor, where things rapidly deteriorated into sheer animosity between him and the guide.

"As you'll see this room houses the collection of family portraits, including work by several masters of British art, depicting five generations of the Thaine family."

She could feel the tension emanating from him, it was building by the second. She turned toward the painting he was staring at and her hand leapt to her mouth. Cullen's image was there on the canvas. Much younger, a teenage boy, but it was him, undeniably.

"Unfortunately, this particular work wasn't dated by the artist," announced the guide, "but we've had our experts look at it and it has been dated to the early 1790s."

"1788," Cullen corrected.

"I'm sorry, did you say something?" The guide quizzed him with a look of annoyance.

"1788. The painting was done in 1788."

The tour guide stared at him for several moments, her lips fastened in a tight line. Then she turned away dismissively and directed the group's attention away from the surly member of the troupe, and back to the painting.

"The Thaine family depicted here are the third generation of the family to be residents in the house. They were responsible for extending the estates, and the generation with perhaps the most infamous Thaine family member," she pointed up in the direction of the two young brothers, as if she wasn't sure which one it was. "Cullen James, who—legend has it—was said to have become a notorious captain of the high seas around the West Indies."

Captain? High seas? A wave of sheer panic hit Lucy. Did this mean he went back and continued with his plans to travel out to the colonies?

"He was like the black sheep of the family, yes," one of the other tourists offered, grinning at the idea of it.

Lucy risked a glance at Cullen. He was shaking his head and casting looks of aspersion at the guide.

"Yes indeed, Cullen Thaine was 'like the black sheep,' although I must stress it is hearsay. Now, let's move along, shall we?"

Lucy's mind was in turmoil. She took a last glance at the family portrait, attempting to commit to memory the image of his mother and father seated, with the two boys and their pretty young sisters standing around them, a hound at their feet.

"Cullen, what do you think it means?"

"It doesn't mean anything. The woman clearly has no idea what she's talking about." He rolled his eyes.

"But it could happen, I mean, if you went back, you don't know what direction your life might go in."

"That is true enough," he agreed, as they followed the red carpet and turned toward the staircase leading up to the second stage of the tour.

He was blatantly unconcerned.

Her blood raced. He was so nonchalant about it. How could he be like that? "Doesn't it matter to you, what becomes of you, of us?"

He was craning his neck to look up at the top of the staircase but glanced away for a second to answer her. "Not right now, it doesn't."

She swallowed. Her chest was tight with anxiety.

The party began to mount the stairs, but he hung back, leaving a fair distance between them and the rest of the group.

"But Cullen, I'm wondering if it will even be possible, you know, I think we might not be able to part when the time comes, because we both have to wish for it..."

"Yes, I had thought of that, my love. Let's not talk about it here."

She felt wretched. In fact, she was almost heart-broken. She almost tripped on the Persian stair carpet. "But I don't know if I'll be able to wish it, truly, with my heart, because I love you so much I can't bear to be apart and that's what counts, the ability to wish for it..."

He ignored her, staring fixedly ahead as they arrived on the landing.

Damn, he was going to leave. He didn't even want to hear her concerns. "Cullen?"

She found herself jolted to a standstill.

"One moment, my love."

He watched as the party ahead of them turned down the corridor, and then jerked his head in the other direction, toward a narrower, gloomier corridor.

She had barely caught her breath and almost dropped her bag, when he hauled her along behind him at sudden, breakneck speed. *What the hell is he up to now?*

The corridor opened out into a smaller landing, and he stopped and dropped her hand. He strode back and forth along the wood paneled walls.

She hitched her bag onto her shoulder, wishing she'd left it in the car. "Cullen, we've got to stick with the tour guide."

He ignored her.

"Cullen, what is the matter with you? Why won't you talk to me?"

He turned and looked at her, attempting to focus on her for a moment. He reached over to her, and drew her to him with a swift scoop of his arm. "One moment, my love, and you'll have all my attention. I promise." He kissed her quickly.

Her body wavered when he freed her again. *What on earth is he up to?*

"And keep an eye out for that damn harridan of a guide," he added, "if I'm caught doing this there will be trouble. They'll claim what I'm looking for is theirs, but it's never been part of this estate."

She was none the wiser about what he was up to, but did as he asked.

He stepped to the right, then to the left, dodging and shifting as he eyed the wood panels with consideration. He seemed to be counting the panels, and then he reached out to touch one panel with his hand. He rapped it with his knuckles, then the one next to it, taking a quick glance down the hallway to where the tour had gone. The rapping sound on the second panel was more hollow.

"Dear God in heaven, I hope I get this right," he murmured. He shut his eyes and put his head back, as if appealing to the heavens. "Let it work."

Lucy stared in awe as he pressed the panel in the bottom left corner, applying pressure and watching with his eyes gleaming as the panel slowly squeaked opened and turned on a central axis.

"Amazing," he whispered, "It worked, even after all this time." He reached into the open slot and withdrew a long leather wrap, as big as his forearm. "Look," he said, blowing the dust off its surface and unrolling the bulging object against one arm.

She watched, mesmerized, as he revealed the contents of the leather wrap and on each turn, another clutch of jewels slid out of its folds. "I don't understand, what is it?"

"It was my mother's," he said, staring down at an exquisite necklace, his thoughts a million miles away. "My mother's jewels, her inheritance."

She glanced over her shoulder, wondering what the hell would happen if the tour guide caught them, now.

"My father didn't want her to wear them," he was saying. "He gave her much more beautiful and valuable things, but to her, these jewels meant the world, they were her mother's before her." He looked at her, seeking her understanding, and his expression was heavy with emotion. "She showed them to me when I was lad, maybe nine years old. I was the second son, I wouldn't inherit all this," he nodded up, indicating the house. "She wanted to hide these away for me, for my future... should I choose to make my own path… Lucy, this is for us."

"I don't understand."

"It's meant to be, all of this. She wanted me to give them to my woman, to my wife."

Her heart constricted as his words sank in.

"I want you to be my wife."

"Wife?" She shook her head. "You mean you'll stay with me?"

He gave a disbelieving laugh. "Lucy love, there's never been any doubt about that. Now, please, say you'll be mine."

Lucy stared at him, mesmerized.

"Say you'll be mine," he demanded.

"But what about Enid, the magic?"

"I don't care how it happened. She was right, we were meant to be together. I want you-forever."

Her heart soared.

"Yes. Yes, I'm yours, but Cullen… are you sure? Really sure? I couldn't bear it if you changed your mind."

"I'm sure. Don't fret." He smoothed her hair back and she could see the deep, honest contentment in his expression. "Forever," he whispered, promised.

"Forever," she repeated, joyously, wriggling into his arms.

"And I thought we might go down the old cave tonight, relive a few memories…"

"Mmm," she purred, her hands roving toward his hips, her fingers latching into the pocket of his jeans. "Sounds fabulous, I can't wait."

The sound of footsteps echoed down the corridor toward them. Reluctantly, his gaze lifted from hers, his brows drawing down and his expression growing guarded. He quickly folded the leather sleeve closed and shoved it into her shoulder bag, his other hand pressing the wood panel shut on its axis, forcing it at the last when it grew stiff and unwilling to lie flat.

Lucy watched in awe as the secret panel closed and became an integral part of the wall again.

His expression changed as the tour guide marched up to them and he acknowledged her presence.

What now? She figured he was right when he said it wasn't the property of the Heritage House consortium—it wouldn't be on their purchase inventory, for a start. But it would be a tough case to argue, especially when the man who claimed rights to the goods said he was from the early eighteen-hundreds.

"I'm sorry, madam, did we drop behind? We were just admiring the wonderful woodwork." He grinned widely at the guide. "I do love a good bit of paneling." He patted the wood with one hand.

The tour guide gave him a dubious look, folding her arms with a disapproving glance.

"Come along my love," he added. "We mustn't miss out on our guide's amusing anecdotes."

The guide forced a tight smile. "You really can't fall out of the guided tour, you might miss something important. Now, do I have your full attention?"

"Madam, for the rest of the tour, my lady betrothed and I are all yours."

He rested his head against Lucy's hair and whispered, "Then you're all mine."

Epilogue

They went to the cliffs on midsummer's morn to make their commitment in the ancient way, handfasting to one another in the pagan style. Enid was to be their witness. She was the one to give them their bond. How could it be anyone else?

As the sun rose, the mist trailed their footsteps, blurring the horizon and masking the telltale signs that showed them where they were in time. Cullen thought that they could be anywhere, and it didn't really matter, as long as they were together. As long as he was with Lucy.

It had taken a while to get used to being alive in Cornwall in the millennium, but he had. His old life had begun to wither away from him. Home is where the heart is, and that was with Lucy. They had agreed to give each other the five years until he would return to his time. His return...the desire to do so had dwindled over time. How could it not? He didn't know exactly when it had happened, but one morning he'd woken up knowing for sure—he could never go back, not without her.

She looked so beautiful, and he couldn't get his fill of her. His mother's favorite gemstones shone at her neck, a simple design of intertwined silver hearts set with small rubies. Lucy had picked it as her favorite, too, and that made him happy. Her hair was garlanded with meadow flowers and her white muslin dress floated about her form so delicately, he thought she looked like an angel. "My angel wench," he whispered possessively.

"My lusty time-traveler." She chuckled as she said it and kissed him, cuddling up against his side and stroking his cotton shirt, for she had insisted he wear the clothes he had traveled through time in.

God, he loved her. This beautiful woman had come through time for him, to give him this life and her love, at home in the land he cherished. Surely no man had ever felt luckier than he did in that moment?

"Am I late?" Enid called over to them, as she climbed out of her mini.

"No," Lucy answered.

"We've got all the time in the world," Cullen added and kissed her forehead.

"I hope you don't mind," Enid said as she walked over to where they stood on the cliffs. "I wore my favorite dress."

"It's beautiful," Lucy whispered mesmerized.

Cullen stared at the ancient garment, a robe of white silk, many centuries old. Would they ever know just how long Enid had been making merry with the hearts of Cornish folk? Her white-streaked flaxen hair was loose about her shoulders, her strange green eyes shining. A silver chain hung at her throat, adorned with a pearl and a piece of carved jet. She was clutching a red velvet cushion and a wicker basket in the other hand.

"I'm so touched to see this moment," Enid said.

"You ought to be," Cullen teased. "It's all your fault."

She threw him a chastising glance, humming happily. "I remembered everything." She set down the basket, which contained a bottle of champagne, glasses, and a camera, and leveled the cushion, arranging the objects they had chosen to fasten to one another: two red ribbons and two ornately-carved, silver Celtic rings. "Ready?" she asked, beaming happily.

"Yes," they replied, in unison.

"Just one thing. I have to ask." She cleared her throat. "As your witness and your mentor, I want to know if this binding of hearts and bodies means you'll be disappearing off together. You know, I'd like some advance warning."

"We're happy here, for the time being," Cullen replied, his mind drifting to images of the high seas, Lucy in his arms aboard a magnificent vessel as it carved its way through the ocean. They had the means to do it now, more than enough with what his mother had left for him. Perhaps they would pursue that adventure, perhaps they wouldn't. Time would tell.

Enid tutted. "I didn't bring you together to have you race off again."

She was teasing. Cullen had long since spotted her mischievous sense of humor. They both had.

"The only thing you can be sure of in life is your heart," Lucy added provocatively, squeezing his hand, "and where it leads, you will follow."

Oh yes, he liked the promise in her eyes. There were many adventures to be had yet with his ladylove.

Enid chuckled under her breath, then she blinked her eyes into the ever-brightening sky and presented them with the cushion. "The time is right," she urged.

He lifted the first ribbon, turning back to Lucy. "Blood of my blood," he recited and tied the red ribbon around Lucy's wrist, "and bone of my bone," he slipped the ring on her finger. "I bind myself to thee and wherever we wander, I will return to this spot each midsummer's day to renew my vow to walk by your side."

Enid offered the cushion to Lucy.

She lifted the second red ribbon. "Blood of my blood..." Her hand shook. He grasped it in his, steadying her, and she finished the job, smiling at him, "And bone of my bone." She slipped the ring onto his finger, and he clutched both her hands in his. "I bind myself to you, now and forever."

Enid wiped a tear from her eyes. "Congratulations. I'm so glad to witness this and I wish you every happiness." She placed her hand over theirs. "Oh, I nearly forgot–the broom! You have to jump the broom. It's tradition."

She turned away and darted back to where she had parked her car, returning a minute later with an old-fashioned broomstick which she set down on the grass in front of them.

"It's supposed to be a witch's broom?" he quizzed.

Enid glared at him in mock annoyance. "Hush now, it's all I had."

"Why am I not surprised?" Lucy responded. She laughed and lifted her skirts, her glance inviting him to take the final step.

He wrapped his arm around her waist and together they jumped over the broom. And then she reached up and kissed him, and he wondered how he could ever have thought of leaving her at all. This was what he wanted, and why wouldn't he? It was pure magic.

About the Author:

Saskia Walker is a British writer who lives with her real life hero, Mark, and their big black cat in the north of England, close to the beautiful landscape of the Yorkshire moors. Because of her parent's nomadic tendencies, Saskia grew up traveling the globe—an only child with a serious book habit. She dreamed of being a writer when she first read romance at the age of 12 and finally began writing seriously in the late 1990s. Since then she's had short fiction published on both sides of the pond and is thrilled to be the first British author writing for Red Sage.

Men you've been dreaming about!

Secrets

Satisfy your desire for more.

*F*eel the wild adventure, fierce passion and the power of love in every *Secrets* Collection story. Red Sage Publishing's romance authors create richly crafted, sexy, sensual, novella-length stories. Each one is just the right length for reading after a long and hectic day.

Each volume in the *Secrets* Collection has four diverse, ultra-sexy, romantic novellas brimming with adventure, passion and love. More adventurous tales for the adventurous reader. The *Secrets* Collection are a glorious mix of romance genre; numerous historical settings, contemporary, paranormal, science fiction and suspense. We are always looking for new adventures.

Reader response to the *Secrets* volumes has been great! Here's just a small sample:

> *"I loved the variety of settings. Four completely wonderful time periods, give you four completely wonderful reads."*

> *"Each story was a page-turning tale I hated to put down."*

> *"I love **Secrets**! When is the next volume coming out? This one was Hot! Loved the heroes!"*

Secrets have won raves and awards. We could go on, but why don't you find out for yourself—order your set of **Secrets** today! See the back for details.

Secrets, Volume 1

Listen to what reviewers say:

"These stories take you beyond romance into the realm of erotica. I found *Secrets* absolutely delicious."

—Virginia Henley,
New York Times Best Selling Author

"*Secrets* is a collection of novellas for the daring, adventurous woman who's not afraid to give her fantasies free reign."

—Kathe Robin, *Romantic Times* Magazine

"…In fact, the men featured in all the stories are terrific, they all want to please and pleasure their women. If you like erotic romance you will love *Secrets*."

—*Romantic Readers* Review

In *Secrets, Volume 1* you'll find:

A Lady's Quest by Bonnie Hamre
Widowed Lady Antonia Blair-Sutworth searches for a lover to save her from the handsome Duke of Sutherland. The "auditions" may be shocking but utterly tantalizing.

The Spinner's Dream by Alice Gaines
A seductive fantasy that leaves every woman wishing for her own private love slave, desperate and running for his life.

The Proposal by Ivy Landon
This tale is a walk on the wild side of love. *The Proposal* will taunt you, tease you, and shock you. A contemporary erotica for the adventurous woman.

The Gift by Jeanie LeGendre
Immerse yourself in this historic tale of exotic seduction, bondage and a concubine's surrender to the Sultan's desire. Can Alessandra live the life and give the gift the Sultan demands of her?

Secrets, Volume 2

Listen to what reviewers say:

"*Secrets* offers four novellas of sensual delight; each beautifully written with intense feeling and dedication to character development. For those seeking stories with heightened intimacy, look no further."

—Kathee Card, *Romancing the Web*

"Such a welcome diversity in styles and genres. Rich characterization in sensual tales. An exciting read that's sure to titillate the senses."

—Cheryl Ann Porter

"*Secrets 2* left me breathless. Sensual satisfaction guaranteed… times four!"

—Virginia Henley, *New York Times* Best Selling Author

In *Secrets, Volume 2* you'll find:

Surrogate Lover by Doreen DeSalvo

Adrian Ross is a surrogate sex therapist who has all the answers and control. He thought he'd seen and done it all, but he'd never met Sarah.

Snowbound by Bonnie Hamre

A delicious, sensuous regency tale. The marriage-shy Earl of Howden is teased and tortured by his own desires and finds there is a woman who can equal his overpowering sensuality.

Roarke's Prisoner by Angela Knight

Elise, a starship captain, remembers the eager animal submission she'd known before at her captor's hands and refuses to become his toy again. However, she has no idea of the delights he's planned for her this time.

Savage Garden by Susan Paul

Raine's been captured by a mysterious and dangerous revolutionary leader in Mexico. At first her only concern is survival, but she quickly finds lush erotic nights in her captor's arms.

Winner of the Fallot Literary Award for Fiction!

Secrets, Volume 3

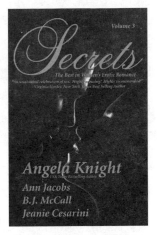

Listen to what reviewers say:

"*Secrets, Volume 3*, leaves the reader breathless. A delicious confection of sensuous treats awaits the reader on each turn of the page!"

—Kathee Card, *Romancing the Web*

"From the FBI to Police Detective to Vampires to a Medieval Warlord home from the Crusade—*Secrets 3* is simply the best!"

—Susan Paul, award winning author

"An unabashed celebration of sex. Highly arousing! Highly recommended!"

—Virginia Henley, *New York Times* Best Selling Author

In *Secrets, Volume 3* you'll find:

The Spy Who Loved Me by Jeanie Cesarini

Undercover FBI agent Paige Ellison's sexual appetites rise to new levels when she works with leading man Christopher Sharp, the cunning agent who uses all his training to capture her body and heart.

The Barbarian by Ann Jacobs

Lady Brianna vows not to surrender to the barbaric Giles, Earl of Harrow. He must use sexual arts learned in the infidels' harem to conquer his bride. A word of caution—this is not for the faint of heart.

Blood and Kisses by Angela Knight

A vampire assassin is after Beryl St. Cloud. Her only hope lies with Decker, another vampire and ex-mercenary. Broke, she offers herself as payment for his services. Will his seductive powers take her very soul?

Love Undercover by B.J. McCall

Amanda Forbes is the bait in a strip joint sting operation. While she performs, fellow detective "Cowboy" Cooper gets to watch. Though he excites her, she must fight the temptation to surrender to the passion.

**Winner of the 1997 Under the Covers
Readers Favorite Award**

Secrets, Volume 4

Listen to what reviewers say:

"Provocative... seductive... a must read!"

—*Romantic Times* Magazine

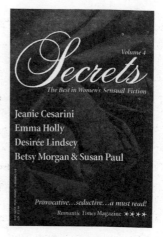

"These are the kind of stories that romance readers that 'want a little more' have been looking for all their lives...."

—*Affaire de Coeur* Magazine

"*Secrets, Volume 4*, has something to satisfy every erotic fantasy... simply sexational!"

—Virginia Henley, *New York Times* Best Selling Author

In *Secrets, Volume 4* you'll find:

An Act of Love by Jeanie Cesarini

Shelby Moran's past left her terrified of sex. International film star Jason Gage must gently coach the young starlet in the ways of love. He wants more than an act—he wants Shelby to feel true passion in his arms.

Enslaved by Desirée Lindsey

Lord Nicholas Summer's air of danger, dark passions, and irresistible charm have brought Lady Crystal's long-hidden desires to the surface. Will he be able to give her the one thing she desires before it's too late?

The Bodyguard by Betsy Morgan and Susan Paul

Kaki York is a bodyguard, but watching the wild, erotic romps of her client's sexual conquests on the security cameras is getting to her—and her partner, the ruggedly handsome James Kulick. Can she resist his insistent desire to have her?

The Love Slave by Emma Holly

A woman's ultimate fantasy. For one year, Princess Lily will be attended to by three delicious men of her choice. While she delights in playing with the first two, it's the reluctant Grae, with his powerful chest, black eyes and hair, that stirs her desires.

Secrets, Volume 5

Listen to what reviewers say:

"Hot, hot, hot! Not for the faint-hearted!"

—Romantic Times Magazine

"As you make your way through the stories, you will find yourself becoming hotter and hotter. *Secrets* just keeps getting better and better."

—Affaire de Coeur Magazine

"*Secrets 5* is a collage of luscious sensuality. Any woman who reads *Secrets* is in for an awakening!"

—Virginia Henley, *New York Times* Best Selling Author

In *Secrets, Volume 5* you'll find:

Beneath Two Moons by Sandy Fraser

Ready for a very wild romp? Step into the future and find Conor, rough and masculine like frontiermen of old, on the prowl for a new conquest. In his sights, Dr. Eva Kelsey. She got away once before, but this time Conor makes sure she begs for more.

Insatiable by Chevon Gael

Marcus Remington photographs beautiful models for a living, but it's Ashlyn Fraser, a young corporate exec having some glamour shots done, who has stolen his heart. It's up to Marcus to help her discover her inner sexual self.

Strictly Business by Shannon Hollis

Elizabeth Forrester knows it's tough enough for a woman to make it to the top in the corporate world. Garrett Hill, the most beautiful man in Silicon Valley, has to come along to stir up her wildest fantasies. Dare she give in to both their desires?

Alias Smith and Jones by B.J. McCall

Meredith Collins finds herself stranded overnight at the airport. A handsome stranger by the name of Smith offers her sanctuary for the evening and she finds those mesmerizing, green-flecked eyes hard to resist. Are they to be just two ships passing in the night?

Secrets, Volume 6

Listen to what reviewers say:

"Red Sage was the first and remains the leader of Women's Erotic Romance Fiction Collections!"
—*Romantic Times* Magazine

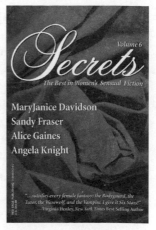

"*Secrets, Volume 6*, is the best of *Secrets* yet. ...four of the most erotic stories in one volume than this reader has yet to see anywhere else. ...These stories are full of erotica at its best and you'll definitely want to keep it handy for lots of re-reading!"
—*Affaire de Coeur* Magazine

"*Secrets 6* satisfies every female fantasy: the Bodyguard, the Tutor, the Werewolf, and the Vampire. I give it Six Stars!"
—Virginia Henley, *New York Times* Best Selling Author

In *Secrets, Volume 6* you'll find:

Flint's Fuse by Sandy Fraser
Dana Madison's father has her "kidnapped" for her own safety. Flint, the tall, dark and dangerous mercenary, is hired for the job. But just which one is the prisoner—Dana will try *anything* to get away.

Love's Prisoner by MaryJanice Davidson
Trapped in an elevator, Jeannie Lawrence experienced unwilling rapture at Michael Windham's hands. She never expected the devilishly handsome man to show back up in her life—or turn out to be a werewolf!

The Education of Miss Felicity Wells by Alice Gaines
Felicity Wells wants to be sure she'll satisfy her soon-to-be husband but she needs a teacher. Dr. Marcus Slade, an experienced lover, agrees to take her on as a student, but can he stop short of taking her completely?

A Candidate for the Kiss by Angela Knight
Working on a story, reporter Dana Ivory stumbles onto a more amazing one—a sexy, secret agent who happens to be a vampire. She wants her story but Gabriel Archer wants more from her than just sex and blood.

Secrets, Volume 7

Listen to what reviewers say:

"Get out your asbestos gloves — *Secrets Volume 7* is… extremely hot, true erotic romance… passionate and titillating. There's nothing quite like baring your secrets!"

—*Romantic Times* Magazine

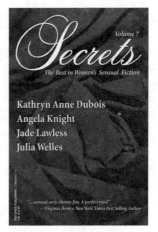

"…sensual, sexy, steamy fun. A perfect read!"
—Virginia Henley,
New York Times Best Selling Author

"Intensely provocative and disarmingly romantic, *Secrets*, *Volume 7*, is a romance reader's paradise that will take you beyond your wildest dreams!"

—Ballston Book House Review

In *Secrets, Volume 7* you'll find:

Amelia's Innocence by Julia Welles

Amelia didn't know her father bet her in a card game with Captain Quentin Hawke, so honor demands a compromise—three days of erotic foreplay, leaving her virginity and future intact.

The Woman of His Dreams by Jade Lawless

From the day artist Gray Avonaco moves in next door, Joanna Morgan is plagued by provocative dreams. But what she believes is unrequited lust, Gray sees as another chance to be with the woman he loves. He must persuade her that even death can't stop true love.

Surrender by Kathryn Anne Dubois

Free-spirited Lady Johanna wants no part of the binding strictures society imposes with her marriage to the powerful Duke. She doesn't know the dark Duke wants sensual adventure, and sexual satisfaction.

Kissing the Hunter by Angela Knight

Navy Seal Logan McLean hunts the vampires who murdered his wife. Virginia Hart is a sexy vampire searching for her lost soul-mate only to find him in a man determined to kill her. She must convince him all vampires aren't created equally.

Winner of the Venus Book Club Best Book of the Year

Secrets, Volume 8

Listen to what reviewers say:

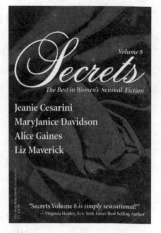

"*Secrets, Volume 8*, is an amazing compilation of sexy stories covering a wide range of subjects, all designed to titillate the senses. …you'll find something for everybody in this latest version of *Secrets*."

—*Affaire de Coeur* Magazine

"*Secrets Volume 8*, is simply sensational!"
—Virginia Henley, *New York Times*
Best Selling Author

"These delectable stories will have you turning the pages long into the night. Passionate, provocative and perfect for setting the mood…."
—*Escape to Romance* Reviews

In *Secrets, Volume 8* you'll find:

Taming Kate by Jeanie Cesarini

Kathryn Roman inherits a legal brothel. Little does this city girl know the town of Love, Nevada wants her to be their new madam so they've charged Trey Holliday, one very dominant cowboy, with taming her.

Jared's Wolf by MaryJanice Davidson

Jared Rocke will do anything to avenge his sister's death, but ends up attracted to Moira Wolfbauer, the she-wolf sworn to protect her pack. Joining forces to stop a killer, they learn love defies all boundaries.

My Champion, My Lover by Alice Gaines

Celeste Broder is a woman committed for having a sexy appetite. Mayor Robert Albright may be her champion—if she can convince him her freedom will mean a chance to indulge their appetites together.

Kiss or Kill by Liz Maverick

In this post-apocalyptic world, Camille Kazinsky's military career rides on her ability to make a choice—whether the robo called Meat should live or die. Meat's future depends on proving he's human enough to live, man enough… to makes her feel like a woman.

Winner of the Venus Book Club Best Book of the Year

Secrets, Volume 9

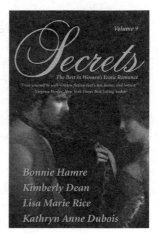

Listen to what reviewers say:

"Everyone should expect only the most erotic stories in a *Secrets* book. …if you like your stories full of hot sexual scenes, then this is for you!"
—Donna Doyle Romance Reviews

"*SECRETS 9*… is sinfully delicious, highly arousing, and hotter than hot as the pages practically burn up as you turn them."
—Suzanne Coleburn, Reader To Reader Reviews/Belles & Beaux of Romance

"Treat yourself to well-written fiction that's hot, hotter, and hottest!"
—Virginia Henley, *New York Times* Best Selling Author

In *Secrets, Volume 9* you'll find:

Wild For You by Kathryn Anne Dubois

When college intern, Georgie, gets captured by a Congo wildman, she discovers this specimen of male virility has never seen a woman. The research possibilities are endless!

Wanted by Kimberly Dean

FBI Special Agent Jeff Reno wants Danielle Carver. There's her body, brains—and that charge of treason on her head. Dani goes on the run, but the sexy Fed is hot on her trail.

Secluded by Lisa Marie Rice

Nicholas Lee's wealth and power came with a price—his enemies will kill anyone he loves. When Isabelle steals his heart, Nicholas secludes her in his palace for a lifetime of desire in only a few days.

Flights of Fantasy by Bonnie Hamre

Chloe taught others to see the realities of life but she's never shared the intimate world of her sensual yearnings. Given the chance, will she be woman enough to fulfill her most secret erotic fantasy?

Secrets, Volume 10

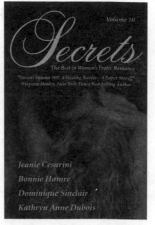

Listen to what reviewers say:

"*Secrets Volume 10*, an erotic dance through medieval castles, sultan's palaces, the English countryside and expensive hotel suites, explodes with passion-filled pages."

—*Romantic Times BOOKclub*

"Having read the previous nine volumes, this one fulfills the expectations of what is expected in a *Secrets* book: romance and eroticism at its best!!"

—*Fallen Angel Reviews*

"All are hot steamy romances so if you enjoy erotica romance, you are sure to enjoy *Secrets, Volume 10*. All this reviewer can say is WOW!!"

—*The Best Reviews*

In *Secrets, Volume 10* you'll find:

Private Eyes by Dominique Sinclair

When a mystery man captivates P.I. Nicolla Black during a stakeout, she discovers her no-seduction rule bending under the pressure of long denied passion. She agrees to the seduction, but he demands her total surrender.

The Ruination of Lady Jane by Bonnie Hamre

To avoid her upcoming marriage, Lady Jane Ponsonby-Maitland flees into the arms of Havyn Attercliffe. She begs him to ruin her rather than turn her over to her odious fiancé.

Code Name: Kiss by Jeanie Cesarini

Agent Lily Justiss is on a mission to defend her country against terrorists that requires giving up her virginity as a sex slave. As her master takes her body, desire for her commanding officer Seth Blackthorn fuels her mind.

The Sacrifice by Kathryn Anne Dubois

Lady Anastasia Bedovier is days from taking her vows as a Nun. Before she denies her sensuality forever, she wants to experience pleasure. Count Maxwell is the perfect man to initiate her into erotic delight.

Secrets, Volume 11

Listen to what reviewers say:

"*Secrets Volume 11* delivers once again with sto-
rylines that include erotic masquerades, ancient
curses, modern-day betrayal and a prince charming looking for a kiss." **4 Stars**

—Romantic Times BOOKclub

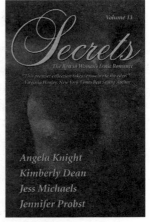

"Indulge yourself with this erotic treat and join the
thousands of readers who just can't get enough. Be
forewarned that *Secrets 11* will whet your appetite
for more, but will offer you the ultimate in pleasurable erotic literature."

—Ballston Book House Review

"*Secrets 11* quite honestly is my favorite anthology from Red Sage so far."

—The Best Reviews

In *Secrets, Volume 11* you'll find:

Masquerade by Jennifer Probst

Hailey Ashton is determined to free herself from her sexual restrictions.
Four nights of erotic pleasures without revealing her identity. A chance to
explore her secret desires without the fear of unmasking.

Ancient Pleasures by Jess Michaels

Isabella Winslow is obsessed with finding out what caused her late husband's
death, but trapped in an Egyptian concubine's tomb with a sexy American
raider, succumbing to the mummy's sensual curse takes over.

Manhunt by Kimberly Dean

Framed for murder, Michael Tucker takes Taryn Swanson hostage—the one
woman who can clear him. Despite the evidence against him, the attraction between them is strong. Tucker resorts to unconventional, yet effective
methods of persuasion to change the sexy ADA's mind.

Wake Me by Angela Knight

Chloe Hart received a sexy painting of a sleeping knight. Radolf of Varik
has been trapped for centuries in the painting since, cursed by a witch. His
only hope is to visit the dreams of women and make one of them fall in love
with him so she can free him with a kiss.

Secrets, Volume 12

Listen to what reviewers say:

"*Secrets Volume 12*, turns on the heat with a seductive encounter inside a bookstore, a temple of naughty and sensual delight, a galactic inferno that thaws ice, and a lightening storm that lights up the English shoreline. Tales of looking for love in all the right places with a heat rating out the charts." **4½ Stars**

—Romantic Times BOOKclub

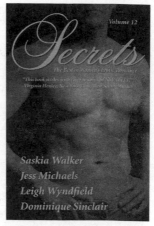

"I really liked these stories. You want great escapism? Read *Secrets, Volume 12*."

—Romance Reviews

In *Secrets, Volume 12* you'll find:

Good Girl Gone Bad by Dominique Sinclair

Reagan's dreams are finally within reach. Setting out to do research for an article, nothing could have prepared her for Luke, or his offer to teach her everything she needs to know about sex. Licentious pleasures, forbidden desires… inspiring the best writing she's ever done.

Aphrodite's Passion by Jess Michaels

When Selena flees Victorian London before her evil stepchildren can institutionalize her for hysteria, Gavin is asked to bring her back home. But when he finds her living on the island of Cyprus, his need to have her begins to block out every other impulse.

White Heat by Leigh Wyndfield

Raine is hiding in an icehouse in the middle of nowhere from one of the scariest men in the universes. Walker escaped from a burning prison. Imagine their surprise when they find out they have the same man to blame for their miseries. Passion, revenge and love are in their future.

Summer Lightning by Saskia Walker

Sculptress Sally is enjoying an idyllic getaway on a secluded cove when she spots a gorgeous man walking naked on the beach. When Julian finds an attractive woman shacked up in his cove, he has to check her out. But what will he do when he finds she's secretly been using him as a model?

Secrets, Volume 13

Listen to what reviewers say:

"In *Secrets Volume 13*, the temperature gets turned up a few notches with a mistaken personal ad, shape-shifters destined to love, a hot Regency lord and his lady, as well as a bodyguard protecting his woman. Emotions and flames blaze high in Red Sage's latest foray into the sensual and delightful art of love." **4½ Stars**

—*Romantic Times BOOKclub*

"The sex is still so hot the pages nearly ignite! Read *Secrets, Volume 13*!"

—*Romance Reviews*

In *Secrets, Volume 13* you'll find:

Out of Control by Rachelle Chase

Astrid's world revolves around her business and she's hoping to pick up wealthy Erik Santos as a client. Only he's hoping to pick up something entirely different. Will she give in to the seductive pull of his proposition?

Hawkmoor by Amber Green

Shape-shifters answer to Darien as he acts in the name of the long-missing Lady Hawkmoor, their hereditary ruler. When she unexpectedly surfaces, Darien must deal with a scrappy individual whose wary eyes hold the other half of his soul, but who has the power to destroy his world.

Lessons in Pleasure by Charlotte Featherstone

A wicked bargain has Lily vowing never to yield to the demands of the rake she once loved and lost. Unfortunately, Damian, the Earl of St. Croix, or Saint as he is infamously known, will not take 'no' for an answer.

In the Heat of the Night by Calista Fox

Haunted by a century-old curse, Molina fears she won't live to see her thirtieth birthday. Nick, her former bodyguard, is hired back into service to protect her from the fatal accidents that plague her family. But *In the Heat of the Night*, will his passion and love for her be enough to convince Molina they have a future together?

Secrets, Volume 14

Listen to what reviewers say:

"*Secrets Volume 14* will excite readers with its diverse selection of delectable sexy tales ranging from a fourteenth century love story to a sci-fi rebel who falls for a irresistible research scientist to a trio of determined vampires who battle for the same woman to a virgin sacrifice who falls in love with a beast. A cornucopia of pure delight!" **4½ Stars**

—*Romantic Times BOOKclub*

"This book contains four erotic tales sure to keep readers up long into the night."

—*Romance Junkies*

In *Secrets, Volume 14* you'll find:

Soul Kisses by Angela Knight

Beth's been kidnapped by Joaquin Ramirez, a sadistic vampire. Handsome vampire cousins, Morgan and Garret Axton, come to her rescue. Can she find happiness with two vampires?

Temptation in Time by Alexa Aames

Ariana escaped the Middle Ages after stealing a kiss of magic from sexy sorcerer, Marcus de Grey. When he brings her back, they begin a battle of wills and a sexual odyssey that could spell disaster for them both.

Ailis and the Beast by Jennifer Barlowe

When Ailis agreed to be her village's sacrifice to the mysterious Beast she was prepared to sacrifice her virtue, and possibly her life. But some things aren't what they seem. Ailis and the Beast are about to discover the greatest sacrifice may be the human heart.

Night Heat by Leigh Wynfield

When Rip Bowhite leads a revolt on the prison planet, he ends up struggling to survive against monsters that rule the night. Jemma, the prison's Healer, won't allow herself to be distracted by the instant attraction she feels for Rip. As the stakes are raised and death draws near, love seems doomed in the heat of the night.

Secrets, Volume 15

Listen to what reviewers say:

"*Secrets Volume 15* blends humor, tension and steamy romance in its newest collection that sizzles with passion between unlikely pairs—a male chauvinist columnist and a librarian turned erotica author; a handsome werewolf and his resisting mate; an unfulfilled woman and a sexy police officer and a Victorian wife who learns discipline can be fun. Readers will revel in this delicious assortment of thrilling tales." **4 Stars**
— *Romantic Times BOOKclub*

"This book contains four tales by some of today's hottest authors that will tease your senses and intrigue your mind."

—*Romance Junkies*

In *Secrets, Volume 15* you'll find:

Simon Says by Jane Thompson

Simon Campbell is a newspaper columnist who panders to male fantasies. Georgina Kennedy is a respectable librarian. On the surface, these two have nothing in common... but don't judge a book by its cover.

Bite of the Wolf by Cynthia Eden

Gareth Morlet, alpha werewolf, has finally found his mate. All he has to do is convince Trinity to join with him, to give in to the pleasure of a were-wolf's mating, and then she will be his... forever.

Falling for Trouble by Saskia Walker

With 48 hours to clear her brother's name, Sonia Harmond finds help from irresistible bad boy, Oliver Eaglestone. When the erotic tension between them hits fever pitch, securing evidence to thwart an international arms dealer isn't the only danger they face.

The Disciplinarian by Leigh Court

Headstrong Clarissa Babcock is sent to the shadowy legend known as The Disciplinarian for instruction in proper wifely obedience. Jared Ashworth uses the tools of seduction to show her how to control a demanding husband, but her beauty, spirit, and uninhibited passion make Jared hunger to keep her—and their darkly erotic nights—all for himself!

Secrets, Volume 16

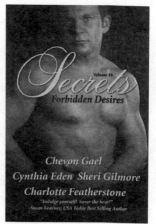

Listen to what reviewers say:

"Blackmail, games of chance, nude beaches and masquerades pave a path to heart-tugging emotions and fiery love scenes in Red Sage's latest collection." **4.5 Stars**

—*Romantic Times BOOKclub*

"Red Sage Publishing has brought to the readers an erotic profusion of highly skilled storytellers in their Secrets Vol. 16. ... This is the best Secrets novel to date and this reviewer's favorite."

—*LoveRomances.com*

In *Secrets, Volume 16* you'll find:

Never Enough by Cynthia Eden

For the last three weeks, Abby McGill has been playing with fire. Bad-boy Jake has taught her the true meaning of desire, but she knows she has to end her relationship with him. But Jake isn't about to let the woman he wants walk away from him.

Bunko by Sheri Gilmoore

Tu Tran is forced to decide between Jack, a man, who promises to share every aspect of his life with her, or Dev, the man, who hides behind a mask and only offers night after night of erotic sex. Will she take the gamble of the dice and choose the man, who can see behind her own mask and expose her true desires?

Hide and Seek by Chevon Gael

Kyle DeLaurier ditches his trophy-fiance in favor of a tropical paradise full of tall, tanned, topless females. Private eye, Darcy McLeod, is on the trail of this runaway groom. Together they sizzle while playing Hide and Seek with their true identities.

Seduction of the Muse by Charlotte Featherstone

He's the Dark Lord, the mysterious author who pens the erotic tales of an innocent woman's seduction. She is his muse, the woman he watches from the dark shadows, the woman whose dreams he invades at night.

Secrets, Volume 17

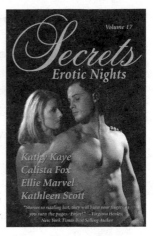

Listen to what reviewers say:

"Readers who have clamored for more *Secrets* will love the mix of alpha and beta males as well as kick-butt heroines who always get their men."
4 Stars
—*Romantic Times BOOKclub*

"Stories so sizzling hot, they will burn your fingers as you turn the pages. Enjoy!"
—Virginia Henley, *New York Times* Best Selling Author

"Red Sage is bringing us another thrilling anthology of passion and desire that will keep you up long into the night."
—*Romance Junkies*

In *Secrets, Volume 17* you'll find:

Rock Hard Candy by Kathy Kaye

Jessica Hennessy, the great, great granddaughter of a Voodoo priestess, decides she's waited long enough for the man of her dreams. A dose of her ancestor's aphrodisiac slipped into the gooey center of her homemade bon bons ought to do the trick.

Fatal Error by Kathleen Scott

Jesse Storm must make amends to humanity by destroying the computer program he helped design that has taken the government hostage. But he must also protect the woman he's loved in secret for nearly a decade.

Birthday by Ellie Marvel

Jasmine Templeton decides she's been celibate long enough. Will a wild night at a hot new club with her two best friends ease the ache inside her or just make it worse? Well, considering one of those best friends is Charlie and she's been having strange notions about their relationship of late… It's definitely a birthday neither she nor Charlie will ever forget.

Intimate Rendezvous by Calista Fox

A thief causes trouble at Cassandra Kensington's nightclub, Rendezvous, and sexy P.I. Dean Hewitt arrives on the scene to help. One look at the siren who owns the club has his blood boiling, despite the fact that his keen instincts have him questioning the legitimacy of her business.

Secrets, Volume 18

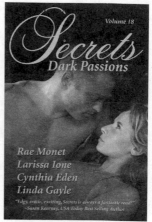

Listen to what reviewers say:

"Fantastic love scenes make this a book to be enjoyed more than once." **4.5 Stars**
— *Romantic Times BOOKclub*

"*Secrets Volume 18* continues [its] tradition of high quality sensual stories that both excite the senses while stimulating the mind."
—CK²S Kwips and Kritiques

"Edgy, erotic, exciting, *Secrets* is always a fantastic read!"
—Susan Kearney, *USA Today* Best Selling Author

In *Secrets, Volume 18* you'll find:

Lone Wolf Three by Rae Monet

Planetary politics and squabbling over wolf occupied territory drain former rebel leader Taban Zias. But his anger quickly turns to desire when he meets, Lakota Blackson. Focused, calm and honorable, the female Wolf Warrior is Taban's perfect mate—now if he can just convince her.

Flesh to Fantasy by Larissa Ione

Kelsa Bradshaw is an intense loner whose job keeps her happily immersed in a fanciful world of virtual reality. Trent Jordan is a laid-back paramedic who experiences the harsh realities of life up close and personal. But when their worlds collide in an erotic eruption can Trent convince Kelsa to turn the fantasy into something real?

Heart Full of Stars by Linda Gayle

Singer Fanta Rae finds herself stranded on a lonely Mars outpost with the first human male she's seen in years. Ex-Marine Alex Decker lost his family and guilt drove him into isolation, but when alien assassins come to enslave Fanta, she and Decker come together to fight for their lives.

The Wolf's Mate by Cynthia Eden

When Michael Morlet finds Katherine "Kat" Hardy fighting for her life in a dark alley, he instantly recognizes her as the mate he's been seeking all of his life, but someone's trying to kill her. With danger stalking them at every turn, will Kat trust him enough to become The Wolf's Mate?

Secrets, Volume 19
Released July 2007

Affliction
by Elisa Adams

Holly Aronson finally believes she's safe and whole in the orbit of sweet Andrew. But when Andrew's life long friend, Shane, arrives, events begin to spiral out of control again. Worse, she's inexplicably drawn to Shane. As she runs for her life, which one will protect her? And whom does she truly love?

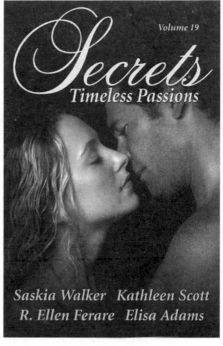

Falling Stars
by Kathleen Scott

Daria is both a Primon fighter pilot and a Primon princess. As a deadly new enemy faces appears, she must choose between her duty to the fleet and the desperate need to forge an alliance through her marriage to the enemy's General Raven.

Toy in the Attic
by R. Ellen Ferare

When Gabrielle checks into the top floor of an old hotel, she discovers a life-sized statue of a nude man. Her unexpected roommate reveals himself to be a talented lover caught by a witch's curse. Can she help him break free of the spell that holds him, without losing her heart along the way?

What You Wish For
by Saskia Walker

Lucy Chambers is renovating her newly purchased historic house. As her dreams about a stranger become more intense, she wishes he were with her now. Two hundred years in the past, the man wishes for companionship and suddenly they find themselves together—in his time.

The Forever Kiss
by Angela Knight

Listen to what reviewers say:

"*The Forever Kiss* flows well with good characters and an interesting plot. … If you enjoy vampires and a lot of hot sex, you are sure to enjoy *The Forever Kiss*."

—*The Best Reviews*

"Battling vampires, a protective ghost and the ever present battle of good and evil keep excellent pace with the erotic delights in Angela Knight's *The Forever Kiss*—a book that absolutely bites with refreshing paranormal humor." **4½ Stars, Top Pick**

—*Romantic Times BOOKclub*

"I found *The Forever Kiss* to be an exceptionally written, refreshing book. … I really enjoyed this book by Angela Knight. … 5 angels!"

—*Fallen Angel Reviews*

"*The Forever Kiss* is the first single title released from Red Sage and if this is any indication of what we can expect, it won't be the last. … The love scenes are hot enough to give a vampire a sunburn and the fight scenes will have you cheering for the good guys."

—*Really Bad Barb Reviews*

In *The Forever Kiss*:

For years, Valerie Chase has been haunted by dreams of a Texas Ranger she knows only as "Cowboy." As a child, he rescued her from the nightmare vampires who murdered her parents. As an adult, she still dreams of him—but now he's her seductive lover in nights of erotic pleasure.

Yet "Cowboy" is more than a dream—he's the real Cade McKinnon—and a vampire! For years, he's protected Valerie from Edward Ridgemont, the sadistic vampire who turned him. Now, Ridgmont wants Valerie for his own and Cade is the only one who can protect her.

When Val finds herself abducted by her handsome dream man, she's appalled to discover he's one of the vampires she fears. Now, caught in a web of fear and passion, she and Cade must learn to trust each other, even as an immortal monster stalks their every move.

Their only hope of survival is… *The Forever Kiss*.

Romantic Times Best Erotic Novel of the Year

It's not just reviewers raving about *Secrets*. See what readers have to say:

"When are you coming out with a new Volume? I want a new one next month!" via email from a reader.

"I loved the hot, wet sex without vulgar words being used to make it exciting." after *Volume 1*

"I loved the blend of sensuality and sexual intensity—HOT!" after *Volume 2*

"The best thing about *Secrets* is they're hot and brief! The least thing is you do not have enough of them!" after *Volume 3*

"I have been extremely satisfied with *Secrets*, keep up the good writing." after *Volume 4*

"Stories have plot and characters to support the erotica. They would be good strong stories without the heat." after *Volume 5*

"*Secrets* really knows how to push the envelop better than anyone else." after *Volume 6*

"These are the best sensual stories I have ever read!" after *Volume 7*

"I love, love, love the *Secrets* stories. I now have all of them, please have more books come out each year." after *Volume 8*

"These are the perfect sensual romance stories!" after *Volume 9*

"What I love about *Secrets Volume 10* is how I couldn't put it down!" after *Volume 10*

"All of the *Secrets* volumes are terrific! I have read all of them up to *Secrets Volume 11*. Please keep them coming! I will read every one you make!" after *Volume 11*

Finally, the men you've been dreaming about!

Give the Gift of Spicy Romantic Fiction

Don't want to wait? You can place a retail price ($12.99) order for any of the *Secrets* volumes from the following:

① **Waldenbooks and Borders Stores**

② **Amazon.com** or **BarnesandNoble.com**

③ **Book Clearinghouse (800-431-1579)**

④ **Romantic Times Magazine** Books by Mail (718-237-1097)

⑤ Special order at other bookstores.

Bookstores: Please contact Bakcr & Taylor Distributors, Ingram Book Distributor, or Red Sage Publishing for bookstore sales.

Order by title or ISBN #:

Vol. 1: 0-9648942-0-3	**Vol. 8:** 0-9648942-8-9	**Vol. 15:** 0-9754516-5-0
ISBN #13 978-0-9648942-0-4	ISBN #13 978-0-9648942-9-7	ISBN #13 978-0-9754516-5-6
Vol. 2: 0-9648942-1-1	**Vol. 9:** 0-9648942-9-7	**Vol. 16:** 0-9754516-6-9
ISBN #13 978-0-9648942-1-1	ISBN #13 978-0-9648942-9-7	ISBN #13 978-0-9754516-6-3
Vol. 3: 0-9648942-2-X	**Vol. 10:** 0-9754516-0-X	**Vol. 17:** 0-9754516-7-7
ISBN #13 978-0-9648942-2-8	ISBN #13 978-0-9754516-0-1	ISBN #13 978-0-9754516-7-0
Vol. 4: 0-9648942-4-6	**Vol. 11:** 0-9754516-1-8	**Vol. 18:** 0-9754516-8-5
ISBN #13 978-0-9648942-4-2	ISBN #13 978-0-9754516-1-8	ISBN #13 978-0-9754516-8-7
Vol. 5: 0-9648942-5-4	**Vol. 12:** 0-9754516-2-6	**Vol. 19:** 0-9754516-9-3
ISBN #13 978-0-9648942-5-9	ISBN #13 978-0-9754516-2-5	ISBN #13 978-0-9754516-9-4
Vol. 6: 0-9648942-6-2	**Vol. 13:** 0-9754516-3-4	**The Forever Kiss:**
ISBN #13 978-0-9648942-6-6	ISBN #13 978-0-9754516-3-2	0-9648942-3-8
Vol. 7: 0-9648942-7-0	**Vol. 14:** 0-9754516-4-2	ISBN #13
ISBN #13 978-0-9648942-7-3	ISBN #13 978-0-9754516-4-9	978-0-9648942-3-5 ($14.00)

Red Sage Publishing Mail Order Form:
(Orders shipped in two to three days of receipt.)

Each volume of *Secrets* retails for $12.99, but you can get it direct via mail order for only $9.99 each. The novel *The Forever Kiss* retails for $14.00, but by direct mail order, you only pay $11.00. Use the order form below to place your direct mail order. Fill in the quantity you want for each book on the blanks beside the title.

_____ *Secrets* Volume 1   _____ *Secrets* Volume 8   _____ *Secrets* Volume 15

_____ *Secrets* Volume 2   _____ *Secrets* Volume 9   _____ *Secrets* Volume 16

_____ *Secrets* Volume 3   _____ *Secrets* Volume 10   _____ *Secrets* Volume 17

_____ *Secrets* Volume 4   _____ *Secrets* Volume 11   _____ *Secrets* Volume 18

_____ *Secrets* Volume 5   _____ *Secrets* Volume 12   _____ *Secrets* Volume 19

_____ *Secrets* Volume 6   _____ *Secrets* Volume 13   _____ *The Forever Kiss*

_____ *Secrets* Volume 7   _____ *Secrets* Volume 14

Total _____ *Secrets* Volumes @ $9.99 each = $_____

Total _____ *The Forever Kiss* @ $11.00 each = $_____

Shipping & handling (in the U.S.) $_____

US Priority Mail: UPS insured:

1–2 books .... $ 5.50   1–4 books $16.00

3–5 books .... $11.50   5–9 books $25.00

6–9 books .... $14.50   10–20 books $29.00

10–20 books $19.00

Sᴜʙᴛᴏᴛᴀʟ $_____

Florida 6% sales tax (if delivered in FL) $_____

TOTAL AMOUNT ENCLOSED $_____

Your personal information is kept private and not shared with anyone.

Name: (please print) _____

Address: (no P.O. Boxes) _____

City/State/Zip: _____

Phone or email: (only regarding order if necessary) _____

Please make check payable to **Red Sage Publishing**. Check must be drawn on a U.S. bank in U.S. dollars. Mail your check and order form to:

Red Sage Publishing, Inc.   **Department S19**   **P.O. Box 4844**   **Seminole, FL 33775**

Or use the order form on our website: **www.redsagepub.com**

Red Sage Publishing Mail Order Form:

(Orders shipped in two to three days of receipt.)

Each volume of *Secrets* retails for $12.99, but you can get it direct via mail order for only $9.99 each. The novel *The Forever Kiss* retails for $14.00, but by direct mail order, you only pay $11.00. Use the order form below to place your direct mail order. Fill in the quantity you want for each book on the blanks beside the title.

_____ *Secrets* Volume 1   _____ *Secrets* Volume 8   _____ *Secrets* Volume 15

_____ *Secrets* Volume 2   _____ *Secrets* Volume 9   _____ *Secrets* Volume 16

_____ *Secrets* Volume 3   _____ *Secrets* Volume 10   _____ *Secrets* Volume 17

_____ *Secrets* Volume 4   _____ *Secrets* Volume 11   _____ *Secrets* Volume 18

_____ *Secrets* Volume 5   _____ *Secrets* Volume 12   _____ *Secrets* Volume 19

_____ *Secrets* Volume 6   _____ *Secrets* Volume 13   _____ *The Forever Kiss*

_____ *Secrets* Volume 7   _____ *Secrets* Volume 14

Total _____ *Secrets* Volumes @ $9.99 each = $_____

Total _____ *The Forever Kiss* @ $11.00 each = $_____

Shipping & handling (in the U.S.) $_____

US Priority Mail:	UPS insured:
1–2 books .... $ 5.50	1–4 books $16.00
3–5 books $11.50	5–9 books $25.00
6–9 books $14.50	10–20 books $29.00
10–20 books $19.00	

SUBTOTAL $_____

Florida 6% sales tax (if delivered in FL) $_____

TOTAL AMOUNT ENCLOSED $_____

Your personal information is kept private and not shared with anyone.

Name: (please print) _____

Address: (no P.O. Boxes) _____

City/State/Zip: _____

Phone or email: (only regarding order if necessary) _____

Please make check payable to **Red Sage Publishing**. Check must be drawn on a U.S. bank in U.S. dollars. Mail your check and order form to:

Red Sage Publishing, Inc.   Department S19   P.O. Box 4844   Seminole, FL 33775

Or use the order form on our website: **www.redsagepub.com**